The Lion of Saint Mark

A Story of Venice in the Fourteenth Century

G. A. Henty

The Lion of Saint Mark: A Story of Venice in the Fourteenth Century

Copyright © 2019 Indo-European Publishing

The present edition is a reproduction of previous publication of this classic work. Minor typographical errors may have been corrected without note, however, for an authentic reading experience the spelling, punctuation, and capitalization have been retained from the original text.

ISBN: 978-1-64439-293-5

CONTENTS

PREFACE

Of all the chapters of history, there are few more interesting or wonderful than that which tells the story of the rise and progress of Venice. Built upon a few sandy islands in a shallow lagoon, and originally founded by fugitives from the mainland, Venice became one of the greatest and most respected powers of Europe. She was mistress of the sea; conquered and ruled over a considerable territory bordering on the Adriatic; checked the rising power of the Turks; conquered Constantinople; successfully defied all the attacks of her jealous rivals to shake her power; and carried on a trade relatively as great as that of England in the present day. I have laid my story in the time not of the triumphs of Venice, but of her hardest struggle for existence—when she defended herself successfully against the coalition of Hungary, Padua, and Genoa—for never at any time were the virtues of Venice, her steadfastness, her patriotism, and her willingness to make all sacrifice for her independence, more brilliantly shown. The historical portion of the story is drawn from Hazlitt's History of the Republic of Venice, and with it I have woven the adventures of an English boy, endowed with a full share of that energy and pluck which, more than any other qualities, have made the British empire the greatest the world has ever seen.

G. A. Henty

CHAPTER 1

VENICE

"I suppose you never have such nights as these in that misty island of yours, Francisco?"

"Yes, we have," the other said stoutly. "I have seen just as bright nights on the Thames. I have stood down by Paul's Stairs and watched the reflection of the moon on the water, and the lights of the houses on the bridge, and the passing boats, just as we are doing now.

"But," he added honestly, "I must confess that we do not have such still, bright nights very often, while with you they are the rule, though sometimes even here a mist rises up and dims the water, just as it does with us."

"But I have heard you say that the stars are not so bright as we have them here."

"No, I do not think they are, Matteo. I do not remember now, but I do know, when I first came here, I was struck with the brightness of the stars, so I suppose there must have been a difference."

"But you like this better than England? You are glad that your father came out here?"

Francis Hammond did not answer at once.

"I am glad he came out," he said after a pause, "because I have seen many things I should never have seen if I had stayed at home, and I have learned to speak your tongue. But I do not know that I like it better than home. Things are different, you see. There was more fun at home. My father had two or three apprentices, whom I used to play with when the shop was closed, and there were often what you would call tumults, but which were not serious. Sometimes there would be a fight between the apprentices of one ward and another. A shout would be raised of 'Clubs!' and all the 'prentices would catch up their sticks and pour out of the shops, and then there would be a fight till the city guard turned out and separated them. Then there used to be the shooting at the butts, and the shows, and the Mayday revels, and all sorts of things. The people were more merry than you are here, and much more free. You see, the barons, who are the same to us that your great families are to you, had no influence in the city. You are a nation of traders, and so are we; but in London the traders have the power, and are

1

absolute masters inside their own walls, caring nothing for the barons, and not much for the king. If anyone did wrong he got an open and fair trial. There was no fear of secret accusations. Everyone thought and said as he pleased. There was no Lion's Mouth, and no Council of Ten."

"Hush! hush! Francisco," the other said, grasping his arm. "Do not say a word against the council. There is no saying who may be listening."

And he looked nervously round to see if anyone was within earshot.

"There it is, you see," his companion said. "So long as we have a safe conscience, in London we are frightened at nothing, whereas here no one can say with certainty that he may not, before tomorrow morning, be lying in the dungeons of St. Mark, without the slightest idea in the world as to what his crime has been."

"There, there, Francisco," Matteo said uneasily. "Do talk about other things. Your notions may do very well in England, but are not safe to discuss here. Of course there are plenty here who would gladly see a change in some matters, but one cannot have everything; and, after all, when one has so much to be proud of, one need not grumble because everything is not just as one would like."

"Yes, you have much to be proud of," Francis Hammond agreed. "It is marvellous that the people of these scattered islets should be masters of the sea, that their alliance should be coveted by every power in Europe, that they should be the greatest trading community in the world. If I were not English I should like to be Venetian."

The speakers were standing at the edge of the water in front of the Palace of St. Mark. In the piazza behind them a throng of people were walking to and fro, gossiping over the latest news from Constantinople, the last rumour as to the doings of the hated rival of Venice, Genoa, or the purport of the letter which had, as everyone knew, been brought by the Bishop of Treviso from the pope to the seignory.

The moon was shining brightly overhead, and glittering in the waters of the lagoon, which were broken into innumerable little wavelets by the continual crossing and recrossing of the gondolas dotting its surface. There was a constant arrival and departure of boats from the steps, fifty yards to the right of the spot where the speakers were standing; but where they had stationed themselves, about halfway between the landing steps and the canal running down by the side of the ducal palace, there were but few people about.

Francis Hammond was a lad between fifteen and sixteen years old. His father was a merchant of London. He was a man of great enterprise and energy, and had four years before determined to leave his junior partner in charge of the business in London, and to come out himself for a time to Venice, so as to buy the Eastern stuffs in which he dealt at the headquarters of the trade, instead of paying such prices as the agents of the Venetian traders might demand in London.

He had succeeded beyond his expectations. In Venice there were constantly bargains to be purchased from ships returning laden with the spoils of some captured Genoese merchantman, or taken in the sack of some Eastern seaport. The prices, too, asked by the traders with the towns of Syria or the Black Sea, were but a fraction of those charged when these goods arrived in London. It was true that occasionally some of his cargoes were lost on the homeward voyage, captured either by the Genoese or the Moorish pirates; but even allowing for this, the profits of the trade were excellent.

The English merchant occupied a good position in Venice. The promptness of his payments, and the integrity of his dealings, made him generally respected; and the fact that he was engaged in trade was no drawback to his social position, in a city in which, of all others, trade was considered honourable, and where members of even the most aristocratic families were, with scarcely an exception, engaged in commerce. There were many foreign merchants settled in Venice, for from the first the republic had encouraged strangers to take up their residence there, and had granted them several privileges and advantages.

Between Venice and England there had always been good feeling. Although jealous of foreigners, England had granted the Venetians liberty to trade in London, Southampton, and some other towns as far back as the year 1304; and their relations had always been cordial, as there were no grounds for jealousy or rivalry between the two peoples; whereas the interference of France, Germany, Austria, and Hungary in the affairs of Italy, had frequently caused uneasiness to Venice, and had on several occasions embroiled her with one or other of the three last named powers. France had as yet taken a very minor part in the continual wars which were waged between the rival cities of Italy, and during the Crusades there had been a close alliance between her and Venice, the troops of the two nations fighting together at the siege of Constantinople, and causing the temporary overthrow of the Greek Empire of the East.

The rise of Venice had been rapid, and she owed her advancement to a combination of circumstances. In the first place, her insular position rendered her almost impervious to attack, and she had therefore no occasion to keep on foot any army, and was able to throw all her strength on to the sea, where Genoa was her only formidable rival. In the second place, her mercantile spirit, and her extensive trade with the East, brought in a steady influx of wealth, and her gold enabled her to purchase allies, to maintain lengthy struggles without faltering, and to emerge unscathed from wars which exhausted the resources, and crippled the powers, of her rivals.

The third source of her success lay in the spirit of her population. Like Rome in her early days, she was never cast down by reverses. Misfortune only nerved her to further exertions, and after each defeat she rose stronger than before. But the cause which, more than all, contributed to give to Venice her ascendancy among the cities of Italy, was her form of government. Democratic at first, as among all communities, it had gradually assumed the character of a close oligarchy, and although nominally ruled by a council containing a large number of members, her destinies were actually in the hands of the Doge, elected for life, and the Council of Ten, chosen from the great body of the council. Thus she had from the first been free from those factions which were the bane of Genoa and Florence. Some of the great families had from time to time come more prominently to the front than others, but none had attained predominant political power, and beyond a few street tumults of slight importance, Venice had not suffered from the popular tumults and uprisings which played so prominent a part in the history of her rivals.

Thus, undisturbed by discord at home, Venice had been able to give all her attention and all her care to her interests abroad, and her affairs, conducted as they were by her wisest citizens, with a single eye to the benefit of the state, had been distinguished by a rare sagacity. Her object had been single and uniform, to protect her own interests, and to prevent any one city on the mainland attaining such a preponderance as would render her a dangerous neighbour. Hence she was always ready to ally herself with the weaker against the stronger, and to aid with money and men any state struggling against an ambitious neighbour. Acting on this principle she by turns assisted Padua against Verona, and Verona against Padua, or either of them when threatened by the growing power of Milan, and at the end of a war she generally came out with an increased territory, and added importance.

4

It is probable that no community was ever governed, for hundreds of years, with such uniform wisdom and sagacity as was Venice; but the advantage was not without drawbacks. The vigilance of the Council of Ten in repressing plots, not unfrequently set on foot by the enemies of the republic, resulted in the adoption of a hateful system of espionage. The city was pervaded with spies, and even secret denunciations were attended to, and the slightest expression of discontent against the ruling authorities was severely punished. On the other hand, comparatively slight attention was paid to private crime. Assassinations were of frequent occurrence, and unless the victim happened to be very powerfully connected, no notice was taken when a man was found to be missing from his usual place, and his corpse was discovered floating in the lagoon. Consequently crimes of this kind were, in the great majority of cases, committed with impunity, and even when traced, the authors, if possessed of powerful protectors, seldom suffered any greater punishment than temporary banishment.

After standing for some time on the Piazzetta, the two lads turned and, entering the square of Saint Mark, mingled with the crowd. It was a motley one. Nobles in silks and satins jostled with fishermen of the lagoons. Natives of all the coasts and islands which owned the sway of Venice, Greeks from Constantinople, Tartar merchants from the Crimea, Tyrians, and inhabitants of the islands of the Aegean, were present in considerable numbers; while among the crowd, vendors of fruit and flowers from the mainland, and of fresh water or cooling drinks, sold their wares. The English lad's companion—Matteo Giustiniani—belonged to one of the leading families of Venice, and was able to name to Francis most of the nobles and persons of importance whom they passed.

"There is Pisani," he said. "Of course you know him. What a jolly, good-tempered looking fellow he is! The sailors would do anything for him, and they say he will have command of the next fleet that puts to sea. I wish I was going with him. There is sure to be a fierce fight when he comes across the Genoese. His father was one of our greatest admirals.

"That noble just behind him is Fiofio Dandolo. What a grand family they have been, what a number of great men they have given to the republic! I should like to have seen the grand old Doge who stormed the walls of Constantinople, and divided the Eastern empire among the crusading barons. He was a hero indeed.

"No; I don't know who that young noble in the green velvet cap and plum coloured dress is. O yes, I do, though; it is Ruggiero

5

Mocenigo; he has been away for the last two years at Constantinople; he was banished for having killed Polo Morosini—he declared it was in fair fight, but no one believed him. They had quarrelled a few days before over some question of the precedence of their families, and Morosini was found dead at the top of the steps close to the church of Saint Paolo. Some people heard a cry and ran up just as Mocenigo leapt into his gondola, but as it rowed off their shouts called the attention of one of the city guard boats which happened to be passing, and it was stopped. As his sword was still wet with blood, he could not deny that he was the author of the deed, but, as I said, he declared it was in fair fight. The Morosinis asserted that Polo's sword was undrawn, but the Mocenigo family brought forward a man, who swore that he was one of the first to arrive, and pick up the sword and place it in its scabbard to prevent its being lost. No doubt he lied; but as Mocenigo's influence in the council was greater than that of the Morosini, the story was accepted. However, the public feeling was so strong that they could not do less than sentence Ruggiero to two years' banishment. I suppose that has just expired, and he has returned from Constantinople. He had a bad reputation before this affair took place, but as his connections are so powerful, I suppose he will be received as if nothing had happened. There are plenty of others as bad as he is."

"It's a scandalous thing," Francis Hammond said indignantly, "that, just because they have got powerful connections, men should be allowed to do, almost with impunity, things for which an ordinary man would be hung. There ought to be one law for the rich as well as the poor."

"So there is as far as the state is concerned," his companion replied. "A noble who plots against the state is as certain of a place in the lowest dungeons as a fisherman who has done the same; but in other respects there is naturally some difference."

"Why naturally?" Francis retorted. "You belong to a powerful family, Giustiniani, and my father is only a trader, but I don't see that naturally you have any more right to get me stabbed in the back, than I have to get you put out of the way."

"Naturally perhaps not," Matteo laughed; "but you see it has become a second nature to us here in Venice. But seriously I admit that the present state of things has grown to be a scandal, and that the doings of some of our class ought to be put down with a strong hand."

"Well, I shall say goodnight now," the English boy said. "My father doesn't like my being out after ten. He keeps up his English habits of shutting up early, and has not learned to turn night into day as you do here in Venice."

"The bell has just tolled the hour, Francis," his father said as he entered.

"I didn't think it was quite so late, father; the Piazza is crowded. I really do not think there is one person in Venice who goes to bed so early as we do. It is so pleasant in the moonlight after the heat of the day."

"That is true enough, Francis, but men are meant to sleep at night and to work in the day. I think our fathers carried this too far when they rang the curfew at eight; but ten is quite late enough for any honest man to be about in the streets, and the hours of the early morning are just as pleasant and far more healthy than those of the evening, especially in a place like this where the mists rise from the water, to say nothing of the chance of meeting a band of wild gallants on their way homewards heated with wine, or of getting a stab in the back from some midnight assassin. However, I do not blame Venice for enjoying herself while she can. She will have more serious matters to attend to soon."

"But she is at peace with every one at present, father. I thought when she signed the treaty with Austria after a year's fighting, she was going to have rest for a time."

"That was only the beginning of the trouble, Francis, and the council knew it well; that was why they made such terms with Austria as they did. They knew that Austria was only acting in accord with Hungary, and Padua, and Genoa. The others were not ready to begin, so Austria came on her own account to get what booty and plunder she could. But the storm is gathering, and will burst before long. But do not let us stand talking here any longer. It is high time for you to be in bed."

But though Francis retired to his room, it was more than an hour before he got into bed. His window looked down upon one of the canals running into the Grand Canal. Gondolas lighted by lanterns, or by torches held by servitors, passed constantly backwards and forwards beneath his window, and by leaning out he could see the passing lights of those on the Grand Canal. Snatches of song and laughter came up to him, and sometimes the note of a musical instrument. The air was soft and balmy, and he felt no inclination for sleep.

Francis thought over what his father had said of the probability of war, as he sat at his window, and wished that he were a couple of years older and could take part in the struggle. The

Venetian fleet had performed such marvels of valour, that, in the days when military service was almost the sole avenue to distinction and fortune, the desire to take part in a naval expedition, which promised unusual opportunities of gaining credit and renown, was the most natural thing possible for a boy of spirit.

Francis was a well built lad of nearly sixteen. He had, until he left London when about twelve years old, taken his full share in the rough sports which formed so good a training for the youths of England, and in which the citizens of London were in no way behind the rest of the kingdom. He had practised shooting with a light bow and arrows, in company with boys of his own age, in the fields outside the city walls; had engaged in many a rough tussle with light clubs and quarterstaffs; and his whole time—except for an hour or two daily which he had, as the son of a well to do citizen, spent in learning to read and write—had been occupied in games and exercises of one kind or other.

Since his arrival in Venice he had not altogether discontinued his former habits. At his earnest solicitation, his father had permitted him to attend the School of Arms, where the sons of patricians and well-to-do merchants learned the use of sword and dagger, to hurl the javelin, and wield the mace and battleaxe; and was, besides, a frequenter of some of the schools where old soldiers gave private lessons in arms to such as could afford it; and the skill and strength of the English lad excited no slight envy among the young Venetian nobles. Often, too, he would go out to one of the sandy islets, and there setting up a mark, practise with the bow. His muscles too, had gained strength and hardness by rowing. It was his constant habit of an evening, when well away from the crowded canals in the gondola, with Giuseppi, the son and assistant of his father's gondolier, to take an oar, for he had thoroughly mastered the difficult accomplishment of rowing well in a gondola; but he only did this when far out from the city, or when the darkness of evening would prevent his figure from being recognized by any of his acquaintances, for no Venetian of good family would demean himself by handling an oar. Francis, however, accustomed to row upon the Thames, could see no reason why he should not do the same in a gondola, and in time he and his companion could send the boat dancing over the water, at a rate which enabled them to overtake and distance most pair-oared boats.

After breakfast next morning he went down to the steps, where Beppo and Giuseppi, in their black cloth suits with red sashes round their waists, were waiting with the gondola in which Mr. Hammond was going out to Malamocco, to examine a cargo which had the day before arrived from Azoph. Giuseppi jumped ashore.

"I have heard of just the gondola to suit you, Messer Francisco, and you can get her a bargain."

"What is she like, Giuseppi?"

"She belongs to a man out at Lido. She was built for the race two years ago, but her owner fell sick and was unable to start. He has not got strong again, and wants to sell his boat, which is far too light for ordinary work. They say she is almost like an eggshell, and you and I will be able to send her along grandly. She cost four ducats, but he will sell her for two."

"That is capital, Giuseppi. This gondola is all well enough for my father, but she is very heavy. This evening we will row over to Lido and look at her."

A few minutes later Mr. Hammond came down. Beppo and his son took off their jackets, and in their snow white shirts and black trousers, set off by the red scarf and a red ribbon round their broad hats, took their places on the bow and stern. Mr. Hammond sat down on the cushions in the middle of the boat, and with an easy, noiseless motion the gondola glided away from the stairs. Francis, with a little sigh, turned away and strolled off for a couple of hours' work with the preceptor, with whom he had continued his studies since he came to Venice.

This work consisted chiefly of learning various languages, for in those days there was little else to learn. Latin was almost universally spoken by educated men in southern Europe, and Greeks, Italians, Spaniards, and Frenchmen were able to converse in this common medium. French Francis understood, for it was the language in use in the court and among the upper classes in England. Italian he picked up naturally during his residence, and spoke it with the facility of a native. He could now converse freely in Latin, and had some knowledge of German. At the same school were many lads of good Venetian families, and it was here that he had first made the acquaintance of Matteo Giustiniani, who was now his most intimate friend.

Matteo, like all the young nobles of Venice, was anxious to excel in military exercises, but he had none of the ardour for really hard work which distinguished his friend. He admired the latter's strength and activity, but could not bring himself to imitate him, in the exercises by which that strength was attained, and had often remonstrated with him upon his fondness for rowing.

"It is not seemly, Francisco, for a gentleman to be labouring like a common gondolier. These men are paid for doing it; but what pleasure there can be in standing up working that oar, till you are drenched with perspiration, I cannot understand. I don't mind getting hot in the School of Arms, because one cannot learn to use the sword and dagger without it, but that's quite another thing from tugging at an oar."

"But I like it, Matteo; and see how strong it has made my muscles, not of the arm only, but the leg and back. You often say you envy me my strength, but you might be just as strong if you chose to work as I do. Besides, it is delightful, when you are accustomed to it, to feel the gondola flying away under your stroke."

"I prefer feeling it fly away under some one else's stroke, Francisco. That is pleasant enough, I grant; but the very thought of working as you do throws me into a perspiration. I should like to be as strong as you are, but to work as a gondolier is too high a price to pay for it."

That evening, Francis crossed the lagoon in the gondola with Giuseppi, to inspect the boat he had heard of. It was just what he wanted. In appearance it differed in no way from an ordinary gondola, but it was a mere shell. The timbers and planking were extremely light, and the weight of the boat was little more than a third of that of other craft. She had been built like a working gondola, instead of in the form of those mostly used for racing, because her owner had intended, after the race was over, to plank her inside and strengthen her for everyday work. But the race had never come off, and the boat lay just as she had come from the hands of her builder, except that she had been painted black, like other gondolas, to prevent her planks from opening. When her owner had determined to part with her he had given her a fresh coat of paint, and had put her in the water, that her seams might close up.

"I don't like parting with her," the young fisherman to whom she belonged said. "I tried her once or twice, and she went like the wind, but I got fever in my bones and I am unlikely to race again, and the times are hard, and I must part with her."

Francis and Giuseppi gave her a trial, and were delighted with the speed and ease with which she flew through the water. On their return Francis at once paid the price asked for her. His father made him a handsome allowance, in order that he might be able to mix, without discomfort, with the lads of good family whom he met at his preceptor's and at the schools of arms. But Francis did not care for strolling in the Piazza, or sitting for hours sipping liquors. Still less did he care for dress or finery. Consequently he had always plenty of money to indulge in his own special fancies.

As soon as the bargain was completed, Giuseppi took his place in the old gondola, while Francis took the oar in his new acquisition,

10

and found to his satisfaction that with scarcely an effort he could dart ahead of his companion and leave him far behind. By nightfall the two gondolas were fastened, side by side, behind the gaily painted posts which, in almost all Venetian houses, are driven into the canal close to the steps, and behind which the gondolas belonging to the house lie safe from injury by passing craft.

"I have bought another gondola, father," Francis said the next morning. "She is a very light, fast craft, and I got her cheap."

"I don't see what you wanted another gondola for, Francis. I do not use mine very much, and you are always welcome to take it when I do not want it."

"Yes, father, but you often use it in the evening, and that is just the time when one wants to go out. You very often only take Beppo with you, when you do not go on business, and I often want a boat that I could take with Giuseppi. Besides, your gondola is a very solid one, and I like passing people."

"Young people always want to go fast," Mr. Hammond said. "Why, I can't make out. However, Francis, I am not sorry that you have got a boat of your own, for it has happened several times lately, that when in the evening I have gone down intending to row round to the Piazzetta, I have found the boat gone, and have had to walk. Now I shall be able to rely on finding Beppo asleep in the boat at the steps. In future, since you have a boat of your own, I shall not be so particular as to your being in at ten. I do not so much mind your being out on the water, only you must promise me that you will not be in the streets after that hour. There are frequent broils as the evening gets on, not to mention the danger of cutthroats in unfrequented lanes; but if you will promise me that you will never be about the streets after half past nine, I will give you leave to stay out on the water till a later hour; but when you come in late be careful always to close and bar the door, and do not make more noise than you can help in coming up to your room."

Francis was much pleased with this concession, for the obligation to return at ten o'clock, just when the temperature was most delightful and the Grand Canal at its gayest, had been very irksome to him. As to the prohibition against being in the streets of Venice after half past nine, he felt that no hardship whatever, as he found no amusement in strolling in the crowded Piazza.

CHAPTER 2

A CONSPIRACY

"Who are those ladies, Matteo?" Francis asked his friend one evening, as the latter, who was sitting with him in his gondola, while Giuseppi rowed them along the Grand Canal, half rose and saluted two girls in a passing gondola.

"They are distant cousins of mine, Maria and Giulia Polani. They only returned a short time since from Corfu. Their father is one of the richest merchants of our city. He has for the last three years been living in Corfu, which is the headquarters of his trade. The family is an old one, and has given doges to Venice. They are two of our richest heiresses, for they have no brothers. Their mother died soon after the birth of Giulia."

"They both look very young," Francis said.

"Maria is about sixteen, her sister two years younger. There will be no lack of suitors for their hands, for although the family is not politically powerful, as it used to be, their wealth would cause them to be gladly received in our very first families."

"Who was the middle-aged lady sitting between them?"

"She is only their duenna," Matteo said carelessly. "She has been with them since they were children, and their father places great confidence in her. And he had need to, for Maria will ere long be receiving bouquets and perfumed notes from many a young gallant."

"I can quite fancy that," Francis said, "for she is very pretty as well as very rich, and, as far as I have observed, the two things do not go very often together. However, no doubt by this time her father has pretty well arranged in his mind whom she is to marry."

"I expect so," agreed Matteo.

"That is the worst of being born of good family. You have got to marry some one of your father's choice, not your own, and that choice is determined simply by the desire to add to the political influence of the family, to strengthen distant ties, or to obtain powerful connections. I suppose it is the same everywhere, Matteo, but I do think that a man or woman ought to have some voice in a matter of such importance to them."

"I think so, too, at the present time," Matteo laughed; "but I don't suppose that I shall be of that opinion when I have a family of sons and daughters to marry.

"This gondola of yours must be a fast one indeed, Francisco, for with only one rower she keeps up with almost all the pair oared boats, and your boy is not exerting himself to the utmost, either."

"She can fly along, I can tell you, Matteo. You shall come out in her some evening when Giuseppi and I both take oars. I have had her ten days now, and we have not come across anything that can hold her for a moment."

"It is always useful," Matteo said, "to have a fast boat. It is invaluable in case you have been getting into a scrape, and have one of the boats of the city watch in chase of you."

"I hope I sha'n't want it for any purpose of that sort," Francis answered, laughing. "I do not think I am likely to give cause to the city watch to chase me."

"I don't think you are, Francisco, but there is never any saying."

"At any rate it is always useful to be able to go fast if necessary, and if we did want to get away, I do not think there are many pair-oared gondolas afloat that would overtake us, though a good four oar might do so. Giuseppi and I are so accustomed to each other's stroke now, that though in a heavy boat we might not be a match for two men, in a light craft like this, where weight does not count for so much, we would not mind entering her for a race against the two best gondoliers on the canals, in an ordinary boat."

A few evenings later, Francis was returning homewards at about half past ten, when, in passing along a quiet canal, the boat was hailed from the shore.

"Shall we take him, Messer Francisco?" Giuseppi asked in a low voice; for more than once they had late in the evening taken a fare.

Francis rowed, like Giuseppi, in his shirt, and in the darkness they were often taken for a pair-oared gondola on the lookout for a fare. Francis had sometimes accepted the offer, because it was an amusement to see where the passenger wished to go—to guess whether he was a lover hastening to keep an appointment, a gambler on a visit to some quiet locality, where high play went on unknown to the authorities, or simply one who had by some error missed his own gondola, and was anxious to return home. It made no difference to him which way he rowed. It was always possible that some adventure was to be met with, and the fare paid was a not unwelcome addition to Giuseppi's funds.

"Yes, we may as well take him," he replied to Giuseppi's question.

"You are in no hurry to get to bed, I suppose?" the man who

had hailed them said as the boat drew up against the wall of the canal.

"It does not make much difference to us, if we are well paid, to keep awake," Giuseppi said.

Upon such occasions he was always the spokesman.

"You know San Nicolo?"

"Yes, I know it," Giuseppi said; "but it is a long row—six miles, if it's a foot."

"You will have to wait there for an hour or two, but I will give you half a ducat for your night's work."

"What do you say, partner?" Giuseppi asked Francis.

"We may as well go," the lad replied after a moment's pause.

The row was certainly a long one, but the night was delightful, and the half ducat was a prize for Giuseppi; but what influenced Francis principally in accepting was curiosity. San Nicolo was a little sandy islet lying quite on the outside of the group of islands. It was inhabited only by a few fishermen; and Francis wondered that a man, evidently by his voice and manner of address belonging to the upper class, should want to go to such a place as this at this hour of the night. Certainly no ordinary motives could actuate him.

As the stranger took his place in the boat, Francis saw by the light of the stars that he was masked; but there was nothing very unusual in this, as masks were not unfrequently worn at night by young gallants, when engaged on any frolic in which they wished their identity to be unrecognized. Still it added to the interest of the trip; and dipping his oar in the water he set out at a slow, steady stroke well within his power. He adopted this partly in view of the length of the row before them, partly because the idea struck him that it might be as well that their passenger should not suspect that the boat was other than an ordinary gondola. The passenger, however, was well satisfied with the speed, for they passed two or three other gondolas before issuing from the narrow canals, and starting across the broad stretch of the lagoon.

Not a word was spoken until the gondola neared its destination. Then the passenger said:

"You row well. If you like the job I may employ you again."

"We are always ready to earn money," Francis said, speaking in a gruff voice quite unlike his own.

"Very well. I will let you know, as we return, what night I shall want you again. I suppose you can keep your mouths shut on occasion, and can go without gossiping to your fellows as to any job on which you are employed?"

"We can do that," Francis said. "It's no matter to us where our

14

customers want to go, if they are willing to pay for it; and as to gossiping, there is a saying, 'A silver gag is the best for keeping the mouth closed.'"

A few minutes later the bow of the gondola ran up on the sandy shore of San Nicolo. The stranger made his way forward and leapt out, and with the words, "It may be two hours before I am back," walked rapidly away.

"Why, Messer Francisco," Giuseppi said when their passenger was well out of hearing, "what on earth possessed you to accept a fare to such a place as this? Of course, for myself, I am glad enough to earn half a ducat, which will buy me a new jacket with silver buttons for the next festa; but to make such a journey as this was too much, and it will be very late before we are back. If the padrone knew it he would be very angry."

"I didn't do it to enable you to earn half a ducat, Giuseppi, although I am glad enough you should do so; but I did it because it seemed to promise the chance of an adventure. There must be something in this. A noble—for I have no doubt he is one—would never be coming out to San Nicolo, at this time of night, without some very strong motive. There can be no rich heiress whom he might want to carry off living here, so that can't be what he has come for. I think there must be some secret meeting, for as we came across the lagoon I saw one or two beats in the distance heading in this direction. Anyhow, I mean to try and find out what it all means."

"You had better not, sir," Giuseppi said earnestly. "If there is any plot on foot we had best not get mixed up in it. No one is too high or too low to escape the vengeance of the council, if found plotting against the state; and before now gondolas, staved in and empty, have been found drifting on the lagoons, and the men who rowed them have never been heard of again. Once in the dungeons of Saint Mark it would be of no use to plead that you had entered into the affair simply for the amusement. The fact that you were not a regular boatman would make the matter all the worse, and the maxim that 'dead men tell no tales' is largely acted upon in Venice.

"I think, sir, the best plan will be to row straight back, and leave our fare to find his way home as best he may."

"I mean to find something out about it if I can, Giuseppi. A state secret may be dangerous, but it may be valuable. Anyhow, there can be no great risk in it. On the water I think we can show our heels to anyone who chases us; and once in Venice, we are absolutely safe, for no one would suspect a gondola of Mr. Hammond, the English merchant, of having any connection with a hired craft with its two gondoliers."

15

"That is true enough, sir; but I don't like it for all that. However, if you have made up your mind to it, there is nothing more to be said."

"Very well. You stay here, and I will go and look round. You had better get the gondola afloat, and be ready to start at the instant, so that, if I should have to run for it, I can jump on board and be off in a moment."

Francis made his way quietly up to the little group of huts inhabited by the fishermen, but in none of them could he see any signs of life—no lights were visible, nor could he hear the murmur of voices. There were, he knew, other buildings scattered about on the island; but he had only the light of the stars to guide him, and, not knowing anything of the exact position of the houses, he thought it better to return to the boat.

"I can find no signs of them, Giuseppi."

"All the better, Messer Francisco. There are some sorts of game, which it is well for the safety of the hunter not to discover. I was very glad, I can tell you, when I heard your whistle, and made out your figure returning at a walk. Now you are back I will take an hour's nap, and I should advise you to do the same."

But Francis had no thought of sleep, and sat down at his end of the gondola, wondering over the adventure, and considering whether or not it would be worth while to follow it up another night. That it was a plot of some sort he had little doubt. There were always in Venice two parties, equally anxious perhaps for the prosperity of the republic, but differing widely as to the means by which that prosperity would be best achieved, and as to the alliances which would, in the long run, prove most beneficial to her. There were also needy and desperate men ready enough to take bribes from any who might offer them, and to intrigue in the interest of Padua or Ferrara, Verona, Milan, or Genoa—whichever might for the time be their paymasters.

Francis was English, but he had been long enough in Venice to feel a pride in the island city, and to be almost as keenly interested in her fortunes as were his companions and friends; and a certain sense of duty, mingled with his natural love of adventure, decided him to follow up the chance which had befallen him, and to endeavour to ascertain the nature of the plot which was, he had little doubt, being hatched at San Nicolo.

In a very few minutes the regular breathing of Giuseppi, who had curled himself up in the bottom of the boat, showed that he had gone to sleep; and he did not stir until, an hour and a half after the return of Francis, the latter heard the fall of footsteps approaching the gondola.

"Wake up, Giuseppi, here comes our fare!"

Francis stood up and stretched himself as the stranger came alongside, as if he too had been fast asleep.

"Take me back to the spot where I hailed you," the fare said briefly, as he stepped into the boat and threw himself back on the cushions, and without a word the lads dipped their oars in the water and the gondola glided away towards Venice.

Just as they reached the mouth of the Grand Canal, and were about to turn into it, a six-oared gondola shot out from under the point, and a voice called out:

"Stop, in the name of the republic, and give an account of yourselves!"

"Row on," the passenger exclaimed, starting up. "Ten ducats if you can set me safely on shore."

Had the lads been real gondoliers, it is probable that even this tempting offer would not have induced them to disregard the order from the galley, for they would have run no slight risk in so doing. But Francis had no desire to be caught, and perhaps imprisoned for a considerable time, until he was able to convince the council that his share of the night's work had been merely the result of a boyish freak. With two strokes of his oar, therefore, he swept the boat's head round, thereby throwing their pursuers directly astern of them; then he and Giuseppi threw their whole weight into the stroke, and the boat danced over the water at a pace very different to that at which it had hitherto proceeded.

But, fast as they went, the galley travelled somewhat faster, the rowers doing their utmost in obedience to the angry orders of their officer; and had the race been continued on a broad stretch of water, it would sooner or later have overhauled the gondola. But Francis was perfectly aware of this, and edged the boat away towards the end of the Piazzetta, and then, shooting her head round, dashed at full speed along the canal by the side of the ducal palace, the galley being at the time some forty yards behind.

"The first to the right," Francis said, and with scarce a pause in their speed, they turned off at right angles up the first canal they came to. Again and again they turned and twisted, regardless of the direction in which the canals took them, their only object being to gain on their pursuers, who lost considerably at each turn, being obliged always to check their speed, before arriving at each angle, to allow the boat to go round.

In ten minutes she was far behind, and they then abated their speed, and turned the boat's head in the direction in which they wished to go.

"By San Paolo," the stranger said, "that was well done! You are masters of your craft, and sent your boat along at a pace which must have astonished those fellows in that lumbering galley. I had no reason to fear them, but I do not care to be interfered with and questioned by these jacks-in-office of the republic."

A few minutes later they reached the place where he embarked, and as he got out he handed the money he had promised to Giuseppi.

"Next Thursday night," he said, "at half past ten."

"It seems a dangerous sort of service, signor," Giuseppi said hesitatingly. "It is no joke to disobey the officers of the republic, and next time we may not be so fortunate."

"It's worth taking a little risk when you are well paid," the other said, turning away, "and it is not likely we shall run against one of the state galleys another night."

"Home, now, Giuseppi," Francis said, "we can talk about it tomorrow. It's the best night's work you ever did in your life, and as I have had a grand excitement we are both contented."

During the next few days Francis debated seriously with himself whether to follow up the adventure; but he finally decided on doing so, feeling convinced that there could be no real danger, even were the boat seized by one of the state galleys; as his story, that he had gone into the matter simply to discover whether any plot was intended against the republic, would finally be believed, as it would be beyond the bounds of probability that a lad of his age could himself have been concerned in such a conspiracy. As to Giuseppi, he offered no remonstrance when Francis told him that he intended to go out to San Nicolo on the following Thursday, for the ten ducats he had received were a sum larger than he could have saved in a couple of years' steady work, and were indeed quite a fortune in his eyes. Another such a sum, and he would be able, when the time came, to buy a gondola of his own, to marry, and set up housekeeping in grand style. As for the danger, if Francis was willing to run it he could do the same; for after all, a few months' imprisonment was the worst that could befall him for his share in the business.

Before the day came Matteo Giustiniani told Francis a piece of news which interested him.

"You remember my cousin Maria Polani, whom we met the other evening on the Grand Canal?"

"Of course I do, Matteo. What of her?"

"Well, what do you think? Ruggiero Mocenigo, whom I pointed out to you on the Piazza—the man who had been banished for two years—has asked for her hand in marriage."

"He is not going to have it, I hope," Francis said indignantly. "It would be a shame, indeed, to give her to such a man as that."

"That is just what her father thought, Francisco, and he refused Ruggiero pretty curtly, and told him, I believe, he would rather see her in her grave than married to him; and I hear there was a regular scene, and Ruggiero went away swearing Polani should regret his refusal."

"I suppose your cousin does not care much about his threats," Francis said.

"I don't suppose he cares much about them," Matteo replied; "but Ruggiero is very powerfully connected, and may do him damage, not to speak of the chance of his hiring a bravo to stab him on the first opportunity. I know my father advised Polani to be very cautious where he went at night for a time. This fellow, Ruggiero, is a dangerous enemy. If he were to get Polani stabbed, it would be next to impossible to prove that it was his doing, however strong the suspicion might be; for mere suspicion goes for nothing against a man with his influence and connections. He has two near relations on the council, and if he were to burn down Polani's mansion, and to carry off Maria, the chances are against his being punished, if he did but keep out of the way for a few months."

As in England powerful barons were in the habit of waging private wars with each other, and the carrying off a bride by force was no very rare event, this state of things did not appear, to Francis, as outrageous as it would do to an English lad of the present day, but he shook his head.

"Of course one understands, Matteo, that everywhere powerful nobles do things which would be regarded as crimes if done by others; but, elsewhere, people can fortify their houses, and call out and arm their retainers, and stand on their guard. But that here, in a city like this, private feuds should be carried on, and men stabbed when unconscious of danger, seems to me detestable."

"Of course it isn't right," Matteo said carelessly, "but I don't know how you are going to put a stop to it; and after all, our quarrels here only involve a life or two, while in other countries nobles go to war with each other, and hundreds of lives, of people who have nothing to do with the quarrel, may be sacrificed."

This was a light in which Francis had hardly looked upon the matter before, and he was obliged to own that even private assassination, detestable as it was, yet caused much less suffering than feudal war. Still, he was not disposed entirely to give in to his friend's opinion.

"That is true, Matteo; but at the same time, in a war it is fair fighting, while a stab in the back is a cowardly business."

"It is not always fair fighting," Matteo replied. "You hear of castles being surprised, and the people massacred without a chance of resistance; of villages being burned, and the people butchered unresistingly. I don't think there is so much more fairness one way than the other. Polani knows he will have to be careful, and if he likes he can hire bravos to put Ruggiero out of the way, just as Ruggiero can do to remove him. There's a good deal to be said for both sides of the question."

Francis felt this was so, and that although he had an abhorrence of the Venetian method of settling quarrels, he saw that as far as the public were concerned, it was really preferable to the feudal method, of both parties calling out their retainers and going to war with each other, especially as assassinations played no inconsiderable part in the feudal struggles of the time.

On the Thursday night the gondola was in waiting at the agreed spot. Francis had thought it probable that the stranger might this time ask some questions as to where they lived and their usual place of plying for hire, and would endeavour to find out as much as he could about them, as they could not but suspect that he was engaged in some very unusual enterprise. He had therefore warned Giuseppi to be very careful in his replies. He knew that it was not necessary to say more, for Giuseppi had plenty of shrewdness, and would, he was sure, invent some plausible story without the least difficulty, possessing, as he did, plenty of the easy mendacity so general among the lower classes of the races inhabiting countries bordering on the Mediterranean. Their fare came down to the gondola a few minutes after the clock had tolled the half hour.

"I see you are punctual," he said, "which is more than most of you men are."

Francis was rowing the bow oar, and therefore stood with his back to the passenger, and was not likely to be addressed by him, as he would naturally turn to Giuseppi, who stood close behind him. As Francis had expected, as soon as they were out on the lagoon the passenger turned to his companion and began to question him.

"I cannot see your faces," he said; "but by your figures you are both young, are you not?"

"I am but twenty-two," Giuseppi said, "and my brother is a year younger."

"And what are your names?"

"Giovanni and Beppo Morani."

"And is this boat your own?"

"It is, signor. Our father died three years ago, leaving us his boat."

"And where do you usually ply?"

"Anywhere, signor, just as the fancy seizes us. Sometimes one place is good, sometimes another."

"And where do you live?"

"We don't live anywhere, signor. When night comes, and business is over, we tie up the boat to a post, wrap ourselves up, and go to sleep at the bottom. It costs nothing, and we are just as comfortable there as we should be on straw in a room."

"Then you must be saving money."

"Yes; we are laying money by. Some day, I suppose, we shall marry, and our wives must have homes. Besides, sometimes we are lazy and don't work. One must have some pleasure, you know."

"Would you like to enter service?"

"No, signor. We prefer being our own masters; to take a fare or leave it as we please."

"Your boat is a very fast one. You went at a tremendous rate when the galley was after us the other night."

"The boat is like others," Giuseppi said carelessly; "but most men can row fast when the alternative is ten ducats one way or a prison the other."

"Then there would be no place where I could always find you in the daytime if I wanted you?"

"No, signor; there would be no saying where we might be. We have sometimes regular customers, and it would not pay us to disappoint them, even if you paid us five times the ordinary fare. But we could always meet you at night anywhere, when you choose to appoint."

"But how can I appoint," the passenger said irritably, "if I don't know where to find you?"

Giuseppi was silent for a stroke or two.

"If your excellency would write in figures, half past ten or eleven, or whatever time we should meet you, just at the base of the column of the palace—the corner one on the Piazzetta—we should be sure to be there sometime or other during the day, and would look for it."

"You can read and write, then?" the passenger asked.

"I cannot do that, signor," Giuseppi said, "but I can make out figures. That is necessary to us, as how else could we keep time with our customers? We can read the sundials, as everyone else can; but as to reading and writing, that is not for poor lads like us."

21

The stranger was satisfied. Certainly every one could read the sundials; and the gondoliers would, as they said, understand his figures if he wrote them.

"Very well," he said. "It is probable I shall generally know, each time I discharge you, when I shall want you again; but should there be any change, I will make the figures on the base of the column at the corner of the Piazzetta, and that will mean the hour at which you are to meet me that night at the usual place."

Nothing more was said, until the gondola arrived at the same spot at which it had landed the passenger on the previous occasion.

"I shall be back in about the same time as before," the fare said when he alighted.

As he strode away into the darkness, Francis followed him. He was shoeless, for at that time the lower class seldom wore any protection to the feet, unless when going a journey over rough ground. Among the gondoliers shoes were unknown; and Francis himself generally took his off, for coolness and comfort, when out for the evening in his boat.

He kept some distance behind the man he was following, for as there were no hedges or inclosures, he could make out his figure against the sky at a considerable distance. As Francis had expected, he did not make towards the village, but kept along the island at a short distance from the edge of the water.

Presently Francis heard the dip of oars, and a gondola ran up on the sands halfway between himself and the man he was following. He threw himself down on the ground. Two men alighted, and went in the same direction as the one who had gone ahead.

Francis made a detour, so as to avoid being noticed by the gondoliers, and then again followed. After keeping more than a quarter of a mile near the water, the two figures ahead struck inshore. Francis followed them, and in a few minutes they stopped at a black mass, rising above the sand. He heard them knock, and then a low murmur, as if they were answering some question from within. Then they entered, and a door closed.

He moved up to the building. It was a hut of some size, but had a deserted appearance. It stood between two ridges of low sand hills, and the sand had drifted till it was halfway up the walls. There was no garden or inclosure round it, and any passerby would have concluded that it was uninhabited. The shutters were closed, and no gleam of light showed from within.

After stepping carefully round it, Francis took his post round the angle close to the door, and waited. Presently he heard footsteps approaching—three knocks were given on the door, and a voice within asked, "Who is there?"

The reply was, "One who is in distress."

The question came, "What ails you?"

And the answer, "All is wrong within."

Then there was a sound of bars being withdrawn, and the door opened and closed again.

There were four other arrivals. The same questions were asked and answered each time. Then some minutes elapsed without any fresh comers, and Francis thought that the number was probably complete. He lay down on the sand, and with his dagger began to make a hole through the wood, which was old and rotten, and gave him no difficulty in piercing it.

He applied his eye to the orifice, and saw that there were some twelve men seated round a table. Of those facing him he knew three or four by sight; all were men of good family. Two of them belonged to the council, but not to the inner Council of Ten. One, sitting at the top of the table, was speaking; but although Francis applied his ear to the hole he had made, he could hear but a confused murmur, and could not catch the words. He now rose cautiously, scooped up the sand so as to cover the hole in the wall, and swept a little down over the spot where he had been lying, although he had no doubt that the breeze, which would spring up before morning, would soon drift the light shifting sand over it, and obliterate the mark of his recumbent figure. Then he went round to the other side of the hut and bored another hole, so as to obtain a view of the faces of those whose backs had before been towards him.

One of these was Ruggiero Mocenigo. Another was a stranger to Francis, and some difference in the fashion of his garments indicated that he was not a Venetian, but, Francis thought, a Hungarian. The other three were not nobles. One of them Francis recognized, as being a man of much influence among the fishermen and sailors. The other two were unknown to him.

As upwards of an hour had been spent in making the two holes and taking observations, Francis thought it better now to make his way back to his boat, especially as it was evident that he would gain nothing by remaining longer. Therefore, after taking the same precautions as before, to conceal all signs of his presence, he made his way across the sands back to his gondola.

"Heaven be praised, you are back again!" Giuseppi said, when he heard his low whistle, as he came down to the boat. "I have been in a fever ever since I lost sight of you. Have you succeeded?"

"I have found out that there is certainly a plot of some sort being got up, and I know some of those concerned in it, but I could hear nothing that went on. Still, I have succeeded better than I expected, and I am well satisfied with the night's work."

23

"I hope you won't come again, Messer Francisco. In the first place, you may not always have the fortune to get away unseen. In the next place, it is a dangerous matter to have to do with conspiracies, whichever side you are on. The way to live long in Venice is to make no enemies."

"Yes, I know that, Giuseppi, and I haven't decided yet what to do in the matter."

A quarter of an hour later, their fare returned to the boat. This time they took a long detour, and, entering Venice by one of the many canals, reached the landing place without adventure. The stranger handed Giuseppi a ducat.

"I do not know when I shall want you again; but I will mark the hour, as agreed, on the pillar. Do not fail to go there every afternoon; and even if you don't see it, you might as well come round here at half past ten of a night. I may want you suddenly."

Before going to sleep that night, Francis thought the matter over seriously, and finally concluded that he would have no more to do with it. No doubt, by crossing over to San Nicolo in the daytime, he might be able to loosen a plank at the back of the hut, or to cut so large an opening that he could hear, as well as see, what was going on within; but supposing he discovered that a plot was on hand in favour of the enemies of Venice, such as Padua or Hungary, what was he to do next? At the best, if he denounced it, and the officers of the republic surrounded the hut when the conspirators were gathered there, arrested them, and found upon them, or in their houses, proofs sufficient to condemn them, his own position would not be enviable. He would gain, indeed, the gratitude of the republic; but as for rewards, he had no need of them. On the other hand, he would draw upon himself the enmity of some eight or ten important families, and all their connections and followers, and his life would be placed in imminent danger. They would be all the more bitter against him, inasmuch as the discovery would not have been made by accident, but by an act of deliberate prying into matters which concerned him in no way, he not being a citizen of the republic.

So far his action in the matter had been a mere boyish freak; and now that he saw it was likely to become an affair of grave importance, involving the lives of many persons, he determined to have nothing further to do with it.

CHAPTER 3

ON THE GRAND CANAL

Giuseppi, next morning, heard the announcement of the determination of Francis, to interfere no further in the matter of the conspiracy at San Nicolo, with immense satisfaction. For the last few nights he had scarcely slept, and whenever he dozed off, dreamed either of being tortured in dungeons, or of being murdered in his gondola; and no money could make up for the constant terrors which assailed him. In his waking moments he was more anxious for his employer than for himself, for it was upon him that the vengeance of the conspirators would fall, rather than upon a young gondolier, who was only obeying the orders of his master.

It was, then, with unbounded relief that he heard Francis had decided to go no more out to San Nicolo.

During the next few days Francis went more frequently than usual to the Piazza of Saint Mark, and had no difficulty in recognizing there the various persons he had seen in the hut, and in ascertaining their names and families. One of the citizens he had failed to recognize was a large contractor in the salt works on the mainland. The other was the largest importer of beasts for the supply of meat to the markets of the city.

Francis was well satisfied with the knowledge he had gained. It might never be of any use to him, but it might, on the other hand, be of importance when least expected.

As a matter of precaution he drew up an exact account of the proceedings of the two nights on the lagoons, giving an account of the meeting, and the names of the persons present, and placed it in a drawer in his room. He told Giuseppi what he had done.

"I do not think there is the least chance of our ever being recognized, Giuseppi. There was not enough light for the man to have made out our features. Still there is nothing like taking precautions, and if—I don't think it is likely, mind—but if anything should ever happen to me—if I should be missing, for example, and not return by the following morning—you take that paper out of my drawer and drop it into the Lion's Mouth. Then, if you are questioned, tell the whole story."

"But they will never believe me, Messer Francisco," Giuseppi said in alarm.

"They will believe you, because it will be a confirmation of my story; but I don't think that there is the least chance of our ever hearing anything further about it."

"Why not denounce them at once without putting your name to it," Giuseppi said. "Then they could pounce upon them over there, and find out all about it for themselves?"

"I have thought about it, Giuseppi, but there is something treacherous in secret denunciations. These men have done me no harm, and as a foreigner their political schemes do not greatly concern me. I should not like to think I had sent twelve men to the dungeons and perhaps to death."

"I think it's a pity you ever went there at all, Messer Francisco."

"Well, perhaps it is, Giuseppi; but I never thought it would turn out a serious affair like this. However, I do wish I hadn't gone now; not that I think it really matters, or that we shall ever hear anything more of it. We may, perhaps, some day see the result of this conspiracy, that is, if its objects are such as I guess them to be; namely, to form a party opposed to war with Hungary, Padua, or Genoa."

For some days after this Francis abstained from late excursions in the gondola. It was improbable that he or Giuseppi would be recognized did their late passenger meet them. Still, it was possible that they might be so; and when he went out he sat quietly among the cushions while Giuseppi rowed, as it would be a pair-oared gondola the stranger would be looking for. He was sure that the conspirator would feel uneasy when the boat did not come to the rendezvous, especially when they found that, on three successive days, figures were marked as had been arranged on the column at the corner of the Piazzetta.

Giuseppi learned indeed, a week later, that inquiries had been made among the gondoliers for a boat rowed by two brothers, Giovanni and Beppo; and the inquirer, who was dressed as a retainer of a noble family, had offered five ducats reward for information concerning it. No such names, however, were down upon the register of gondoliers licensed to ply for hire. Giuseppi learned that the search had been conducted quietly but vigorously, and that several young gondoliers who rowed together had been seen and questioned.

The general opinion, among the boatmen, was that some lady must have been carried off, and that her friends were seeking for a clue as to the spot to which she had been taken.

One evening Francis had been strolling on the Piazza with Matteo, and had remained out later than he had done since the night of his last visit to San Nicolo. He took his seat in the gondola, and when Giuseppi asked him if he would go home, said he would first take a turn or two on the Grand Canal as the night was close and sultry.

There was no moon now, and most of the gondolas carried torches. Giuseppi was paddling quietly, when a pair-oared gondola shot past them, and by the light of the torch it carried, Francis recognized the ladies sitting in it to be Maria and Giulia Polani with their duenna; two armed retainers sat behind them. They were, Francis supposed, returning from spending the evening at the house of some of their friends. There were but few boats now passing along the canal.

Polani's gondola was a considerable distance ahead, when Francis heard a sudden shout of, "Mind where you are going!"

Then there was a crash of two gondolas striking each other, followed by an outburst of shouts and cries of alarm, with, Francis thought, the clash of swords.

"Row, Giuseppi!" he exclaimed, leaping from his seat and catching up the other oar; and with swift and powerful strokes the two lads drove the gondola towards the scene of what was either an accident, or an attempt at crime.

They had no doubt which it was when they arrived at the spot. A four-oared gondola lay alongside that of the Polanis, and the gondoliers with their oars, and the two retainers with their swords, had offered a stout resistance to an armed party who were trying to board her from the other craft, but their resistance was well nigh over by the time Francis brought his gondola alongside.

One of the retainers had fallen with a sword thrust through his body, and a gondolier had been knocked overboard by a blow from an oar. The two girls were standing up screaming, and the surviving retainer was being borne backwards by three or four armed men, who were slashing furiously at him.

"Quick, ladies, jump into my boat!" Francis exclaimed as he came alongside, and, leaning over, he dragged them one after the other into his boat, just as their last defender fell.

With a fierce oath the leader of the assailants was about to spring into the gondola, when Francis, snatching up his oar, smote him with all his strength on the head as he was in the act of springing, and he fell with a heavy splash into the water between the boats.

A shout of alarm and rage rose from his followers, but the gondolas were now separated, and in another moment that of Francis was flying along the canal at the top of its speed.

"Calm yourselves, ladies," Francis said. "There is no fear of pursuit. They will stop to pick up the man I knocked into the canal, and by the time they get him on board we shall be out of their reach."

"What will become of the signora?" the eldest girl asked, when they recovered a little from their agitation.

"No harm will befall her, you may be sure," Francis said. "It was evidently an attempt to carry you off, and now that you have escaped they will care nothing for your duenna. She seemed to have lost her head altogether, for as I lifted you into the boat she clung so fast to your garments that I fancy a portion of them were left in her grasp."

"Do you know where to take us? I see you are going in the right direction?" the girl asked.

"To the Palazzo Polani," Francis said. "I have the honour of being a friend of your cousin, Matteo Giustiniani, and being with him one day when you passed in your gondola, he named you to me."

"A friend of Matteo!" the girl repeated in surprise. "Pardon me, signor, I thought you were two passing gondoliers. It was so dark that I could not recognize you; and, you see, it is so unusual to see a gentleman rowing."

"I am English, signora, and we are fond of strong exercise, and so after nightfall, when it cannot shock my friends, I often take an oar myself."

"I thank you, sir, with all my heart, for my sister and myself, for the service you have rendered us. I can hardly understand what has passed, even now it seems like a dream. We were going quietly along home, when a large dark gondola dashed out from one of the side canals, and nearly ran us down. Our gondolier shouted to warn them, but they ran alongside, and then some men jumped on board, and there was a terrible fight, and every moment I expected that the gondola would have been upset. Beppo was knocked overboard, and I saw old Nicolini fall; and then, just as it seemed all over, you appeared suddenly by our side, and dragged us on board this boat before I had time to think."

"I am afraid I was rather rough, signora, but there was no time to stand on ceremony. Here is the palazzo."

The boat was brought up by the side of the steps. Francis leapt ashore and rang the bell, and then assisted the girls to land. In a minute the door was thrown open, and two servitors with torches appeared. There was an exclamation of astonishment as they saw the young ladies alone with a strange attendant.

"I will do myself the honour of calling tomorrow to inquire if you are any the worse for your adventure, signora."

"No, indeed," the eldest girl said. "You must come up with us and see our father. We must tell him what has happened; and he will be angry indeed, did we suffer our rescuer to depart without his having an opportunity of thanking him."

Francis bowed and followed the girls upstairs. They entered a large, very handsomely furnished apartment where a tall man was sitting reading.

"Why, girls," he exclaimed as he rose, "what has happened? you look strangely excited. Where is your duenna? and who is this young gentleman who accompanies you?"

"We have been attacked, father, on our way home," both the girls exclaimed.

"Attacked?" Signor Polani repeated. "Who has dared to venture on such an outrage?"

"We don't know, father," Maria said. "It was a four-oared gondola that ran suddenly into us. We thought it was an accident till a number of men, with their swords drawn, leaped on board. Then Nicolini and Francia drew their swords and tried to defend us, and Beppo and Jacopo both fought bravely too with their oars; but Beppo was knocked overboard, and I am afraid Nicolini and Francia are killed, and in another moment they would have got at us, when this young gentleman came alongside in his gondola, and dragged us on board, for we were too bewildered and frightened to do anything. One of them—he seemed the leader of the party—tried to jump on board, but our protector struck him a terrible blow with his oar, and he fell into the water, and then the gondola made off, and, so far as we could see, they did not chase us."

"It is a scandalous outrage, and I will demand justice at the hands of the council.

"Young sir, you have laid me under an obligation I shall never forget. You have saved my daughter from the worst calamity that could befall her. Who is it to whom I am thus indebted?"

"My name is Francis Hammond. My father is an English merchant who has, for the last four years, established himself here."

"I know him well by repute," Polani said. "I trust I shall know more of him in the future.

"But where is your duenna, girls?"

"She remained behind in the gondola, father; she seemed too frightened to move."

"The lady seemed to have lost her head altogether," Francis said. "As I was lifting your daughters into my gondola, in a very hasty and unceremonious way—for the resistance of your servitors was all but overcome, and there was no time to be lost—she held so tightly to their robes that they were rent in her hands."

29

Signor Polani struck a gong.

"Let a gondola be manned instantly," he said, "and let six of you take arms and go in search of our boat. Let another man at once summon a leech, for some of those on board are, I fear, grievously wounded, if not killed."

But there was no occasion to carry out the order concerning the boat, for before it was ready to start the missing gondola arrived at the steps, rowed by the remaining gondolier. The duenna was lifted out sobbing hysterically, and the bodies of the two retainers were then landed. One was dead; the other expired a few minutes after being brought ashore.

"You did not observe anything particular about the gondola, Maria, or you, Giulia?"

"No, father, I saw no mark or escutcheon upon it, though they might have been there without my noticing them. I was too frightened to see anything; it came so suddenly upon us."

"It was, as far as I noticed, a plain black gondola," Francis said. "The men concerned in the affair were all dressed in dark clothes, without any distinguishing badges."

"How was it you came to interfere in the fray, young gentleman? Few of our people would have done so, holding it to be a dangerous thing, for a man to mix himself up in a quarrel in which he had no concern."

"I should probably have mixed myself up in it, in any case, when I heard the cry of women," Francis replied; "but, in truth, I recognized the signoras as their gondola passed mine, and knew them to be cousins of my friend Matteo Giustiniani. Therefore when I heard the outcry ahead, I naturally hastened up to do what I could in the matter."

"And well you did it," Polani said heartily. "I trust that the man you felled into the water is he who is the author of this outrage. I do not think I need seek far for him. My suspicions point very strongly in one direction, and tomorrow I will lay the matter before the council and demand reparation."

"And now, signor, if you will permit me I will take my leave," Francis said. "The hour is late, and the signoras will require rest after their fright and emotion."

"I will see you tomorrow, sir. I shall do myself the honour of calling early upon your father, to thank him for the great service you have rendered me."

Signor Polani accompanied Francis to the steps, while two servants held torches while he took his seat in the gondola, and remained standing there until the barque had shot away beyond the circle of light.

"We seem fated to have adventures, Giuseppi."

"We do indeed, Messer Francisco, and this is more to my liking than the last. We arrived just at the nick of time; another half minute and those young ladies would have been carried off. That was a rare blow you dealt their leader. I fancy he never came up again, and that that is why we got away without being chased."

"I am of that opinion myself, Giuseppi."

"If that is the case we shall not have heard the last of it, Messer Francisco. Only someone of a powerful family would venture upon so bold a deed, as to try to carry off ladies of birth on the Grand Canal, and you may find that this adventure has created for you enemies not to be despised."

"I can't help it if it has," Francis said carelessly. "On the other hand, it will gain for me an influential friend in Signor Polani, who is not only one of the richest merchants of Venice, but closely related to a number of the best families of the city."

"His influence will not protect you against the point of a dagger," Giuseppi said. "Your share in this business cannot but become public, and I think that it would be wise to give up our evening excursions at present."

"I don't agree with you, Giuseppi. We don't go about with torches burning, so no one who meets us is likely to recognize us. One gondola in the dark is pretty much like another, and however many enemies I had, I should not be afraid of traversing the canals."

The next morning, at breakfast time, Francis related to his father his adventure of the previous evening.

"It is a mistake, my son, to mix yourself up in broils which do not concern you; but in the present instance it may be that your adventure will turn out to be advantageous to your prospects. Signor Polani is one of the most illustrious merchants of Venice. His name is known everywhere in the East, and there is not a port in the Levant where his galleys do not trade. The friendship of such a man cannot but be most useful to me.

"Upon the other hand, you will probably make some enemies by your interference with the plans of some unscrupulous young noble, and Venice is not a healthy city for those who have powerful enemies; still I think that the advantages will more than balance the risk.

"However, Francis, you must curb your spirit of adventure. You are not the son of a baron or count, and the winning of honour and glory by deeds of arms neither befits you, nor would be of advantage to you in any way. A trader of the city of London should be distinguished for his probity and his attention to business; and

31

methinks that, ere long, it will be well to send you home to take your place in the counting house under the eye of my partner, John Pearson.

"Hitherto I have not checked your love for arms, or your intercourse with youths of far higher rank than your own; but I have been for some time doubting the wisdom of my course in bringing you out here with me, and have regretted that I did not leave you in good hands at home. The events of last night show that the time is fast approaching when you can no longer be considered a boy, and it will be better for you to turn at once into the groove in which you are to travel, than to continue a mode of life which will unfit you for the career of a city trader."

Francis knew too well his duty towards his father to make any reply, but his heart sank at the prospect of settling down in the establishment in London. His life there had not been an unpleasant one, but he knew that he should find it terribly dull, after the freedom and liberty he had enjoyed in Venice. He had never, however, even to himself, indulged the idea that any other career, save that of his father, could be his; and had regarded it as a matter of course that, some day, he would take his place in the shop in Cheapside.

Now that it was suddenly presented to him as something which would shortly take place, a feeling of repugnance towards the life came over him. Not that he dreamt for a moment of trying to induce his father to allow him to seek some other calling. He had been always taught to consider the position of a trader of good standing, of the city of London, as one of the most desirable possible. The line between the noble and the citizen was so strongly marked that no one thought of overstepping it. The citizens of London were as proud of their position and as tenacious of their rights as were the nobles themselves. They were ready enough to take up arms to defend their privileges and to resist oppression, whether it came from king or noble; but few indeed, even of the wilder spirits of the city, ever thought of taking to arms as a profession.

It was true that honour and rank were to be gained, by those who rode in the train of great nobles to the wars, but the nobles drew their following from their own estates, and not from among the dwellers in the cities; and, although the bodies of men-at-arms and archers, furnished by the city to the king in his wars, always did their duty stoutly in the field, they had no opportunity of distinguishing themselves singly. The deeds which attracted attention, and led to honour and rank, were performed by the esquires and candidates for the rank of knighthood, who rode behind the barons into the thick of the French chivalry.

Therefore Francis Hammond had never thought of taking to the profession of arms in his own country; though, when the news arrived in Venice of desperate fighting at sea with the Genoese, he had thought, to himself, that the most glorious thing in life must be to command a well-manned galley, as she advanced to the encounter of an enemy superior in numbers. He had never dreamed that such an aspiration could ever be satisfied—it was merely one of the fancies in which lads so often indulge.

Still, the thought that he was soon to return and take his place in the shop in Chepe was exceedingly unpleasant to him.

Soon after breakfast the bell at the water gate rang loudly, and a minute later the servant entered with the news that Signor Polani was below, and begged an interview. Mr. Hammond at once went down to the steps to receive his visitor, whom he saluted with all ceremony, and conducted upstairs.

"I am known to you by name, no doubt, Signor Hammond, as you are to me," the Venetian said, when the first formal greetings were over. "I am not a man of ceremony, nor, I judge, are you; but even if I were, the present is not an occasion for it. Your son has doubtless told you of the inestimable service, which he rendered to me last night, by saving my daughters, or rather my eldest daughter—for it was doubtless she whom the villains sought—from being borne off by one of the worst and most disreputable of the many bad and disreputable young men of this city."

"I am indeed glad, Signor Polani, that my son was able to be of service to you. I have somewhat blamed myself that I have let him have his own way so much, and permitted him to give himself up to exercises of arms, more befitting the son of a warlike noble than of a peaceful trader; but the quickness and boldness, which the mastery of arms gives, was yesterday of service, and I no longer regret the time he has spent, since it has enabled him to be of aid to the daughters of Signor Polani."

"A mastery of arms is always useful, whether a man be a peace-loving citizen, or one who would carve his way to fame by means of his weapons. We merchants of the Mediterranean might give up our trade, if we were not prepared to defend our ships against the corsairs of Barbary, and the pirates who haunt every inlet and islet of the Levant now, as they have ever done since the days of Rome. Besides, it is the duty of every citizen to defend his native city when attacked. And lastly, there are the private enemies, that every man who rises but in the smallest degree above his fellows is sure to create for himself.

"Moreover, a training in arms, as you say, gives readiness and quickness, it enables the mind to remain calm and steadfast amidst dangers of all sorts, and, methinks, it adds not a little to a man's dignity and self respect to know that he is equal, man to man, to any with whom he may come in contact. Here in Venice we are all soldiers and sailors, and your son will make no worse merchant, but rather the better, for being able to wield sword and dagger.

"Even now," he said with a smile, "he has proved the advantage of his training; for, though I say it not boastfully, Nicholas Polani has it in his power to be of some use to his friends, and foremost among them he will henceforward count your brave son, and, if you will permit him, yourself.

"But you will, I trust, excuse my paying you but a short visit this morning, for I am on my way to lay a complaint before the council. I have already been round to several of my friends, and Phillipo Giustiniani and some six others, nearest related to me, will go with me, being all aggrieved at this outrage to a family nearly connected. I crave you to permit me to take your son with me, in order that he may be at hand, if called upon, to say what he knows of the affair."

"Assuredly it is his duty to go with you if you desire it; although I own I am not sorry that he could see, as he tells me, no badge or cognizance which would enable him to say aught which can lead to the identification of those who would have abducted your daughter. It is but too well known a fact that it is dangerous to make enemies in Venice, for even the most powerful protection does not avail against the stab of a dagger."

"That is true enough," the merchant said. "The frequency of assassinations is a disgrace to our city; nor will it ever be put down until some men of high rank are executed, and the seignory show that they are as jealous of the lives of private citizens, as they are of the honour and well being of the republic."

Francis gladly threw aside his books when he was told that Signor Polani desired him to accompany him, and was soon seated by the side of the merchant in his gondola.

"How old are you, my friend?" the merchant asked him, as the boat threaded the mazes of the canals.

"I am just sixteen, signor."

"No more!" the merchant said in surprise. "I had taken you for well-nigh two years older. I have but just come from the Palazzo Giustiniani, and my young kinsman, Matteo, tells me that in the School of Arms there are none of our young nobles who are your match with rapier or battleaxe."

34

"I fear, sir," Francis said modestly, "that I have given up more time to the study of arms than befits the son of a sober trader."

"Not at all," the Venetian replied. "We traders have to defend our rights and our liberties, our goods and our ships, just as much as the nobles have to defend their privileges and their castles. Here in Venice there are no such distinctions of rank as there are elsewhere. Certain families, distinguished among the rest by their long standing, wealth, influence, or the services they have rendered to the state, are of senatorial rank, and constitute our nobility; but there are no titles among us. We are all citizens of the republic, with our rights and privileges, which cannot be infringed even by the most powerful; and the poorest citizen has an equal right to make himself as proficient in the arms, which he may be called upon to wield in defence of the state, as the Doge himself. In your country also, I believe, all men are obliged to learn the use of arms, to practise shooting at the butts, and to make themselves efficient, if called upon to take part in the wars of the country. And I have heard that at the jousts, the champions of the city of London have ere now held their own against those of the court."

"They have done so," Francis said; "and yet, I know not why, it is considered unseemly for the sons of well-to-do citizens to be too fond of military exercises."

"The idea is a foolish one," the Venetian said hotly. "I myself have, a score of times, defended my ships against corsairs and pirates, Genoese, and other enemies. I have fought against the Greeks, and been forced to busy myself in more than one serious fray in the streets of Constantinople, Alexandria, and other ports, and have served in the galleys of the state. All men who live by trade must be in favour of peace; but they must also be prepared to defend their goods, and the better able they are to do it, the more the honour to them.

"But here we are at the Piazzetta."

A group of nobles were standing near the landing place, and Signor Polani at once went up to them, and introduced Francis to them as the gentleman who had done his daughter and their kinswoman such good service. Francis was warmly thanked and congratulated by them all.

"Will you wait near the entrance?" Signor Polani said. "I see that my young cousin, Matteo, has accompanied his father, and you will, no doubt, find enough to say to each other while we are with the council."

The gentlemen entered the palace, and Matteo, who had remained respectfully at a short distance from the seniors, at once joined his friend.

"Well, Francis, I congratulate you heartily, though I feel quite jealous of you. It was splendid to think of your dashing up in your gondola, and carrying off my pretty cousins from the clutches of that villain, Ruggiero Mocenigo, just as he was about to lay his hands on them."

"Are you sure it was Ruggiero, Matteo?"

"Oh, there can't be any doubt about it. You know, he had asked for Maria's hand, and when Polani refused him, had gone off muttering threats. You know what his character is. He is capable of any evil action; besides, they say that he has dissipated his patrimony, in gaming and other extravagances at Constantinople, and is deep in the hands of the Jews. If he could have succeeded in carrying off Maria it would more than have mended his fortunes, for she and her sister are acknowledged to be the richest heiresses in Venice. Oh, there is not a shadow of doubt that it's he.

"You won't hear me saying anything against your love of prowling about in that gondola of yours, since it has brought you such a piece of good fortune—for it is a piece of good fortune, Francis, to have rendered such a service to Polani, to say nothing of all the rest of us who are connected with his family. I can tell you that there are scores of young men of good birth in Venice, who would give their right hand to have done what you did."

"I should have considered myself fortunate to have been of service to any girls threatened by violence, though they had only been fishermen's daughters," Francis said; "but I am specially pleased because they are relatives of yours, Matteo."

"To say nothing to their being two of the prettiest girls in Venice," Matteo added slyly.

"That counts for something too, no doubt," Francis said laughing, "though I didn't think of it.

"I wonder," he went on gravely, "whether that was Ruggiero whom I struck down, and whether he came up again to the surface. He has very powerful connections, you know, Matteo; and if I have gained friends, I shall also have gained enemies by the night's work."

"That is so," Matteo agreed. "For your sake, I own that I hope that Ruggiero is at present at the bottom of the canal. He was certainly no credit to his friends; and although they would of course have stood by him, I do not think they will feel, at heart, in any way displeased to know that he will trouble them no longer. But if his men got him out again, I should say you had best be careful, for Ruggiero is about the last man in Venice I should care to have as an enemy. However, we won't look at the unpleasant side of the matter, and will hope that his career has been brought to a close."

"I don't know which way to hope," Francis said gravely. "He will certainly be a dangerous enemy if he is alive; and yet the thought of having killed a man troubles me much."

"It would not trouble me at all if I were in your place," Matteo said. "If you had not killed him, you may be very sure that he would have killed you, and that the deed would have caused him no compunction whatever. It was a fair fight, just as if it had been a hostile galley in mid-sea; and I don't see why the thought of having rid Venice of one of her worst citizens need trouble you in any way."

"You see I have been brought up with rather different ideas to yours, Matteo. My father, as a trader, is adverse to fighting of all kinds—save, of course, in defence of one's country; and although he has not blamed me in any way for the part I took, I can see that he is much disquieted, and indeed speaks of sending me back to England at once."

"Oh, I hope not!" Matteo said earnestly. "Hitherto you and I have been great friends, Francis, but we shall be more in future. All Polani's friends will regard you as one of themselves; and I was even thinking, on my way here, that perhaps you and I might enter the service of the state together, and get appointed to a war galley in a few years."

"My father's hair would stand up at the thought, Matteo; though, for myself, I should like nothing so well. However, that could never have been. Still I am sorry, indeed, at the thought of leaving Venice. I have been very happy here, and I have made friends, and there is always something to do or talk about; and the life in London would be so dull in comparison. But here comes one of the ushers from the palace."

The official came up to them, and asked if either of them was Messer Francisco Hammond, and, finding that he had come to the right person, requested Francis to follow him.

CHAPTER 4

CARRIED OFF

It was with a feeling of considerable discomfort, and some awe, that Francis Hammond followed his conductor to the chamber of the Council. It was a large and stately apartment. The decorations were magnificent, and large pictures, representing events in the wars of Venice, hung round the walls. The ceiling was also superbly painted. The cornices were heavily gilded. Curtains of worked tapestry hung by the windows, and fell behind him as he entered the door.

At a table of horseshoe shape eleven councillors, clad in the long scarlet robes, trimmed with ermine, which were the distinguishing dress of Venetian senators, were seated—the doge himself acting as president. On their heads they wore black velvet caps, flat at the top, and in shape somewhat resembling the flat Scotch bonnet. Signor Polani and his companions were seated in chairs, facing the table.

When Francis entered the gondolier was giving evidence as to the attack upon his boat. Several questions were asked him when he had finished, and he was then told to retire. The usher then brought Francis forward.

"This is Messer Francisco Hammond," he said.

"Tell your story your own way," the doge said.

Francis related the story of the attack on the gondola, and the escape of the ladies in his boat.

"How came you, a foreigner and a youth, to interfere in a fray of this kind?" one of the councillors asked.

"I did not stop to think of my being a stranger, or a youth," Francis replied quietly. "I heard the screams of women in distress, and felt naturally bound to render them what aid I could."

"Did you know who the ladies were?"

"I knew them only by sight. My friend Matteo Giustiniani had pointed them out to me, on one occasion, as being the daughters of Signor Polani, and connections of his. When their gondola had passed mine, a few minutes previously, I recognized their faces by the light of the torches in their boat."

"Were the torches burning brightly?" another of the council asked; "because it may be that this attack was not intended against them, but against some others."

"The light was bright enough for me to recognize their faces at a glance," Francis said, "and also the yellow and white sashes of their gondoliers."

"Did you see any badge or cognizance, either on the gondola or on the persons of the assailants?"

"I did not," Francis said. "They certainly wore none. One of the torches in the Polani gondola had been extinguished in the fray, but the other was still burning, and, had the gondoliers worn coloured sashes or other distinguishing marks, I should have noticed them."

"Should you recognize, were you to see them again, any of the assailants?"

"I should not," Francis said. "They were all masked."

"You say you struck down the one who appeared to be their leader with an oar, as he was about to leap into your boat. How was it the oar was in your hand instead of that of your gondolier?"

"I was myself rowing," Francis said. "In London, rowing is an amusement of which boys of all classes are fond, and since I have been out here with my father I have learned to row a gondola; and sometimes, when I am out of an evening, I take an oar as well as my gondolier, enjoying the exercise and the speed at which the boat goes along. I was not rowing when the signora's boat passed me, but upon hearing the screams, I stood up and took the second oar, to arrive as quickly as possible at the spot. That was how it was that I had it in my hand, when the man was about to leap into the boat."

"Then there is nothing at all, so far as you know, to direct your suspicion against anyone as the author of this attack?"

"There was nothing," Francis said, "either in the gondola itself, or in the attire or persons of those concerned in the fray, which could give me the slightest clue as to their identity."

"At any rate, young gentleman," the doge said, "you appear to have behaved with a promptness, presence of mind, and courage— for it needs courage to interfere in a fray of this sort—beyond your years; and, in the name of the republic, I thank you for having prevented the commission of a grievous crime. You will please to remain here for the present. It may be that, when the person accused of this crime appears before us, you may be able to recognize his figure."

It was with mixed feelings that Francis heard, a minute or two later, the usher announce that Signor Ruggiero Mocenigo was without, awaiting the pleasure of their excellencies.

"Let him enter," the doge said.

The curtains fell back, and Ruggiero Mocenigo entered with a haughty air. He bowed to the council, and stood as if expecting to be questioned.

"You are charged, Ruggiero Mocenigo," the doge said, "with being concerned in an attempt to carry off the daughters of Signor Polani, and of taking part in the killing of three servitors of that gentleman."

"On what grounds am I accused?" Ruggiero said haughtily.

"On the ground that you are a rejected suitor for the elder lady's hand, and that you had uttered threats against her father, who, so far as he knows, has no other enemies."

"This seems somewhat scanty ground for an accusation of such gravity," Ruggiero said sneeringly. "If every suitor who grumbles, when his offer is refused, is to be held responsible for every accident which may take place in the lady's family, methinks that the time of this reverend and illustrious council will be largely occupied."

"You will remember," the doge said sternly, "that your previous conduct gives good ground for suspicion against you. You have already been banished from the state for two years for assassination, and such reports as reached us of your conduct in Constantinople, during your exile, were the reverse of satisfactory. Had it not been so, the prayers of your friends, that your term of banishment might be shortened, would doubtless have produced their effect."

"At any rate," Ruggiero said, "I can, with little difficulty, prove that I had no hand in any attempt upon Signor Polani's daughters last night, seeing that I had friends spending the evening with me, and that we indulged in play until three o'clock this morning—an hour at which, I should imagine, the Signoras Polani would scarcely be abroad."

"At what time did your friends assemble?"

"At nine o'clock," Ruggiero said. "We met by agreement in the Piazza, somewhat before that hour, and proceeded together on foot to my house."

"Who were your companions?"

Ruggiero gave the names of six young men, all connections of his family, and summonses were immediately sent for them to attend before the council.

"In the meantime, Messer Francisco Hammond, you can tell us whether you recognize in the accused one of the assailants last night."

40

"I cannot recognize him, your excellency," Francis said; "but I can say certainly that he was not the leader of the party, whom I struck with my oar. The blow fell on the temple, and assuredly there would be marks of such a blow remaining today."

As Francis was speaking, Ruggiero looked at him with a cold piercing glance, which expressed the reverse of gratitude for the evidence which he was giving in his favour, and something like a chill ran through him as he resumed his seat behind Signor Polani and his friends.

There was silence for a quarter of an hour. Occasionally the members of the council spoke in low tones to each other, but no word was spoken aloud, until the appearance of the first of the young men who had been summoned. One after another they gave their evidence, and all were unanimous in declaring that they had spent the evening with Ruggiero Mocenigo, and that he did not leave the room, from the moment of his arrival there soon after nine o'clock, until they left him at two in the morning.

"You have heard my witnesses," Ruggiero said, when the last had given his testimony; "and I now ask your excellencies, whether it is right that a gentleman, of good family, should be exposed to a villainous accusation of this kind, on the barest grounds of suspicion?"

"You have heard the evidence which has been given, Signor Polani," the doge said. "Do you withdraw your accusation against Signor Mocenigo?"

"I acknowledge, your excellency," Signor Polani said, rising, "that Ruggiero Mocenigo has proved that he took no personal part in the affair, but I will submit to you that this in no way proves that he is not the author of the attempt. He would know that my first suspicion would fall upon him, and would, therefore, naturally leave the matter to be carried out by others, and would take precautions to enable him to prove, as he has done, that he was not present. I still maintain that the circumstances of the case, his threats to me, and the fact that my daughter will naturally inherit a portion of what wealth I might possess, and that, as I know and can prove, Ruggiero Mocenigo has been lately reduced to borrowing money of the Jews, all point to his being the author of this attempt, which would at once satisfy his anger against me, for having declined the honour of his alliance, and repair his damaged fortunes."

There were a few words of whispered consultation between the councillors, and the doge then said:

"All present will now retire while the council deliberates. Our decision will be made known to the parties concerned, in due time."

On leaving the palace, Signor Polani and his friends walked together across the Piazza, discussing the turn of events.

"He will escape," Polani said. "He has two near relations on the council, and however strong our suspicions may be, there is really no proof against him. I fear that he will go free. I feel as certain as ever that he is the contriver of the attempt; but the precautions he has taken seem to render it impossible to bring the crime home to him. However, it is no use talking about it any more, at present.

"You will, I hope, accompany me home, Signor Francisco, and allow me to present you formally to my daughters. They were too much agitated, last night, to be able to thank you fully for the service you had rendered them.

"Matteo, do you come with us."

Three days passed, and no decision of the council had been announced, when, early in the morning, one of the state messengers brought an order that Francis should be in readiness, at nine o'clock, to accompany him. At that hour a gondola drew up at the steps. It was a covered gondola, with hangings, which prevented any from seeing who were within. Francis took his seat by the side of the official, and the gondola started at once.

"It looks very much as if I was being taken as a prisoner," Francis said to himself. "However, that can hardly be, for even if Ruggiero convinced the council that he was wholly innocent of this affair, no blame could fall on me, for I neither accused nor identified him. However, it is certainly towards the prisons we are going."

The boat, indeed, was passing the Piazzetta without stopping, and turned down the canal behind, to the prisons in rear of the palace. They stopped at the water gate, close to the Bridge of Sighs, and Francis and his conductor entered. They proceeded along two or three passages, until they came to a door where an official was standing. A word was spoken, and they passed in.

The chamber they entered was bare and vaulted, and contained no furniture whatever, but at one end was a low stone slab, upon which something was lying covered with a cloak. Four of the members of the council were standing in a group, talking, when Francis entered. Signor Polani, with two of his friends, stood apart at one side of the chamber. Ruggiero Mocenigo also, with two of his companions, stood on the other side.

Francis thought that the demeanour of Ruggiero was somewhat altered from that which he had assumed at the previous investigation, and that he looked sullen and anxious.

"We have sent for you, Francisco Hammond, in order that you may, if you can, identify a body which was found last night, floating in the Grand Canal."

One of the officials stepped forward and removed the cloak, showing on the stone slab the body of a young man. On the left temple there was an extensive bruise, and the skin was broken.

"Do you recognize that body?"

"I do not recognize the face," Francis said, "and do not know that I ever saw it before."

"The wound upon the temple which you see, is it such as, you would suppose, would be caused by the blow you struck an unknown person, while he was engaged in attacking the gondola of Signor Polani?"

"I cannot say whether it is such a wound as would be caused by a blow with an oar," Francis said; "but it is certainly, as nearly as possible, on the spot where I struck the man, just as he was leaping, sword in hand, into my gondola."

"You stated, at your examination the other day, that it was on the left temple you struck the blow."

"I did so. I said at once that Signor Ruggiero Mocenigo could not have been the man who led the assailants, because had he been so he would assuredly have borne a mark from the blow on the left temple."

"Look at the clothes. Do you see anything there which could lead you to identify him with your assailant?"

"My assailant was dressed in dark clothes, as this one was. There was but one distinguishing mark that I noticed, and this is wanting here. The light of the torch fell upon the handle of a dagger in his girdle. I saw it but for a moment, but I caught the gleam of gems. It was only a passing impression, but I could swear that he carried a small gold or yellow metal-handled dagger, and I believe that it was set with gems, but to this I should not like to swear."

"Produce the dagger found upon the dead man," one of the council said to an official.

And the officer produced a small dagger with a fine steel blade and gold handle, thickly encrusted with gems.

"Is this the dagger?" the senator asked Francis.

"I cannot say that it is the dagger," Francis replied; "but it closely resembles it, if it is not the same."

"You have no doubt, I suppose, seeing that wound on the temple, the dagger found in the girdle, and the fact that the body has evidently only been a few days in the water, that this is the man whom you struck down in the fray on the canal?"

"No, signor, I have no doubt whatever that it is the same person."

"That will do," the council said. "You can retire; and we thank you, in the name of justice, for the evidence you have given."

Francis was led back to the gondola, and conveyed to his father's house. An hour later Signor Polani arrived.

"The matter is finished," he said, "I cannot say satisfactorily to me, for the punishment is wholly inadequate to the offence, but at any rate he has not got off altogether unpunished. After you left, we passed from the prison into the palace, and then the whole council assembled, as before, in the council chamber. I may tell you that the body which was found was that of a cousin and intimate of Ruggiero Mocenigo. The two have been constantly together since the return of the latter from Constantinople. It was found, by inquiry at the house of the young man's father, that he left home on the evening upon which the attack was committed, saying that he was going to the mainland, and might not be expected to return for some days.

"The council took it for granted, from the wound in his head, and the fact that a leech has testified that the body had probably been in the water about three days, that he was the man that was stunned by your blow, and drowned in the canal. Ruggiero urged that the discovery in no way affected him; and that his cousin had, no doubt, attempted to carry off my daughter on his own account. There was eventually a division among the council on this point, but Maria was sent for, and on being questioned, testified that the young man had never spoken to her, and that, indeed, she did not know him even by sight; and the majority thereupon came to the conclusion that he could only have been acting as an instrument of Ruggiero's.

"We were not in the apartment while the deliberation was going on, but when we returned the president announced that, although there was no absolute proof of Ruggiero's complicity in the affair, yet that, considering his application for my daughter's hand, his threats on my refusal to his request, his previous character, and his intimacy with his cousin, the council had no doubt that the attempt had been made at his instigation, and therefore sentenced him to banishment from Venice and the islands for three years."

"I should be better pleased if they had sent him back to Constantinople, or one of the islands of the Levant," Mr. Hammond said. "If he is allowed to take up his abode on the mainland, he may be only two or three miles away, which, in the case of a man of his description, is much too near to be pleasant for those who have incurred his enmity."

44

"That is true," Signor Polani agreed, "and I myself, and my friends, are indignant that he should not have been banished to a distance, where he at least would have been powerless for fresh mischief. On the other hand, his friends will doubtless consider that he has been hardly treated. However, as far as my daughters are concerned, I will take good care that he shall have no opportunity of repeating his attempt; for I have ordered them, on no account whatever, to be absent from the palazzo after the shades of evening begin to fall, unless I myself am with them; and I shall increase the number of armed retainers in the house, by bringing some of my men on shore from a ship which arrived last night in port. I cannot believe that even Ruggiero would have the insolence to attempt to carry them off from the house by force; but when one has to deal with a man like this, one cannot take too great precautions."

"I have already ordered my son, on no account, to be out after nightfall in the streets. In his gondola I do not mind, for unless the gondoliers wear badges, it is impossible to tell one boat from another after dark. Besides, as he tells me, his boat is so fast that he has no fear whatever of being overtaken, even if recognized and chased. But I shall not feel comfortable so long as he is here, and shall send him back to England on the very first occasion that offers."

"I trust that no such occasion may occur just yet, Signor Hammond. I should be sorry, indeed, for your son to be separated so soon from us. We must talk the matter over together, and perhaps between us we may hit on some plan by which, while he may be out of the reach of the peril he has incurred on behalf of my family, he may yet be neither wasting his time, nor altogether separated from us."

For the next fortnight Francis spent most of his time at the Palazzo Polani. The merchant was evidently sincere in his invitation to him to make his house his home; and if a day passed without the lad paying a visit, would chide him gently for deserting them. He himself was frequently present in the balcony, where the four young people—for Matteo Giustiniani was generally of the party—sat and chatted together, the gouvernante sitting austerely by, with at times a strong expression of disapproval on her countenance at their laughter and merriment, although—as her charges' father approved of the intimacy of the girls with their young cousin and this English lad—she could offer no open objections. In the afternoon, the party generally went for a long row in a four-oared gondola, always returning home upon the approach of evening.

To Francis this time was delightful. He had had no sister of his own; and although he had made the acquaintance of a number of lads in Venice, and had accompanied his father to formal entertainments at the houses of his friends, he had never before been intimate in any of their families. The gaiety and high spirits of the two girls, when they were in the house, amused and pleased him, especially as it was in contrast to the somewhat stiff and dignified demeanour which they assumed when passing through the frequented canals in the gondola.

"I do not like that woman Castaldi," Francis said one evening as, after leaving the palazzo, Giuseppi rowed them towards the Palazzo Giustiniani, where Matteo was to be landed.

"Gouvernantes are not popular, as a class, with young men," Matteo laughed.

"But seriously, Matteo, I don't like her; and I am quite sure that, for some reason or other, she does not like me. I have seen her watching me, as a cat would watch a mouse she is going to spring on."

"Perhaps she has not forgiven you, Francisco, for saving her two charges, and leaving her to the mercy of their assailants."

"I don't know, Matteo. Her conduct appeared to me, at the time, to be very strange. Of course, she might have been paralysed with fright, but it was certainly curious the way she clung to their dresses, and tried to prevent them from leaving the boat."

"You don't really think, Francis, that she wanted them to be captured?"

"I don't know whether I should be justified in saying as much as that, Matteo, and I certainly should not say so to anyone else, but I can't help thinking that such was the case. I don't like her face, and I don't like the woman. She strikes me as being deceitful. She certainly did try to prevent my carrying the girls off and, had not their dresses given way in her hands, she would have done so. Anyhow, it strikes me that Ruggiero must have had some accomplice in the house. How else could he have known of the exact time at which they would be passing along the Grand Canal? For, that the gondola was in waiting to dash out and surprise them, there is no doubt.

"I was asking Signora Giulia, the other day, how it was they were so late, for she says that her father never liked their being out after dusk in Venice, though at Corfu he did not care how late they were upon the water. She replied that she did not quite know how it happened. Her sister had said, some time before, that she thought it

46

was time to be going, but the gouvernante—who was generally very particular—had said that there was no occasion to hurry, as their father knew where they were, and would not be uneasy. She thought the woman must have mistaken the time, and did not know how late it was.

"Of course, this proves nothing. Still I own that, putting all the things together, I have my suspicions."

"It is certainly curious, Francisco, though I can hardly believe it possible that the woman could be treacherous. She has been for some years in the service of the family, and my cousin has every confidence in her."

"That may be, Matteo; but Ruggiero may have promised so highly that he may have persuaded her to aid him. He could have afforded to be generous, if he had been successful."

"There is another thing, by the bye, Francisco, which did not strike me at the time; but now you speak of it, may be another link in the chain. I was laughing at Maria about their screaming, and saying what a noise the three of them must have made, and she said, 'Oh, no! there were only two of us—Giulia and I screamed for aid at the top of our voices; but the signora was as quiet and brave as possible, and did not utter a sound.'"

"That doesn't agree, Matteo, with her being so frightened as to hold the girls tightly, and almost prevent their escape, or with the row she made, sobbing and crying, when she came back. Of course there is not enough to go upon; and I could hardly venture to speak of it to Signor Polani, or to accuse a woman, in whom he has perfect confidence, of such frightful treachery on such vague grounds of suspicion. Still I do suspect her; and I hope, when I go away from Venice, you will, as far as you can, keep an eye upon her."

"I do not know how to do that," Matteo said, laughing; "but I will tell my cousins that we don't like her, and advise them, in future, not on any account to stay out after dusk, even if she gives them permission to do so; and if I learn anything more to justify our suspicions, I will tell my cousin what you and I think, though it won't be a pleasant thing to do. However, Ruggiero is gone now, and I hope we sha'n't hear anything more about him."

"I hope not, Matteo; but I am sure he is not the man to give up the plan he has once formed easily, any more than he is to forgive an injury.

"However, here we are at your steps. We will talk the other matter over another time. Anyhow, I am glad I have told you what I thought, for it has been worrying me. Now that I find you don't think my ideas about her are altogether absurd, I will keep my eyes more open than ever in future. I am convinced she is a bad one, and I only hope we may be able to prove it."

"You have made me very uncomfortable, Francisco," Matteo said as he stepped ashore; "but we will talk about it again tomorrow."

"We shall meet at your cousin's in the evening. Before that time, we had better both think over whether we ought to tell anyone our suspicions, and we can hold a council in the gondola on the way back."

Francis did think the matter over that night. He felt that the fact told him by Giulia, that the gouvernante had herself been the means of their staying out later than usual on the evening of the attack, added great weight to the vague suspicions he had previously entertained; and he determined to let the matter rest no longer, but that the next day he would speak to Signor Polani, even at the risk of offending him by his suspicions of a person who had been, for some years, in his confidence. Accordingly, he went in the morning to the palazzo, but found that Signor Polani was absent, and would not be in until two or three o'clock in the afternoon. He did not see the girls, who, he knew, were going out to spend the day with some friends.

At three o'clock he returned, and found that Polani had just come in.

"Why, Francisco," the merchant said when he entered, "have you forgotten that my daughters will be out all day?"

"No, signor, I have not forgotten that, but I wish to speak to you. I dare say you will laugh at me, but I hope you will not think me meddlesome, or impertinent, for touching upon a subject which concerns you nearly."

"I am sure you will not be meddlesome or impertinent, Francisco," Signor Polani said reassuringly, for he saw that the lad was nervous and anxious. "Tell me what you have to say, and I can promise you beforehand that, whether I agree with you or not in what you may have to say, I shall be in no way vexed, for I shall know you have said it with the best intentions."

"What I have to say, sir, concerns the Signora Castaldi, your daughters' gouvernante. I know, sir, that you repose implicit confidence in her; and your judgment, formed after years of intimate knowledge, is hardly likely to be shaken by what I have to tell you. I spoke to Matteo about it, and, as he is somewhat of my opinion, I have decided that it is, at least, my duty to tell you all the circumstances, and you can then form your own conclusions."

48

Francis then related the facts known to him. First, that the assailants of the gondola must have had accurate information as to the hour at which they would come along; secondly, that it was at the gouvernante's suggestion that the return had been delayed much later than usual; lastly, that when the attack took place, the gouvernante did not raise her voice to cry for assistance, and that she had, at the last moment, so firmly seized their dresses, that it was only by tearing the girls from her grasp that he had been enabled to get them into the boat.

"There may be nothing in all this," he said when he had concluded. "But at least, sir, I thought that it was right you should know it; and you will believe me, that it is only anxiety as to the safety of your daughters that has led me to speak to you."

"Of that I am quite sure," Signor Polani said cordially, "and you were perfectly right in speaking to me. I own, however, that I do not for a moment think that the circumstances are more than mere coincidences. Signora Castaldi has been with me for upwards of ten years. She has instructed and trained my daughters entirely to my satisfaction. I do not say that she is everything that one could wish, but, then, no one is perfect, and I have every confidence in her fidelity and trustworthiness. I own that the chain you have put together is a strong one, and had she but lately entered my service, and were she a person of whom I knew but little, I should attach great weight to the facts, although taken in themselves they do not amount to much. Doubtless she saw that my daughters were enjoying themselves in the society of my friends, and in her kindness of heart erred, as she certainly did err, in allowing them to stay longer than she should have done.

"Then, as to her not crying out when attacked, women behave differently in cases of danger. Some scream loudly, others are silent, as if paralysed by fear. This would seem to have been her case. Doubtless she instinctively grasped the girls for their protection, and in her fright did not even perceive that a boat had come alongside, or know that you were a friend trying to save them. That someone informed their assailants of the whereabouts of my daughters, and the time they were coming home, is clear; but they might have been seen going to the house, and a swift gondola have been placed on the watch. Had this boat started as soon as they took their seat in the gondola on their return, and hastened, by the narrow canals, to the spot where their accomplices were waiting, they could have warned them in ample time of the approach of the gondola with my daughters.

"I have, as you may believe, thought the matter deeply over, for it was evident to me that the news of my daughters' coming must have reached their assailants beforehand. I was most unwilling to suspect treachery on the part of any of my household, and came to the conclusion that the warning was given in the way I have suggested.

"At the same time, Francisco, I thank you deeply for having mentioned to me the suspicions you have formed, and although I think that you are wholly mistaken, I certainly shall not neglect the warning, but shall watch very closely the conduct of my daughters' gouvernante, and shall take every precaution to put it out of her power to play me false, even while I cannot, for a moment, believe she would be so base and treacherous as to attempt to do so."

"In that case, signor, I shall feel that my mission has not been unsuccessful, however mistaken I may be, and I trust sincerely that I am wholly wrong. I thank you much for the kind way in which you have heard me express suspicions of a person in your confidence."

The gravity with which the merchant had heard Francis' story vanished immediately he left the room, and a smile came over his face.

"Boys are boys all the world over," he said to himself, "and though my young friend has almost the stature of a man, as well as the quickness and courage of one, and has plenty of sense in other matters, he has at once the prejudices and the romantic ideas of a boy. Had Signora Castaldi been young and pretty, no idea that she was treacherous would have ever entered his mind; but what young fellow yet ever liked a gouvernante, who sits by and works at her tambour frame, with a disapproving expression on her face, while he is laughing and talking with a girl of his own age. I should have felt the same when I was a boy. Still, to picture the poor signora as a traitoress, in the pay of that villain Mocenigo, is too absurd. I had the greatest difficulty in keeping my gravity when he was unfolding his story. But he is an excellent lad, nevertheless. A true, honest, brave lad, with a little of the bluffness that they say all his nation possess, but with a heart of gold, unless I am greatly mistaken."

At seven o'clock, Francis was just getting into his gondola to go round again to Signor Polani's, when another gondola came along the canal at the top of its speed, and he recognized at once the badge of the Giustiniani. It stopped suddenly as it came abreast of his own boat, and Matteo, in a state of the highest excitement, jumped from his own boat into that of Francis.

"What is the matter, Matteo? What has happened?"

"I have terrible news, Francisco. My cousins have both disappeared."

"Disappeared!" Francis repeated in astonishment "How have they disappeared?"

"Their father has just been round to see mine. He is half mad with grief and anger. You know they had gone to spend the day at the Persanis?"

"Yes, yes," Francis exclaimed; "but do go on, Matteo. Tell me all about it, quickly."

"Well, it seems that Polani, for some reason or other, thought he would go and fetch them himself, and at five o'clock he arrived there in his gondola, only to find that they had left two hours before. You were right, Francisco, it was that beldam Castaldi. She went with them there in the morning, and left them there, and was to have come in the gondola for them at six. At three o'clock she arrived, saying that their father had met with a serious accident, having fallen down the steps of one of the bridges and broken his leg, and that he had sent her to fetch them at once.

"Of course, they left with her instantly. Polani questioned the lackeys, who had aided them to embark. They said that the gondola was not one of his boats, but was apparently a hired gondola, with a closed cabin. The girls had stopped in surprise as they came down the steps, and Maria said, 'Why, this is not our gondola!'

"Castaldi replied, 'No, no; our own gondolas had both gone off to find and bring a leech, and as your father was urgently wanting you, I hailed the first passing boat. Make haste, dears, your father is longing for you.'

"So they got on board at once, and the gondola rowed swiftly away. That is all I know about it, except that the story was a lie, that their father never sent for them, and that up to a quarter of an hour ago they had not reached home."

CHAPTER 5

FINDING A CLUE

"This is awful, Matteo," Francis said, when his friend had finished his story. "What is to be done?"

"That is just the thing, Francisco. What is to be done? My cousin has been already to the city magistrates, to tell them what has taken place, and to request their aid in discovering where the girls have been carried to. I believe that he is going to put up a proclamation, announcing that he will give a thousand ducats to whomsoever will bring information which will enable him to recover the girls. That will set every gondolier on the canals on the alert, and some of them must surely have noticed a closed gondola rowed by two men, for at this time of year very few gondolas have their covers on. It seems to be terrible not to be able to do anything, so I came straight off to tell you."

"You had better send your gondola home, Matteo. It may be wanted. We will paddle out to the lagoon and talk it over. Surely there must be something to be done, if we could but think of it.

"This is terrible, indeed, Matteo," he repeated, after they had sat without speaking for some minutes. "One feels quite helpless and bewildered. To think that only yesterday evening we were laughing and chatting with them, and that now they are lost, and in the power of that villain Mocenigo, who you may be sure is at the bottom of it.

"By the way," he said suddenly, "do you know where he has taken up his abode?"

"I heard that he was at Botonda, near Chioggia, a week ago, but whether he is there still I have not the least idea."

"It seems to me that the thing to do is to find him, and keep him in sight. He will probably have them hidden away somewhere, and will not go near them for some time, for he will know that he will be suspected, and perhaps watched."

"But why should he not force Maria to marry him at once?" Matteo said. "You see, when he has once made her his wife he will be safe, for my cousin would be driven then to make terms with him for her sake."

"He may try that," Francis said; "but he must know that Maria has plenty of spirit, and may refuse to marry him, threaten her as he will. He may think that, after she has been kept confined for some time, and finds that there is no hope of escape, except by consenting to be his wife, she may give way. But in any case, it seems to me that the thing to be done is to find Ruggiero, and to watch his movements."

"I have no doubt my cousin has already taken steps in that direction," Matteo said, "and I feel sure that, in this case, he will receive the support of every influential man in Venice, outside the Mocenigo family and their connections. The carrying off of ladies, in broad daylight, will be regarded as a personal injury in every family. The last attempt was different. I do not say it was not bad enough, but it is not like decoying girls from home by a false message. No one could feel safe, if such a deed as this were not severely punished."

"Let us go back again, Matteo. It is no use our thinking of anything until we know what has really been done, and you are sure to be able to learn, at home, what steps have been taken."

On reaching home Matteo learned that Polani, accompanied by two members of the council, had already started in one of the swiftest of the state galleys for the mainland. A council had been hastily summoned, and, upon hearing Polani's narrative, had dispatched two of their number, with an official of the republic, to Botonda. If Ruggiero was found to be still there, he was to be kept a prisoner in the house in which he was staying, under the strictest watch. If he had left, orders were to be sent, to every town in the Venetian dominions on the mainland, for his arrest when discovered, and in that case he was to be sent a prisoner, strongly guarded, to Venice.

Other galleys had been simultaneously dispatched to the various ports, ordering a strict search of every boat arriving or leaving, and directing a minute investigation to be made as to the occupants of every boat that had arrived during the evening or night. The fact that a thousand ducats were offered, for information which would lead to the recovery of the girls, was also to be published far and wide.

The news of the abduction had spread, and the greatest indignation was excited in the city. The sailors from the port of Malamocco came over in great numbers. They regarded this outrage on the family of the great merchant as almost a personal insult. Stones were thrown at the windows of the Palazzo Mocenigo, and an attack would have been made upon it, had not the authorities sent down strong guards to protect it. Persons belonging to that house, and the families connected with it, were assaulted in the streets, and all Venice was in an uproar.

"There is one comfort," Giuseppi said, when he heard from Francis what had taken place. "Just at present, Mocenigo will have

53

enough to think about his own affairs without troubling about you. I have been in a tremble ever since that day, and have dreamed bad dreams every night."

"You are more nervous for me than I am for myself, Giuseppi; but I have been careful too, for although Ruggiero himself was away his friends are here, and active, too, as you see by this successful attempt. But I think that at present they are likely to let matters sleep. Public opinion is greatly excited over the affair, and as, if I were found with a stab in my back, it would, after what has passed, be put down to them, I think they will leave me alone."

"I do hope, father," Francis said at breakfast the next morning, "that there may be no opportunity of sending me back to England, until something is heard of the Polanis."

"I have somewhat changed my mind, Francis, as to that matter. After what Signor Polani said the other day, I feel that it would be foolish for me to adhere to that plan. With his immense trade and business connections he can do almost anything for you, and such an introduction into business is so vastly better than your entering my shop in the city, that it is best, in every way, that you should stay here for the present. Of course, for the time he will be able to think of nothing but his missing daughters; but at any rate, you can remain here until he has leisure to pursue the subject, and to state, further than he did the other day, what he proposes for you. My own business is a good one for a London trader, but it is nothing by the side of the transactions of the merchant princes at Venice, among the very first of whom Signor Polani is reckoned."

Francis was greatly pleased at his father's words. He had, ever since Polani had spoken to him, been pondering the matter in his mind. He knew that to enter business under his protection would be one of the best openings that even Venice could afford; but his father was slow to change his plans, and Francis greatly feared that he would adhere to his original plan.

"I was hoping, father, that you would think favourably of what Signor Polani said, although, of course, I kept silence, knowing that you would do what was best for me. And now I would ask you if you will, until this matter is cleared up, excuse me from my tasks. I should learn nothing did I continue at them, for my mind would be ever running upon Signor Polani's daughters, and I should be altogether too restless to apply myself. It seems to me, too, that I might, as I row here and there in my gondola, obtain some clue as to their place of concealment."

"I do not see how you could do that, Francis, when so many others, far better qualified than yourself, will be on the lookout. Still, as I agree with you that you are not likely to apply your mind diligently to your tasks, and as, indeed, you will shortly be giving them up altogether, I grant your request."

Polani returned in the evening to Venice. Ruggiero Mocenigo had been found. He professed great indignation at the accusation brought against him, of being concerned in the abduction of the ladies, and protested furiously when he heard that, until they were found, he was to consider himself a prisoner. Signor Polani considered that his indignation was feigned, but he had no doubt as to the reality of his anger at finding that he was to be confined to his house under a guard.

Immediately after his return, Polani sent his gondola for Francis. He was pacing up and down the room when the lad arrived.

"Your suspicions have turned out correct, as you see, Francis. Would to Heaven I had acted upon them at once, and then this would not have happened. It seemed to me altogether absurd, when you spoke to me, that the woman I have for years treated as a friend should thus betray me. And yet your warning made me uneasy, so much so that I set off myself to fetch them home at five o'clock, only to find that I was too late. I scarcely know why I have sent for you, Francis, except that as I have found, to my cost, that you were more clear sighted in this matter than I, I want to know what you think now, and whether any plan offering even a chance of success has occurred to you. That they have been carried off by the friends of Mocenigo I have no doubt whatever."

"I fear, signor," Francis said, "that there is little hope of my thinking of anything that has not already occurred to you. It seems to me hardly likely that they can be in the city, although, of course, they may be confined in the house of Mocenigo's agents. Still, they would be sure that you would offer large rewards for their discovery, and would be more likely to take them right away. Besides, I should think that it was Mocenigo's intention to join them, wherever they may be, as soon as he learned that they were in the hands of his accomplices. Your fortunate discovery that they had gone, so soon after they had been carried off, and your going straight to him armed with the order of the council, probably upset his calculations, for it is likely enough that his agents had not arrived at the house, and that he learned from you, for the first time, that his plans had succeeded. Had you arrived two or three hours later, you might have found him gone."

"That is what I calculated, Francisco. His agents had but four hours' start of me. They would, no doubt, carry the girls to the place of concealment chosen, and would then bear the news to him; whereas I, going direct in one of the state gondolas, might reach him before they did, and I feel assured that I did so.

"It was nigh midnight when I arrived, but he was still up, and I doubt not awaiting the arrival of the villains he had employed. My first step was to set a watch round the house, with the order to arrest any who might come and inquire for him. No one, however, came.

"The news, indeed, of the sudden arrival of a state galley, at that hour, had caused some excitement in the place, and his agents might well have heard of it upon their arrival. I agree with you in thinking they are not in the town, but this makes the search all the more difficult. The question is, what ought we to do next?"

"The reward that you have offered will certainly bring you news, signor, if any, save those absolutely concerned, have observed anything suspicious; but I should send to all the fishing villages, on the islets and on the mainland, to publish the news of the reward you have offered. Beyond that, I do not see that anything can be done; and I, too, have thought of nothing else since Matteo brought me the news of their being carried off. It will be of no use, that I can see, going among the fishermen and questioning them, because, with such a reward in view, it is certain that anyone who has anything to tell will come, of his own accord, to do so."

"I know that is the case already, Francisco. The authorities have been busy all day with the matter, and a score of reports as to closed gondolas being seen have reached them; but so far nothing has come of it. Many of these gondolas have been traced to their destinations, but in no case was there anything to justify suspicion. Happily, as long as Mocenigo is in confinement, I feel that no actual harm will happen to the girls; but the villain is as crafty as a fox, and may elude the vigilance of the officer in charge of him. I am going to the council, presently, to urge that he should be brought here as a prisoner; but from what I hear there is little chance of the request being complied with. His friends are already declaiming on the injustice of a man being treated as a criminal, when there is no shadow of proof forthcoming against him; and the disturbances last night have angered many who have no great friendship for him, but who are indignant at the attack of the populace upon the house of a noble. So you see that there is but faint chance that they would bring him hither a prisoner."

"I think, sir, that were I in your case, I should put some trusty men to watch round the house where he is confined; so that in case he should escape the vigilance of his guards they might seize upon him. Everything depends, as you say, upon his being kept in durance."

"I will do so, Francisco, at once. I will send to two of my officers at the port, and tell them to pick out a dozen men on whom they can rely, to proceed to Botonda, and to watch closely everyone who enters or leaves the house, without at the same time making themselves conspicuous. At any rate, they will be handy there in case Mocenigo's friends attempt to rescue him by force, which might be done with success, for the house he occupies stands at a short distance out of the town, and the official in charge of Mocenigo has only eight men with him.

"Yes, your advice is excellent, and I will follow it at once. Should any other idea occur to you, pray let me know it immediately. You saved my daughters once, and although I know there is no reason why it should be so, still, I feel a sort of belief that you may, somehow, be instrumental in their again being brought back to me."

"I will do my best, sir, you may depend upon it," Francis said earnestly. "Were they my own sisters, I could not feel more strongly interested in their behalf."

Francis spent the next week almost entirely in his gondola. Starting soon after daybreak with Giuseppi, he would row across to the villages on the mainland, and make inquiries of all sorts there; or would visit the little groups of fishermen's huts, built here and there on posts among the shallows. He would scan every house as he passed it, with the vague hope that a face might appear at the window, or a hand be waved for assistance. But, during all that time, he had found nothing which seemed to offer the slightest clue, nor were the inquiries set on foot by Signor Polani more successful. Every piece of information which seemed to bear, in the slightest degree, upon the affair was investigated, but in no case was it found of the slightest utility.

One evening he was returning late, tired by the long day's work, and discouraged with his utter want of success, when, just as he had passed under the Ponto Maggiore, the lights on the bridge fell on the faces of the sitters in a gondola coming the other way. They were a man and a woman. The latter was closely veiled. But the night was close and oppressive, and, just at the moment when Francis' eyes fell upon her, she lifted her veil for air. Francis recognized her instantly. For a moment he stopped rowing, and then dipped his oar in as before. Directly the other gondola passed through the bridge behind him, and his own had got beyond the circle of light, he swept it suddenly round.

Giuseppi gave an exclamation of surprise.

"Giuseppi, we have luck at last. Did you notice that gondola we met just now? The woman sitting in it is Castaldi, the woman who betrayed the signoras."

"What shall we do, Messer Francisco?" Giuseppi, who had

become almost as interested in the search as his master, asked. "There was only a single gondolier and one other man. If we take them by surprise we can master them."

"That will not do, Giuseppi. The woman would refuse to speak, and though they could force her to do so in the dungeons, the girls would be sure to be removed the moment it was known she was captured. We must follow them, and see where they go to. Let us get well behind them, so that we can just make them out in the distance. If they have a suspicion that they are being followed, they will land her at the first steps and slip away from us."

"They are landing now, signor," Giuseppi exclaimed directly afterwards. "Shall we push on and overtake them on shore?"

"It is too late, Giuseppi. They are a hundred and fifty yards away, and would have mixed in the crowd, and be lost, long before we should get ashore and follow them. Row on fast, but not over towards that side. If the gondola moves off, we will make straight for the steps and try to follow them, though our chance of hitting upon them in the narrow lanes and turnings is slight indeed.

"But if, as I hope, the gondola stops at the steps, most likely they will return to it in time. So we will row in to the bank a hundred yards farther up the canal and wait."

The persons who had been seen in the gondola had disappeared when they came abreast of it, and the gondolier had seated himself in the boat, with the evident intention of waiting. Francis steered his gondola at a distance of a few yards from it as he shot past, but did not abate his speed, and continued to row till they were three or four hundred yards farther up the canal. Then he turned the gondola, and paddled noiselessly back until he could see the outline of the boat he was watching.

An hour elapsed before any movement was visible. Then Francis heard the sound of footsteps, and could just make out the figures of persons descending the steps and entering the gondola. Then the boat moved out into the middle of the canal, where a few boats were still passing to and fro. Francis kept his gondola close by the bank, so as to be in the deep shade of the houses. The boat they were following again passed under the Ponto Maggiore, and for some distance followed the line of the Grand Canal.

"Keep your eye upon it, Giuseppi. It is sure to turn off one way or the other soon, and if it is too far ahead of us when it does so, then it may give us the slip altogether."

But the gondola continued its course the whole length of the canal, and then straight on until, nearly opposite Saint Mark's, it passed close to a larger gondola, with four rowers, coming slowly in the other direction; and it seemed to Francis that the two boats paused when opposite each other, and that a few words were exchanged.

Then the boat they were watching turned out straight into the lagoon. It was rather lighter here than in the canal, bordered on each side by houses, and Francis did not turn the head of his gondola for a minute or two.

"It will be very difficult to keep them in sight out here without their making us out," Giuseppi said.

"Yes, and it is likely enough that they are only going out there in order that they may be quite sure that they are not followed, before striking off to the place they want to go to. They may possibly have made us out, and guess that we are tracking them. They would be sure to keep their eyes and ears open."

"I can only just make them out now, Messer Francisco, and as we shall have the buildings behind us, they will not be able to see us as well as we can see them. I think we can go now."

"We will risk it, at any rate, Giuseppi. I have lost sight of them already, and it will never do to let them give us the slip."

They dipped their oars in the water, and the gondola darted out from the shore. They had not gone fifty strokes when they heard the sound of oars close at hand.

"To the right, Giuseppi, hard!" Francis cried as he glanced over his shoulder.

A sweep with both oars brought the gondola's head, in a moment, almost at right angles to the course that she had been pursuing; and the next sent her dancing on a new line, just as a four-oared gondola swept down upon them, missing their stern by only three or four feet. Had they been less quick in turning, the iron prow would have cut right through their light boat.

Giuseppi burst into a torrent of vituperation at the carelessness of the gondoliers who had so nearly run into them, but Francis silenced him at once.

"Row, Giuseppi. It was done on purpose. It is the gondola the other spoke to."

Their assailant was turning also, and in a few seconds was in pursuit. Francis understood it now. The gondola they had been following had noticed them, and had informed their friends, waiting off Saint Mark's, of the fact. Intent upon watching the receding boat, he had paid no further attention to the four-oared craft, which had made a turn, and lay waiting in readiness to run them down, should they follow in the track of the other boat.

Francis soon saw that the craft behind them was a fast one, and rowed by men who were first-rate gondoliers. Fast as his own boat was flying through the water, the other gained upon them steadily. He was heading now for the entrance to the Grand Canal, for their pursuer, in the wider sweep he had made in turning, was nearer to the Piazza than they were, and cut off their flight in that direction.

"Keep cool, Giuseppi," he said. "They will be up to us in a minute or two. When their bow is within a yard or two of us, and I say, 'Now!' sweep her head straight round towards the lagoon. We can turn quicker than they can. Then let them gain upon us, and we will then turn again."

The gondola in pursuit came up hand over hand. Francis kept looking over his shoulder, and when he saw its bow gliding up within a few feet of her stern he exclaimed "Now!" and, with a sudden turn, the gondola again swept out seaward.

Their pursuer rushed on for a length or two before she could sweep round, while a volley of imprecations and threats burst from three men who were standing up in her with drawn swords. Francis and Giuseppi were now rowing less strongly, and gaining breath for their next effort. When the gondola again came up to them they swept round to the left, and as their pursuers followed they headed for the Grand Canal.

"Make for the steps of Santa Maria church. We will jump out there and trust to our feet."

The two lads put out all their strength now. They were some three boats' lengths ahead before their pursuers were fairly on their track. They were now rowing for life, for they knew that they could hardly succeed in doubling again, and that the gondola behind them was so well handled, that they could not gain on it at the turnings were they to venture into the narrow channels. It was a question of speed alone, and so hard did they row that the gondola in pursuit gained but slowly on them, and they were still two lengths ahead when they dashed up to the steps of the church.

Simultaneously they sprang on shore, leaped up the steps, and dashed off at the top of their speed, hearing, as they did so, a crash as the gondola ran into their light craft. There was a moment's delay, as the men had to step across their boat to gain the shore, and they were fifty yards ahead before they heard the sound of their pursuers' feet on the stone steps; but they were lightly clad and shoeless, and carried nothing to impede their movements, and they had therefore little fear of being overtaken.

After racing on at the top of their speed for a few minutes, they stopped and listened. The sound of their pursuers' footsteps died away in the distance; and, after taking a few turns to put them off their track, they pursued their way at a more leisurely pace.

"They have smashed the gondola," Giuseppi said with a sob, for he was very proud of the light craft.

"Never mind the gondola," Francis said cheerfully. "If they had smashed a hundred it would not matter."

"But the woman has got away and we have learned nothing," Giuseppi said, surprised at his master's cheerfulness.

"I think we have learned something, Giuseppi. I think we have learned everything. I have no doubt the girls are confined in that hut on San Nicolo. I wonder I never thought of it before; but I made so sure that they would be taken somewhere close to where Mocenigo was staying, that it never occurred to me that they might hide them out there. I ought to have known that that was just the thing they would do, for while the search would be keen among the islets near the land, and the villages there, no one would think of looking for them on the seaward islands.

"I have no doubt they are there now. That woman came ashore to report to his friends, and that four-oared boat which has chased us was in waiting off Saint Mark's, to attack any boat that might be following them.

"We will go to Signor Polani at once and tell him what has happened. I suppose it is about one o'clock now, but I have not noticed the hour. It was past eleven before we first met the gondola, and we must have been a good deal more than an hour lying there waiting for them."

A quarter of an hour's walking took them to the palazzo of Polani. They rang twice at the bell at the land entrance, before a face appeared at the little window of the door, and asked who was there.

"I wish to see Signor Polani at once," Francis said.

"The signor retired to rest an hour ago," the man said.

"Never mind that," Francis replied. "I am Francis Hammond, and I have important news to give him."

As soon as the servitor recognized Francis' voice, he unbarred the door.

"Have you news of the ladies?" he asked eagerly.

"I have news which will, I hope, lead to something," Francis replied.

A moment later the voice of Polani himself, who, although he had retired to his room, had not yet gone to sleep, was heard at the top of the grand stairs, inquiring who it was who had come so late; for although men had been arriving all day, with reports from the various islands and villages, he thought that no one would come at this hour unless his news were important.

Francis at once answered:

"It is I, Signor Polani, Francis Hammond. I have news which I think may be of importance, although I may be mistaken. Still, it is certainly news that may lead to something."

The merchant hurried down.

"What is it, Francisco? What have you learned?"

"I have seen the woman Castaldi, and have followed her. I do not know for certain where she was going, for we have been chased by a large gondola, and have narrowly escaped with our lives. Still, I have a clue to their whereabouts."

Francis then related the events of the evening.

"But why did you not run into the boat and give the alarm at once, Francisco? Any gondolas passing would have given their assistance, when you declared who she was, for the affair is the talk of the city. If that woman were in our power we should soon find means to make her speak."

"Yes, signor; but the moment she was known to be in your power, you may be sure that they would remove your daughters from the place where they have been hiding them. I thought, therefore, the best plan would be to track them. No doubt we should have succeeded in doing so, had it not been for the attack upon us by another gondola."

"You are right, no doubt, Francisco. Still, it is unfortunate, for I do not see that we are now any nearer than we were before, except that we know that this woman is in the habit of coming into the city."

"I think we are nearer, sir, for I had an adventure some time ago that may afford a clue to their hiding place."

He then told the merchant how he had, one evening, taken a man out to San Nicolo, and had discovered that a hut in that island was used as a meeting place by various persons, among whom was Ruggiero Mocenigo.

"I might have thought of the place before, signor; but, in fact, it never entered my mind. From the first, we considered it so certain that the men who carried off your daughters would take them to some hiding place where Mocenigo could speedily join them, that San Nicolo never entered my mind. I own that it was very stupid, for it seems now to me that the natural thing for them to do, would be to take them in the very opposite direction to that in which the search for them would be made."

The story had been frequently interrupted by exclamations of surprise by Polani. At its conclusion, he laid his hand on Francis' shoulder.

"My dear boy," he said, "How can I thank you! You seem to me to be born to be the preserver of my daughters. I cannot doubt that your suspicion is correct, and that they are confined in this hut at San Nicolo. How fortunate that you did not denounce this conspiracy—for conspiracy no doubt it is—that you discovered, for, had you done so, some other place would have been selected for the girls' prison."

"I would not be too sanguine, sir. The girls may not be in this hut, still we may come on some clue there which may lead us to them. If not, we will search the islands on that side as closely as we have done those on the mainland."

"Now, shall I send for the gondoliers and set out at once? There are ten or twelve men in the house, and it is hardly likely that they will place a guard over them of anything like this strength, as of course they will be anxious to avoid observation by the islanders."

"I do not think I would do anything tonight, sir," Francis said. "The gondola that chased us will be on the alert. They cannot, of course, suspect in the slightest that we have any clue to the hiding place of your daughters. Still, they might think that, if we were really pursuing the other gondola, and had recognized the woman Castaldi, we might bring the news to you, and that a stir might be made. They may therefore be watching to see if anything comes of it; and if they saw a bustle and gondolas setting out taking the direction of the island, they might set off and get there first, for it is a very fast craft, and remove your daughters before we reach the hut.

"I should say wait till morning. They may be watching your house now, and if, in an hour or two, they see all is quiet, they will no doubt retire with the belief that all danger is at an end. Then, in the morning, I would embark the men in two or three gondolas, but I would not start from your own steps, for no doubt your house is watched. Let the men go out singly, and embark at a distance from here, and not at the same place. Once out upon the lagoon, they should row quietly towards San Nicolo, keeping a considerable distance apart, the men lying down in the bottom as the boats approach the island, so that if anyone is on watch he will have no suspicion.

"As I am the only one that knows the position of the hut, I will be with you in the first gondola. We will not land near the hut, but pass by, and land at the other end of the island. The other gondolas will slowly follow us, and land at the same spot. Then three or four men can go along by the sea face, with orders to watch any boats hauled up upon the shore there, and stop any party making down towards them. The rest of us will walk straight to the hut, and, as it lies among sand hills, I hope we shall be able to get quite close to it before our approach is discovered."

"An excellent plan, Francisco, though I am so impatient that the night will seem endless to me; but certainly your plan is the best. Even if the house is watched, and you were seen to enter, if all remains perfectly quiet they will naturally suppose that the news you brought was not considered of sufficient importance to lead to any action. You will, of course, remain here till morning?"

"I cannot do that, sir, though I will return the first thing. There is, lying on my table, a paper with the particulars and names of the persons I saw meet in this hut, and a request to my father that, if I do not return in the morning, he will at once lay this before the council. I place it there every day when I go out, in order that, if I should be seized and carried off by Mocenigo's people, I should have some means of forcing them to let me go.

"Although I know absolutely nothing of the nature of the conspiracy, they will not know how much I am aware of, or what particulars I may have given in the document; and as I could name to them those present, and among them is the envoy of the King of Hungary, now in the city, they would hardly dare harm me, when they knew that if they did so this affair would be brought before the council."

"It was an excellent precaution, Francisco. Why, you are as prudent and thoughtful as you are courageous!"

"It was not likely to be of much use, sir," Francis said modestly. "I was very much more likely to get a stab in the back than to be carried off. Still, it was just possible that Mocenigo might himself like to see his vengeance carried out, and it was therefore worth my while guarding against it. But, as you see, it will be necessary for me to be back sometime before morning."

"At any rate, Francisco, you had better wait here until morning breaks. Your room is not likely to be entered for some hours after that; so while I am preparing for our expedition, you can go out and make your way to the Grand Canal, hail an early gondola, and be put down at your own steps, when, as you have told me, you can enter the house without disturbing anyone. Then you can remove that paper, and return here in the gondola. We will start at seven. There will be plenty of boats about by that time, and the lagoon will be dotted by the fishermen's craft, so that our gondolas will attract no attention."

"Perhaps that will be the best plan, signor; and, indeed, I should not be sorry for a few hours' sleep, for Giuseppi and I have been in our boat since a very early hour in the morning, and were pretty well tired out before this last adventure began."

CHAPTER 6

THE HUT ON SAN NICOLO

At seven o'clock all was in readiness for a start. Signor Polani set out alone in his gondola, and picked up Francis, and four men, at a secluded spot some distance from the house. A messenger had been sent, two hours before, to the captain of one of the merchant ships lying in the port. He at once put ten men into a large boat, and rowed down to within half a mile of the island. Here a grapnel was thrown overboard, most of the men lay down in the bottom, and the captain, according to his instructions, kept a sharp lookout to see that no boat left San Nicolo—his instructions being to overhaul any boat coming out, and to see that no one was concealed on board it.

There he remained until Polani's gondola rowed past him. After it had gone a few hundred yards, the grapnel was got up, the men took to their oars and followed the gondola, keeping so far behind that it would not seem there was any connection between them.

Francis made for the narrow channel which separated San Nicolo from the next island, and then directed the gondola to be run ashore, where a low sand hill, close by, hid them from the sight of anyone on the lookout. A few minutes later the ship's boat arrived.

Francis now led the way direct for the hut, accompanied by Polani and six men, while four sailors advanced, at a distance of a hundred yards on either flank, to cut off anyone making for the water.

"We may as well go fast," he said, "for we can scarcely get there without being seen by a lookout, should there be one on the sand hills, and the distance is so short that there will be no possibility of their carrying your daughters off, before we get there."

"The faster the better," the merchant said. "This suspense is terrible."

Accordingly, the party started at a brisk run. Francis kept his eyes on the spot where he believed the hut lay.

"I see no one anywhere near there," he said, as they came over one of the sand ridges. "Had there been anyone on the watch I think we should see him now."

On they ran, until, passing over one of the sand hills, Francis came to a standstill. The hut lay in the hollow below them.

"There is the house, signor. Now we shall soon know."

They dashed down the short slope, and gathered round the door.

"Within there, open!" the merchant shouted, hammering with the hilt of his sword on the door.

All was silent within.

"Break it down!" he said; and two of the sailors, who had brought axes with them, began to hew away at the door.

A few blows, and it suddenly opened, and two men dressed as fishermen appeared in the doorway.

"What means this attack upon the house of quiet people?" they demanded.

"Bind them securely," Polani said, as he rushed in, followed closely by Francis, while those who followed seized the men.

Polani paused as he crossed the threshold, with a cry of disappointment—the hut was empty. Francis was almost equally disappointed.

"If they are not here, they are near by," Francis said to Polani. "Do not give up hope. I am convinced they are not far off; and if we search we may find a clue. Better keep your men outside. We can search more thoroughly by ourselves."

The merchant told his men, who had seized and were binding the two occupants of the hut, to remain outside. The inside of the hut differed in no way from the ordinary dwelling of fishermen, except that a large table stood in the middle of it, and there were some benches against the walls. Some oars stood in one corner, and some nets were piled close to them. A fire burned in the open hearth, and a pot hung over it, and two others stood on the hearth.

"Let us see what they have got here," Francis said, while the merchant leaned against the table with an air of profound depression, paying no attention to what he was doing.

"A soup," Francis said, lifting the lid from the pot over the fire, "and, by the smell, a good one."

Then he lifted the other pots simmering among the burning brands.

"A ragout of kid and a boiled fish. Signor Polani, this is no fisherman's meal. Either these men expect visitors of a much higher degree than themselves, or your daughters are somewhere close.

"Oh! there is a door."

"It can lead nowhere," Polani said. "The sand is piled up to the roof on that side of the house."

"It is," Francis agreed; "but there may be a lower room there, completely covered with the sand. At any rate, we will see."

He pushed against the door, but it did not give in the slightest.

"It may be the sand," he said. "It may be bolts."

He went to the outside door, and called in the sailors with the hatchets.

"Break open that door," he said.

"There is a space behind," he exclaimed, as the first blow was given. "It is hollow, I swear. It would be a different sound altogether if sand was piled up against it."

A dozen blows and the fastenings gave, and, sword in hand, the merchant and Francis rushed through.

Both gave a shout of delight. They were in a room built out at the back of the hut. It was richly furnished, and hangings of Eastern stuffs covered the walls. A burning lamp hung from the ceiling. Two men stood irresolute with drawn swords, having apparently turned round just as the door gave way; for as it did so, two figures struggled to their feet from a couch behind them, for some shawls had been wrapped round their heads, and with a cry of delight rushed forward to meet their rescuers. Seated at the end of the couch, with bowed down head, was another female figure.

"Maria—Giulia!" the merchant exclaimed, as, dropping his sword, he clasped his daughters in his arms.

Francis, followed by the two sailors with hatchets, advanced towards the men.

"Drop your swords and surrender," he said. "Resistance is useless. There are a dozen men outside."

The men threw their swords down on the ground.

"Lead them outside, and bind them securely," Francis said.

For the next minute or two, few words were spoken. The girls sobbed with delight on their father's breast, while he himself was too moved to do more than murmur words of love and thankfulness. Francis went quietly out and spoke to the captain, who went in to the inner room, touched the sitting figure on the shoulder, and, taking her by the arm, led her outside.

"Come in, Francis," Polani called a minute later.

"My dears, it is not me you must thank for your rescue. It is your English friend here who has again restored you to me. It is to him we owe our happiness, and that you, my child, are saved from the dreadful fate of being forced to be the wife of that villain Mocenigo.

"Embrace him, my dears, as a brother, for he has done more than a brother for you. And now tell me all that has happened since I last saw you."

"You know, father, the message that was brought us, that you had been hurt and wanted us home?"

"Yes, my dears, that I learned soon afterwards. I went at five o'clock to fetch you home, and found that you had gone, and why."

"Well, father, directly we had taken our seats in the cabin of the gondola, our gouvernante closed the doors, and soon afterwards she slid to the two shutters before the windows. We cried out in surprise at finding ourselves in the dark, but she bade us be quiet, in a tone quite different to any in which she had ever spoken to us before. We were both frightened, and tried to push back the shutters and open the door, but they were fastened firmly. I suppose there was some spring which held them. Then we screamed; but I could feel that the inside was all thickly padded. I suppose our voices could not be heard outside. I thought so, because once I thought I heard the gondoliers singing, but it was so faint that I could not be sure. Then the air seemed stiflingly close, and I fainted; and when I came to myself one of the windows was open, and Giulia said she had promised we would not scream, but I think we were beyond the canals then, for I could see nothing but the sky as we passed along. When I was better the windows were almost shut again, so that we could not see out, though a little air could get in; then the gondola went on for a long time.

"At last it stopped, and she said we must be blindfolded. We said we would not submit to it, and she told us unless we let her do it, the men would do it. So we submitted, and she wrapped shawls closely over our heads. Then we were helped ashore, and walked some distance. At last the shawls were taken off our heads, and we found ourselves here, and here we have been ever since."

"You have not been ill treated in any way, my children?" the merchant asked anxiously.

"Not at all, father. Until today, nobody has been into this room besides ourselves and that woman. The door was generally left a little open for air, for you see there are no windows here. She used to go into the next room and come back with our food. We could see men moving about in there, but they were very quiet, and all spoke in low tones.

"You may think how we upbraided our gouvernante for her treachery, and threatened her with your anger. She told us we should never be found, and that I might as well make up my mind to marry Ruggiero Mocenigo, for if I did not consent quietly, means would be found to compel me to do so. I said I would die first, but she used to laugh a cruel laugh, and say he would soon be here with the priest, and that it mattered not whether I said yes or no. The ceremony would be performed, and then Ruggiero would sail away with me to the East, and I should be glad enough then to make peace between him and you. But he never came. I think she became anxious, for she went away twice for three or four hours, and locked us in here when she went.

"That, father, is all we know about it. Where are we?"

"You are at San Nicolo."

"On the island!" Maria exclaimed in surprise. "She told us we were on the mainland. And now, how did you find us?"

"I will tell you as we go home, Maria."

"Yes, that will be better, father. Giulia and I long for a breath of fresh air, and the sight of the blue sky."

"Giulia has not had so much to frighten her as you have," her father said.

"Yes, I have, father; for she said I was to go across the seas with Maria, and that Ruggiero would soon find a husband for me among his friends. I told her she was a wicked woman, over and over again, and we told her that we were sure you would forgive, and even reward her, if she would take us back again to you. When she was away, we thought we would try to make our escape behind, and we made a little hole in the boards; but the sand came pouring in, and we found we were underground, though how we got there we didn't know, for we had not come down any steps. So we had to give up the idea of escape."

"You are partly underground," her father said, "for, as you will see when you get out, the sand has drifted up at the back of the hut to the roof, and has altogether hidden this part of the hut; so that we did not know that there was more than one room, and I should never have thought of breaking into that door, had it not been for Francisco. And now come along, my dears. Let us wait here no longer."

The sailors and servitors broke into a cheer as the girls came out of the hut.

"Shall we put a torch to this place?" Francis asked Polani.

"No, Francisco. It must be searched thoroughly first.

"Captain Lontano, do you order four of your men to remain here, until some of the officials of the state arrive. If anyone comes before that, they must seize them and detain them as prisoners. The state will investigate the matter to the bottom."

Now that they were in the open air, the merchant could see that the close confinement and anxiety had told greatly upon his daughters. Both were pale and hollow eyed, and looked as if they had suffered a long illness. Seeing how shaken they were, he ordered one of the retainers to go to the gondola, and tell the men to row it round to the nearest point to the hut. The party then walked along down to the shore.

In a few minutes the gondola arrived. Polani, his two daughters, and Francis took their places in it. The four men, bound hand and foot, were laid in the bottom of the ship's boat; the gouvernante was made to take her place there also, and the sailors were told to follow closely behind the gondola, which was rowed at a very slow pace.

On the way, Polani told his daughters of the manner in which Francis had discovered the place of concealment.

"Had it not been for him, my dears, we should certainly not have found you, and that villain would have carried out his plans, sooner or later. He would either have given his guards the slip, or, when no evidence was forthcoming against him, they would have been removed. He would then have gone outside the jurisdiction of the republic, obtained a ship with a crew of desperadoes, sailed round to the seaward side of San Nicolo, and carried you off. Nothing could have saved you, and your resistance would, as that woman told you, have been futile."

"We shall be grateful to you all our lives, Francisco," Maria said. "We shall pray for you always, night and morning.

"Shall we not, Giulia?"

"Yes, indeed," the young girl said simply. "We shall love him all our lives."

"Answer for yourself, Giulia," Maria said with a laugh, her spirits returning in the bright sunshine and fresh air. "When Francisco asks for my love, it will be quite soon enough to say what I think about it."

"I should never have courage enough to do that, signora. I know what you would say too well."

"What should I say?" Maria asked.

"You would say I was an impudent boy."

Maria laughed.

"I cannot think of you as a boy any longer, Francisco," she said more gravely. "I have, perhaps, regarded you as a boy till now, though you did save us so bravely before; but you see you are only my own age, and a girl always looks upon a boy of her own age as ever so much younger than she is herself. Besides, too, you have none of the airs of being a man, which some of my cousins have;

and never pay compliments or say pretty things, but seem altogether like a younger brother. But I shall think you a boy no more. I know you better now."

"But I am a boy," Francis said, "and I don't want to be thought anything else. In England we keep young longer than they do here, and a boy of my age would not think of speaking to his elders, unless he was first addressed.

"What are you going to do with your prisoners, signor?"

"I shall take them direct to my house, and then go and report the recovery of my daughters, and their capture. Officials will at once be sent, with a gondola, to take them off to the prison. There can be no question now as to the part Mocenigo has played in this business, and no doubt he will be brought here a prisoner at once. Even his nearest connections will not dare to defend conduct so outrageous, especially when public indignation has been so excited.

"You do not know, girls, what a stir has been caused in the city on your account. If it had not been for the citizen guard, I believe the Mocenigo Palace would have been burned down; and Ruggiero's connections have scarcely dared to show their faces in the streets, since you have been missing. You see, every father of a family felt personally grieved, for if the nobles were permitted, with impunity, to carry off the daughters of citizens, who could feel safe?

"When this is all over I shall take you, for a time, back to our home in Corfu. It is not good for girls to be the subject of public talk and attention."

"I shall be very glad, father," Giulia said. "I love our home at Corfu, with its gardens and flowers, far better than the palazzo here. The air is always soft and balmy, while here it is so hot sometimes by day, and so damp and foggy in the evening. I shall be glad to go back again."

"And you, Maria?"

"I shall be very happy there, father, but I like Venice best."

"You are getting to an age to enjoy gaiety, Maria; and it is natural you should do so. However, it will not be necessary for you to be long absent. In a city like Venice there are always fresh subjects for talk, and the most exciting piece of scandal is but a three days' wonder. A few weeks at Corfu will restore your nerves, which cannot but have been shaken by what you have gone through, and you will come back here more disposed than ever to appreciate the gaieties of Venice."

"As long as it is for only a few weeks, father, I shall not care; for you know I am very fond, too, of our beautiful home there. Still, I do like Venice."

They had now reached the steps of the Palazzo Polani. They had not proceeded by way of the Grand Canal, as the merchant was anxious that his daughters should reach their home unrecognized, as, had they been noticed, it would have given rise to no little excitement, and they had had more than enough of this, and needed quiet and repose. Besides, until the prisoners were in the safe custody of the officials of the state, it was in every way desirable that the events of the morning should remain unknown.

Their return home created quite a tumult of joy in the house. The preparations that had been made had been kept a profound secret, as the merchant could not be sure but that some other member of his household was in the pay of Mocenigo. Thus, until the girls alighted at the steps, none in the house were aware that any clue had been obtained as to their hiding place. The women ran down with cries of joy. The men would have shouted and cheered, had not Polani held up his hand.

"The signoras have had more than enough excitement," he said. "They are grateful to you for your goodwill and affection, but for the present they need quiet. They may have more to go through today. I pray you that no word, as to their return, be said outside the house. I would not that the news were whispered in the city, till the seignory decide what is to be done in the matter."

As soon as the girls had gone upstairs to their rooms, the ship's boat came alongside, and the prisoners were carried into the house, glances of indignation and anger being cast at the gouvernante, who had, as soon as she was placed on board the boat, closely veiled herself; and some of the women broke out into threats and imprecations.

"Captain Lontano, the servants will show you a room where your men can guard the prisoners. You had better remain with them yourself. Let no one, except your own men, enter the room."

Giuseppi was on the steps, and Francis stepped up to him and eagerly asked, "What news of the gondola?"

"I found her, stove in and full of water, behind the piles close to the steps. Someone must have pushed her there, to be out of the way of the traffic. She has several holes in her bottom, besides being stove in at the gunwale where the other boat struck her. They must have thrust the ends of their oars through her planks, out of sheer spite, when they found that we had escaped them. Father and I have towed her round to your steps, but I doubt whether she is worth repairing."

"Well, we can't help it, Giuseppi. She has done her work; and if every two ducats I lay out were to bring in as good a harvest, I should have no reason to complain."

Having seen the prisoners safely placed, the merchant returned.

"I think, Francisco, you must go with me. They will be sure to want to question you."

"I shall have to say what were my reasons for thinking your daughters were hid in that hut, signor," Francis said as the gondola rowed towards Saint Mark's; "and I can only do that by telling of that secret meeting. I do not want to denounce a number of people, besides Ruggiero. I have no evidence against them, and do not know what they were plotting, nor have I any wish to create for myself more enemies. It is quite enough to have incurred the enmity of all the connections of the house of Mocenigo."

"That is true enough, Francisco, but I do not see how it is to be avoided. Unfortunately, you did recognize others besides Ruggiero."

"Quite so, signor, and I am not going to tell a lie about it, whatever the consequences may be. Still, I wish I could get out of it."

"I wish you could, Francis, but I do not see any escape for it, especially as you say you did not recognize Ruggiero as the passenger you carried."

"No, signor, I did not. It might have been he, but I cannot say. He was wrapped in a cloak, and I did not see his features."

"It is a pity, Francisco, for had you known him, the statement that, moved by curiosity, you followed him and saw him into that hut, would have been sufficient without your entering into the other matter. Most of my countrymen would not hesitate about telling a lie, to avoid mixing themselves up further in such a matter, for the dangers of making enemies are thoroughly appreciated here; but you are perfectly right, and I like your steady love of the truth, whatever the consequences to yourself; but certainly as soon as the matter is concluded, it will be better for you to quit Venice for a time."

"Are you going to the council direct, signor?"

"No. I am going first to the magistrates, to tell them that I have in my hands five persons, who have been engaged in carrying off my daughters, and beg them to send at once to take them into their custody. Then I shall go before the council, and demand justice upon Mocenigo, against whom we have now conclusive evidence. You will not be wanted at the magistracy. My own evidence, that I found them keeping guard over my daughters, will be quite

73

sufficient for the present, and after that the girls' evidence will be sufficient to convict them, without your name appearing in the affair at all.

"I will try whether I cannot keep your name from appearing before the council also. Yes, I think I might do that; and as a first step, I give you my promise not to name you, unless I find it absolutely necessary. You may as well remain here in the gondola until I return."

It was upwards of an hour before Signor Polani came back to the boat.

"I have succeeded," he said, "in keeping your name out of it. I first of all told my daughters' story, and then said that, having obtained information that Ruggiero, before he was banished from Venice, was in the habit of going sometimes at night to a hut on San Nicolo, I proceeded thither, and found my daughters concealed in the hut whose position had been described to me. Of course, they inquired where I had obtained the information; but I replied that, as they knew, I had offered a large reward which would lead to my daughters' discovery, and that this reward had attracted one in the secret of Mocenigo, but that, for the man's own safety, I had been compelled to promise that I would not divulge his name.

"Some of the council were inclined to insist, but others pointed out that, for the ends of justice, it mattered in no way how I obtained the information. I had, at any rate, gone to the island and found my daughters there; and their evidence, if it was in accordance with what I had stated, was amply sufficient to bring the guilt of the abduction of my daughters home to Ruggiero, against whom other circumstances had already excited suspicion. A galley has already started for the mainland, with orders to bring him back a prisoner, and the girls are to appear to give evidence tomorrow. The woman, Castaldi, is to be interrogated by the council this afternoon, and I have no doubt she will make a full confession, seeing that my daughters' evidence is, in itself, sufficient to prove her guilt, and that it can be proved, from other sources, that it was she who inveigled them away by a false message from me."

"I am glad indeed, signor, that I am not to be called, and that this affair of the conspiracy is not to be brought up. I would, with your permission, now return home. Giuseppi took a message to my father from me, the first thing, explaining my absence; and I told him, when we left your house, to go at once to tell him that your daughters had been recovered, and that I should return before long. Still, he will want to hear from me as to the events of the night."

"Will you also tell him, Francisco, that I will call upon him this afternoon. I have much to say to him."

"I am glad Signor Polani is coming," Mr. Hammond said, when his son gave him the message. "I am quite resolved that you shall quit Venice at once. I do not wish to blame you for what you have done, which, indeed, is likely to have a favourable effect upon your fortunes; but that, at your age, you have mixed yourself up in adventures of this kind, taken part in the affairs of great houses, and drawn upon yourself the enmity of one of the most powerful families of Venice, is altogether strange and improper for a lad of your years, and belonging to the family of a quiet trader. I have been thinking about it all this morning, and am quite resolved that the sooner you are out of Venice the better. If I saw any way of sending you off before nightfall I would do so.

"Signor Polani has, you say, so far concealed from the council the fact that you have been mixed up in this business; but there is no saying how soon it may come out. You know that Venice swarms with spies, and these are likely, before many hours, to learn the fact of your midnight arrival at Polani's house; and as no orders were given for the preparation of this expedition to the island before that time, it will not need much penetration to conclude that you were the bearer of the news that led to the discovery of the maidens. Besides which, you accompanied the expedition, and acted as its guide to the hut. Part of this they will learn from the servants of the house, part of it they may get out from the sailors, who, over their wine cups, are not given to reticence. The council may not have pressed Polani on this point, but, take my word for it, some of them, at least, will endeavour to get to the bottom of it, especially Mocenigo's connections, who will naturally be alarmed at the thought that there is somewhere a traitor among their own ranks.

"The affair has become very serious, Francis, and far beyond the compass of a boyish scrape, and no time must be lost in getting you out of Venice. I have no doubt Polani will see the matter in the same light, for he knows the ways of his countrymen even better than I do."

The interview between the two traders was a long one. At its conclusion Francis was sent for.

"Francis," his father said, "Signor Polani has had the kindness to make me offers of a most generous nature."

"Not at all, Messer Hammond," the Venetian interrupted. "Let there be no mistake upon that score. Your son has rendered me services impossible for me ever to repay adequately. He has laid me under an obligation greater than I can ever discharge. At the same time, fortunately, I am in a position to be able to further his interests in life.

"I have proposed, Francisco, that you shall enter my house at once. You will, of course, for some years learn the business, but you will do so in the position which a son of mine would occupy, and when you come of age, you will take your place as a partner with me.

"Your father will return to England. He informs me that he is now longing to return to his own country, and has for some time been thinking of doing so. I have proposed to him that he shall act as my agent there. Hitherto I have not traded direct with England; in future I shall do so largely. Your father has explained to me somewhat of his transactions, and I see there is good profit to be made on trade with London, by a merchant who has the advantage of the advice and assistance of one, like your father, thoroughly conversant in the trade. Thus, I hope that the arrangement will be largely to our mutual advantage. As to yourself, you will probably be reluctant to establish yourself for life in this country; but there is no reason why, in time, when your father wishes to retire from business, you should not establish yourself in London, in charge of the English branch of our house."

"I am most grateful to you for your offer, signor, which is vastly beyond anything that my ambition could ever have aspired to. I can only say that I will try my best to do justice to your kindness to me."

"I have no fear as to that, Francisco," the merchant said. "You have shown so much thoughtfulness, in this business, that I shall have no fear of entrusting even weighty affairs of business in your hands; and you must remember always that I shall still consider myself your debtor. I thoroughly agree with your father's views as to the necessity for your leaving Venice, as soon as possible. In a few months this matter will have blown over, the angry feelings excited will calm down, and you will then be able to come and go in safety; but at present you were best out of the town, and I have, therefore, arranged with your father that you shall embark tonight on board the Bonito, which sails tomorrow. You will have much to say to your father now, but I hope you will find time to come round, and say goodbye to my daughters, this evening."

"Your adventures, Francis," Mr. Hammond said when the merchant had left them, "have turned out fortunate, indeed. You have an opening now beyond anything we could have hoped for. Signor Polani has expressed himself most warmly. He told me that I need concern myself no further with your future, for that would now be his affair. The arrangement that he has made with me, will enable me to hold my head as high as any in the City, for it will give me almost a monopoly of the Venetian trade; and although he said that he had long been thinking of entering into trade direct with England, there is no doubt that it is his feeling towards you, which has influenced him now in the matter.

"My business here has more than answered my expectations, in one respect, but has fallen short in another. I have bought cheaply, and the business should have been a very profitable one; but my partner in London is either not acting fairly by me, or he is mismanaging matters altogether. This offer, then, of Signor Polani is in every respect acceptable. I shall give up my own business and start anew, and selling, as I shall, on commission, shall run no risk, while the profits will be far larger than I could myself make, for Polani will carry it on on a great scale.

"As for you, you will soon learn the ways of trade, and will be able to come home and join me, and eventually succeed me in the business.

"No fairer prospect could well open to a young man, and if you show yourself as keen in business, as you have been energetic in the pursuits you have adopted, assuredly a great future is open to you, and you may look to be one of the greatest merchants in the city of London. I know not yet what offers Polani may make you here, but I hope that you will not settle in Venice permanently, but will always remember that you are an Englishman, and the son of a London citizen, and that you will never lose your love for your native land.

"And yet, do not hurry home for my sake. Your two brothers will soon have finished their schooling, and will, of course, be apprenticed to me as soon as I return; and if, as I hope, they turn out steady and industrious; they will, by the time they come to man's estate, be of great assistance to me in the business.

"And now, you will be wanting to say goodbye to your friends. Be careful this last evening, for it is just when you are thinking most of other matters, that sudden misfortune is likely to come upon you."

Delighted with his good fortune—rather because it opened up a life of activity, instead of the confinement to business that he had dreaded, than for the pecuniary advantages it offered—Francis ran downstairs and, leaping into his father's gondola, told Beppo to take him to the Palazzo Giustiniani. On the way he told Beppo and his son that the next day he was leaving Venice, and was going to enter the service of Signor Polani.

Giuseppi ceased rowing, and, throwing himself down at the bottom of the gondola, began to sob violently, with the abandonment to his emotions common to his race. Then he suddenly sat up.

"If you are going, I will go too, Messer Francisco. You will want a servant who will be faithful to you. I will ask the padrone to let me go with you.

"You will let me go, will you not, father? I cannot leave our young master, and should pine away, were I obliged to stop here to work a gondola; while he may be wanting my help, for Messer Francisco is sure to get into adventures and dangers. Has he not done it here in Venice? and is he not sure to do it at sea, where there are Genoese and pirates, and perils of all kinds?

"You will take me with you, will you not, Messer Francisco? You will never be so hard hearted as to go away and leave me behind?"

"I shall be very glad to have you with me, Giuseppi, if your father will give you leave to go. I am quite sure that Signor Polani will make no objection. In the first place, he would do it to oblige me, and in the second, I know that it is his intention to do something to your advantage. He has spoken to me about it several times, for you had your share of the danger when we first rescued his daughters, and again when we were chased by that four-oared gondola. He has been too busy with the search for his daughters to give the matter his attention, but I know that he is conscious of his obligation to you, and that he intends to reward you largely. Therefore, I am sure that he will offer no objection to your accompanying me.

"What do you say, Beppo?"

"I do not like to stand in the way of the lad's wishes, Messer Francisco; but, you see, he is of an age now to be very useful to me. If Giuseppi leaves me, I shall have to hire another hand for the gondola, or to take a partner."

"Well, we will talk it over presently," Francis said. "Here we are at the steps of the palazzo, and here comes Matteo himself. It is lucky I was not five minutes later, or I should have missed him."

CHAPTER 7

ON BOARD A TRADER

"Have you heard the news, Francisco? My cousins are rescued! I have been out this morning and have only just heard it, and I was on the point of starting to tell you."

"Your news is old, Matteo. I knew it hours ago."

"And I hear," Matteo went on, "that Polani found them in a hut on San Nicolo. My father cannot think how he came to hear of their hiding place. He says Polani would not say how he learned the news. My father supposes he heard it from some member of Ruggiero's household."

Francis hesitated for a moment. He had at first been on the point of telling Matteo of the share he had had in the recovery of the girls; but he thought that although his friend could be trusted not to repeat the news wilfully, he might accidentally say something which would lead to the fact being known, and that as Polani had strongly enjoined the necessity of keeping the secret, and had himself declined to mention, even to the council, the source from which he obtained his information, he would look upon him as a babbler, and unworthy of trust, did he find that Matteo had been let into the secret.

"It does not much matter who it is Polani learned the news from. The great point is, he has found his daughters safe from all injury, and I hear has brought back with him the woman who betrayed them. It is fortunate indeed that he took such prompt measures with Ruggiero, and thus prevented his escaping from the mainland, and making off with the girls, as of course he intended to do."

"My father tells me," Matteo said, "that a state gondola has already been dispatched to bring Ruggiero a prisoner here, and that even his powerful connections will not save him from severe punishment, for public indignation is so great at the attempt, that his friends will not venture to plead on his behalf."

"And now I have my bit of news to tell you, Matteo. Signor Polani has most generously offered me a position in his house, and I am to sail tomorrow in one of his ships for the East."

"I congratulate you, Francisco, for I know, from what you have often said, that you would like this much better than going back to England. But it seems very sudden. You did not know anything about it yesterday, and now you are going to start at once. Why, when can it have been settled? Polani has been absent since daybreak, engaged in this matter of the girls, and has been occupied ever since with the council."

"I have seen him since he returned," Francis replied; "and though it was only absolutely settled this morning, he has had several interviews with my father on the subject. I believe he and my father thought that it was better to get me away as soon as possible, as Ruggiero's friends may put down the disgrace which has befallen him to my interference in his first attempt to carry off the girls."

"Well, I think you are a lucky fellow anyhow, Francisco, and I hope that I may be soon doing something also. I shall speak to my father about it, and ask him to get Polani to let me take some voyages in his vessels, so that I may be fit to become an officer in one of the state galleys, as soon as I am of age. Where are you going now?"

"I am going round to the School of Arms, to say goodbye to our comrades. After that I am going to Signor Polani's to pay my respects to the signoras. Then I shall be at home with my father till it is time to go on board. He will have left here before I return from my voyage, as he is going to wind up his affairs at once and return to England."

"Well, I will accompany you to the school and to my cousin's," Matteo said. "I shall miss you terribly here, and shall certainly do all I can to follow your example, and get afloat. You may have all sorts of adventures, for we shall certainly be at war with Genoa before many weeks are over, and you will have to keep a sharp lookout for their war galleys. Polani's ships are prizes worth taking, and you may have the chance of seeing the inside of a Genoese prison before you return."

After a visit to the School of Arms, the two friends were rowed to Signor Polani's. The merchant himself was out, but they were at once shown up to the room where the girls were sitting.

"My dear cousins," Matteo said as he entered, "I am delighted to see you back safe and well. All Venice is talking of your return. You are the heroines of the day. You do not know what an excitement there has been over your adventure."

"The sooner people get to talk about something else the better, Matteo," Maria said, "for we shall have to be prisoners all day till something else occupies their attention. We have not the least desire to be pointed at, whenever we go out, as the maidens who were carried away. If the Venetians were so interested in us, they had much better have set about discovering where we were hidden away before."

"But everyone did try, I can assure you, Maria. Every place has been ransacked, high and low. Every gondolier has been questioned and cross questioned as to his doings on that day. Every fishing village has been visited. Never was such a search, I do believe. But who could have thought of your being hidden away all the time at San Nicolo! As for me, I have spent most of my time in a gondola, going out and staring up at every house I passed, in hopes of seeing a handkerchief waved from a casement. And so has Francisco; he has been just as busy in the search as anyone, I can assure you."

"Francisco is different," Maria said, not observing the signs Francis was making for her to be silent. "Francisco has got eyes in his head, and a brain in his skull, which is more, it seems, than any of the Venetians have; and had he not brought father to our hiding place, there we should have remained until Ruggiero Mocenigo came and carried us away."

"Francisco brought your father the news!" Matteo exclaimed in astonishment. "Why, was it he who found you out, after all?"

"Did you not know that, Matteo? Of course it was Francisco! As I told you, he has got brains; and if it had not been for him, we should certainly never have been rescued. Giulia and I owe him everything—don't we, Giulia?"

"Forgive me for not telling you, Matteo," Francis said to his astonished friend; "but Signor Polani, and my father, both impressed upon me so strongly that I should keep silent as to my share in the business, that I thought it better not even to mention it to you at present. It was purely the result of an accident."

"It was nothing of the sort," Maria said. "It was the result of your keeping your eyes open and knowing how to put two and two together. I did not know, Francisco, that it was a secret. We have not seen our father since we have returned, and I suppose he thought we should see nobody until he saw us again, and so did not tell us that we were not to mention your name in the affair; but we will be careful in future."

"But how was it, Francisco?" Matteo asked. "Now I know so much as this, I suppose I can be told the rest. I can understand well enough why it was to be kept a secret, and why my cousin is anxious to get you out of Venice at once."

Francis related the manner in which he first became acquainted with the existence of the hut on the island, and the fact of its being frequented by Ruggiero Mocenigo; and how, on catching sight of the gouvernante in a gondola, and seeing her make out across the lagoons, the idea struck him that the girls were confined in the hut.

"It is all very simple, you see, Matteo," he concluded.

"I will never say anything against learning to row a gondola in future," Matteo said, "for it seems to lead to all sorts of adventures; and unless you could have rowed well, you would never have got back to tell the story. But it is certain that it is a good thing you are leaving Venice for a time, for Ruggiero's friends may find out the share you had in it from some of my cousin's servants. You may be sure that they will do their best to discover how he came to be informed of the hiding place, and he is quite right to send you off at once."

"What! are you going away, Francisco?" the two girls exclaimed together.

"I am sailing tomorrow in one of your father's ships, signoras."

"And you are not coming back again?" Maria exclaimed.

"I hope to have the pleasure of seeing you again before very long, signora. I am entering your father's service for good, and shall be backwards and forwards to Venice as the ship comes and goes. My father is returning to England, and Signor Polani has most kindly requested me to make my home with him whenever I am in port."

"That is better," Maria said. "We should have a pretty quarrel with papa if he had let you go away altogether, after what you have done for us—

"Shouldn't we, Giulia?"

But Giulia had walked away to the window, and did not seem to hear the question.

"That will be very pleasant," Maria went on; "for you will be back every two or three months, and I shall take good care that papa does not send the ship off in a hurry again. It will be almost as good as having a brother; and I look upon you almost as a brother now, Francisco—and a very good brother, too. I don't think that man will molest us any more. If I thought there was any chance of it, I should ask papa to keep you for a time, because I should feel confident that you would manage to protect us somehow."

"I do not think there is the slightest chance of more trouble from him," Francis said. "He is sure of a long term of imprisonment for carrying you off."

"That is the least they can do to him, I should think," Maria said indignantly. "I certainly shall not feel comfortable while he is at large."

After half an hour's talk Francis and his friend took their leave.

"You certainly were born with a silver spoon in your mouth," Matteo said as they took their seats in the gondola, "and my cousin does well to get you out of Venice at once, for I can tell you there are scores of young fellows who would feel jealous at your position with my cousins."

"Nonsense!" Francis said, colouring. "How can you talk so absurdly, Matteo? I am only a boy, and it will be years before I could think of marriage. Besides, your cousins are said to be the richest heiresses in Venice; and it is not because I have been able to be of some slight service to them, that I should venture to think of either of them in that way."

"We shall see," Matteo laughed. "Maria is a little too old for you, I grant, but Giulia will do very well; and as you have already come, as Maria says, to be looked upon by them as a brother and protector, there is no saying as to how she may regard you in another two or three years."

"The thing is absurd, Matteo," Francis said impatiently. "Do not talk such nonsense any more."

Matteo lay back in his seat and whistled.

"I will say no more about it at present, Francisco," he said, after a pause; "but I must own that I should be well content to stand as high in the good graces of my pretty cousins as you do."

The next morning Francis spent some time with his father talking over future arrangements.

"I have no doubt that I shall see you sometimes, Francis; for Polani will be sure to give you an opportunity of making a trip to England, from time to time, in one of his ships trading thither. Unless anything unexpected happens, your future appears assured. Polani tells me he shall always regard you in the light of a son; and I have no fear of your doing anything to cause him to forfeit his good opinion of you. Do not be over adventurous, for even in a merchant ship there are many perils to be met with. Pirates swarm in the Mediterranean, in spite of the efforts of Venice to suppress them; and when war is going on, both Venice and Genoa send out numbers of ships whose doings savour strongly of piracy. Remember that the first duty of the captain of a merchant ship is to save his vessel and cargo, and that he should not think of fighting unless he sees no other method of escape open to him.

"It is possible that, after a time, I may send one of your brothers out here, but that will depend upon what I find of their disposition when I get home; for it will be worse than useless to send a lad of a headstrong disposition out to the care of one but a few years older than himself. But this we can talk about when you come over to England, and we see what position you are occupying here.

"I fear that Venice is about to enter upon a period of great difficulty and danger. There can be little doubt that Genoa, Padua, and Hungary are leagued against her; and powerful as she is, and great as are her resources, they will be taxed to the utmost to carry her through the dangers that threaten her. However, I have faith in her future, and believe that she will weather the storm, as she has done many that have preceded it.

"Venice has the rare virtue of endurance—the greatest dangers, the most disastrous defeats, fail to shake her courage, and only arouse her to greater efforts. In this respect she is in the greatest contrast to her rival, Genoa, who always loses heart the moment the tide turns against her. No doubt this is due, in no slight extent, to her oligarchic form of government. The people see the nobles, who rule them, calm and self possessed, however great the danger, and remain confident and tranquil; while in Genoa each misfortune is the signal for a struggle between contending factions. The occasion is seized to throw blame and contumely upon those in power, and the people give way to alternate outbursts of rage and depression.

"I do not say there are no faults in the government of Venice, but taking her altogether there is no government in Europe to compare with it. During the last three hundred years, the history of every other city in Italy, I may say of every other nation in Europe, is one long record of intestine struggle and bloodshed, while in Venice there has not been a single popular tumult worthy of the name. It is to the strength, the firmness, and the moderation of her government that Venice owes her advancement, the respect in which she is held among nations, as much as to the commercial industry of her people.

"She alone among nations could for years have withstood the interdict of the pope, or the misfortunes that have sometimes befallen her. She alone has never felt the foot of the invader, or bent her neck beneath a foreign yoke to preserve her existence. Here, save only in matters of government, all opinions are free, strangers of all nationalities are welcome. It is a grand city and a grand people, Francis, and though I shall be glad to return to England I cannot but feel regret at leaving it.

"And now, my boy, it is time to be going off to your ship. Polani said she would sail at ten o'clock. It is now nine, and it will take you half an hour to get there. I am glad to hear that Giuseppi is going with you. The lad is faithful and attached to you, and may be of service. Your trunk has already been sent on board, so let us be going."

On arriving at the ship, which was lying in the port of Malamocco, they found that she was just ready for sailing. The last bales of goods were being hoisted on board, and the sailors were preparing to loosen the sails.

The Bonito was a large vessel, built for stowage rather than speed. She carried two masts with large square sails, and before the wind would probably proceed at a fair rate; but the art of sailing close hauled was then unknown, and in the event of the wind being unfavourable she would be forced either to anchor or to depend upon her oars, of which she rowed fifteen on either side. As they mounted on to the deck they were greeted by Polani himself.

"I have come off to see the last of your son, Messer Hammond, and to make sure that my orders for his comfort have been carried out.

"Captain Corpadio, this is the young gentleman of whom I have spoken to you, and who is to be treated in all respects as if he were my son. You will instruct him in all matters connected with the navigation of the ship, as well as in the mercantile portion of the business, the best methods of buying and selling, the prices of goods, and the methods of payment.

"This is your cabin, Francisco."

He opened the door of a roomy cabin in the poop of the ship. It was fitted up with every luxury.

"Thank you very much indeed, Signor Polani," Francis said. "The only fault is that it is too comfortable. I would as lief have roughed it as other aspirants have to do."

"There was no occasion, Francisco. When there is rough work to be done, you will, I have no doubt, do it; but as you are going to be a trader, and not a sailor, there is no occasion that you should do so more than is necessary. You will learn to command a ship just as well as if you began by dipping your hands in tar. And it is well that you should learn to do this, for unless a man can sail a vessel himself, he is not well qualified to judge of the merits of men he appoints to be captains; but you must remember that you are going

85

as a representative of my house, and must, therefore, travel in accordance with that condition.

"You will be sorry to hear that bad news has just been received from the mainland. The state galley sent to fetch Ruggiero Mocenigo has arrived with the news that, on the previous night, a strong party of men who are believed to have come from Padua, fell upon the guard and carried off Ruggiero. My sailors came up and fought stoutly, but they were overpowered, and several of them were killed; so Ruggiero is again at large.

"This is a great disappointment to me. Though the villain is not likely to show his face in the Venetian territory again, I shall be anxious until Maria is safely married, and shall lose no time in choosing a husband for her. Unless I am mistaken, her liking is turned in the direction of Rufino, brother of your friend Matteo Giustiniani, and as I like none better among the suitors for her hand, methinks that by the time you return you will find that they are betrothed.

"And now I hear the sailors are heaving the anchor, and therefore, Messer Hammond, it is time we took to our boats."

There was a parting embrace between Francis and his father. Then the merchants descended into their gondolas, and lay waiting alongside until the anchor was up, the great sails shaken out, and the Bonito began to move slowly through the water towards the entrance of the port. Then, with a final wave of the hand, the gondolas rowed off and Francis turned to look at his surroundings. The first object that met his eye was Giuseppi, who was standing near him waving his cap to his father.

"Well, Giuseppi, what do you think of this?"

"I don't know what to think yet, Messer Francisco. It all seems so big and solid one does not feel as if one was on the water. It's more like living in a house. It does not seem as if anything could move her."

"You will find the waves can move her about when we get fairly to sea, Giuseppi, and the time will come when you will think our fast gondola was a steady craft in comparison. How long have you been on board?"

"I came off three hours ago, signor, with the boat that brought the furniture for your cabin. I have been putting that to rights since. A supply of the best wine has been sent off, and extra stores of all sorts, so you need not be afraid of being starved on the voyage."

"I wish he hadn't sent so much," Francis said. "It makes one feel like a milksop. Whose cabin is it I have got?"

"I believe that it is the cabin usually used by the supercargo, who is in charge of the goods and does the trading, but the men say the captain of this ship has been a great many years in Polani's employment, and often sails without a supercargo, being able to manage the trading perfectly well by himself. But the usual cabin is only half the size of yours, and two have been thrown into one to make it light and airy."

"And where do you sleep, Giuseppi?"

"I am going to sleep in the passage outside your door, Messer Francisco."

"Oh, but I sha'n't like that!" Francis said. "You ought to have a better place than that."

Giuseppi laughed.

"Why, Messer Francisco, considering that half my time I slept in the gondola, and the other half on some straw in our kitchen, I shall do capitally. Of course I could sleep in the fo'castle with the crew if I liked, but I should find it hot and stifling there. I chose the place myself, and asked the captain if I could sleep there, and he has given me leave."

In an hour the Bonito had passed through the Malamocco Channel, and was out on the broad sea. The wind was very light, and but just sufficient to keep the great sails bellied out. The sailors were all at work, coiling down ropes, washing the decks, and making everything clean and tidy.

"This is a good start, Messer Hammond," the captain said, coming up to him. "If this wind holds, we shall be able to make our course round the southern point of Greece, and then on to Candia, which is our first port. I always like a light breeze when I first go out of port, it gives time for everyone to get at home and have things shipshape before we begin to get lively."

"She does not look as if she would ever get lively," Francis said, looking at the heavy vessel.

"She is lively enough in a storm, I can tell you," the captain said, laughing. "When she once begins to roll she does it in earnest, but she is a fine sea boat, and I have no fear of gales. I wish I could say as much of pirates. However, she has always been fortunate, and as we carry a stout crew she could give a good account of herself against any of the small piratical vessels that swarm among the islands, although, of course, if she fell in with two or three of them together it would be awkward."

"How many men do you carry altogether, captain?"

"Just seventy. You see she rows thirty oars, and in case of

87

need we put two men to each oar, and though she doesn't look fast she can get along at a fine rate when the oars are double banked. We have shown them our heels many a time. Our orders are strict. We are never to fight if we can get away by running."

"But I suppose you have to fight sometimes?" Francis asked.

"Yes, I have been in some tough fights several times, though not in the Bonito, which was only built last year. Once in the Lion we were attacked by three pirates. We were at anchor in a bay, and the wind was blowing on the shore, when they suddenly came round the headland, so there was no chance of running, and we had to fight it out. We fought for five hours before they sheered off, pretty well crippled, and one of them in flames, for we carried Greek fire.

"Three or four times they nearly got a footing on deck, but we managed to beat them off somehow. We lost a third of our crew. I don't think there was a man escaped without a wound. I was laid up for three months, after I got home, with a slash on the shoulder, which pretty nigh took off my left arm. However, we saved the ship and the cargo, which was a valuable one, and Messer Polani saw that no one was the worse for his share in the business. There's no more liberal-hearted man in the trade than he is, and whatever may be the scarcity of hands in the port, there is never any difficulty in getting a good crew together for his vessels.

"Of course there are the roughs with the smooths. Some years ago I was in prison for six months, with all my crew, in Azoff. It was the work of those rascally Genoese, who are always doing us a bad turn when they have the chance, even when we are at peace with them. They set the mind of the native khan—that is the prince of the country—against us by some lying stories that we had been engaged in smuggling goods in at another port. And suddenly, in the middle of the night, in marched his soldiers on board my ship, and two other Venetian craft lying in the harbour, and took possession of them, and shut us all up in prison. There we were till Messer Polani got news, and sent out another ship to pay the fine demanded. That was no joke, I can tell you, for the prison was so hot and crowded, and the food so bad, that we got fever, and pretty near half of us died before our ransom came. Then at Constantinople the Genoese stirred the people up against us once or twice, and all the sailors ashore had to fight for their lives. Those Genoese are always doing us mischief."

"But I suppose you do them mischief sometimes, captain. I imagine it isn't all one side."

"Of course, we pay them out when we get a chance," the

88

captain replied. "It isn't likely we are going to stand being always put upon, and not take our chance when it comes. We only want fair trade and no favour, while those rascals want it all to themselves. They know they have no chance with us when it comes to fair trading."

"You know, captain, that the Genoese say just the same things about the Venetians, that the Venetians do about them. So I expect that there are faults on both sides."

The captain laughed.

"I suppose each want to have matters their own way, Messer Hammond, but I don't consider the Genoese have any right to come interfering with us, to the eastward of Italy. They have got France and Spain to trade with, and all the western parts of Italy. Why don't they keep there? Besides, I look upon them as landsmen. Why, we can always lick them at sea in a fair fight."

"Generally, captain. I admit you generally thrash them. Still, you know they have sometimes got the better of you, even when the force was equal."

The captain grunted. He could not deny the fact.

"Sometimes our captains don't do their duty," he said. "They put a lot of young patricians in command of the galleys, men that don't know one end of a ship from the other, and then, of course, we get the worst of it. But I maintain that, properly fought, a Venetian ship is always more than a match for a Genoese."

"I think she generally is, captain, and I hope it will always prove so in the future. You see, though I am English, I have lived long enough in Venice to feel like a Venetian."

"I have never been to England," the captain said, "though a good many Venetian ships go there every year. They tell me it's an island, like Venice, only a deal bigger than any we have got in the Mediterranean. Those who have been there say the sea is mighty stormy, and that, sailing up from Spain, you get tremendous tempests sometimes, with the waves ever so much bigger than we have here, and longer and more regular, but not so trying to the ships as the short sharp gales of these seas."

"I believe that is so, captain, though I don't know anything about it myself. It is some years since I came out, and our voyage was a very calm one."

Three days of quiet sailing, and the Bonito rounded the headlands of the Morea, and shaped her course to Candia. The voyage was a very pleasant one to Francis. Each day the captain brought out the list of cargo, and instructed him in the prices of each description of goods, told him of the various descriptions of merchandise which they would be likely to purchase at the different ports at which they were to touch, and the prices which they would probably have to pay for them. A certain time, too, was devoted each day to the examination of the charts of the various ports and islands, the captain pointing out the marks which were to be observed on entering and leaving the harbours, the best places for anchorage, and the points where shelter could be obtained should high winds come on.

After losing sight of the Morea the weather changed, clouds banked up rapidly in the southwest, and the captain ordered the great sails to be furled.

"We are going to have a serious gale," he said to Francis, "which is unusual at this period of the year. I have thought, for the last two days, we were going to have a change, but I hoped to have reached Candia before the gale burst upon us. I fear that this will drive us off our course."

By evening it was blowing hard, and the sea got up rapidly. The ship speedily justified the remarks of the captain on her power of rolling, and the oars, at which the men had been labouring since the sails were furled, were laid in.

"It is impossible to keep our course," the captain said, "and we must run up among the islands, and anchor under the lee of one of them. I should recommend you to get into your bed as soon as possible. You have not learned to keep your legs in a storm. I see that lad of yours is very ill already, but as you show no signs of suffering thus far, you will probably escape."

It was some time, however, before Francis went below. The scene was novel to him, and he was astonished at the sight of the waves, and at the manner in which they tossed the great ship about, as if she were an eggshell. But when it became quite dark, and he could see nothing but the white crests of the waves and the foam that flew high in the air every time the bluff bows of the ship plunged down into a hollow, he took the captain's advice and retired to his cabin.

He was on deck again early. A gray mist overhung the water. The sea was of a leaden colour, crested with white heads. The waves were far higher than they had been on the previous evening, and as they came racing along behind the Bonito each crest seemed as if it would rise over her stern and overwhelm her. But this apprehension was soon dispelled, as he saw how lightly the vessel rose each time. Although showing but a very small breadth of sail, she was running along at a great rate, leaving a white streak of foam behind her. The captain was standing near the helm, and Francis made his way to him.

"Well, captain, and how are you getting on, and where are we?" he asked, cheerfully.

"We are getting on well enough, Messer Francisco, as you can see for yourself. The Bonito is as good a sea boat as ever floated, and would not care for the wind were it twice as strong as it is. It is not the storm I am thinking about, but the islands. If we were down in the Mediterranean I could turn into my cot and sleep soundly; but here it is another matter. We are somewhere up among the islands, but where, no man can say. The wind has shifted a bit two or three times during the night, and, as we are obliged to run straight before it, there is no calculating to within a few miles where we are. I have tried to edge out to the westward as much as I could, but with this wind blowing and the height of the ship out of water, we sag away to leeward so fast that nothing is gained by it.

"According to my calculation, we cannot be very far from the west coast of Mitylene. If the clouds would but lift, and give us a look round for two minutes, we should know all about it, as I know the outline of every island in the Aegean; and as over on this side you are always in sight of two or three of them, I should know all about it if I could get a view of the land. Now, for aught we know, we may be running straight down upon some rocky coast."

The idea was not a pleasant one, and Francis strained his eyes, gazing through the mist.

"What should we do if we saw land, captain?" he asked presently.

"Get out the oars, row her head round, and try to work either to the right or left, whichever point of land seemed easiest to weather. Of course, if it was the mainland we were being driven on there would be no use, and we should try and row into the teeth of the gale, so as to keep her off land as long as possible, in the hope of the wind dropping. When we got into shallow water we should drop our anchors, and still keep on rowing to lessen the strain upon them. If they gave, there would be an end to the Bonito. But if, as I think, we are driving towards Mitylene, there is a safe harbour on this side of the island, and I shall certainly run into it. It is well sheltered and landlocked."

Two more hours passed, and then there was a startling transformation. The clouds broke suddenly and cleared off, as if by magic, and the sun streamed brightly out. The wind was blowing as strong as ever, but the change in the hue of sky and sea would at once have raised the spirits of the tired crew, had not a long line of land been seen stretching ahead of them at a distance of four or five miles.

"Just as I thought," the captain exclaimed as he saw it. "That is Mitylene, sure enough, and the entrance to the harbour I spoke of lies away there on that beam."

The oars were at once got out, the sail braced up a little, and the Bonito made for the point indicated by the captain, who himself took the helm.

Another half hour and they were close to land. Francis could see no sign of a port, but in a few minutes the Bonito rounded the end of a low island, and a passage opened before her. She passed through this and found herself in still water, in a harbour large enough to hold the fleet of Venice. The anchor was speedily let drop.

"It seems almost bewildering," Francis said, "the hush and quiet here after the turmoil of the storm outside. To whom does Mitylene belong?"

"The Genoese have a trading station and a castle at the other side of the island, but it belongs to Constantinople. The other side of the island is rich and fertile, but this, as you see, is mountainous and barren. The people have not a very good reputation, and if we had been wrecked we should have been plundered, if not murdered.

"You see those two vessels lying close to the shore, near the village? They are pirates when they get a chance, you may be quite sure. In fact, these islands swarm with them. Venice does all she can to keep them down, but the Genoese, and the Hungarians, and the rest of them, keep her so busy that she has no time to take the matter properly in hand, and make a clean sweep of them."

CHAPTER 8

AN ATTACK BY PIRATES

A boat was lowered, and the captain went ashore with a strong crew, all armed to the teeth. Francis accompanied him. The natives were sullen in their manner, but expressed a willingness to trade, and to exchange hides and wine for cloth.

"We may as well do a little barter," the captain said, as they rowed back towards the ship. "The port is not often visited, and the road across the island is hilly and rough, so they ought to be willing to sell their goods cheaply."

"They did not seem pleased to see us, nevertheless," Francis said.

"No; you see the Genoese have got a footing in the island, and of course they represent us to the natives as being robbers, who would take their island if we got the chance. All round these coasts and islands the people are partisans either of Venice or Genoa. They care very little for Constantinople, although they form part of the empire. Constantinople taxes them heavily, and is too weak to afford them protection. Of course they are Greeks, but the Greeks of the islands have very little in common, beyond their language, with the Greeks of Constantinople. They see, too, that the Turks are increasing in power, and they know that, if they are to be saved from falling into the hands of the Moslem, it is Venice or Genoa who will protect them, and not Constantinople, who will have enough to do to defend herself.

"As to themselves, they would naturally prefer Venice, because Venice is a far better mistress than Genoa; but of course, when the Genoese get a footing, they spread lies as to our tyranny and greed, and so it comes that the people of the islands are divided in their wishes, and that while we are gladly received in some of them, we are regarded with hate and suspicion in others."

Trade at once began, and continued until evening.

"How long do you expect to stay here, captain?" Francis asked.

"That must depend upon the wind. It may go down tomorrow, it may continue to blow strong for days, and it is no use our attempting to work down to Candia until it changes its direction. I should hope, however, that in a day or two we may be off. We are doing little more than wasting our time here."

A strong watch was placed on deck at nightfall.

"Why, surely, captain, there is no fear of an attack! War has not yet been proclaimed with Genoa, although there is little doubt it will be so in a few weeks, or perhaps a few days."

"There is never a real peace between Venice and Genoa in these seas," the captain said, "and as war is now imminent, one cannot be too watchful. State galleys would not be attacked, but merchant vessels are different. Who is to inquire about a merchant ship! Why, if we were attacked and plundered here, who would be any the wiser? We should either have our throats cut, or be sent to rot in the dungeons of Genoa. And not till there was an exchange of prisoners, perhaps years hence, would any in Venice know what had befallen us. When weeks passed, and no news came to Venice of our having reached Candia, it would be supposed that we had been lost in the storm.

"Signor Polani would run his pen through the name of the Bonito, and put her down as a total loss, and there would be an end of it, till those of us who were alive, when the prison doors were opened, made their way back to Venice. No, no, Messer Francisco. In these eastern waters one must always act as if the republic were at war. Why, did not Antonio Doria, in a time of profound peace, attack and seize eight Venetian ships laden with goods, killing two of the merchants on board, and putting the ships at a ransom? As to single vessels missing, and never heard of, their number is innumerable.

"It is all put down to pirates; but trust me, the Genoese are often at the bottom of it. They are robbers, the Genoese. In fair trade we can always beat them, and they know it, and so they are always seeking a pretext for a quarrel with us."

Francis smiled quietly at the bigoted hatred which the captain bore the Genoese, but thought it useless to argue with him. The next morning he came up on deck soon after daybreak.

"I see one of those vessels has taken her departure," he said, as he glanced towards the spot where they had been lying.

"So she has," the captain said. "I had not noticed that before. I wonder what that fellow has gone for? No good, you may be sure. Why, it is blowing hard outside still, as you may see by the rate those light clouds travel. He would never have put to sea without having a motive, and he must have had a strong crew on board, to row out in the teeth of the gale far enough to make off the land. That fellow is up to mischief of some sort."

A few minutes later the captain ordered a boat to be lowered, and rowed out to the rocky islet at the mouth of the harbour, and landing, climbed up the rocks and looked out to sea. In half an hour he returned to the ship.

"It is no use," he said to Francis. "The wind is blowing straight into the passage, and we could not row the Bonito out against it. It was different with that craft that went out yesterday evening, for I have no doubt she started as soon as it became dark. She was low in the water, and would not hold the wind; besides, no doubt they lowered the masts, and with a strong crew might well have swept her out. But with the Bonito, with her high sides and heavy tonnage, it could not be done."

"What do you think she went out for, captain?"

"It is likely enough that she may have gone to one of the other islands, and may return with a dozen other craft, pirates like herself. The news that a Venetian merchant ship, without consorts, is weather bound here, would bring them upon us like bees.

"It is a dangerous thing, this sailing alone. I have talked it over several times with the master. Other merchants generally send their ships in companies of eight or ten, and they are then strong enough to beat off any attack of pirates. Messer Polani always sends his vessels out singly. What he says is this: 'A single ship always travels faster than a convoy, because these must go at the rate of the slowest among them. Then the captain is free to go where he will, without consulting others, according as he gets news where trade is to be done, and when he gets there he can drive his own bargains without the competition of other ships.

"So you see there are advantages both ways. The padrone's ships run greater risks, but, if they get through them safely, they bring home much larger profits than do those of others. As a rule, I prefer sailing singly; but just at the present time I should be well pleased to see half a dozen consorts lying alongside."

Three times during the day the captain paid a visit to the rocky island. On his return for the last time before nightfall he said to Francis:

"The wind is certainly falling. I hope that tomorrow morning we shall be able to get out of this trap. I am convinced that there is danger."

"You see nothing else, do you, captain, beyond the departure of that craft, to make you think that there is danger?"

"Yes, I have seen two things," the captain said. "In the first place, the demeanour of the people has changed. They do not seem more unfriendly than they were before, but as I moved about the place today, it seemed to me that there was a suppressed excitement—people gathered together and talked earnestly, and separated if any of our crew happened to go near them; even laughed when they thought that none of us were looking, and looked serious and sullen if we turned round. I am convinced that they are expecting something to happen.

"I have another reason for suspecting it. I have kept a sharp watch on that high hill behind the village; they tell me there is nothing at the top except some curious stones, that look as if they had once been trees, so there is nothing they can want to go up for. Several times today I have made out the figures of men climbing that hill. When they got to the top they stood for some time as if they were looking out over the sea, and then came down again without doing anything. Now, men do not climb such a hill as that merely for exercise. They went up because they expected to see something, and that something could only be a fleet of pirate boats from the other islands. I would give a year's pay if we could get out of this place this evening, but it cannot be done, and we must wait till tomorrow morning. I will try then, even though I risk being driven on the rocks. However, if they do come tonight they will not catch us asleep."

Orders were issued that the whole crew were to remain in readiness for attack, and that those whose watch was below were to sleep with their arms beside them. The lower ports were all closed, a strong watch was kept on deck, and it was certain that, whatever happened, the Bonito would not be taken by surprise.

Being assured by the captain that it was not probable that any attack would be made before morning, as the pirates, not knowing their exact position, would wait until the first gleam of daylight enabled them to make out where she was lying, and to advance in order against her, Francis lay down on his couch, leaving orders that, if asleep, he was to be called two hours before daybreak. He slept but little, however, getting up frequently and going out to ascertain if any sounds indicated the presence of an enemy.

Upon one of these occasions he found that the person leaning next to him against the bulwark, and gazing towards the mouth of the harbour, was Giuseppi.

"Have you been here long, Giuseppi?"

"Since you were out last, Messer Francisco. I thought I would wait a bit, and listen."

"And have you heard anything?"

"I have heard sounds several times."

"What sort of sounds, Giuseppi?"

"Such a sound as is made when the sails and yards are lowered. I have heard it over and over again when out at night on the lagoons near the port. There is no mistake in the creaking of the blocks as the halyards run through them. I am sure, that since I have been here several vessels have brought up inside the mouth of the harbour. Some of the sailors have heard the same noises, so there cannot be any mistake about it. If the captain likes, I will take a small boat and row out, and find out all about them."

"I will ask the captain, Giuseppi."

The captain, however, said that there would be no use in this being done.

"Whether there are few or whether there are many of them, we must wait till morning before we go out. There will be no working out that channel in the dark, even if we were unopposed."

"But they must have managed to come in," Francis said.

"No doubt some of their comrades in the other barque, or people from the village, show a light out there to guide them in. Besides, the wind is favourable to them and against us. No, young sir, there is nothing to do but to wait. In the morning, if there are but few of them, we will try to break through and gain the sea. If there are many we will fight here, as then all hands will be available for the combat, while if we were rowing, half of them would be occupied with the oars. If your lad were to go as he proposes he might fall into the hands of the enemy, and as the information he could gather would be in any case of no use, it is best he should remain where he is."

The hours seemed long until the first tinge of daylight appeared in the sky. All hands were on deck now, for the news that vessels had been arriving in the port had convinced all that danger really threatened them. It was not until half an hour later that they were able to make out some dark objects, lying in under the shadow of the islet across the mouth of the harbour.

"There they are, Messer Francisco," the captain said. "Ten of them, as far as I can make out; but there may be more, for likely enough some of them are lying side by side. There may, too, be some round a corner, where we cannot see them. Another half hour we shall know all about it."

Francis was half surprised that the captain did not order the oars to be put out and lashed in that position, for it was a recognized plan for preventing a ship from being boarded by an enemy, who could thus only approach her at the lofty poop and forecastle.

"Are you not going to get out the oars to keep them off?"

"No, Messer Francisco. In the first place, our sides are so high out of water that the pirates will have a difficulty in boarding us in any case. In the second place, if we get the oars out and they row full at them, sooner or later they will break them off; and it is all important that we should be able to row. I have been thinking the matter over, and my idea is, as soon as they advance, to get three or four oars at work on either side, so as to move her gradually through the water towards the harbour mouth. The rowers will be charged to let their oars swing alongside whenever any of their craft dash at them. We shall want every oar, as well as our sails, to get away when we are once outside. I do not think we have much chance of finally beating them off if we stop and fight here. But if we can do so for a time, and can manage to creep out of the harbour, all may be well."

When daylight fairly broke they were able to make out their enemy. The vessels were of all sizes, from long, low craft, carrying great sails and long banks of oars, down to boats of a few tons burden. All seemed crowded with men.

"None of them are anything like as high out of the water as the Bonito," the captain said, "and they will find it very difficult to climb up our sides. Still the odds against us are serious, but we shall give them a warmer reception than they expect. They will hardly calculate either on our being so strong handed, or so well prepared for them."

Everything was indeed ready for the combat. Two or three barrels of the compound known as Greek fire had been brought up from the hold, and the cooks had heated cauldrons full of pitch. Thirty men with bows and arrows were on the poop, and the rest, with spears, axes, and swords, stood along the bulwarks.

"We may as well get as near the entrance as we can before the fight begins," the captain said. "Get up the anchor, and as soon as it is aboard, get out four oars on each side."

The anchor had already been hove short, and was soon in its place. Then the oars dipped into the water, and slowly the Bonito moved towards the mouth of the harbour. Scarcely had the oars touched the water, than a bustle was perceived on board the piratical ships. Oars were put out, and in two or three minutes the pirates were under way, advancing at a rapid pace towards the Bonito.

The crew made no reply to the shouts and yells of the pirates, but, in accordance with the orders of the captain, remained in a stooping position, so that the figure of the captain, as he hauled up the flag with the lion of Venice to the masthead, was alone visible to the pirates. As these approached volleys of arrows were shot at the Bonito, but not a shot replied until they were within fifty yards of the ship.

Then the captain gave the word. The archers sprang to their feet, and from their eminence poured their arrows thick and fast on to the crowded decks of the pirates. The captain gave the word to the rowers, and they relinquished their oars, which swung in by the side of the vessel.

A moment later two of the largest craft of the pirates dashed alongside. The instant they did so they were saluted with showers of boiling pitch, while pots full of Greek fire were thrown down upon them. Those who tried to climb up the side of the Bonito were speared with lances or cut down with battleaxes.

The combat was of short duration. Many of those on whom the boiling pitch had fallen jumped overboard in their agony, while others did the same to escape the Greek fire, which they in vain endeavoured to extinguish. The fire quickly spread to the woodwork, and in five minutes after the beginning of the fight, the two craft dropped astern from the Bonito, with the flames already rising fiercely from them.

In the meantime the other vessels had not been idle, and a storm of missiles was poured upon the Bonito. The fate which befell their comrades, however, showed them how formidable was the vessel they had regarded as an easy prey, and when the first assailants of the Bonito dropped astern, none of the others cared to take their places.

"Man the oars again!" the captain ordered, and the Bonito again moved forward, her crew stooping behind the bulwarks, while the archers only rose from time to time to discharge their shafts.

"The thing I am most afraid of," the captain said to Francis, who was standing beside him, "is, that they will ram us with their prows. The Bonito is strongly built, but the chances are that they would knock a hole in her."

"I should think, captain, that if we were to get up some of those bales of cloth, and fasten ropes to them, we might lower them over the side and so break the shock."

"It is worth trying, anyhow," the captain said.

And a score of the sailors were at once sent down to fetch up the bales. Ropes were fastened round these, and they were laid along by the bulwarks in readiness for being lowered instantly. Ten bales were placed on each side, and three men told off to each bale.

By this time they were halfway to the mouth of the harbour, and the preparations were completed just in time, for the small boats suddenly drew aside, and two of the largest of the pirates' craft, each rowed by twenty-four oars, dashed at her, one on each side. The captain shouted the order, and the men all sprang to their feet. It was seen at once that the vessels would both strike about midships. Three bales on either side were raised to the bulwarks, and lowered down with the ropes until close to the water's edge and closely touching each other. Francis sprang on to the bulwark and superintended the operations on one side, while the captain did the same on the other.

"A few feet more astern, lads. That is right. Now, keep the bales touching. You are just in the line."

An instant later the Bonito reeled from the shock of two tremendous blows. The bows of the pirates were stove in, but the thick bales enabled the Bonito to withstand the shock, although her sides creaked, the seams started, and the water flowed in freely. But of this the crew thought little. They were occupied in hurling darts, arrows, and combustibles into the pirates as these backed off, in an already sinking condition.

"Now I think we can go," the captain said, and ordered the whole of the oars to be manned.

They were speedily got out, and the Bonito made her way out through the mouth of the harbour. The pirates, in their lighter boats, rowed round and round her, shooting clouds of arrows, but not venturing to come to close quarters, after the fate which had befallen the four largest vessels of their fleet.

As soon as they were clear of the islet the sails were hoisted. The wind had fallen much during the night, and had worked round to the east, and under sails and oars the Bonito left the island, none of the pirates venturing to follow in pursuit. The oars were soon laid in, and the men, with mallets and chisels, set to work to caulk the seams through which the water was making its way. The casualties were now inquired into, and it was found that six men had been shot dead, and that nine-and-twenty had received wounds more or less severe from the arrows of the pirates.

Francis had been twice wounded while superintending the placing of the bales. One arrow had gone through his right leg, another had struck him in the side and glanced off a rib.

"This won't do, Messer Francisco," the captain said as he assisted Giuseppi to bandage the wounds. "Signor Polani placed you on board to learn something of seamanship and commerce, not to make yourself a target for the arrows of pirates. However, we have to thank you for the saving of the Bonito, for assuredly she would have been stove in, had not the happy thought of hanging those bales overboard struck you. It would be of no use against war galleys, whose beaks are often below the waterline, but against craft like these pirates it acts splendidly, and there is no doubt that you saved the ship from destruction, and us from death, for after the burning of the two first vessels that attacked us, you may be sure they would have shown but little mercy. I can't think how you came to think of it."

"Why, I have read in books, captain, of defenders of walls hanging over trusses of straw, to break the blows of battering rams and machines of the besiegers. Directly you said they were going to ram us it struck me we might do the same, and then I thought that bales of cloth, similar to those you got up on deck to trade with the islanders would be just the thing."

"It was a close shave," the captain said. "I was leaning over, and saw the whole side of the ship bend beneath the blow, and expected to hear the ribs crack beneath me. Fortunately the Bonito was stronger built than her assailants, and their bows crumpled in before her side gave; but my heart was in my mouth for a time, I can tell you."

"So was mine, captain. I hardly felt these two arrows strike me. They must have been shot from one of the other boats. Then I could not help laughing to see the way in which the men at the oars tumbled backwards at the moment when their vessel struck us. It was as if an invisible giant had swept them all off their seats together."

The wind continued favourable until they arrived at Candia, where the captain reported, to the commander of a Venetian war galley lying in the port, the attack that had been made upon him; and the galley at once started for the scene of the action, to destroy any pirates she might find there or among the neighbouring islands, or in the various inlets and bays of the mainland.

Having delivered their letters and landed a portion of their cargo for the use of Polani's agents in the islands, the Bonito proceeded to Cyprus. For some weeks she cruised along the coast of Syria, trading in the various Turkish ports, for Venice, although she had shared in some of the crusades, was now, as she had often been before, on friendly terms with the Turks. Her interests all lay in that direction. She carried on a large trade with them; and in the days when she lay under the interdict of the pope, and all Europe stood aloof from her, she drew her stores of provisions from the Moslem ports, and was thus enabled successfully to resist the pressure which she suffered from the interdict. She foresaw, too, the growing power of the Turks, and perceived that in the future they would triumph over the degenerate Greek empire at Constantinople. She had spent her blood and treasure freely in maintaining that empire; but the weakness and profligacy of its emperors, the intestine quarrels and disturbances which were forever going on, and the ingratitude with which she had always treated Venice, had completely alienated the Venetians from her. Genoa had, indeed, for many years exercised a far more preponderating influence at Constantinople than Venice had done.

Having completed the tour of the Syrian ports, the Bonito sailed north, with the intention of passing the Dardanelles and Bosphorus, and proceeding to Azoph.

When she reached the little island of Tenedos, a few miles from the entrance to the strait, she heard news which compelled the captain to alter his intentions. A revolution had broken out in Constantinople, aided by the Genoese of Pera. The cruel tyrant Calojohannes the 5th had been deposed, and his heir Andronicus, whom he had deprived of sight and thrown into a dungeon, released and placed on the throne.

As a reward for the services she had rendered him, Andronicus issued a decree conferring Tenedos upon Genoa. The news had just arrived when the Bonito entered the port, and the town was in a ferment. There were two or three Venetian warships in the harbour; but the Venetian admiral, being without orders from home as to what part to take in such an emergency, remained neutral. The matter was, however, an important one, for the possession of Tenedos gave its owners the command of the Dardanelles, and a fleet lying there could effectually block the passage.

The people thronged up to the governor's house with shouts of "Down with Genoa!" The governor, being unsupported by any Greek or Genoese troops, bowed to the popular will, and declared that he did not recognize the revolution that had taken place in Constantinople, and refused to submit to the decree of Andronicus. Donato Trono, a Venetian merchant resident in the island, and other Venetians, harangued the people, and pointed out to them that alone they could not hope to resist the united forces of Greece and Genoa, and that their only hope of safety lay in placing themselves under the protection of Venice. The people, seeing the justice of the arguments of the Venetians, and preferring the Venetian rule to that of Genoa, agreed to the proposal. The banner of St. Mark was raised amid great enthusiasm, and the island declared subject to Venice.

A Genoese galley in port immediately set sail, and quickly carried the news to Constantinople, where the emperor at once threw the whole of the Venetian residents into prison. As soon as the news of this reached Tenedos the captain of the Bonito held a consultation with Francis.

"It is evident, Messer Francisco, that we cannot proceed upon our northward voyage. We should be captured and held at Constantinople; and, even did we succeed in passing at night, we should fall into the hands of the Genoese—who are far stronger in the Black Sea than we are—for if Venice accepts the offer of the people of this place, and takes possession of the island, Genoa is sure to declare war.

"I think, then, that we had better make our way back to Venice with what cargo we have on board, and there get fresh orders from the padrone. We have not done badly so far, and it is better to make sure of what we have got than to risk its loss, for at any day we may fall in with the Genoese fleet sailing hither."

Francis quite agreed with the captain's opinion, and the Bonito sailed for the south. They touched, on their way, at several islands, and the news that an early outbreak of hostilities between Genoa and Venice was probable—in which case there would be an almost complete cessation of trade—produced so strong a desire, on the part of the islanders, to lay in a store of goods, that the captain was able to dispose of the rest of his cargo on good terms, and to fill up his ship with the produce of the islands.

Thus the Bonito was deep in the water when she re-entered the port of Venice after an absence of about three months. As soon as the anchor was dropped the captain, accompanied by Francis, hired a gondola, and rowed into the city to give an account to Signor Polani of the success of his voyage, and to lay before him a list of the cargo with which the Bonito was laden. The merchant received them with great cordiality, and embraced Francis with the affection of a father.

"Do you go at once into the salon, Francisco. You will find my daughters expecting you there, for the news came an hour ago that the Bonito was entering port. Of course, we heard from the letters from Candia of your adventures with the pirates, and the gallant way in which the Bonito defeated them.

"You will find, captain, that I have ordered an extra month's pay to be given to all on board.

"The captain did full justice, Francisco, in his account of the matter, to your quickness in suggesting a method by which the effort of the ramming of the enemy was neutralized, and for the courage you showed in carrying out your idea; but we will talk of that afterwards. He and I have business to transact which will occupy us for some time, so the sooner you go the better."

Francis at once took himself off and joined the girls, who received him with the heartiest greeting.

"We were glad indeed, Francis," Maria said, "when our father told us that the Bonito was signalled as entering the port. No letters have come for some time, and we feared that you must have entered the Dardanelles, and reached Constantinople, before the news arrived there of that affair at Tenedos, in which case you would no doubt have been seized and thrown into the dungeons."

"We were at Tenedos when the affair took place," Francis said, "and have had no opportunity since of sending a letter by any ship likely to be here before us. The outbreak made us alter our plans, for, of course, it would not have been safe to have sailed farther when the emperor was so enraged against Venice. I need hardly tell you I was not sorry when we turned our faces again towards Venice. I have enjoyed the voyage very much, and have had plenty to occupy me. Still, three months at a time is long enough, and I was beginning to long for a sight of Venice."

"For a sight of Venice and—" Maria repeated, holding up her finger reprovingly.

"And of you both," Francis said smiling. "I did not think it necessary to put that in, because you must know that you are Venice to me."

"That is much better," Maria said approvingly. "I think you have improved since you have been away. Do you not think so, Giulia?"

"I don't think that sort of nonsense is an improvement," Giulia said gravely. "Any of the young Venetian gallants can say that sort of thing. We do not want flattery from Francisco."

"You should say you do not want it, Giulia," Maria said, laughing. "I like it, I own, even from Francisco. It may not mean anything, but it is pleasant nevertheless; besides, one likes to think that there is just a little truth in it, not much, perhaps, but just a little in what Francisco said, for instance. Of course we are not all Venice to him. Still, just as we are pleased to see him, he is pleased to see us; and why shouldn't he say so in a pretty way? It's all very well for you to set up as being above flattery, Giulia, but you are young yet. I have no doubt you will like it when you get as old as I am."

Giulia shook her head decidedly.

"I always think," she said, "when I hear a man saying flattering things to a girl, that it is the least complimentary thing he can do, for it is treating her as if he considers that she is a fool, otherwise he would never say such outrageous nonsense to her."

"There, Francisco," Maria laughed, "you are fairly warned now. Beware how you venture to pay any compliment to Giulia in future.

"It would be a dull world if every one were to think as you do, Giulia, and to say exactly as they meant. Fancy a young man saying to you: 'I think you are a nice sort of girl, no prettier than the rest, but good tempered and pleasant, and to be desired because your father is rich!' A nice sort of way that would be to be made love to!"

"There is no occasion for them to say anything at all," Giulia said indignantly. "We don't go about saying to them, 'I think you are good looking, and well mannered, and witty;' or, 'I like you because they say you are a brave soldier and a good swordsman.' Why should they say such things to us? I suppose we can tell if anyone likes us without all that nonsense."

"Perhaps so," the elder girl assented; "and yet I maintain it's pleasant, and at any rate it's the custom, and as it's the custom, we must put up with it.

"What do you say, Francisco?"

"I don't know anything about it," Francis said. "Certainly some of the compliments I have heard paid were barefaced falsehoods, and I have wondered how men could make them, and how women could even affect to believe in them; but, on the other hand, I suppose that when people are in love, they really do think the person they are in love with is prettier and more charming, or braver and more handsome, than anyone else in the world, and that though it may be flattery, it is really true in the opinion of the person who utters it."

"And now let us leave the matter alone for the present, Francisco. We are dying to hear all about your adventures, and especially that fight with the pirates. The captain, in his letter, merely said that you were attacked and beat the pirates off, and that you would have been sunk if it hadn't been that, at your suggestion, they lowered bales of cloth over to break the shock; and that so many men were killed and so many wounded; and that you were hit twice by arrows, but the wounds were healing. That's all he said, for papa read that portion of his letter out to us. Now we want a full and particular account of the affair."

Francis gave a full account of the fight, and then related the other incidents of the voyage.

"We know many of the ports you touched at," Maria said when he had finished, "for when we were little girls, papa took us sometimes for voyages in his ships, when the times were peaceful and there was no danger. Now let us order a gondola, and go for a row. Papa is sure to be occupied for ever so long with your captain."

CHAPTER 9

THE CAPTURE OF THE LIDO

Signor Polani told Francis, that evening, that he was much pleased with the report that the captain had given of his eagerness to acquire information both in mercantile and nautical matters, and of the manner in which he had kept the ship's books, and the entries of the sales, and purchases of goods.

"Many young fellows at your age, Francis, when there was no compulsion for them to have taken these matters into their charge, would have thought only of amusement and gaiety when they were in port, and I am glad to see that you have a real interest in them. Whatever the line in life a young man takes up, he will never excel in it unless he goes into it with all his heart, and I am very glad to see that you have thrown yourself so heartily into your new profession. The Bonito made a most satisfactory voyage, far more so than I anticipated, when I found that she would not be able to carry out the programme I had laid down for her; but the rise in the prices in the latter part of your voyage have more than made up for the loss of the trade in the Black Sea; and you have done as much in the three months you were absent, as I should have expected had you been, as I anticipated, six months away.

"You will be some little time before you start again, as I wish to see how matters are going before I send the Bonito out upon another adventure. At present nothing is settled here. That there will be war with Genoa before long is certain, but we would rather postpone it as long as possible, and the senate has not yet arrived at the decision to accept the offer of Tenedos. Negotiations are going on with Genoa and Constantinople, but I have little hope that anything will come of them.

"It is getting late in the season now, and the war will hardly break out until next spring; but I have no doubt the struggle will then begin, and preparations are going on with all speed in the dockyards. We are endeavouring to obtain allies, but the combination is so strong against Venice that we are meeting with little success, and Ferrara is really the only friend on whom we can rely, and she is not in a position to aid us materially, in such a struggle as this will be.

"I am glad to tell you that the affair in which you were concerned, before you sailed, has now completely dropped. Nothing has been heard of Mocenigo since he made his escape.

"A decree of banishment was passed against him, but where he is we know not. That wretched woman was sentenced to four years' imprisonment, but upon my petition she will be released at the end of six months, on her promise that she will not again set foot in the territory of the republic. As Mocenigo has not been brought to trial, there will be no further official inquiry into the matter, and I have not been further questioned as to the source from which I obtained my information as to the girls' hiding place. Your share in the matter is therefore altogether unsuspected, and I do not think that there is any further danger to you from Mocenigo's partisans."

"I should be glad enough to remain in Venice a fortnight or so, sir," Francis said. "But if, at the end of that time, you have any vessel going out, I shall prefer to go in her. Now that my studies are over, I shall very soon get tired of doing nothing. Perhaps in a few years I may care more for the gaieties of Venice, but certainly at present I have no interest in them, and would rather be at sea. Matteo tells me that you have promised he shall make a few voyages in your ships, and that you have told him he shall go in one of them shortly. If so, it would be very pleasant to us both if we can sail together."

"I will arrange it so, Francisco. It would be for the benefit of my cousin—who is a good lad, but harebrained, and without ballast—for you to go with him. I should indeed have proposed it, but the vessel in which I have decided he shall sail will be ready for sea in another ten days or so, and I thought that you would prefer a longer stay in Venice before you again set sail. If, however, it is your wish to be off again so soon, I will arrange for you both to sail together.

"This time you will go officially as my supercargo, since you now understand the duties. The captain of the vessel in which you will sail is a good sailor and a brave man, but he has no aptitude for trade, and I must have sent a supercargo with him. Your decision to go relieves me of this, for which I am not sorry, for men who are at once good supercargos, and honest men, are difficult to get."

The fortnight passed rapidly, and Francis enjoyed his stay at the merchant's greatly, but he was not sorry when, at the end of ten days, Polani told him that the lading of the vessel would begin the next day, and that he had best go on board early and see the cargo shipped, so that he might check off the bales and casks as they were sent on board, and see where each description of goods was stowed away.

"I think, papa, it is too bad of you, sending Francisco away so soon," Maria said, when at their evening meal she learned the news of his early departure.

"It is his own doing," her father said. "It is he who wants to go, not I who send him. I consider that it is entirely your fault."

"Our fault!" the two girls repeated in surprise.

"Certainly. If you had made Venice sufficiently pleasant to him, he would not wish to leave. I am too busy to see about such things, and I left it to you to entertain him. As he is in such a hurry to get away again, it is evident that you have not succeeded in doing so."

"Indeed, Signor Polani, your daughters have been everything that is kind, but I have no taste for assemblies and entertainments. I feel out of place there, amid all the gaily dressed nobles and ladies, and no sooner do I get there, than I begin to wonder how anyone can prefer the heated rooms, and clatter of tongues, to the quiet pleasure of a walk backwards and forwards on the deck of a good ship. Besides, I want to learn my profession, and there is so much to learn in it that I feel I have no time to lose."

"I am right glad to see your eagerness in that direction, Francisco, and I did but jest with my daughters. You have not yet asked me what is the destination of the Lido, for that is the name of your new vessel. This time you are going quite in a new direction. In the spring we are certain to have war with Genoa, and as Parma and Hungary will probably both take side against us, we may find ourselves cut off from the mainland, and, in case of a disaster happening to our fleet, in sore straits for food. I am, therefore, going to gather into my warehouses as much grain as they will hold. This will both be a benefit to the state, and will bring me good profit, for the price of wheat will be high in the city if we are leaguered on the land side.

"The Lido will go down to Sicily, and fill up there with corn. You will have to use care before entering port, for with war now certain, both parties will begin to snap up prizes when they get the chance. So you must keep a sharp lookout for Genoese galleys. If you find the coast is too closely watched, you will go to the Moorish ports. We are friends with them at present, though doubtless, as soon as Genoa and ourselves get to blows, they will be resuming their piratical work. Thus you will, this time, take in a much smaller amount of cargo, as you will have to pay for the most part in gold."

It mattered little to Francis where he voyaged; but Matteo, who had been greatly delighted at the thought of sailing with his friend, was much disappointed when he heard that they were only going to fetch grain from Sicily.

"Why, it is nothing to call a voyage," he said in tones of disgust, when Francis told him the destination of the Lido. "I had hoped we were going to make a long voyage, and touch at all sorts of places, just as you did last time."

"I do not see that it matters much, Matteo; and we shall learn navigation just as well from one course as another. The voyage will not be a long one, unless we meet with unfavourable winds; but there's no saying what may happen, and you may meet with adventure, even on a voyage to Sicily and back."

The trip down to Sicily was quickly made. Francis had worked hard on his first voyage, and was now able to make daily calculations as to the run made, the course steered, and the position of the ship, and found that these tallied closely with those of the captain. Matteo and he shared a large and handsome cabin, and the time passed pleasantly as the vessel ran down the coast of Italy. Once out of the Adriatic a sharp lookout was kept, but the coast of Sicily was made without seeing any sails of a suspicious character.

The lads were struck with surprise and admiration when, on coming on deck in the morning, they saw the great cone of Etna lying ahead of them. Neither of them had ever seen a mountain of any size, and their interest in the scene was heightened by a slight wreath of smoke, which curled up from the summit of the hill.

"It is well worth a voyage, if it were only to see that mountain," Francis said. "What an immense height it is, and how regular in its shape!"

"And yet," Matteo said, "those who have journeyed from Italy into France tell me that there are mountains there beside which Etna is as nothing. These mountains are a continuation of the range of hills which we can see from Venice. Their tops are always covered with snow, and cannot be ascended by man; whereas it is easy, they say, to reach the top of Etna."

"Yes, that looks easy enough," Francis agreed. "It seems such a regular slope, that one could almost ride up; but I dare say, when you are close you would find all sorts of difficult places."

"I should like to try," Matteo said. "What a grand view there would be from the top!

"Is the port we are going to try first, captain, anywhere near the foot of the mountain?"

"No, I am going round the southern part of the island. On this side the ground is less fertile, and we should have difficulty in obtaining a cargo. But even were we to put into a port on this side, you would not be able to climb Mount Etna.

"Sicily has been an unfortunate country. Its great natural

wealth has rendered it an object of desire, to all its neighbours. It was the battleground of the Romans and Carthaginians. Pisa, Genoa, and Naples have all contended for its possession; and the Moors frequently make descents upon its coasts. It has seldom enjoyed a peaceful and settled government. The consequence is that general lawlessness prevails in the districts remote from the towns; while in the forests that clothe the side of Mount Etna, there are numerous hordes of bandits who set the authorities at defiance, levy blackmail throughout the surrounding villages, and carry off wealthy inhabitants, and put them to ransom. No one in his senses would think of ascending that mountain, unless he had something like an army with him."

"I should like to try it, all the same," Matteo asserted. "If there are woods all over it, it is not likely one would happen to meet with any of these people. I should like, above all things, to get to the top of that hill."

"It would be harder work than you think, young sir," the captain said. "You have no idea from this distance what the height is, or what a long journey it is to ascend to the top. I have been told that it is a hundred and twenty miles round its foot."

"I don't think you would like it, Matteo, if you were to try it," Francis said laughing. "You know you are as lazy as you can be, and hate exerting yourself. I am sure that, before you got a quarter the distance up that mountain, you would have only one wish, and that would be to be at the bottom again."

"I don't know," Matteo said. "I hate exerting myself uselessly—wasting my strength, as you do, in rowing at an oar, or anything of that sort; but to do anything great, I would not mind exertion, and would go on until I dropped."

"That is all very well, Matteo; but to do anything great, you have got to do small things first. You could never wield a sword for five minutes unless you had practised with it; and you will never succeed in accomplishing any feats requiring great strength and endurance, if you do not practise your muscles on every occasion. You used to grumble at the height when you came up to my room in the old house, and I suppose Etna is something like two hundred times as high."

"That does sound a serious undertaking," Matteo said, laughing; "and I am afraid that I shall never see the view from the top of Etna. Certainly I shall not, if it will be necessary beforehand to be always exercising my muscles by running up the stairs of high houses."

The next day they were off Girgenti, the port at which they

110

hoped to obtain a cargo. They steered in until they encountered a fishing boat, and learned from those on board that there was no Genoese vessel in port, nor, as far as the men knew, any state galleys anywhere in the neighbourhood. Obtaining this news, they sailed boldly into the port and dropped anchor.

Francis, who had received before starting a list of houses with whom Signor Polani was in the habit of doing business, at once rowed ashore, Matteo and Giuseppi accompanying him. His business arrangements were soon completed. The harvest had been a good one, and there was an abundance of corn to be had at a cheap rate. In half an hour he arranged for as large a quantity as the Lido would carry.

The work of loading soon commenced, and in four days the ship was full up to the hatches. Francis went on shore to settle the various accounts, and was just making the last payment when Matteo ran into the office.

"Four Genoese galleys are entering the bay!"

Francis ran out, and saw four Genoese galleys rowing in.

"It is too late to escape. Even were we empty we could not get away; but laden as the Lido is, they could row three feet to her one."

"What shall we do, Francisco?"

Francis stood for half a minute thinking.

"You had better stay here, Matteo. I will row out to the ship, and send most of the men on shore. If they seize the ship, they may not take those on board prisoners; but if they do, there is no reason why they should take us all."

"You had better come on shore too, Francisco, and leave the captain in charge. You can do no good by staying there; and Polani would be more concerned at your capture than he would at the loss of a dozen ships. If you could do any good, it would be different; but as it is, it would be foolish to risk capture."

"I will see," Francis said. "At any rate, do you stop here."

Jumping into a boat, he rowed towards the Lido, which was lying but a cable's length from the shore. As he neared her, he shouted to the men to lower the boats.

"Captain," he said, "I do not know whether there is any danger of being captured by the Genoese. But it is useless to run any unnecessary risk. Therefore send all the crew but three or four men on shore. If the Genoese board us, we have our papers as peaceful traders buying wheat; but if, in spite of that, they capture us, we must take our chance."

"Surely you are not thinking of stopping, Messer Francisco. The padrone would be terribly vexed if you were taken. He specially ordered me, before we started, to see that no unnecessary risk was run, and to prevent you from thrusting yourself into danger. Therefore, as captain of the ship, I must insist that you go on shore."

"I think I ought to stay here," Francis said.

"I do not think so," the captain said firmly, "and I will not suffer it. I have to answer for your safety to the padrone; and if you do not go by yourself, I shall order the men to put you into one of the boats by force. I mean no disrespect; but I know my duty, and that is to prevent you from falling into the hands of the Genoese."

"I will not oblige you to use force, captain," Francis said, smiling, "and will do as you wish me."

In five minutes the men were all—save four, whom the captain had selected—in the boat, and rowing towards shore. Matteo was awaiting them when they landed.

"That is right, Francisco. I was half afraid you would stay on board. I know how obstinate you are whenever you take a thing into your head."

"The captain was more obstinate still, Matteo, and said that unless I came away he would send me on shore by force; but I don't like deserting the ship."

"That is nonsense, Francisco. If the Genoese take her, they take her, and your remaining on board could not do any good. What are you going to do now?"

"We will at once leave the place with the men, Matteo, and retire into the country behind. It is not likely the Genoese would land and seize us here, but they might do so, or the inhabitants, to please Genoa, might seize us and send us on board. At any rate, we shall be safer in the country."

The men had, by the captain's orders, brought their arms ashore on leaving the ship. This was the suggestion of Francis, who said that, were they unarmed, the people might seize them and hand them over to the Genoese. At the head of this party, which was about fifty strong, Francis marched up through the little town and out into the country. He had really but little fear, either that the Genoese would arrest them on shore, or that the people would interfere with them, for they would not care to risk the anger of Venice by interfering in such a matter. He thought it probable, however, that if his men remained in the town, broils would arise between them and any of the Genoese sailors who might land.

As soon as the Genoese galleys came up to the head of the bay, a boat was lowered and rowed to the Lido, at whose masthead the Venetian flag was flying. An officer, followed by six men, climbed up on to the deck.

"Are you the captain of this ship?" the officer asked as the captain approached him.

"I am," the captain said.

"What ship is it?"

"It is the Lido, the property of Messer Polani, a merchant of Venice, and laden with a cargo of wheat."

"Then you are my prisoner," the Genoese said. "I seize this vessel as lawful prize."

"There is peace between the republics," the captain said. "I protest against the seizure of this ship, as an act of piracy."

"We have news that several of our ships have been seized by the Venetians," the officer said; "and we therefore capture this vessel in reprisal. Where are your crew?"

"There are only four on board," the captain said. "We have filled up our cargo, and were going to sail tomorrow, and therefore the rest of the crew were allowed to go on shore; and I do not think it is likely that they will return now," for one of the Genoese sailors had hauled down the flag of Venice, and had replaced it with that of Genoa.

The Genoese officer briefly examined the vessel.

"Whom have you here on board with you?" he asked, struck with the furniture and fittings of Francis' cabin.

"This is the cabin of Matteo Giustiniani, a young noble of Venice, who is making his first voyage, in order to fit himself for entering the service of the state: and of Francisco Hammond, who stands high in the affections of my patron."

The Genoese uttered an angry exclamation. The name of Polani was well known in Genoa as one of the chief merchants of Venice and as belonging to a ducal house, while the family of Giustiniani was even more illustrious; and had these passengers fallen into his hands, a ransom might have been obtained greatly exceeding the value of the Lido and her cargo. Leaving four of his men on board he went off to the galley of the officer commanding the fleet, and presently returned with a large boat full of sailors.

"You and your men can go ashore," he said to the captain. "The admiral does not deem you worth the trouble of carrying to Genoa; but be quick, or you will have to swim to shore."

As the Lido's boats had all gone ashore, the captain hailed a fishing boat which was passing, and with the four sailors was rowed to shore, well content that he had escaped the dungeons of Genoa. He rightly imagined that he and his men were released solely on account of the paucity of their numbers. Had the whole crew been captured, they would have been carried to Genoa; but the admiral did not care to bring in five prisoners only, and preferred taking the ship alone.

Francis, with his party, followed the line of the coast, ascending the hills which rose steeply from the edge of the sea at a short distance from the town. He had brought with him from the town a supply of food sufficient for four or five days, and encamped in a little wood near the edge of the cliff. From this they had a view of the port, and could watch the doings of the Genoese galleys. Fires were lit and meat cooked over them; and just as the meal was prepared the captain and the four sailors joined them, amid a hearty cheer from the crew.

"I have made my protest," the captain said as he took his seat by the side of Francis, "and the padrone can make a complaint before the council if he thinks fit to do so; but there is small chance that he will ever recover the Lido, or the value of her cargo."

"I don't like losing the ship," Francis said. "Of course, it is only a stroke of bad fortune, and we could neither fly nor defend ourselves. Still one hates arriving home with the story that one has lost the ship."

"Yes," the captain agreed. "Messer Polani is a just man, yet no one cares to employ men who are unlucky; and the worst of it is that the last ship I commanded was wrecked. Many men would not have employed me again, although it wasn't my fault. But after this second affair, in a few months' time, I shall get the name of being an unlucky man, and no one in his senses would employ a man who is always losing his ships."

"Do you think that there is any chance of our recapturing it, captain?"

"Not the least in the world," the captain replied. "Even supposing that we could get on board, and overpower the Genoese without being heard, and get her out of the port without being seen, we should not get away. Laden as she is with grain, she will sail very slowly, and the Genoese would overtake her in a few hours; and I needn't tell you that then there would be very little mercy shown to any on board."

"That is true enough," Francis said. "Still, I do not like the idea of losing the Lido."

After the meal was over Francis rose, and asked Matteo to accompany him on a stroll along the cliffs, Giuseppi as usual following them. They walked along until they rounded the head of the bay, and were able to look along the coast for some distance. It was steep and rocky, and worn into a number of slight indentations. In one of these rose a ledge of rocks at a very short distance from the shore.

"How much further are we going, Francis?" Matteo said when they had walked a couple of miles.

"About a quarter of a mile, Matteo. I want to examine that ledge of rocks we saw from the first point."

"What on earth do you want to look at them for, Francis? You certainly are the most curious fellow I ever met. You scoffed at me when I said I should like to go up Mount Etna, and now here you are, dragging me along this cliff, just to look at some rocks of no possible interest to any one."

"That is the point to be inquired into, Matteo. I think it's possible they may prove very interesting."

Matteo shrugged his shoulders, as he often did when he felt too lazy to combat the eccentric ideas of his English friend.

"There we are," Francis said at last, standing on the edge of the cliff and looking down. "Nothing could be better."

"I am glad you think so, Francisco," Matteo said, seating himself on the grass. "I hope you intend to stay some little time to admire them, for I own that I should like a rest before I go back."

Francis stood looking at the rocks. The bay was a shallow one, and was but five or six hundred yards from point to point, the rocks rising nearly in a line between the points, and showing for about two hundred yards above water, and at about the same distance from the cliffs behind them.

"What height do you think those rocks are above the water, Giuseppi?"

"It is difficult to judge, signor, we are so high above them; but I should think in the middle they must be ten or twelve feet."

"I should think it likely they were more than double that, Giuseppi; but we shall see better when we get down to the bottom. I daresay we shall find a place where we can clamber down somewhere."

"My dear Francisco," Matteo said earnestly, "is anything the matter with you? I begin to have doubts of your sanity. What on earth do these rocks matter to you, one way or the other? or what can you care whether they are thirty inches or thirty feet above the water?

"They do not differ from other rocks, as far as I can see. They are very rugged and very rough, and would be very awkward if they lay out at sea instead of in this little bay, where they are in nobody's way. Is it not enough that you have tramped two miles to have a look at them, which means four miles, as we have got to return somehow? And now you talk about climbing down that break-neck cliff to have a look at them close!"

But Francis paid no attention to Matteo's words. He was gazing down into the clear smooth water, which was so transparent that every stone and pebble at the bottom could be seen.

"The water looks extremely shallow, Giuseppi. What do you think?"

"It seems to me, signor, that there is not a foot of water between the rocks and the shore."

"It does look so, Giuseppi; but it is possible that the transparency of the water deceives us, and that there may be ten or twelve feet of water there. However, that is what we must go down and find out. Now the first thing is to look about, and find some point at which we can get down to the beach."

"Well, I will lie down and take a nap till you come back," Matteo said in a tone of resignation. "I have no interest either in these rocks or in the water; and as far as I can protest, I do so against the whole proceeding, which to me savours of madness."

"Don't you understand, you silly fellow, what I am thinking about?" Francis said impatiently.

"Not in the smallest degree, Francisco; but do not trouble to tell me—it makes no matter. You have some idea in your head. Carry it out by all means; only don't ask me to cut my hands, tear my clothes, and put myself into a perspiration by climbing down that cliff."

"My idea is this, Matteo. There is no chance of carrying off the Lido by speed from the Genoese; but if we could get her out of the bay we might bring her round here and lay her behind those rocks, and the Genoese would pass by without dreaming she was there. Half a mile out those rocks would look as if they form part of the cliff, and none would suspect there was a passage behind them."

"That is something like an idea!" Matteo said, jumping to his feet. "Why did you not tell me of it before? You have quite alarmed me. Seriously, I began to think that you had become a little mad, and was wondering whether I had not better go back and fetch the captain and some of his men to look after you.

"Now let us look at your rocks again. Why, man, there is not water enough to float a boat between them and the shore, much less the Lido, which draws nine foot of water now she is loaded."

"I don't know, Matteo. Looking down on water from a height is very deceiving. If it is clear and transparent, there is nothing to enable you to judge its depth. At any rate it is worth trying. Before we go down, we will cut some long stiff rods with which we can measure the depth. But we have first to find a place where we can get down to the water."

116

After a quarter of an hour's search, they found a point where the descent seemed practicable. A little stream had worn a deep fissure in the face of the rock. Shrubs and bushes had grown up in the crevices and afforded a hold for the hands, and there appeared no great difficulty in getting down. Before starting they cut three stiff slender rods twelve feet in length. They then set to work to make the descent. It was by no means difficult, and in a few minutes they stood by the edge of the water.

"It is a great advantage, the path being so easy," Francis said, "for in case they did discover the ship we could land and climb to the top before they had time to come to shore, and once there we could keep the whole force in those galleys at bay. Now for the main point, the depth of the water."

Matteo shook his head.

"It is useless to take the trouble to undress, Francis," he said, as the latter threw off his jacket. "Giuseppi can wade out to the rocks without wetting his knees."

"Giuseppi can try if he likes," Francis said, "but I will wager he will not get far."

Giuseppi, as convinced as Matteo of the shallowness of the water, stepped into it, but was surprised to find that, before he had gone many paces, the water was up to his waist.

"Well, I wouldn't have believed it if I hadn't seen it," Matteo said when he returned, "but I think he must have got into a deep hole among the rocks. However, we shall soon see," and he too began to undress.

In a few minutes the three lads were swimming out towards the rocks which, as Francis had anticipated, rose from twenty to thirty feet above the level of the sea. The water deepened fast, and for the last thirty or forty yards, they were unable to touch the bottom, even when thrusting down their rods to the fullest depth. They then tried the depth in the passages at the end of the rocks, and found that there was ample water for the Lido. When they ascertained this to their satisfaction they swam back to the shore.

"I shall believe you in future, Francis, even if you assert that the moon is made of cheese. I could have taken an oath that there was not a foot of water between those rocks and the shore."

"I hardly ventured to hope that it was as deep as it is," Francis said, "but I know how deceiving clear water is, when you look down upon it from a height. However, that point is settled."

"But they would see our masts above the rocks, Francisco. They are sure to keep a sharp lookout as they go along."

"We must take the masts out of her," Francis said. "I don't

know how it is to be done, but the captain will know, and if that can't be managed we must cut them down. There is no difficulty about that.

"Now we will make our way back again, it will be dark in a couple of hours' time. Everything depends upon whether they have towed the Lido out and anchored her among their galleys. If they have, I fear the scheme is impracticable, but if they let her remain where she is lying, we might get her out without being noticed, for there is no moon."

As they began to ascend the cliff, Francis stopped suddenly.

"We should never be able to find this place in the dark," he said.

"Giuseppi, you must stay here. Do you collect a quantity of dried sticks, and lay them in readiness at that point opposite the ledge. We will show a light as we come along, that is if we succeed in getting the Lido out, and directly you see it set fire to the sticks. The fire will be a guide to us as to the position of the rocks."

"Perhaps I had better take the sticks off to the ledge, Messer Francisco, and light my fire on the rock at the end. The water is deep a few yards out, as we found, so you could sail close to the fire and then round behind the rocks without danger."

"That will be the best way, Giuseppi; but how will you get the sticks off without wetting them?"

"I will make a bundle three or four times as big as I want," Giuseppi said, "and then half of them will be dry. I can put my clothes on them and the tinder. I will answer for the fire, but I would rather have been with you in your adventure."

"There will be no danger there, Giuseppi, so you need not be anxious about us. It has to be done quietly and secretly, and there will be no fighting. These Genoese are too strong to think of that; and if we are discovered in the attempt, or as we make off, we shall take to our boats again and row straight on shore.

"Keep a sharp lookout for us, we will hoist two lights, one above the other, to prevent your mistaking any fishing boat which may be coming along for us.

"Now, Matteo, for a climb. We have no time to lose."

The two lads climbed to the top of the cliff, and then started at a brisk pace along the top, and in half an hour reached the wood.

"We were beginning to wonder what had become of you," the captain said as they joined him.

"We have been settling how to carry off the Lido," Francis said, "and have arranged everything."

The captain laughed.

"If we could fly with her through the air, you might get her away, but I see no other way. I have been thinking it over since you left. With luck we might get her safely out of the bay, but the galleys row four feet to our one, and as they would be sure to send some one way, and some the other, along the coast; they would pick us up again in two or three hours after daylight."

"Nevertheless we have settled it, captain. We have found a place where we can hide her, and the Genoese might search the coast for a month without finding her."

"If that be so it is possible," the captain said eagerly, "and you may be sure you will not find us backward in doing our best."

Francis described the nature and position of the rock which would afford a shelter, and the means by which they had ascertained that there was plenty of water for the Lido behind it.

"It seems plausible," the captain said when he had concluded, "and I am quite ready to make the attempt, if, in your opinion, it can be done. You are Messer Polani's representative, and for my own sake as well as his, I would do anything which promises a chance of recapturing the ship. Besides, as you say, there is little danger in it, for we can take to the boats and make for the shore if discovered.

"The Lido is still lying where we anchored her. They can have no fear of a recapture, for they would know that they could overtake us easily enough. I daresay they intend to sail tomorrow morning, and did not think it worth the trouble to get up the anchor and tow her out to where they are lying."

The details of the expedition were now discussed and arranged, and the men told off to their various duties, and at eleven o'clock at night, when all in the town were fast asleep, the party quitted the bivouac and marched down again to the port.

CHAPTER 10

RECAPTURED

No one was astir in the streets as the band marched through, and they reached the port without encountering a single person. A small boat was chosen, and in this the captain, Francis, Matteo, and two of the strongest and most powerful of the sailors embarked. It was thought unlikely that, lying, as the Lido did, within a couple of hundred yards of the Genoese galleys, any very vigilant watch would be kept, and not more than two sailors would probably be on deck.

The dark mass of the ship could just be made out from the shore, and when all was ready the two sailors with their oars pushed her off with all their strength, and then stood perfectly quiet.

The impetus was sufficient. The boat moved so slowly through the water, indeed, before they reached the ship, that Francis thought it would be necessary for the men to row a stroke or two; but the boat still moved on, until at last it touched the side of the ship. All had removed their boots before starting, and they now clambered up the sides without making the slightest noise.

Once on deck they stood perfectly quiet, listening. Presently they heard a murmur of voices on the other side of the vessel. Very quietly they crept towards the sound, and at length made out two figures leaning over the bulwarks, talking.

Each man's work had been settled, and there was no confusion. One of the sailors and Francis stole towards one of the men, while the other and Matteo approached the second. The captain stood with his sword bared, in readiness to cut down any other man who might be on deck.

The Genoese did not look round. Francis gave the word, "Now," and in a moment the two sailors seized them from behind with a grasp of iron, while the lads at the same moment passed bandages tightly round their mouths, and before the Genoese were quite aware of what had happened, they were lying, bound hand and foot, gagged upon the deck.

The party now made a search, but found no one else about. They then secured and fastened down the hatch of the forecastle by coiling ropes upon it, quietly opened the door leading to the poop cabins, and entering, seized and bound two officers sleeping there without the slightest noise or resistance.

Then they took a light from the cabin and showed it towards

120

the shore. At the signal the sailors, who had already taken their places in the boats, at once rowed out to the vessel. When all were on board, the boats were fastened alongside, in case it should be necessary to abandon the ship again.

The cable was then cut. One of the sailors had already ascended the shrouds, and poured oil over the blocks through which the halyards ran, so that the sails should ascend noiselessly. The wind was very light, scarcely enough to belly out the sails, but it was fortunately in the right direction, and the Lido began to steal through the water.

Not a word had been spoken since they first started, but Francis now whispered to the captain, "I think I can make out the Genoese ships."

"So can I," the captain said, "but they cannot see us. They are against the skyline, while we are in the shadow of the shore. So far all is perfectly safe, and if this breath of wind will but carry us far enough out to be able to use our oars without their hearing us, we shall certainly get away."

The progress of the Lido was so slow, that it was nearly an hour before the captain said that he thought they were now fairly round the point of the bay, and could use their oars.

"We had better tow," he said; "the sweeps make a noise that can be heard miles away on a calm night like this, whereas, if they are careful, men in a boat can row almost noiselessly."

Ten of the men accordingly took their places in one of the large boats in which they had come on board, and a rope being passed down to them they began rowing at the head of the ship.

"We may as well lower the sails," the captain said, "they are doing no good now. Indeed I think it is a current rather than the wind that has helped us so far."

"I will put two lanterns over the side," Francis said. "We may have gone farther than we think, and it would never do to pass our hiding place."

The men in the boat rowed vigorously, but it was slow work towing the deeply-laden vessel. At last, however, a light burst suddenly up from the shore.

"There is Giuseppi," Francis exclaimed. "We are further out than we thought we were. He must be fully a mile and a half away."

The men in the boat were told to row direct for the light, and some of the sweeps were got out and helped the vessel through the water. As they drew near, they could make out Giuseppi throwing fresh wood on the fire.

"You can steer within ten yards of where he is standing, captain, and directly you are abreast of him, put your helm hard to port. You had better get the sweeps in now, the less way she has on her the better."

"All well?" Giuseppi hailed, as they came within fifty yards of it.

"All well, Giuseppi! There has been no fighting, so you have lost nothing. Put all your wood on the fire, we want as much light as we can to get in."

The flames shot up high, and the captain had no difficulty in rounding the corner of the rocks, and bringing up his vessel behind them. A kedge was dropped, and the men in the boat rowed to the end of the rocks, and brought off Giuseppi.

"I was beginning to be anxious," the lad said, as he joined them on deck, "and when I first saw your signal I took you for a fishing boat. You were so far off that the two lights looked like one, but by dint of gazing I made them out at last, and then lit the fire."

"Now, captain," Francis said, "we have a good deal to do before morning, for I take it it will be no easy matter to get out the masts."

"There would be no difficulty in getting the masts out," the captain answered. "I have only to knock out the wedges, and loosen the stays, and get up a tripod made of three spars to lift them out; but I don't see how they are to be got in again."

"How is that, captain? I should have thought it no more difficult to get a mast in than to take it out."

"Nor would it be so, under ordinary circumstances," the captain replied; "but you see, our hold is full of grain, and as the mast comes out, the hole it leaves will fill up, and there will be no getting it down again to step it on the keel without discharging the cargo."

"Yes, I see that, captain. Then you think we had better cut down the masts; but in that case how are we to raise them?"

"We will cut them off about six feet above the deck, Messer Francisco; then when we want to set sail again, we have only to rear the masts up by the side of the stumps, and lash them securely. Of course they will be six feet shorter than before, but that is of little consequence."

"Then so let it be," Francis said, "the sooner we begin the better."

Just at this moment there was a violent knocking against the hatch of the forecastle.

"I had forgotten all about the sailors," the captain said,

laughing. "I suppose the men who were to relieve the watch have woke up, and finding they could not get out, have aroused their comrades."

"Shall we leave them there, or take them out and bind them?" Matteo asked.

"We had better have them up," the captain said. "I don't suppose there are more than twenty of them, and it would be best to bind them, and put them down in the hold with the corn, otherwise they may manage to break out when we are not expecting it, and might give us some trouble."

Accordingly, the sailors gathered round the hatch. The ropes were then removed, and the hatch taken off.

"What fooling are you up to?" one of the Genoese exclaimed, angrily, as they rushed up on deck. "You have nearly stifled us down below putting on the hatch and fastening it."

He stopped abruptly as, on gaining the deck, he saw a crowd of armed figures round him, for a lantern had been placed so as to throw a light upon the spot.

"You are prisoners," the captain said. "It is useless to attempt resistance."

"Help, help, treachery!" one of the Genoese shouted at the top of his voice.

"It is useless for you to shout," the captain said, "you are miles away from your fleet. Now, do you surrender, or are we to attack you?"

Taken by surprise, and unarmed, the Genoese who had gained the deck sullenly replied that they surrendered. They were bound and led away, and the others ordered to come up on deck. There were found to be four-and-twenty in all, and these were soon laid side by side on the grain in the hold, the hatch being left off to give them air. The masts were then cut through, and were with some trouble lowered to the deck.

"There is nothing more to be done now," the captain said, "and I think we can all safely turn in till morning."

He then ordered the under officer to place two men on watch on the rocks, and two men on deck, two men to stand as sentinels over the prisoners, and the rest to lie down. He directed that he should be roused at the earliest streak of daylight.

The lads were soon fast asleep, and could hardly believe that the night was over, when Giuseppi awakened them with the news that day was breaking. They were soon on deck, and found that the crew were already astir. The sentinels on the rock were at once ordered to lie down, so that they could command a view of the sea, without exposing themselves to sight. The boats were drawn up alongside, and everything put in readiness for instant debarkation, and then the party waited for the appearance of the Genoese galleys.

"They will be along in less than an hour," the captain said. "It is light enough now for the watch to have discovered that the Lido is missing, and it will not be many minutes before they are under way. They will calculate that we can have but five or six hours' start at the utmost, and that three hours' rowing will bring them up to us."

"I have no fear whatever of their discovering us as they go along," Francis said. "The only fear is that, after rowing for three or four hours and seeing no sign of us, they will guess that we are hidden somewhere under the cliffs, and will come back along the shore, searching every bay."

"There is a chance of that," the captain agreed, "but I should think only a chance. When the party who come this way find they do not overtake us, they will suppose that we have sailed to the west, and that on their return they will find us in the hands of their comrades; and when these also come back empty handed they will conclude that we have sailed straight out to sea. Of course they may have sent a galley southward also, but will conclude that that has somehow missed us when it returns without news. I hardly think that the idea, that we may be hidden so close to them, will enter their minds, and the only fear I entertain is that some peasant may happen to come to the edge of the cliff and see us lying here, and may take the news back to Girgenti."

"Yes, there is certainly a danger of that," Francis said. "I think, captain, it would be the best plan to land twenty men at once. Giuseppi will show them the way up the cliff, and then they must take their station, at short distances apart, along the edge of the cliff, from point to point of this little bay, with orders to seize any one who may approach and bring him down here. They must, of course, be told to lie down, as a line of sentries along the top of the cliff might attract the attention of somebody on the galleys, and lead to a search."

"Yes, I think that will be a wise precaution," the captain agreed.

"Thomaso, do you take twenty men and post them as you hear Messer Francisco say. Tell them to lie in the bushes and keep out of sight, and on no account to show themselves, unless someone comes along sufficiently near to look over the edge of the cliff."

"Giuseppi," Francis said, "do you act as guide to the party. You will have plenty of time to get to the top and to return before the galleys come along."

A quarter of an hour later the captain, with Matteo and Francis, landed on the ledge, and took the place of the sentries, and in twenty minutes a simultaneous exclamation burst from them, as a Genoese galley was seen rowing rapidly along.

"They have sent only one galley," Francis said. "Of course, they would know that it was sufficiently strong to overpower us without difficulty. I suppose one has gone west, and the others have put out to sea in different directions. That certainly was the best course they could have adopted, and it is very lucky that we did not attempt to escape seaward, for they would assuredly have had us. I suppose, captain, you intend to sail tonight."

"Certainly," the captain replied. "We will get everything in readiness for hoisting the masts as soon as the galley has passed us on its way back. There is no fear of their coming along again later on, for the men will have had an eight hours' row of it; the first part, at any rate, at full speed. Besides, they will not know, until all the galleys return, that we have not been found, so I think it will be quite safe to get up the masts as soon as they have passed. Then directly it is dark we will man our oars and row to the southwest. We shall be far away before morning, even if they look further for us, which they are hardly likely to do."

"How about the prisoners, captain?"

"We have no choice but to take them with us, Messer Francisco. I am sure I do not want to be bothered with them, but we cannot land them before we leave, or they would carry the news to Girgenti in an hour, and we should be caught the first thing in the morning."

It was late in the afternoon before the galley was seen returning, rowing slowly and heavily.

"I expect," the captain said, "they kept up the racing pace at which they started for some four hours. By that time they must have been completely worn out, and no doubt they anchored and waited for some hours for the men to feed and rest themselves, for from the hurry with which they started you may be sure that they did not wait to break their fast.

"I would give a month's pay to be in that harbour this evening. What tempers they must be in when they find, after all their toil, that we have slipped through their fingers, How they will talk the matter over, and discuss which way we went. How the men in each ship will say that the others cannot have used their eyes or exerted themselves, else we must have been overtaken. Messer Francisco, I am indebted to you, not only for having saved the ship, but for giving me a joke, which I shall laugh over whenever I think of it. It will be a grand story to tell over the wine cups, how we cheated a whole Genoese fleet, and carried off the Lido from under their noses. What a tale it will be to relate to a Genoese, when we meet in some port after the war is over; it will be enough to make him dance with rage.

"Now, lads," he went on, turning to the men, "stand to your tackle. The moment that galley gets out of sight round the point, up with the mast."

Ten minutes later the masts were up, stout ropes were lashed round them and the stumps, and wedges driven in to tighten the cords to the utmost. The rigging was of the simplest description, and before dark everything was in readiness for hoisting the sails.

"I don't think they can make us out now," the captain said.

"I don't think they could," Francis agreed; "but we had better wait another quarter of an hour. It would be absurd to run any risk after everything has turned out so well; but the men can get into the boats and tow us out through the channel, then we can hoist the boats on board, and by that time it should be nearly dark enough."

"I think there will be a breeze presently," the captain said, "and from the right direction. However, the men won't mind working hard for a bit. They have had an easy time for the last two days."

The oars were all manned, and the men set to work with hearty goodwill. They were delighted at their escape from the island, for they might have been there some time before they got a passage back; and still more pleased at having tricked the Genoese; and the Lido, heavy laden as she was, moved at a steady pace through the water, under the impulsion of the oars.

For an hour they rowed parallel with the shore, as, had they made out to sea, they might possibly have been seen by one of the galleys, returning late from the search for them. At the end of that time the captain turned her head from shore. As soon as they got well out from under the shelter of the land the breeze made itself felt, and the sails were hoisted.

For a time the men kept on rowing, but the breeze increased rapidly, and the captain ordered the oars to be laid in. A double allowance of wine was served out, and an hour or two spent in song and hilarity; then the watch below was sent down, and Francis and Matteo turned into their cots.

In the morning the breeze was blowing strong. The sails had been taken off the mainmast, but that on the foremast was dragging the Lido through the water at a good rate of speed, and before night they were off Cape Spartivento. The wind held till next morning, when they were abreast of the Gulf of Taranto. Then came a long spell of calms or baffling winds, and it was a fortnight before the campaniles of Venice were seen rising apparently from the water.

"I have been anxious about you," Signor Polani said when Francis arrived. "One of our galleys brought the report that a Genoese fleet was cruising on the coast of Sicily, and as, although war had not yet been openly declared, both parties were making prizes, I was afraid that they might have snapped you up."

"They did snap us up," Francis said smiling. "They caught us in the port of Girgenti, and the standard of Genoa waved over the Lido."

"But how can that be," Polani said, "when you have returned in her? For she was signalled as approaching the port hours ago. You could hardly have persuaded the Genoese by fair words to release a prize that they had once taken.

"Eh, captain?"

"No, that is not the Genoese way, nor ours either," the captain said. "We did better than that, signor. We recaptured her, and carried her off from under their noses."

"You are joking," Polani said, "for they signalled the Lido as returning laden, and a laden ship could never get away from state galleys, however long her start. A fat pig might as soon try to escape from a hunting dog."

"That is so, Messer Polani, and we did not trust to our speed. We tricked them famously, sir. At least, when I say we did, Messer Francisco hcrc did, for the credit is due solely to him. If it had not been for this young gentleman, I and the crew would now have bccn camping out in the forests of Sicily, without the slightest prospect of being able to make our way home, and the Lido would now be moored in the port of Genoa."

"That is so, Cousin Polani," Matteo said. "It is to Francisco that we owe our escape, and you owe the safety of the Lido and her cargo."

"It was just a happy idea that occurred to me," Francis said, "as it would assuredly have occurred to Captain Pesoro, if he had been with us, or to anyone else, and after I had first suggested it the captain carried out all the arrangements."

"Not at all, Messer Francisco," the captain said obstinately. "I had no part or hand in the business, beyond doing what you suggested, and you would have got the Lido off just as well if I hadn't been there."

"Well, I will judge for myself when I hear," Polani said. "But, as it must be an interesting story, my daughters would like to hear it also. So, come into the next room and tell the tale, and I will order up a flagon of Cyprus wine to moisten your throats."

"First of all," the captain began, after the girls had greeted Francis, and all had taken their seats, "I must tell how the Lido was captured."

And he then related how the Genoese fleet had suddenly appeared before them, and how, seeing the impossibility of escape, he had sent all on shore with the exception of four sailors, and how he had, with them, been released and sent on shore.

"That's the Genoese all over," Polani said. "If they could have sent forty prisoners home they would have done so; but the fact that there were only five on board, when they took the vessel, would seem to them to detract from the credit of the capture."

The captain then told how, fearing that the people of Girgenti might give them all up to the Genoese, or that fights might ensue among the Genoese sailors who landed, he had marched the crew away out of the town.

"Now, captain," Matteo broke in, "I will tell the next bit, because I was with Francis when he found a hiding place."

He then related how Francis had seen the ledge of rocks in the distance, and had dragged him along the cliff two miles to observe them more closely; and how he had come to the conclusion that his companion had lost his senses. Then he described the exact position, and the clearness of the water, and how he had been convinced that there was not depth to float a rowboat inside the rocks; and how they had gone down, swum out, fathomed the water, and then returned to the wood.

The captain then took up the tale again, and completed it to the end.

"There is no doubt you were right, captain," Polani said, "and that it is entirely Francisco's quickness of observation, readiness of plan, and determination to see if his ideas could be carried into effect, which saved the Lido. That he possessed these qualities is not new to me, for I have already greatly benefited by them. If he had not been born a peaceful trader, he would have made a great captain some day; but the qualities which would distinguish a man in war are also useful in peace, and I think it fully as honourable to be a successful merchant, as a successful soldier."

"Henceforth, Francisco, I shall no longer consider you as in leading strings, and shall feel that I can confide important business to you, young as you are."

The next voyage that Francis made was to Jaffa, and this was accomplished without adventure. On his return, he found that Venice was in a state of excitement—war had at last been declared, and every effort was being made to fit out a fleet which could cope with that of Genoa.

The command was entrusted to Vettore Pisani, who was invested in the church of Saint Mark with the supreme command of the fleet by the doge himself, who handed to the admiral the great banner of Venice, with the words:

"You are destined by God to defend with your valour this republic, and to retaliate upon those who have dared to insult her and to rob her of that security which she owes to the virtue of her ancestors. Wherefore, we confide to you this victorious and great standard, which it will be your duty to restore to us unsullied and triumphant."

Carlo Zeno, a noble, who had gained a high reputation in various capacities, was appointed commissioner and captain general of Negropont. The three first divisions of those inscribed in the register, as liable to serve in the navy, were called out, and on the 24th of April Pisani sailed from Venice with fourteen war galleys.

Pisani enjoyed the highest popularity among the people of Venice. His manner was that of a bluff hearty sailor. He was always ready to share in the hardships of his men, and to set them an example of good temper and cheerfulness, as well as of bravery. He was quick tempered, and when in a passion cared nothing whom he struck.

When governor of Candia, he had got into a serious scrape, by striking Pietro Cornaro, an officer of the republic, from whom he happened to differ on some point of routine. He was a relative of the Doge Andrea Contarini, and had been employed not only as an officer in the navy, but as a military engineer and as a diplomatist, and in each capacity had shown equal talent.

He was connected with the Polani family, and was at their house several times before he sailed. Here he heard from his kinsman an account of the manner in which Francisco had saved the Bonito from being rammed by the pirates, and how he had succeeded in getting the Lido out of the hands of the Genoese; and he was so much pleased that he offered to take him with him in his galley, but Polani advised Francis not to accept the offer.

"It is quite true," he said, "that most of our noble families are, like myself, engaged in commerce; and that one day they are trading as merchants and the next fighting under the state; but at present, if you take my advice, you will stick to the peaceful side of the profession; especially as, being an Englishman, you are in no way called upon to serve the state. In another five or six years, if we are then at war, it will be different. I have frequently offered galleys for the service of the state, and you can then take the command of one, and will, I have no doubt, distinguish yourself; but were you to enter now, you might remain in the service of the state for some years, and would be losing your time as a merchant.

"There are countries in which, when a man once takes up the profession of arms, he remains a soldier all his life, and may not only achieve honour but wealth and wide possessions. It is not so in Venice. Here we are all citizens as well as all soldiers if need be. We fight for the state while a war lasts, and then return to our peaceful avocations. Even my kinsman, Pisani, may be admiral of the fleet today, and a week hence may be a private citizen. Therefore, my lad, I think it would be very foolish of you to give up commerce at present to take military service."

"I quite agree with you, signor," Francis said, although, in truth, for a moment he had felt a strong mind to accept the offer of Pisani. "I am just beginning to learn a little of trade, and desire nothing better than to be a successful merchant; though I confess that I should like to take part in such a glorious sea fight as that which is likely to take place soon."

"Yes, and perhaps be killed in the first engagement, Francis, for neither skill nor bravery avail against a bolt from a Genoese crossbow. No, my lad, be content with trade, especially since you have seen already that even the life of a trader has plenty of incident and excitement. What with storms, what with pirates, what with the enemies of the state and the treachery of the native peoples with whom we trade, there is no lack of adventure in the life of a Venetian merchant."

Francis felt that this was true, and that he had in the past six months had fully his share in adventures. His stay on shore this time extended over a month, and it was not until three weeks after Pisani sailed that he again set out.

The notice was a short one. Polani had been sent for to attend the council early in the morning, and on his return he said to Francis:

"You must go down to the port at once, Francis. News has

been received from Pisani that he has sailed almost into the port of Genoa, without finding the fleet of Fieschi. The Genoese have been in a terrible state of panic. The Lord of Fiesole, who is our ally, is menacing the city by land; the Stella Company of Condottieri, which is in our pay, is also marching against them; and the news that Pisani was close at hand seems to have frightened them out of their senses. Their first step, as usual, has been to depose their doge and choose another.

"However, that is not the point. Pisani has written asking that some ships with provisions and stores shall be sent out to him. They are to go through the Straits of Messina and up the coast of Italy until he meets them. His force is far too small for him to think of making an attack upon Genoa. He will wait in the neighbourhood of the city for a short time in hopes of Fieschi's fleet returning. If it does not do so he will come down the coast searching for it, and as he does not wish to put in port, he desires the stores mentioned to be sent out to him.

"I have placed the Bonito at their service, and have promised that she shall be ready to sail tomorrow morning, if they will send the stores on board today. Three other merchants placed ships at their disposal, but these may not sail for a day or two. They are particularly anxious that the Bonito shall start at once, as, in addition to provisions, she will carry a store of javelins, arrows, and other missiles of which there was not a sufficiency in the arsenal when Pisani sailed.

"You will have a strong party on board, as speed is required, and the oars must be kept going until you join the fleet. Therefore I shall place the crew of the Lido on board as well as the Bonito's own complement, and this will bring the number up to a hundred men. The captain has had an accident, and will not be able to go in charge, therefore the Lido's captain will command. This time I shall appoint you specifically second in command, as well as my representative. Now get off on board as quickly as you can, for there is enough to keep you at work, till tomorrow morning, to get everything in readiness for a start. You had best run in and say goodbye to my daughters, as it may be that you will not find time to return before sailing. You can send your boy ashore for what things you require. Matteo will accompany you."

A few minutes later, Francis was on his way to the port, leaving Giuseppi to charter a gondola and follow with his trunks. As Polani had said, he was occupied without intermission until the time for sailing next morning. The barges of the state kept coming alongside with stores and provisions from the arsenal; while other boats brought out the ship's stores; and Francis had to take a note of all that came on board.

The captain superintended the setting up of the rigging, and the getting of the ship into working order; while the under officers saw to the hoisting in and storing of the cargo. Gangs of men were at work tarring the sides of the ship, for she had only two days before returned from a trip to Spain; and a number of sailors were unloading the cargo from one hatchway, while her fresh freight was being taken in at the other.

It seemed well nigh impossible that she could be ready to sail at the hour named, but everyone worked with a will, and by daybreak things were almost in order. Polani himself came down to the port as soon as it was light, and expressed satisfaction at the work which had been done; and half an hour afterwards the anchor was weighed.

Just as the sails had been hoisted, Matteo arrived.

"You are only just in time, Matteo," Polani said. "Why did you not come off yesterday and help?"

"I was out," Matteo said, "when your message came, and only returned just in time to go to the entertainment at the ducal palace. I knew I could be of no use on board while they were only getting in the cargo."

"You will never be of any use on board, Matteo, if you go to entertainments when there's work to be done. You could have taken the marks on the bales as they came on board, just as well as another. I suppose you thought that the dirt and dust wouldn't suit a fine gentleman like you! Another time, unless you come on board when sent for, and make yourself as useful as you can, while the ship is fitting out and loading, you will not sail in her. One part of the duty is just as important as the other, and seamanship does not consist solely in strolling up and down the deck, and watching a vessel sail for her destination."

Matteo was abashed at the reproach, but soon recovered his usual spirits after Polani had left, when the vessel was under way.

"My cousin was rather in a sharp mood this morning," he said with a laugh to Francis; "but really I did not think I could be of any good, and the entertainment was a grand one. Everyone was there, and I should have been very sorry to have missed it."

"Everyone to his taste, Matteo. For my part, I would very much rather have been at work here all night watching the cargo got in and checking it off, than have been standing about doing nothing in the palace."

"Doing nothing!" Matteo repeated indignantly. "Why, I was talking to someone the whole time I was there."

"Talking about what, Matteo?"

"The heat, and the music, and the costumes, and the last bit of scandal at the Piazza."

"I don't call that talk. I call it chatter. And now, Matteo, I shall leave you to your own devices, for I am going to turn in and get a sleep for a few hours."

"You look as if you wanted it," Matteo said; "but I think that you stand in even more need of a wash. You are grimy with dust. It is just as well that my cousin Giulia did not come on board with her father this morning, for the sight of your face would have given her quite a shock, and would have dissipated any illusions she may have had that you were a good-looking fellow."

Francis went off to his cabin with a laugh, and took Matteo's advice as to the wash before he turned in. In a few minutes he was asleep, and did not wake until Giuseppi came to say that the midday meal was just ready.

The Bonito made a rapid voyage. The winds were light, and for the most part favourable, and the twenty-four oars were kept going night and day, the men relieving each other every two hours, so that they had six hours' rest between the spells of rowing.

When they rounded the southern point of Italy a sharp lookout was kept for the fleet of Fieschi, but they passed through the straits without catching sight of a single vessel carrying the Genoese flag. The most vigilant watch was now kept for Pisani's galleys, and they always anchored at the close of day, lest they should pass him in the dark.

Occasionally they overhauled a fishing boat, and endeavoured to obtain news of the two squadrons; but beyond the fact that Fieschi had been seen steering north some days before, and that no signs had been seen of Pisani's returning fleet, they could learn nothing.

CHAPTER 11

THE BATTLE OF ANTIUM

"We are running very far north," the captain said on the 29th of May. "We are near Antium now, and are getting into what we may call Genoese waters. If anything has occurred to prevent Pisani carrying out his intention of sailing back along this coast, or if he has passed us on the way up, our position would be a hazardous one, for as soon as he has rowed away the Genoese galleys will be on the move again, and even if we do not fall in with Fieschi, we may be snapped up by one of their cruisers."

"It is rather risky, captain," Francis agreed; "but our orders are distinct. We were to sail north till we met Pisani, and we must do so till we are within sight of the walls of Genoa. If we then see he is not lying off the port, we shall put about and make our way back again."

"Yes, if they give us the chance, Messer Francisco; but long before we are sufficiently near to Genoa to make out whether Pisani is lying off the port, they will see us from the hills, and will send off a galley to bring us in. However, we must take our chance, and if we get into a scrape I shall look to you confidently to get us out again."

"I should advise you not to count on that," Francis said, laughing. "It is not always one gets such a lucky combination of circumstances as we did at Girgenti."

At last, they obtained news from a fishing boat that Fieschi's fleet had passed, going northward, on the previous day, and was now lying in the bay of Antium. As Antium lay but a few miles north, they held a consultation as to the best method to pursue. If they sailed on there was a risk of capture; but that risk did not appear to be very great. The Genoese admiral would not expect to find a Venetian merchant ship so near to Genoa, and they might be able to pass without being interfered with. On the other hand, news might possibly have come of the departure of store ships from Venice for Pisani's fleet, and in that case a strict lookout would certainly be kept, and it would be necessary to keep so far to sea as to be out of sight of the Genoese; but in that case there would be a risk of their missing Pisani's fleet on the way down.

"I think," the captain said, after a long debate, "that we had better anchor here close under the shore tonight. If I am not mistaken, we shall have a gale in the morning. I do not like the look of the sky. Tomorrow we shall see how the weather is, and can then come to a decision."

By morning, as the captain had predicted, the wind was blowing strongly, and a heavy sea was running, and it was agreed to keep along under the lee of the shore until they could obtain a view of the Bay of Antium, and see if the fleet of Fieschi was still there. If so, they would tack and run back some distance, and make straight out to sea, so as to pass along four or five miles from the shore, as it would be unlikely in the extreme that the Genoese admiral would send a galley out to overhaul a passing ship in such weather.

They sailed along till they neared the slight depression known as the Bay of Antium, and then bore farther out to sea. Suddenly a fleet was seen running down the coast at some distance away.

"'Bout ship," the captain cried. "The Genoese have been cruising further north, and are coming down the coast. In such weather as this, the Bonito ought to be able to get away from them."

"It may be Pisani's fleet," Francis said, as the ship was put round.

"It is possible," the captain agreed; "but we cannot run the risk of stopping until we make inquiries."

"No, captain; but, at least, if we run a mile or so out to sea, we should be able to see round the point, and discover whether Fieschi's galleys are there."

The captain assented. The vessel's head was turned from the land. In ten minutes there was a joyous shout on board the Bonito, for the Genoese fleet was seen lying in the bay. The distant fleet must then form that of Pisani.

"See!" Francis exclaimed. "The Genoese have just caught sight of them, and are hoisting sail. They are either going to meet them or to run away. Our vessels are the most numerous; but no, there is not much difference. Pisani has fourteen ships, but some must be lagging behind, or have been lost. How many do you make them out to be, captain?"

"I think there are only nine," the captain answered, "and that is just the number of the Genoese."

"Then Fieschi will fight, if he is not a coward," Matteo said; "but, in that case, why are they making out to sea?"

"Fieschi may not care to be attacked at anchor," the captain replied. "That would give all the advantage to us. Besides, if they were beaten there would be but little chance of any of them escaping. No, he is right to make out to sea, but blowing as it is, it will be next to impossible for him to fight there. Two vessels could hardly get alongside to board in such a sea as this. I expect Fieschi thinks that we shall never attack him in such a storm; but Pisani would fight if it were a hurricane."

It did indeed seem almost impossible to fight in such a sea. The Bonito was rolling, gunwale under. Her sail had been reduced to its smallest proportions, and yet, when the squalls struck her she was laid completely over on her side. But the rival admirals were too anxious to fight to be deterred by the difficulty, and both were bent upon bringing on an action at once.

"I would give anything to be on board one of our galleys," Matteo said. "It is horrible standing here doing nothing, when such a fight as this is going to begin."

"Cannot we edge down towards them, captain?" Francis asked. "I do not mean that we should take part in the fight, for we have but a hundred men, and the galleys must each carry at least three times as many. Still, we might be near enough to see something, and perhaps to give succour to any disabled ship that drops out of the fight."

"I will do so if you like, Messer Francisco," the captain said. "If you will take the responsibility. But if our side gets the worst of it, you must remember that the Bonito may be captured."

"I don't think there's much chance of Pisani being beaten by an enemy no stronger than himself," Francis said; "and even if they should be victorious, the Genoese will certainly have enough on their hands, with repairing damages and securing prisoners, to think of setting off in chase of a ship like ours."

"That is true enough," the captain agreed, for he was indeed as anxious as Francis and Matteo to witness the struggle.

The vessels on both sides were under canvas, for it was impossible to row in such a sea. As soon as they approached each other, both fleets broke up, and the vessels each singling an opponent out, the combat began. It was a singular one, and differed widely from ordinary sea fights of the time, in which the combatants always tried to grapple with their enemies and carry them by boarding. This was almost impossible now, for it seemed that the vessels would be dashed in pieces like eggshells were they to strike each other. Clouds of missiles were poured from one to the other. The archers plied their bows. Great machines hurled javelins and big stones, and the crash of the blows of the latter, against the sides of the ships, sounded even above the noise of the wind and waves, and the shouting of the combatants. As for the cannon with which all the galleys were armed, they were far too cumbrous and unmanageable to be worked in such weather. Sometimes one vessel, lifted on the crest of a wave while its opponent lay in a hollow, swept its decks with terrible effect; while a few seconds later the advantage was on the other side.

For a long time, neither party seemed to gain any advantage. Great numbers were killed on both sides, but victory did not incline either way, until the mast of one of the Venetian galleys was struck by a heavy stone and went over the side. She at once fell out of the line of the battle, her opponent keeping close to her, pouring in volumes of missiles, while the sea, taking her on the broad side, washed numbers of her crew overboard. Her opponent, seeing that she was altogether helpless, left her to be taken possession of afterwards, and made for Pisani's galley, which was distinguished by its flag at the masthead, and was maintaining a desperate conflict with the galley of Fieschi.

The admiral's ship was now swept with missiles from both sides, and when his adversaries saw that his crew was greatly weakened, they prepared to close, in spite of the state of the sea. If Pisani himself could be captured, there would remain but seven Venetian ships to the nine Genoese, and victory was certain.

The captain of the Bonito had lashed together some heavy spars and thrown them overboard, having fastened a strong rope to them, and was riding head to the waves by means of this sea anchor, at a distance of about half a mile from the conflict. A cry of grief and rage had arisen when the crew saw that one of their galleys was disabled, and their excitement became intense when they saw the unequal struggle which Pisani was maintaining.

"They are preparing to board, captain," Francis said. "We must go to the admiral's aid. If his ship is captured, the battle is lost."

"I am ready, Messer Francisco, if you authorize me."

"Certainly I do," Francis said. "The loss or capture of the Bonito is as nothing in comparison to the importance of saving Pisani."

The captain gave the order for the hawser to be cut, and the sail hoisted. A cheer broke from the crew as they saw what was to be done. Their arms had been served out at the beginning of the contest, and they now seized them, and gathered in readiness to take part in the fight.

The two Genoese galleys had thrown their grapnels and made fast, one on each side of Pisani's galley. The bulwarks were stove in

137

and splintered as the vessels rolled, and the rigging of the three ships became entangled. The Genoese sprang on to the deck of Pisani's galley, with shouts of triumph, but they were met by the admiral himself, wielding a mighty battleaxe, and the survivors of his crew.

The combat was still raging when the Bonito sailed swiftly up. Her sails were lowered as she came alongside, and she was lashed to one of the galleys. But this manoeuvre was not performed without loss. As she approached, with the Venetian flag flying at her masthead, the Genoese archers on the poop of the galley, who had hitherto been pouring their missiles among Pisani's men, turned round and opened fire upon this new foe. Their arrows did far more execution here than they had done among the armour clad soldiers of the state. The captain fell dead with an arrow which struck him full in the throat, and ten or twelve of the sailors fell on the deck beside him.

"Pour in one volley," Francis shouted; "then throw down your bows, and take to your axes and follow me."

The instant the vessel was lashed, Francis sprang on to the deck of the galley. Matteo was by his side, Giuseppi just behind, and the whole crew followed. Climbing first upon the poop, they fell upon the archers, who, after a short struggle, were cut down; then, descending again to the waist of the galley, they leaped on to the deck of Pisani's ship, and fell upon the rear of the Genoese.

These were taken completely by surprise. Absorbed in the struggle in which they were engaged, they had noticed neither the approach of the Bonito, nor the struggle on board their own galley, and supposed that another of the Venetian warships had come up to the assistance of their admiral.

Taken then by surprise, and finding themselves thus between two bands of foes, they fought irresolutely, and the crew of the Bonito, with their heavy axes, cut down numbers of them, and fighting their way through the mass, joined the diminished force of Pisani.

The admiral shouted the battle cry of "Saint Mark!" His followers, who had begun to give way to despair, rallied at the arrival of this unlooked-for reinforcement, and the whole fell upon the Genoese with fury. The latter fought stoutly and steadily now, animated by the voice and example of Fieschi himself; but their assurance of victory was gone, and they were gradually beaten back to the deck of their admiral's ship. Here they made desperate efforts to cut the lashings and free the vessel; but the yards had got interlocked and the rigging entangled, and the Venetians sprang on to the deck of the ship, and renewed the conflict there.

For some time the struggle was doubtful. The Genoese had still the advantage in numbers, but they were disheartened at the success, which they had deemed certain, having been so suddenly and unexpectedly snatched from their grasp.

The presence of Pisani, in itself, doubled the strength of the Venetians. He was the most popular of their commanders, and each strove to imitate the example which he set them.

After ten minutes' hard fighting, the result was no longer doubtful. Many of the Genoese ran below. Others threw down their arms, and their admiral, at last, seeing further resistance was hopeless, lowered his sword and surrendered.

No sooner had resistance ceased than Pisani turned to Francis, who had been fighting by his side:

"I thank you, in the name of myself and the republic," he said. "Where you have sprung from, or how you came here, I know not. You seemed to me to have fallen from heaven to our assistance, just at the moment when all was lost. Who are you? I seem to know your face, though I cannot recall where I have seen it."

"I am Francis Hammond, Messer Pisani. I had the honour of seeing you at the house of my patron, Signor Polani, and you were good enough to offer to take me with you to sea."

"Oh, I remember now!" Pisani said. "But how came you here?"

"I came in the Bonito, one of Polani's ships. She is lying outside the farther of the Venetian galleys. We bring from Venice some of the stores for which you sent. We were lying off, watching the battle, until we saw that you were sore beset and in need of help, and could then no longer remain inactive. Our captain was killed by an arrow as we ranged up alongside of the galley, and I am now in command. This is my friend, Matteo Giustiniani, a volunteer on board the Bonito."

"I remember you, Master Matteo," Pisani said, as he shook him by the hand. "I have seen you often at your father's house. I shall have to give him a good account of you, for I saw you fighting bravely.

"But we will talk more of this afterwards. We must set to work to separate the galleys, or we shall have them grinding each other to pieces. Then we must hasten to the assistance of our friends."

The Genoese prisoners were all fastened below, and the Venetians then set to work to cut the lashings and free the rigging of the ships. Francis kept only twenty men on board the Bonito. The remainder were distributed between the two captured Genoese galleys, and the admiral turned his attention to the battle.

But it was already almost over. The sight of the Venetian flag, at the mastheads of the admiral's ship and the other galley, struck dismay into the Genoese. Five of their ships immediately hoisted all canvas and made off, while the other two, surrounded by the Venetian galleys, hauled down their flags.

The battle had been a sanguinary one, and but eight hundred men were found alive on board the four galleys captured. The fight is known in history as the battle of Porto d'Anzo. The struggle had lasted nearly the whole day, and it was growing dark when the Venetian fleet, with their prizes, anchored under shelter of the land.

All night long the work of attending upon the wounded went on, and it was daybreak before the wearied crews lay down for repose. In the afternoon, Pisani hoisted a signal for the captains of the galleys to come on board; and in their presence he formally thanked Francis, in the name of the republic, for the aid he had afforded him at the most critical moment. Had it not been for that aid, he acknowledged that he and his crew must have succumbed, and the victory would assuredly have fallen to the Genoese.

After the meeting was over he took Francis into his cabin, and again offered him a post in his own ship.

"Were your merit properly rewarded," he said, "I would appoint you at once to the command of a galley; but to do so would do you no service, for it would excite against you the jealousy of all the young nobles in the fleet. Besides, you are so young, that although the council at home cannot but acknowledge the vastness of the service you have rendered, they might make your age an excuse for refusing to confirm the appointment; but if you like to come as my third officer, I can promise you that you shall have rapid promotion, and speedily be in command of a galley. We Venetians have no prejudice against foreigners. They hold very high commands, and, indeed, our armies in the field are frequently commanded by foreign captains."

Francis thanked the admiral heartily for his offer, but said that his father's wishes, and his own, led him to adopt the life of a merchant, and that, under the patronage of Messer Polani, his prospects were so good that he would not exchange them, even for a command under the state of Venice.

"You are quite right, lad," the admiral said. "All governments are ungrateful, and republics most of all. Where all are supposed to be equal, there is ever envy and jealousy against one who rises above the rest. The multitude is fickle and easily led; and the first change of fortune, however slight, is seized upon by enemies as a cause of complaint, and the popular hero of today may be an exile tomorrow. Like enough I shall see the inside of a Venetian prison some day."

"Impossible, signor!" Francis exclaimed. "The people would tear to pieces anyone who ventured to malign you."

"Just at present, my lad; just at present. But I know my countrymen. They are not as light hearted and fickle as those of Genoa; but they are easily led, and will shout 'Abasso!' as easily as 'Viva!' Time will show. I was within an ace of being defeated today; and you may not be close at hand to come to my rescue next time. And now to business.

"Tomorrow morning I will set the crews to get out your stores, and distribute them as required, and will place four hundred prisoners in your hold, and you shall carry them to Venice with my despatches announcing the victory. The other four hundred Genoese I shall send, in the galley that was dismasted yesterday, to Candia, to be imprisoned there. I shall send prize crews home in the galleys we have captured; and as soon as they are refitted and manned, and rejoin me, I shall sail in search of Doria and his fleet. I shall first cruise up the Adriatic, in case he may have gone that way to threaten Venice, and I can the more easily receive such reinforcements as may have been prepared for me."

The following day was spent in unloading the vessel. This was accomplished by nightfall. The prisoners were then put on board. Francis at once ordered sail to be set, and the Bonito was started on her homeward voyage.

As soon as the Bonito was signalled in sight, Signor Polani went down to the port to meet her, to ascertain where she had fallen in with the fleet, for there was great anxiety in Venice, as no news had been received from Pisani for more than ten days. The vessel had just passed through the entrance between the islands, when the gondola, with her owner, was seen approaching. Francis went to the gangway to receive him.

"Why, what has happened, Francisco?" Polani asked, as the boat neared the side of the ship. "Half your bulwark is carried away, and the whole side of the ship is scraped and scored. She looks as if she had been rubbing against a rock."

"Not quite so bad as that, Messer Polani. She has been grinding against a Genoese galley."

"Against a Genoese galley!" the merchant repeated in

surprise, stopping in his passage up the rope ladder, which had been lowered for him. "Why, how is that? But never mind that now. First tell me what is the news from the fleet?"

"There is great news," Francis replied. "The admiral fell in with Fieschi off Antium. There were nine ships on each side, and the battle took place in a storm. We were victorious, and captured four of the Genoese galleys, with Fieschi himself and eight hundred prisoners. The rest fled. Fieschi is now in my cabin, and four hundred prisoners in the hold."

"This is indeed great news," the merchant said, "and will be an immense relief to Venice. We were getting very anxious, for had Pisani been defeated, there was nothing to prevent the Genoese ravaging our coasts, and even assailing Venice itself. But where is the captain?"

"I regret to say, sir, that he has been killed, as well as twenty-seven of the sailors, and many of the others are more or less severely wounded. I am the bearer of despatches from the admiral to the council."

"Then get into my gondola, and come along at once," Polani said. "I deeply regret the death of the captain and sailors. You shall tell me all about it as we come along. We must not delay a moment in carrying this great news ashore. Have you got the despatches?"

"Yes, signor. I put them into my doublet when I saw you approaching, thinking that you would probably wish me to take them on shore at once."

"And now tell me all about the battle," the merchant said as soon as they had taken their seats in the gondola. "You say there were nine ships on either side. Pisani sailed away with fourteen. Has he lost the remainder?"

"They came up next day," Francis replied. "The fleet was in a port north of Antium when the news came that Fieschi's fleet was there. Five of the galleys had been dismantled, and were under repair, and Pisani would not wait for them to be got into fighting order, as he was afraid lest Fieschi might weigh anchor and escape if he delayed an hour. He learned that the Genoese had nine ships with him, and as he had himself this number ready for sea, he sailed at once.

"The weather was stormy, and the sea very high, when he appeared within sight of Antium. Fieschi sailed boldly out to meet him. The battle lasted all day, for it was next to impossible to board; but in the end, as I say, four Genoese galleys surrendered and the rest fled. It was a terrible sight; for it seemed at every moment as if the waves would hurl the vessels against each other, and so break them into fragments; but in no case did such an accident happen."

"Why, you speak as if you saw it, Francisco! Had you joined the admiral before the battle took place?"

"No, signor. We arrived near Antium on the evening before the fight, and heard of Fieschi's presence there. Therefore we anchored south of the promontory. In the morning we put out, intending to sail well out to sea and so pass the Genoese, who were not likely, in such weather, to put out to question a sail passing in the distance; but as we made off from land we saw Pisani's fleet approaching. Then, as Fieschi put to sea and we saw that the battle was imminent, there was nothing for us to do but to lie to, and wait for the battle to be over, before we delivered our stores, having little doubt that Pisani would be victorious."

"Then had the battle gone the other way," the merchant said, "the Bonito at the present moment would probably be lying a prize in the harbour of Genoa!"

"We did not lose sight of the probability of that, signor, but thought that, if the Genoese should gain a victory, they would be too busy with their prizes and prisoners, if not too crippled, to pursue us, and we reckoned that in such weather the Bonito would be able to sail quite as fast as any of the Genoese."

"And now, tell me about your affairs, Francisco. Where was it you fell in with the Genoese galley, and by what miracle did you get off?"

"It was in the battle, sir. One of the Venetian galleys had dropped out of the fight disabled, and its opponent went to the assistance of their admiral's ship, which was engaged with Pisani. They attempted to board him on both sides, and, seeing that he was in great peril, and that if his ship was taken the battle would be as bad as lost, we thought that you yourself would approve of our going to his assistance. This we did, and engaged one of their galleys; and, as her crew were occupied with the admiral, we took them by surprise, and created such a diversion that he succeeded, with what assistance we could give him, in capturing both his opponents."

"That was done well indeed," Polani said warmly. "It was a risky matter, indeed, for you, with sailors unprotected by armour, to enter into a combat with the iron-clad soldiers of Genoa.

"And so the captain and twenty-seven of the men were killed! You must have had some brisk fighting!"

"The captain, and many of the men, were shot by the Genoese archers as we ranged up alongside their vessel. The others were killed in hand-to-hand fighting."

143

"And my cousin Matteo, what has become of him?" Polani asked suddenly. "I trust he is not among the killed!"

"He is unharmed," Francis replied. "He fought gallantly, and the admiral, the next day, offered to take him on board his own ship, many of the volunteers serving on board having been killed. Matteo, of course, accepted the offer."

"He would have done better to have stayed on board my ship for another two years," Polani said, "and learned his business. He would have made a far better sailor than he can ever become on board a state galley; but I never expected him to stick to it. He has no earnestness of purpose, and is too particular about his dress to care about the rough life of a real seaman."

"He has plenty of courage, sir, and I have always found him a staunch friend."

"No doubt he has courage," the merchant said. "He comes of good blood and could hardly be a coward. I think he is a good-hearted lad, too, and will, I have no doubt, make a brave commander of a galley; but more than that Matteo is never likely to become."

"Your daughters are well, I hope?" Francis asked.

"Quite well; but you will not find them at home—they sailed three days ago, in the Lido, for Corfu. They are going to stay for a time at my villa there. That affair of last year shook them both, and I thought it better that they should go away for a change—the hot months here are trying, and often unhealthy. I will go over myself next week to be with them."

They were now approaching the Piazzetta, and Polani shouted out, to various acquaintances he met in passing gondolas, the news that Pisani had gained a great victory, and had captured the Genoese admiral with four of his galleys. The gondolas at once changed their course, and accompanied them, to gather further details of the fight. The news was shouted to other passing boats, and by the time they reached the steps of the Piazzetta, a throng was round them.

Those on shore shouted out the news, and it spread rapidly from mouth to mouth. The shopkeepers left their stores, and the loungers on the Piazzetta ran up, and it was with difficulty that Polani and Francis could make their way, through the shouting and excited crowd, to the entrance of the ducal palace.

Polani at once led Francis to the doge, to whom he gave an account of the action. Messengers were immediately despatched to some of the members of the council, for it was to them that the despatches had to be delivered. As soon as a sufficient number to transact the business had arrived at the palace, the doge himself led Francis to the council chamber.

"Is the news that we heard, shouted in the streets as we came thither, true, your highness?" one of the councillors asked as they entered. "That our fleet has gained a victory over the Genoese?"

"I am happy to say that it is quite true; but this young gentleman is the bearer of despatches from the admiral, and these will doubtless give us all particulars."

"Admiral Pisani has chosen a strange messenger for so important a despatch," one of the party hostile to the admiral said. "It is usual to send despatches of this kind by a trusted officer, and I do not think it respectful, either to the council or the republic, to send home the news of a victory by a lad like this."

"The admiral apparently chose this young gentleman because, owing to the death of his captain, he was in command of the ship which Messer Polani placed at the service of the republic, and which was present at the fight. The admiral intended, as I hear, to set out at once in search of the fleet of Doria, and doubtless did not wish to weaken himself by despatching a state galley with the news. But perhaps he may explain the matter in his despatches."

Several other councillors had by this time arrived, and the despatches were opened. The admiral's account of the engagement was brief, for he was fonder of the sword than the pen. He stated that, having obtained news that Fieschi's fleet was at anchor under the promontory of Antium, he sailed thither with nine ships, these being all that were at the moment fit to take to sea; that Fieschi had sailed out to meet him, and that an engagement had taken place in the storm, which prevented the ships from pursuing their usual tactics, and compelled them to fight with missiles at a distance. The despatch then went on:

"We fought all day, and the upshot of it was, we captured four of their galleys, the admiral himself, and eight hundred prisoners. Fortunately it is unnecessary for me to give your seignory the details of the fighting, as these can be furnished you by Messer Francisco Hammond, who will hand you these despatches. He was a witness of the action on the Bonito, which had that morning arrived at Antium with some of the stores you despatched me. I have selected this young gentleman as the bearer of these despatches, because it is to him I entirely owe it that I am not at the present moment a prisoner in Genoa, and to him the republic owes that we yesterday won a victory.

"I was attacked by Fieschi and by another galley, and, in spite

145

of the weather, they cast grapnels on to my ship and boarded me. I had already lost half of my crew by their missiles, and things were going very badly with us, when the Bonito came up to our assistance, and grappled with one of the galleys. Her captain was killed, but Messer Hammond—of whom Polani has so high an opinion that he had appointed him second in command—led his men to my rescue. They boarded the galley and slew those who remained on board, and then, crossing on to my ship, fell upon the rear of the Genoese who were pressing us backwards. His sailors, undefended as they were by armour, fought like demons with their axes, and, led by Messer Hammond, cut their way through the enemy and joined me.

"This reinforcement gave fresh strength and spirit to my men, who had a minute before thought that all was lost. Together we fell upon the Genoese, before they could recover from their surprise, beat them back into their admiral's ship, and following them there forced them to surrender. Messer Hammond fought by my side, and although but a lad in years, he showed himself a sturdy man-at-arms, and behaved with a coolness and bravery beyond praise. I hereby recommend him to your gracious consideration, for assuredly to him it is due that it is I, and not Fieschi, who is writing to announce a victory."

A murmur of surprise from the councillors greeted the reading of this portion of the letter. When it was concluded, the doge was the first to speak.

"You have indeed deserved well of the republic, Messer Hammond, for we know that Admiral Pisani is not one to give undue praise, or to exaggerate in aught.

"This is news to me, signors, as well as to you, for in his narrative to me of the events of the fight, he passed over his own share in it, though Messer Polani, who accompanied him, did say that his ship had taken some part in the fight, and that the captain and twenty-seven men had been killed.

"Now, young sir, as the admiral has referred us to you for a detailed narrative of the battle, we will thank you to tell us all you witnessed, omitting no detail of the occurrences."

Francis accordingly gave a full account of the action, and gave great praise to his crew for the valour with which they had fought against the heavy armed Genoese. When he had concluded the doge said:

"We thank you for your narrative, Messer Hammond, as well as for the great service you have rendered the state. Will you now leave us, as we have much to debate on regarding this and other matters, and to arrange for the reinforcements for which, I see by his letter, the admiral asks.

"Will you ask Messer Polani to remain in attendance for a while, as we wish to consult with him as to ships and other matters? As to yourself, we shall ask you to come before us again shortly."

After Francis had left, the council first voted that five ducats should be given to every man of the crew of the Bonito, and that the widows of those who had been slain should be provided for, at the expense of the state. They deferred the question as to the honours which should be conferred upon Francis, until they had consulted Polani.

State barges were at once sent off to bring in the prisoners from the ship, and preparations made for their accommodation, for Venice always treated prisoners taken in war with the greatest kindness, an example which Genoa was very far from following.

Then Polani was sent for, and the question of stores and ships gone into. Orders were issued for redoubled activity in the arsenal, and it was arranged that several ships, belonging to Polani and others, should be at once purchased for the service of the state.

Then they asked him for his opinion as to the reward which should be given to Francis. Upon the merchant expressing his ignorance of any special service his young friend had rendered, the passage from Pisani's letter relating to him was read out.

"The lad is as modest as he is brave," the merchant said, "for although, of course, he told me that the ship had taken some part in the fight, and had done what it could to assist the admiral, in which service the captain and twenty-seven men had lost their lives, I had no idea of the real nature of the encounter. I feel very proud of the service he has rendered the state, for he has rendered me as a private individual no less important service, and I regard him as my adopted son, and my future partner in my business. Such being the case, signors, he needs no gift of money from the state."

"He has not, of course, being still a minor, taken up his papers of naturalization as a citizen?" the doge said.

"No, your highness, nor is it his intention to do so. I spoke to him on the subject once, and he said that, although he regarded Venice with affection, and would at all times do everything in his power for the state, he could not renounce his birthplace, as an Englishman, by taking an oath of allegiance to another state, and that probably he should after a time return to his native country. I pointed out to him that, although foreigners were given every facility for trade in Venice, it would be a grievous disadvantage to him in the islands, and especially with countries such as Egypt, the Turks, and the Eastern empire, with whom we had treaties; as, unless he were a Venetian, he would be unable to trade with them.

"He fully saw the force of my argument, but persisted in his determination. If you ask my opinion, therefore, signors, and you do not think the honour too great, I would suggest that the highest and most acceptable honour that could be bestowed upon him, would be that which you have at various times conferred upon foreign personages of distinction, namely, to grant him the freedom of Venice, and inscribe his name upon the list of her citizens, without requiring of him the renunciation of his own country, or the taking the oath of allegiance."

"The honour is assuredly a great and exceptional one," the doge said, "but so is the service that he has rendered. He has converted what would have been a defeat into a victory, and has saved Venice from a grave peril.

"Will you retire for a few minutes, signor, and we will then announce to you the result of our deliberations on the matter."

CHAPTER 12

IN MOCENIGO'S POWER

It was fully an hour before Polani was recalled to the council chamber. He saw at once, by the flushed and angry faces of some of the council, that the debate had been a hot one. At this he was not surprised, for he knew that the friends and connections of Ruggiero Mocenigo would vehemently oppose the suggestion he had made.

The doge announced the decision.

"The council thank you for your suggestion, Signor Polani, and have resolved, by a majority, to confer upon Messer Francisco Hammond the high honour of placing his name upon the list of the citizens of Venice, without requiring from him the oaths of allegiance to the state. As such an honour has never before been conferred, save upon personages of the highest rank, it will be a proof of the gratitude which Venice feels towards one who has done her such distinguished service. The decree to that effect will be published tomorrow."

The merchant retired, highly gratified. The honour was a great and signal one, and the material advantages considerable. The fact that Francis was a foreigner had been the sole obstacle which had presented itself to him, in associating him with his business, for it would prevent Francis from trading personally with any of the countries in which Venetian citizens enjoyed special advantages.

Francis was immensely gratified, when he heard from the merchant of the honour to be conferred upon him. It was of all others the reward he would have selected, had a free choice been given him, but it was so great and unusual an honour, that he could indeed scarcely credit it when the merchant told him the result of his interviews with the council. The difficulty which his being a foreigner would throw in the way of his career as a merchant in Eastern waters, had been frequently in his mind, and would, he foresaw, greatly lessen his usefulness, but that he should be able to obtain naturalization, without renouncing his allegiance to England, he had never even hoped.

"It is a very high honour, doubtless," Polani said, "but no whit higher than you deserve. Besides, after all, it costs Venice nothing, and money is scarce at present. At any rate, I can congratulate myself as well as you, for I foresaw many difficulties in our way. Although the ships carrying the Venetian flag could enter the ports of all countries trading with us, you would personally be liable to arrest, at any time, on being denounced as not being a native of Venice, which you assuredly would be by my rivals in trade."

The next day a bulletin was published, giving the substance of Pisani's despatch, and announcing that, in token of the gratitude of the republic for the great service he had rendered, Messer Hammond would be at once granted the freedom of Venice, and his name inserted on the list of her citizens.

During these two days the delight of Venice at the news of the victory had been extreme. The houses had been decorated with flags, and the bells of all the churches had peeled out joyously. Crowds assembled round the Polani Palace, and insisted upon Francis making his appearance, when they greeted him with tremendous shouts of applause. Upon the evening of the second day he said to Polani:

"Have you any ship fit for sea, signor, because if so, I pray you to send me away, no matter where. I cannot stand this. Since the decree was published, this morning, I have not had a moment's peace, and it is too absurd, when I did no more than any sailor on board the ship. If it went on, I should very soon be heartily sorry I ever interfered on behalf of the admiral."

The merchant smiled.

"I have half promised to take you with me to the reception at the Persanis' this evening, and have had a dozen requests of a similar nature for every night this week and next."

"Then, if you have no ship ready, signor, I will charter a fishing boat, engage a couple of men, and go off for a fortnight. By the end of that time something fresh will have happened."

"I can send you off, if you really wish it, Francisco, the first thing tomorrow morning. I am despatching a small craft with a message to my agent in Corfu, and with letters for my daughters. They will be delighted to see you, and indeed, I shall be glad to know that you are with them, until I can wind up several affairs which I have in hand, and join them myself. She is fast, and you should be at Corfu in eight-and-forty hours after sailing."

Francis gladly embraced the offer, and started the next morning. The vessel was a small one, designed either to sail or row. Her crew consisted of twenty men, who rowed sixteen sweeps when the wind was light or unfavourable. She was an open boat, except that she was decked at each end, a small cabin being formed aft for the captain, and any passengers there might be on board, while the crew stowed themselves in the little forecastle.

When the boat was halfway across, a sail was seen approaching, and the captain recognized her as one of Polani's vessels.

"In that case," Francis said, "we may as well direct our course so as to pass them within hailing distance. When you approach them, hoist the Polani flag, and signal to them to lay to."

This was done, and the two craft brought up within thirty yards of each other. The captain appeared at the side of the vessel, and doffed his cap when he recognized Francis.

"Have you any news from the East?" the latter asked.

"But little, signor. A few Genoese pirates are among the islands, and are reported to have made some captures, but I have seen none. There is nothing new from Constantinople. No fresh attempt has been made by the emperor to recapture Tenedos."

"Did you touch at Corfu on your way back?"

"I left there yesterday, signor. A strange craft has been reported as having been seen on the coast. She carries no flag, but from her appearance she is judged to be a Moor."

"But we are at peace with the Moors," Francis said, "and it is years since they ventured on any depredations, excepting on their own waters."

"That is so, signor, and I only tell you what was the report at Corfu. She appeared to be a swift craft, rowing a great many oars. Her movements certainly seem mysterious, as she has several times appeared off the coast. Two vessels which sailed from Cyprus, and were to have touched at Corfu, had not arrived there when I left, and they say that several others are overdue. I do not say that has anything to do with the strange galley, but it is the general opinion in Corfu that it has something to do with it, and I am the bearer of letters from the governor to the seignory, praying that two or three war ships may at once be sent down to the island."

"It looks strange, certainly," Francis said; "but I cannot believe that any Moorish pirates would be so daring as to come up into Venetian waters."

"I should not have thought so either, signor; but it may be that, knowing there is war between Venice and Genoa, and that the state galleys of the republics, instead of being scattered over the seas, are now collected in fleets, and thinking only of fighting each other, they might consider it a good opportunity for picking prizes."

"It is a good opportunity, certainly," Francis said; "but they would know that Venice would, sooner or later, reckon with them; and would demand a four-fold indemnity for any losses her merchants may have suffered.

"However, I will not detain you longer. Will you tell Signor Polani that you met us, and that we were making good progress, and hoped to reach Corfu some time tomorrow?"

"This is a curious thing about this galley," the captain of the boat said to Francis, as the men again dipped their oars into the water, and the boat once more proceeded on the way.

"It is much more likely to be a Genoese pirate than a Moor," Francis said. "They may have purposely altered their rig a little, in order to deceive vessels who may sight them. It is very many years since any Moorish craft have been bold enough to commit acts of piracy on this side of Sicily. However, we must hope that we shall not fall in with her, and if we see anything answering to her description we will give it a wide berth. Besides, it is hardly likely they would interfere with so small a craft as ours, for they would be sure we should be carrying no cargo of any great value."

"Twenty Christian slaves would fetch money among the Moors," the captain said. "Let us hope we shall see nothing of them; for we should have no chance of resistance against such a craft, and she would go two feet to our one."

The next morning Francis was aroused by a hurried summons from the captain. Half awake, and wondering what could be the cause of the call, for the boat lay motionless on the water, he hurried out from the little cabin. Day had just broken, the sky was aglow with ruddy light in the east.

"Look there, signor!" the captain said, pointing to the south. "The watch made them out a quarter of an hour since, but, thinking nothing of it, they did not call me. What do you think of that?"

Two vessels were lying in close proximity to each other, at a distance of about two miles from the boat. One of them was a large trader, the other was a long galley rigged quite differently to those of either Venice or Genoa.

"That is the craft they were speaking of," the captain said. "There is no mistaking her. She may be an Egyptian or a Moor, but certainly she comes from the African coast."

"Or is got up in African fashion," Francis said. "She may be, as we agreed yesterday, a Genoese masquerading in that fashion, in order to be able to approach our traders without their suspicions being aroused. She looks as if she has made a captive of that vessel. I imagine she must have come up to her late yesterday evening, and has been at work all night stripping her. I hope she is too busy to attend to us."

The sail had been lowered the instant the captain caught sight of the vessels, for there was scarcely enough wind to fill it, and the men were now rowing steadily.

"I do not think she could have taken much of her cargo out. She is very deep in the water."

"Very deep," Francis agreed. "She seems to me to be deeper than she did three minutes ago."

"She is a great deal deeper than when we first caught sight of her," one of the sailors said. "She stood much higher in the water than the galley did, and now, if anything, the galley stands highest."

"See!" the captain exclaimed suddenly, "the galley is rowing her oars on the port bow, and bringing her head round. She has noticed us, and is going to chase us! We have seen too much.

"Row, men—it is for life! If they overtake us it is a question between death, and slavery among the Moors."

A sudden exclamation from one of the men caused the captain to glance round again at the galley. She was alone now on the water—the trader had sunk!

"Do you take the helm, signor," the captain said. "All hands will help at the oars."

Some of the oars were double banked, and beneath the strength of the twenty men, the boat moved fast through the water. The galley was now rowing all her oars, and in full pursuit. For a quarter of an hour not a word was spoken. Every man on board was doing his utmost. Francis had glanced backwards several times, and at the end of a quarter of an hour, he could see that the distance between the boat and her pursuer had distinctly lessened.

"Is she gaining on us?" the captain asked, for the cabin in the stern hid the galley from the sight of the oarsmen.

"She is gaining," Francis said quietly, "but not rapidly. Row steadily, my lads, and do not despair. When they find how slowly they gain, they may give up the chase and think us not worth the trouble.

"Jacopo," he said to an old sailor who was rowing in the bow, and who already was getting exhausted from the exertion, "do you lay in your oar and come aft. I will take your place."

At the end of an hour the galley was little more than a quarter of a mile away.

"We had better stop," the captain said. "We have no chance of getting away, and the longer the chase the more furious they will be. What do you think, signor?"

"I agree with you," Francis replied. "We have done all that we could. There is no use in rowing longer."

The oars fell motionless in the water, and a few minutes later the long galley came rushing up by their side.

"A fine row you have given us, you dogs!" a man shouted angrily as she came alongside. "If you haven't something on board that will pay us for the chase we have had, it will be the worse for you. What boat is that?"

"It is the Naxos, and belongs to Messer Polani of Venice. We are bound to Corfu, and bear letters from the padrone to his agent there. We have no cargo on board."

"The letters, perhaps, may be worth more than any cargo such a boat would carry. So come on board, and let us see what the excellent Polani says to his agent. Now, make haste all of you, or it will be the worse for you."

It was useless hesitating. The captain, Francis, and the crew stepped on board the galley.

"Just look round her," the captain said to one of his sailors. "If there is anything worth taking, take it, and then knock a hole in her bottom with your axe."

Francis, as he stepped on board the galley, looked round at the crew. They were not Genoese, as he had expected, but a mixture of ruffians from all the ports in the Mediterranean, as he saw at once by their costumes. Some were Greeks from the islands, some Smyrniots, Moors, and Spaniards; but the Moors predominated, nearly half the crew belonging to that race.

Then he looked at the captain, who was eagerly perusing the documents the captain had handed him. As his eye fell upon him, Francis started, for he recognized at once the man whose designs he had twice thwarted, Ruggiero Mocenigo, and felt that he was in deadly peril.

After reading the merchant's communication to his agent, Ruggiero opened the letter addressed to Maria. He had read but a few lines when he suddenly looked up, and then, with an expression of savage pleasure in his face, stepped up to Francis.

"So, Messer Hammond, the good Polani sends you to stay for a while with his daughters! Truly, when I set out in chase this morning of that wretched rowboat, I little deemed that she carried a prize that I valued more than a loaded caravel! It is to you I owe it that I am an exile, instead of being the honoured son-in-law of the wealthy Polani. It was your accursed interference that brought all my misfortunes upon me; but thank Heaven my vengeance has come at last!

"Take them all below," he said, turning to his men. "Put the heaviest irons you have got on this fellow, and fasten them with staples into the deck.

"You thought I was going to hang you, or throw you overboard," he went on, turning to Francis. "Do not flatter yourself that your death will be so easy a one—you shall suffer a thousand torments before you die!"

Francis had not spoken a word since Ruggiero first turned to him, but had stood with a tranquil and almost contemptuous expression upon his face; but every nerve and muscle of his body were strained, and in readiness to spring into action. He had expected that Ruggiero would at once attack him, and was determined to leap upon him, and to sell his life as dearly as possible.

The sailors seized Francis and his companions, and thrust them down into the hold, which was already crowded with upwards of a hundred captives. He was chained with heavy manacles. In obedience to Ruggiero's orders, staples were driven through the links of his chain deep into the deck, so that he was forced to remain in a sitting or lying posture. The captain of the Naxos came and sat beside him.

"Who is this pirate captain, Messer Francisco, who thus knows and has an enmity against you? By his speech he is surely a Venetian. And yet, how comes a Venetian in command of a pirate?"

"That man is Ruggiero Mocenigo—the same who twice attempted to carry off Messer Polani's daughters. The second time he succeeded, and would have been tried for the offence by the state had he not, aided by a band of Paduans, escaped from the keeping of his guard."

"Of course I heard of it, signor. I was away at sea at the time, but I heard how you came up at the moment when the padrone's gondoliers had been overcome, and rescued his daughters. And this is that villain Mocenigo, a disgrace to his name and family!"

"Remember the name, captain, and tell it to each of your men, so that if they ever escape from this slavery, into which, no doubt, he intends to sell you, they may tell it in Venice that Ruggiero Mocenigo is a pirate, and an ally of the Moors. As for me, there is, I think, but small chance of escape; but at any rate, if you ever reach Venice, you will be able to tell the padrone how it was that we never arrived at Corfu, and how I fell into the hands of his old enemy. Still, I do not despair that I may carry the message myself. There is many a slip between the cup and the lip, and Mocenigo may have cause, yet, to regret that he did not make an end of me as soon as he got me into his hands."

"It may be so," the captain said, "and indeed I cannot think that so brave a young gentleman is destined to die, miserably, at the hands of such a scoundrel as this man has shown himself to be. As for death, did it come but speedily and sharply, I would far sooner die than live a Moorish slave. Santa Maria, how they will wonder at home, when the days go on, and the Naxos does not return, and how at last they will give up all hope, thinking that she has gone down in a sudden squall, and never dreaming that we are sold as slaves to the Moors by a countryman!"

"Keep up your heart, captain. Be sure that when the war with

Genoa is over, Venice will take the matter in hand. As you know, a vessel has already carried tidings thither of the depredation of a Moorish cruiser, and she will take vengeance on the Moors, and may even force them to liberate the captives they have taken; and besides, you may be sure that the padrone, when he hears of the Moorish galley, and finds we never reached Corfu although the weather continued fine, will guess that we have fallen into her hands, and will never rest till he finds where we have been taken, and will ransom those who survive at whatever price they may put upon them."

"He will do his best, I know. He is a good master to serve. But once a prisoner among the Moors, the hope of one's ever being heard of again is slight. Sometimes, of course, men have been ransomed; but most, as I have heard, can never be found by their friends, however ready they may be to pay any ransom that might be asked. It just depends whether they are sold to a Moor living in a seaport or not. If they are, there would be no great difficulty in hearing of them, but if they are sold into the interior, no inquiries are ever likely to discover them."

"You must hope for the best," Francis said. "Chances of escape may occur, and I have heard that Christian captives, who have been released, say that the Moors are for the most part kind masters."

"I have heard so, too," the captain said; "and anyhow, I would rather be a Moorish slave than lie in a Genoese dungeon. The Genoese are not like us. When we take prisoners we treat them fairly and honourably, while they treat their prisoners worse than dogs. I wish I could do something for you, Messer Francisco. Your case is a deal worse than ours.

"Listen, they are quarrelling up on deck!"

There was indeed a sound of men in hot dispute, a trampling of feet, a clash of steel, and the sound of bodies falling.

"It is not possible that one of our cruisers can have come up, and is boarding the pirate," the captain said, "for no sail was in sight when we were brought here. I looked round the last thing before I left the deck. What can they be fighting about?"

"Likely enough, as to their course. They have probably, from what we heard, taken and sunk several ships, and some may be in favour of returning to dispose of their booty, while others may be for cruising longer. I only hope that scoundrel Ruggiero is among those we heard fall. They are quiet now, and one party or the other has evidently got the best of it. There, they are taking to the oars again."

Several days passed. Sometimes the oars were heard going,

but generally the galley was under sail. The sailors brought down food and water, morning and evening, but paid no other attention to the captives. Francis discussed, with some of the other prisoners, the chances of making a sudden rush on to the deck, and overpowering the crew; but all their arms had been taken from them, and the galley, they calculated, contained fully a hundred and fifty men. They noticed, too, when the sailors brought down the food, a party armed and in readiness were assembled round the hatchway.

At all other times the hatchway was nearly closed, being only left sufficiently open to allow a certain amount of air to pass down into the hold, and by the steady tramp of steps, up and down, they knew that two sentries were also on guard above. Most of the prisoners were so overcome with the misfortune which had befallen them, and the prospect of a life in hopeless slavery, that they had no spirit to attempt any enterprise whatever, and there was nothing to do but to wait the termination of the voyage.

At the end of six days there was a bustle on deck, and the chain of the anchor was heard to run out. Two or three hours afterwards the hatchway was taken off. When the rest had ascended, two men came below with hammers, and drew the staples which fastened Francis to the deck.

On going up, he was at first so blinded with the glare of the sunshine—after six days in almost total darkness—that he could scarce see where he was. The ship was lying at anchor in a bay. The shores were low, and a group of houses stood abreast of where the ship was anchored. By their appearance Francis saw at once that he was on the coast of Africa, or of some island near it.

The prisoners were ordered to descend into the boats which lay alongside, some sailors taking their places with them. Ruggiero was not at first to be seen, but just as Francis was preparing to take his place in the boat, he came out from the cabin. One of his arms was in a sling, and his head bandaged.

"Take special care of that prisoner," he said to the men. "Do not take off his chains, and place a sentinel at the door of the place of his confinement. I would rather lose my share of all the spoil we have taken, than he should escape me!"

The shackles had been removed from the rest of the captives, and on landing they were driven into some huts which stood a little apart from the village. Francis was thrust into a small chamber with five or six companions. The next morning the other prisoners were called out, and Francis was left alone by himself all day. On their return in the evening, they told him that all the prisoners had been employed in assisting to get out the cargo, with which the vessel was crammed, and in carrying it to a large storehouse in the village.

"They must have taken a rich booty, indeed," said one of the prisoners, who had already told Francis that he was the captain of the vessel they had seen founder. "I could tell pretty well what all the bales contain, by the manner of packing, and I should say that there were the pick of the cargoes of a dozen ships there. All of us here belong to three ships, except those taken with you; but from the talk of the sailors, I heard that they had already sent off two batches of captives, by another ship which was cruising in company of them. I also learned that the quarrel, which took place just after you were captured, arose from the fact that the captain wished a party to land, to carry off two women from somewhere in the island of Corfu; but the crew insisted on first returning with the booty, urging, that if surprised by a Venetian galley, they might lose all the result of their toil. This was the opinion of the majority, although a few sided with the captain, being induced to do so by the fact that he offered to give up all his share of the booty, if they would do so.

"The captain lost his temper and drew his sword, but he and his party were quickly overpowered. He has kept to his cabin ever since, suffering, they say, more from rage than from his wounds. However, it seems that as soon as we and the cargo have been sold, they are to start for Corfu to carry out the enterprise. We are on an island not very far from Tunis, and a fast-rowing boat started early this morning to the merchants with whom they deal, for it seems that a certain amount of secrecy is observed, in order that if any complaints are made by Venice, the Moorish authorities may disclaim all knowledge of the matter."

Two days later the prisoners captured were again led out, their guards telling them that the merchants who had been expected had arrived. Giuseppi, who had hitherto borne up bravely, was in an agony of grief at being separated from Francis. He threw himself upon the ground, wept, tore his hair, and besought the guards to let him share his master's fate, whatever that might be. He declared that he would kill himself were they separated; and the guards would have been obliged to use force, had not Francis begged Giuseppi not to struggle against fate, but to go quietly, promising again and again that, if he himself regained his freedom, he would not rest until Giuseppi was also set at liberty. At last the lad yielded, and suffered himself to be led away, in a heartbroken state, by the guards.

None of the captives returned to the hut, and Francis now turned his whole thoughts to freeing himself from his chains. He had already revolved in his mind every possible mode of escape. He had tried the strong iron bars of the window, but found that they were so rigidly fixed and embedded in the stonework, that there was no hope of escape in this way; and even could he have got through the window, the weight of his shackles would have crippled him.

He was fastened with two chains, each about two feet six inches long, going from the wrist of the right hand to the left ankle, and from the left hand to the right ankle. Thus he was unable to stand quite upright, and anything like rapid movement was almost impossible. The bottom of the window came within four feet of the ground, and it was only by standing on one leg, and lifting the other as high as he could, that he was able to grasp one of the bars to try its strength.

The news he had heard from his fellow prisoner almost maddened him, and he thought far less of his own fate, than of that of the girls, who would be living in their quiet country retreat in ignorance of danger, until suddenly seized by Mocenigo and his band of pirates.

He had, on the first day, tried whether it was possible to draw his hand through the iron band round his wrist, but had concluded it could not be done, for it was riveted so tightly as to press upon the flesh. Therefore there was no hope of freeing himself in that manner. The only possible means, then, would be to cut through the rivet or chain, and for this a tool would be required.

Suddenly an idea struck him. The guard who brought in his food was a Sicilian, and was evidently of a talkative disposition, for he had several times entered into conversation with the captives. In addition to a long knife, he carried a small stiletto in his girdle, and Francis thought that, if he could obtain this, he might possibly free himself. Accordingly, at the hour when he expected his guard to enter, Francis placed himself at his window, with his face against the bars. When he heard the guard come in, and, as usual, close the door behind him, he turned round and said:

"Who is that damsel there? She is very beautiful, and she passes here frequently. There she is, just going among those trees."

The guard moved to the window and looked out.

"Do you see her just going round that corner there? Ah! She is gone."

The guard was pressing his face against the bars, to look in the direction indicated, and Francis, who was already standing on his left leg, with the right raised so as to give freedom to the hand next to the man, had no difficulty in drawing the stiletto from its sheath, and slipping it into his trousers.

"You were just too late," he said, "but no doubt you often see her."

"I don't see any beautiful damsels about in this wretched place," the man replied. "I suppose she is the daughter of the head man in the village. They say he has some good-looking ones, but he takes pretty good care that they are not about when we are here. I suppose she thought she wouldn't be seen along that path. I will keep a good lookout for her in future."

"Don't frighten her away," Francis said, laughing. "She is the one pleasant thing I have in the day to look at."

After some more talk the man retired, and Francis examined his prize. It was a thin blade of fine steel, and he at once hid it in the earth which formed the floor of the hut.

An hour later the guard opened the door suddenly. It was now dusk, and Francis was sitting quietly in a corner.

"Bring a light, Thomaso," the guard shouted to his comrade outside. "It is getting dark in here."

The other brought a torch, and they carefully examined the floor of the cell.

"What is it that you are searching for?" Francis asked.

"I have dropped my dagger somewhere," the man replied. "I can't think how it fell out."

"When did you see it last?"

"Not since dinner time. I know I had it then. I thought possibly I might have dropped it here, and a dagger is not the sort of plaything one cares about giving to prisoners."

"Chained as I am," Francis said, "a dagger would not be a formidable weapon in my hands."

"No," the man agreed. "It would be useless to you, unless you wanted to stick it into your own ribs."

"I should have to sit down to be able to do even that."

"That is so, lad. It is not for me to question what the captain says, I just do as I am told. But I own it does seem hard, keeping a young fellow like you chained up as if you were a wild beast. If he had got Pisani or Zeno as a prisoner, and wanted to make doubly sure that they would not escape, it would be all well enough, but for a lad like you, with one man always at the door, and the window barred so that a lion couldn't break through, I do think it hard to keep you chained like this; and the worst of it is, we are going to have to stop here to look after you till the captain gets back, and that may be three weeks or a month, who knows!"

"Why don't you keep your mouth shut, Philippo?" the other

man growled. "It's always talk, talk with you. We are chosen because the captain can rely upon us."

"He can rely upon anyone," Philippo retorted, "who knows that he will get his throat cut if he fails in his duty."

"Well, come along," the other said, "I don't want to be staying here all night. Your dagger isn't here, that's certain, and as I am off guard at present, I want to be going."

As soon as he was left alone, Francis unearthed the dagger, feeling sure that no fresh visit would be made him that evening. As he had hoped, his first attempt showed him that the iron of the rivet was soft, and the keen dagger at once notched off a small piece of the burred end. Again and again he tried, and each time a small piece of metal flew off. After each cut he examined the edge of the dagger, but it was well tempered, and seemed entirely unaffected.

He now felt certain that, with patience, he should be able to cut off the projecting edges of the rivets, and so be able to free his hands. He, therefore, now examined the fastenings at the ankles. These were more heavy, and on trying them, the iron of the rivet appeared to be much harder than that which kept the manacles together. It was, however, now too dark to see what he was doing, and concealing the dagger again, he lay down with a lighter heart than he had from the moment of his capture.

Even if he found that the lower fastenings of the chain defied all his efforts, he could cut the rivets at the wrists, and so free one end of each chain. He could then tie the chains round his legs, and their weight would not be sufficient to prevent his walking.

CHAPTER 13

THE PIRATES' RAID

As soon as it was daylight next morning, Francis was up and at work. His experiments of the evening before were at once confirmed. Three or four hours' work would enable him to free his wrists, but he could make no impression on the rivets at his ankles. After a few trials he gave this up as hopeless, for he was afraid, if he continued, he would blunt the edge of the dagger.

For an hour he sat still, thinking, and at last an idea occurred to him. Iron could be ground by rubbing it upon stone, and if he could not cut off the burr of the rivet with the dagger, he might perhaps be able to wear it down, by rubbing it with a stone.

He at once turned to the walls of his cell. These were not built of the unbaked clay so largely used for houses of the poorer class in Northern Egypt, but had evidently been constructed either as a prison, or more probably as a strong room where some merchant kept valuable goods. It was therefore constructed of blocks of hard stone.

It seemed to Francis that this was sandstone, and to test its quality, he sat down in the corner where the guard had, the night before, placed his supply of food and water. First he moistened a portion of the wall, then he took up a link of his chain, and rubbed for some time against it. At last, to his satisfaction, a bright patch showed that the stone was capable of wearing away iron. But in vain did he try to twist his legs so as to rub the rivet against the wall, and he gave up the attempt as impossible.

It was clear, then, that he must have a bit of the stone to rub with. He at once began to dig with the dagger in the earth at the foot of the wall, to see if he could find any such pieces. For a long time he came across no chips, even of the smallest size. As he worked, he was most careful to stamp down the earth which he had moved, scattering over it the sand, of which there was an abundance in the corners of the room, to obliterate all traces of his work.

When breakfast time approached he ceased for a while, but after the meal had been taken, he recommenced the task. He met with little success till he reached the door, but here he was more fortunate. A short distance below the surface were a number of pieces of stone of various sizes, which, he had no doubt, had been cut from the blocks to allow for the fixing of the lintel and doorpost. He chose half a dozen pieces of the handiest sizes, each having a flat surface. Then replacing the earth carefully, he took one of the pieces in his hand, and moistening it with water, set to work.

He made little progress. Still the stone did wear the iron, and he felt sure that, by perseverance, he should succeed in wearing off the burrs. All day he worked without intermission, holding a rag wrapped round the stone to deaden the sound. He worked till his fingers ached so that he could no longer hold it, then rested for an hour or two, and resumed his work. When his guard brought his dinner he asked him when the galley was to sail again.

"It was to have gone today," the man said, "but the captain has been laid up with fever. He has a leech from Tunis attending him, and, weak as he is, he is so bent on going that he would have had himself carried on board the ship, had not the leech said that, in that case, he would not answer for his life, as in the state his blood is in, his wounds would assuredly mortify did he not remain perfectly quiet. So he has agreed to delay for three days."

Francis was unable to work with the stone at night, for in the stillness the sound might be heard; but for some hours he hacked away with the dagger at the rivets on his manacles. The next morning he was at work as soon as the chirrup of the cicadas began, as these, he knew, would completely deaden any sound he might make. By nighttime the rivet ends on the irons round his ankles were worn so thin, that he felt sure that another hour's work would bring them level with the iron, and before he went to sleep the rivets on the wrist were in the same condition.

He learned from his guard, next morning, that the captain was better, that he was to be taken on board in the cool of the evening, and that the vessel would start as soon as the breeze sprang up in the morning. In the afternoon his two guards entered, and bade him follow them. He was conducted to the principal house in the village, and into a room where Ruggiero Mocenigo was lying on a couch.

"I have sent for you," Ruggiero said, "to tell you that I have not forgotten you. My vengeance has been delayed from no fault of mine, but it will be all the sweeter when it comes. I am going to fetch Polani's daughters. I have heard that, since you thrust yourself between me and them, you have been a familiar in the house, that Polani treats you as a member of the family, and that you are in high favour with his daughters. I have kept myself informed of what happened in Venice, and I have noted each of these things down in the account of what I owe you. I am going to fetch Polani's

163

daughters here, and to make Maria my wife, and then I will show her how I treat those who cross my path. It will be a lesson to her, as well as for you. You shall wish yourself dead a thousand times before death comes to you."

"I always knew that you were a villain, Ruggiero Mocenigo," Francis said quietly, "although I hardly thought that a man who had once the honour of being a noble of Venice, would sink to become a pirate and renegade. You may carry Maria Polani off, but you will never succeed through her in obtaining a portion of her father's fortune, for I know that, the first moment her hands are free, she will stab herself to the heart, rather than remain in the power of such a wretch."

Ruggiero snatched up a dagger from a table by his couch as Francis was speaking, but dropped it again.

"Fool," he said. "Am I not going to carry off the two girls? and do you not see that it will tame Maria's spirit effectually, when she knows that if she lays hands on herself, she will but shift the honour of being my wife from herself to her sister?"

As the laugh of anticipated triumph rang in Francis's ears, the latter, in his fury, made a spring forward to throw himself upon the villain, but he had forgotten his chains, and fell headlong on to the floor.

"Guards," Ruggiero shouted, "take this fellow away, and I charge you watch over him securely, and remember that your lives shall answer for his escape."

"There is no need for threats, signor," Philippo said. "You can rely on our vigilance, though, as far as I see, if he had but a child to watch him he would be safe in that cell of his, fettered as he is."

Ruggiero waved his hand impatiently, and the two men withdrew with their prisoner.

"If it were not that I have not touched my share of the booty of our last trip," Philippo said as they left the house, "I would not serve him another day. As it is, as soon as the galley returns, and we get our shares of the money, and of the sum he has promised if this expedition of his is successful, I will be off. I have had enough of this. It is bad enough to be consorting with Moors, without being abused and threatened as if one was a dog."

As soon as he was alone again, Francis set to work, and by the afternoon the ends of the four rivets were worn down level with the iron, and it needed but a pressure to make the rings spring open. Then he waited for the evening before freeing himself, as by some chance he might again be visited, and even if free before nightfall he could not leave the house.

164

Philippo was later than usual in bringing him his meal, and Francis heard angry words passing between him and his comrade, because he had not returned to relieve him sooner.

"Is everything ready for the start?" Francis asked the man as he entered.

"Yes, the crew are all on board. The boat is to be on shore for the captain at nine o'clock, and as there is a little breeze blowing, I expect they will get up sail and start at once."

After a few minutes' talk the man left, and Francis waited until it became almost dark, then he inserted the dagger between the irons at the point of junction. At the first wrench they flew apart, and his left hand was free. A few minutes' more work and the chains lay on the ground.

Taking them up, he rattled them together loudly. In a minute he heard the guard outside move and come to the door, then the key was inserted in the lock and the door opened.

"What on earth are you doing now?" Philippo asked as he entered.

Francis was standing close to the door, so that as his guard entered he had his back to him, and before the question was finished he sprang upon him, throwing him headlong to the ground with the shock, and before the astonished man could speak he was kneeling upon him, with the point of the dagger at his throat.

"If you make a sound, or utter a cry," he exclaimed, "I will drive this dagger into your throat."

Philippo could feel the point of the dagger against his skin, and remained perfectly quiet.

"I do not want to kill you, Philippo. You have not been harsh to me, and I would spare your life if I could. Hold your hands back above your head, and put your wrists together that I may fasten them. Then I will let you get up."

Philippo held up his hands as requested, and Francis bound them tightly together with a strip of twisted cloth. He then allowed him to rise.

"Now, Philippo, I must gag you. Then I will fasten your hands to a bar well above your head, so that you can't get at the rope with your teeth. I will leave you here till your comrade comes in the morning."

"I would rather that you killed me at once, signor," the man said. "Thomaso will be furious at your having made your escape, for he will certainly come in for a share of the fury of the captain. There are three or four of the crew remaining behind, and no doubt they will keep me locked up till the ship returns, and in that case the captain will be as good as his word. You had better kill me at once."

"But what am I to do, Philippo? I must ensure my own safety. If you will suggest any way by which I can do that, I will."

"I would swear any oath you like, signor, that I will not give the alarm. I will make straight across the island, and get hold of a boat there, so as to be well away before your escape is known in the morning."

"Well, look here, Philippo. I believe you are sincere, and you shall take the oath you hold most sacred."

"You can accompany me, signor, if you will. Keep my hands tied till we are on the other side of the island, and stab me if I give the alarm."

"I will not do that, Philippo. I will trust you altogether; but first take the oath you spoke of."

Philippo swore a terrible oath, that he would abstain from giving the alarm, and would cross the island and make straight for the mainland. Francis at once cut the bonds.

"You will lose your share of the plunder, Philippo, and you will have to keep out of the way to avoid the captain's rage. Therefore I advise you, when you get to Tunis, to embark in the first ship that sails. If you come to Venice, ask for me, and I will make up to you for your loss of booty, and put you in the way of leading an honest life again. But before going, you must first change clothes with me. You can sell mine at Tunis for enough to buy you a dozen suits like yours; but you must divide with me what money you now have in your possession, for I cannot start penniless."

"I thank you for your kindness," the man said. "You had it in your power, with a thrust of the dagger, to make yourself safe, and you abstained. Even were it not for my oath, I should be a treacherous dog, indeed, were I to betray you. I do not know what your plans are, signor, but I pray you to follow my example, and get away from this place before daylight. The people here will all aid in the search for you, and as the island is not large, you will assuredly be discovered. It has for many years been a rendezvous of pirates, a place to which they bring their booty to sell to the traders who come over from the mainland."

"Thank you for your advice, Philippo, and be assured I shall be off the island before daybreak, but I have some work to do first, and cannot therefore accompany you."

"May all the saints bless you, signor, and aid you to get safe away! Assuredly, if I live, I will ere long present myself to you at

Venice—not for the money which you so generously promised me, but that I may, with your aid, earn an honest living among Christians."

By this time the exchange of clothes was effected, the six ducats in Philippo's purse—the result of a little private plundering on one of the captured vessels—divided; and then they left the prison room, and Philippo locked the door after them.

"Is there any chance of Thomaso returning speedily?" Francis asked. "Because, if so, he might notice your absence, and so give the alarm before the ship sets sail, in which case we should have the whole crew on our tracks."

"I do not think that he will. He will be likely to be drinking in the wine shop for an hour or two before he returns. But I tell you what I will do, signor. I will resume my place here on guard until he has returned. He will relieve me at midnight, and in the darkness will not notice the change of clothes. There will still be plenty of time for me to cross the island, and get out of sight in the boat, before the alarm is given, which will not be until six o'clock, when I ought to relieve him again. As you say, if the alarm were to be given before the vessel sails, they might start at once to cut us off before we reach the mainland, for they would make sure that we should try to escape in that direction."

"That will be the best plan, Philippo; and now goodbye."

Francis walked down to the shore. There were no boats lying there of a size he could launch unaided, but presently he heard the sound of oars, and a small fishing boat rowed by two men approached.

"Look here, lads," he said. "I want to be put on board the ship. I ought to have been on board three hours ago, but took too much wine, and lay down for an hour or two and overslept myself. Do you think you can row quietly up alongside so that I can slip on board unnoticed? If so I will give you a ducat for your trouble."

"We can do that," the fishermen said. "We have just come from the ship now, and have sold them our catch of today. There were half a dozen other boats lying beside her, bargaining for their fish. Besides they are taking on board firewood and other stores that have been left till the last moment. So jump in and we will soon get you there."

In a few minutes they approached the side of the ship.

"I see you have got half a dozen fish left in your boat now," Francis said.

"They are of no account," one of the men said. "They are good

167

enough for our eating, but not such as they buy on board a ship where money is plentiful. You are heartily welcome to them if you have a fancy for them."

"Thank you," Francis said. "I will take two or three of them, if you can spare them. I want to play a trick with a comrade."

As the fishermen said, there were several boats lying near the vessel, and the men were leaning over the sides bargaining for fish. Handing the fishermen their promised reward, Francis sprang up the ladder to the deck. He was unnoticed, for other men had gone down into the boats for fish.

Mingling with the sailors, he gradually made his way to the hatchway leading into the hold, descended the ladder, and stowed himself away among a quantity of casks, some filled with wine and some with water, at the farther end of the hold; and as he lay there devoutly thanked God that his enterprise had been so far successful.

Men came down from time to time with lanterns, to stow away the lately-arrived stores, but none came near the place where Francis was hidden. The time seemed long before he heard the clank of the capstan, and knew the vessel was being hove up to her anchors. Then, after a while, he heard the creaking of cordage, and much trampling of feet on the deck above, and knew that she was under way. Then he made himself as comfortable as he could, in his cramped position, and went off to sleep.

When he woke in the morning, the light was streaming down the hatch, which was only closed in rough weather, as it was necessary frequently to go down into it for water and stores. Francis had brought the fish with him as a means of subsistence during the voyage, in case he should be unable to obtain provisions, but for this there was no occasion, as there was an abundance of fruit hanging from the beams, while piles of bread were stowed in a partition at one end of the hold. During the day, however, he did not venture to move, and was heartily glad when it again became dark, and he could venture to get out and stretch himself. He appropriated a loaf and some bunches of grapes, took a long drink from a pail placed under the tap of a water butt, and made his way back to his corner. After a hearty meal he went out again for another drink, and then turned in to sleep.

So passed six days. By the rush of water against the outside planks, he could always judge whether the vessel was making brisk way or whether she was lying becalmed. Once or twice, after nightfall, he ventured up on deck, feeling certain that in the darkness there was no fear of his being detected. From conversation he overheard on the seventh evening, he learned that Corfu had been sighted that day. For some hours the vessel's sails had been lowered, and she had remained motionless; but she was now again making for the land, and in the course of another two hours a landing was to be made.

The boats had all been got in readiness, and the men were to muster fully armed. Although, as they understood, the carrying off of two girls was their special object, it was intended that they should gather as much plunder as could be obtained. The island was rich, for many wealthy Venetians had residences there. Therefore, with the exception of a few men left on board to take care of the galley, the whole were to land. A picked boat's crew were to accompany the captain, who was now completely convalescent. The rest were to divide in bands and scatter over the country, pillaging as they went, and setting fire to the houses. It was considered that such consternation would be caused that nothing like resistance could be offered for some time, and by daybreak all hands were to gather at the landing place.

How far this spot was from the town, Francis had no means of learning. There was a store of spare arms in the hold, and Francis, furnishing himself with a sword and large dagger, waited until he heard a great movement overhead, and then went upon deck and joined a gang of men employed in lowering one of the boats. The boat was a large one, rowing sixteen oars and carrying some twenty men seated in the stern. Here Francis took his place with the others. The boat pushed off and waited until four others were launched and filled. Then the order was given, and the boats rowed in a body towards the shore. The men landed and formed under their respective officers, one man remaining in each boat to keep it afloat.

Francis leaped ashore, and while the men were forming up, found no difficulty in slipping away unnoticed. As he did not know where the path was, and was afraid of making a noise, he lay down among the rocks until he heard the word of command to start given. Then he cautiously crept out, and, keeping far enough in the rear to be unseen, followed the sound of their footsteps. By the short time which had elapsed between the landing and the start, he had no doubt they were guided by some persons perfectly acquainted with the locality, probably by some natives of the island among the mixed crew.

Francis had, during his voyage, thought over the course he should pursue on landing; and saw that, ignorant as he was of the country, his only hope was in obtaining a guide who would conduct him to Polani's villa before the arrival of Mocenigo and his band. The fact that the crew were divided into five parties, which were to proceed in different directions, and that he did not know which of them was commanded by the captain, added to the difficulty. Had they kept together he might, after seeing the direction in which they were going, make a detour and get ahead of them. But he might now follow a party going in an entirely wrong direction, and before he could obtain a guide, Mocenigo's band might have gone so far that they could not be overtaken before they reached the villa.

There was nothing to do but to get ahead of all the parties, in the hope of coming upon a habitation before going far. As soon, therefore, as the last band had disappeared, he started at a run. The country was open, with few walls or fences; therefore on leaving the road he was able to run rapidly forwards, and in a few minutes knew that he must be ahead of the pirates. Then he again changed his course so as to strike the road he had left.

After running for about a mile he saw a light ahead of him, and soon arrived at a cottage. He knocked at the door, and then entered. The occupants of the room—a man and woman, a lad, and several children—rose to their feet at the sudden entrance of the stranger.

"Good people," Francis said. "I have just landed from a ship, and am the bearer of important messages to the Signoras Polani. I have lost my way, and it is necessary that I should go on without a moment's delay. Can you tell me how far the villa of Polani is distant?"

"It is about three miles from here," the man said.

"I will give a ducat to your son if he will run on with me at once."

The man looked doubtful. The apparel and general appearance of Francis were not prepossessing. He had been six days a prisoner in the hold without means of washing.

"See," he said, producing a ducat, "here is the money. I will give it you at once if you will order your son to go with me, and to hurry at the top of his speed."

"It's a bargain," the man said.

"Here, Rufo! start at once with the signor."

"Come along, signor," the boy said; and without another word to the parents Francis followed him out, and both set off at a run along the road.

Francis had said nothing about pirates to the peasants, for he knew that, did he do so, such alarm would be caused that they would think of nothing but flight, and he should not be able to obtain a guide. It was improbable that they would be molested. The pirates were bent upon pillaging the villas of the wealthy, and would not risk the raising of an alarm by entering cottages where there was no chance of plunder.

After proceeding a few hundred yards, the lad struck off by a byroad at right angles to that which they had been following, and by the direction he took Francis felt that he must at first have gone far out of his way, and that the party going direct to the villa must have had a considerable start. Still, he reckoned that as he was running at the rate of three feet to every one they would march, he might hope to arrive at the house well before them.

Not a word was spoken as they ran along. The lad was wondering, in his mind, as to what could be the urgent business that could necessitate its being carried at such speed; while Francis felt that every breath was needed for the work he had to do. Only once or twice he spoke, to ask how much further it was to their destination.

The last answer was cheering:

"A few hundred paces farther."

"There are the lights, signor. They have not gone to bed. This is the door."

Francis knocked with the pommel of his sword, keeping up a loud continuous knocking. A minute or two passed, and then a face appeared at the window above.

"Who is it that knocks so loudly at this time of night?"

"It is Francisco Hammond. Open instantly. Danger threatens the signoras. Quick, for your life!"

The servant recognized the voice, and ran down without hesitation and unbarred the fastening; but for a moment he thought he must have been mistaken, as Francis ran into the lighted hall.

"Where are the ladies?" he asked. "Lead me to them instantly."

But as he spoke a door standing by was opened, and Signor Polani himself, with the two girls, appeared. They had been on the point of retiring to rest when the knocking began, and the merchant, with his drawn sword, was standing at the door, when he recognized Francis' voice.

They were about to utter an exclamation of pleasure at seeing him, and of astonishment, not only at his sudden arrival, but at his appearance, when Francis burst out:

"There is no time for a word. You must fly instantly. Ruggiero Mocenigo is close at my heels with a band of twenty pirates."

The girls uttered a cry of alarm, and the merchant exclaimed:

"Can we not defend the house, Francisco? I have eight men here, and we can hold it till assistance comes."

"Ruggiero has a hundred," Francis said, "and all can be brought up in a short time—you must fly. For God's sake, do not delay, signor. They may be here at any moment."

"Come, girls," Polani said.

"And you, too," he went on, turning to the servants, whom the knocking had caused to assemble. "Do you follow us. Resistance would only cost you your lives.

"Here, Maria, take my hand.

"Francisco, do you see to Giulia.

"Close the door after the last of you, and bolt it. It will give us a few minutes, before they break in and discover that we have all gone.

"Which way are the scoundrels coming?"

Francis pointed in the direction from which he had come, and the whole party started at a fast pace in the other direction. They had not been gone five minutes, when a loud and sudden knocking broke on the silence of the night.

"It was a close thing, indeed, Francisco," the merchant said, as they ran along close to each other. "At present I feel as if I was in a dream; but you shall tell us all presently."

They were, by this time, outside the grounds of the villa, and some of the servants, who knew the country, now took the lead. In a few minutes the merchant slackened his pace.

"We are out of danger now," he said. "They will not know in which direction to search for us; and if they scatter in pursuit we could make very short work of any that might come up with us."

"I do not know that you are out of danger," Francis said. "A hundred men landed. Mocenigo, with twenty, took the line to your house, but the rest have scattered over the country in smaller bands, bent on murder and pillage. Therefore, we had best keep on as fast as we can, until well beyond the circle they are likely to sweep—that is, unless the ladies are tired."

"Tired!" Maria repeated. "Why, Giulia and I go for long walks every day, and could run for an hour, if necessary."

"Then come on, my dears," the merchant said. "I am burning to know what this all means; and I am sure you are equally curious; but nothing can be said till you are in safety."

Accordingly, the party again broke into a run. A few minutes later one of the servants, looking back, exclaimed:

172

"They have fired the house, signor. There are flames issuing from one of the lower windows."

"I expected that," the merchant said, without looking back. "That scoundrel would, in any case, light it in his fury at finding that we have escaped; but he has probably done so, now, in hopes that the light will enable him to discover us. It is well that we are so far ahead, for the blaze will light up the country for a long way round."

"There is a wood a little way ahead, signor," the servant said. "Once through that we shall be hidden from sight, however great the light."

Arrived at the wood, they again broke into a walk. A few hundred yards beyond the wood was some rising ground, from which they could see far over the country.

"Let us stop here," the merchant said. "We are safe now. We have placed two miles between ourselves and those villains."

The villa was now a mass of flames. Exclamations of fury broke from the men servants, while the women cried with anger at the sight of the destruction.

"Do not concern yourselves," the merchant said. "The house can be rebuilt, and I will see that none of you are the poorer for the loss of your belongings.

"Now, girls, let us sit down here and hear from Francisco how it is that he has once again been your saviour."

"Before I begin, signor, tell me whether there are any ships of war in the port, and how far that is distant from us?"

"It is not above six miles on the other side of the island. That is to say, we have been going towards it since we left the villa.

"See," he broke off, "there are flames rising in three or four directions. The rest of those villains are at their work."

"But are there any war galleys in the port?" Francis interrupted.

"Yes. Three ships were sent here, on the report that a Moorish pirate had been cruising in these waters, and that several vessels were missing. When the story first came I did not credit it. The captain of the ship who brought the news told me he had met you about halfway across, and had told you about the supposed pirate. A vessel arrived four days later, and brought letters from my agent, but he said no word about your boat having arrived.

"Then I became uneasy; and when later news came, and still no word of you, I felt sure that something must have befallen you; that possibly the report was true, and that you had fallen into the hands of the pirates. So I at once started, in one of the galleys which the council were despatching in answer to the request of the governor here."

"In that case, signor, there is not a moment to lose. The governor should be informed that the pirate is lying on the opposite coast, and that his crew have landed, and are burning and pillaging. If orders are issued at once, the galleys could get round before morning, and so cut off the retreat of these miscreants."

"You are quite right," Polani said, rising at once. "We will go on without a moment's delay! The girls can follow slowly under the escort of the servants."

"Oh, papa," Maria exclaimed, "you are not going to take Francisco away till we have heard his story! Can you not send forward the servants with a message to the governor?"

"No, my dear. The governor will have gone to bed, and the servants might not be able to obtain admittance to him. I must go myself. It is for your sakes, as well as for my own. We shall never feel a moment's safety, as long as this villain is at large. Francisco's story will keep till tomorrow.

"As to your gratitude and mine, that needs no telling. He cannot but know what we are feeling, at the thought of the almost miraculous escape you have had from falling into the hands of your persecutor.

"Now come along, Francisco.

"One of you men who knows the road had better come with us. Do the rest of you all keep together.

"Two miles further, girls, as you know, is a villa of Carlo Maffene. If you feel tired, you had best stop and ask for shelter there. There is no fear that the pirates will extend their ravages so far. They will keep on the side of the island where they landed, so as to be able to return with their booty before daybreak to the ship."

CHAPTER 14

THE END OF THE PERSECUTOR

Signor Polani was so well known, that upon his arrival at the governor's house the domestics, upon being aroused, did not hesitate to awaken the governor at once. The latter, as soon as he heard that the pirates had landed and were devastating the other side of the island, and that their ship was lying close in to the coast under the charge of a few sailors only, at once despatched a messenger to the commander of the galleys; ordering them to arouse the crews and make ready to put out to sea instantly. He added that he, himself, should follow his messenger on board in a few minutes, and should accompany them. He then issued orders that the bell should toll to summon the inhabitants to arms; and directed an officer to take the command, and to start with them at once across the island, and to fall upon the pirates while engaged in their work of pillage. They were to take a party with them with litters to carry Polani's daughters to the town, and an apartment was to be assigned to them in his palace, until his return.

While he was issuing this order, refreshments had been placed upon the table, and he pressed Polani and his companions to partake of these before starting.

Francis needed no second invitation. He had been too excited, at the news he had heard on board the ship, to think of eating; and he now remembered that it was a good many hours since he had taken his last meal. He was but a few minutes, however, in satisfying his hunger. By the time he had finished, the governor had seen that his orders had been carried out.

Two hundred armed citizens had already mustered in companies, and were now on the point of setting out, burning with indignation at what they had heard of the depredations which the pirates had committed. After seeing his preparations complete the governor, accompanied by Polani and Francis, made his way down to the port, and was rowed out to the galleys.

Here he found all on the alert. The sails were ready for hoisting, and the men were seated at the benches, ready to aid with oars the light wind which was blowing. The governor now informed the commander of the vessels the reason of the sudden orders for sailing. The news was passed to the captains of the other two vessels, and in a very few minutes the anchors were weighed, and the vessels started on their way.

Francis was closely questioned as to the spot at which the pirate vessel was lying, but could only reply that, beyond the fact that it was some four miles from Polani's villa, he had no idea of the locality.

"But can you not describe to us the nature of the coast?" the commander said.

"That I cannot," Francis replied; "for I was hidden away in the hold of the vessel, and did not come on deck until after it was dark, at which time the land abreast of us was only a dark mass."

"Signor Polani has informed me," the governor said, "that, although your attire does not betoken it, you are a dear friend of his; but he has not yet informed me how it comes that you were upon this pirate ship."

"He has been telling me as we came along," Polani replied; "and a strange story it is. He was on his voyage hither in the Naxos, which, as you doubtless remember, was a little craft of mine, which should have arrived here a month since. As we supposed, it was captured by the pirates, the leader of whom is Ruggiero Mocenigo, who, as of course you know, made his escape from the custody of the officers of the state, they being overpowered by a party of Paduans. The sentence of banishment for life has been passed against him, and, until I heard from my friend here that he was captain of the pirate which has been seen off this island, I knew not what had become of him.

"Those on board the Naxos were taken prisoners, and confined in the pirate's hold, which they found already filled with captives taken from other ships. The pirate at once sailed for Africa, where all the prisoners were sold as slaves to the Moors, my friend here alone excepted, Mocenigo having an old feud with him, and a design to keep him in his hands. Learning that a raid was intended upon Corfu, with the special design of carrying off my daughters, whom Mocenigo had twice previously tried to abduct, Francisco managed to get on board the vessel, and conceal himself in her hold, in order that he might frustrate the design. He managed, in the dark, to mingle with the landing party; and then, separating from them, made his way on ahead, and fortunately was able to obtain a guide to my house, which he reached five minutes only before the arrival of the pirates there."

"Admirable, indeed! And we are all vastly indebted to him, for had it not been for him, we should not have known of the doings of these scoundrels until too late to cut off their retreat; and, once away in their ship again, they might long have preyed upon our commerce, before one of our cruisers happened to fall in with them.

"As for Ruggiero Mocenigo, he is a disgrace to the name of a Venetian; and it is sad to think that one of our most noble families should have to bear the brand of being connected with a man so base and villainous. However, I trust that his power of ill doing has come to an end.

"Is the vessel a fast one, signor?"

"I cannot say whether she sails fast," Francis replied; "but she certainly rows fast."

"I trust that we shall catch her before she gets under way," the commander of the galleys said. "Our vessels are not made for rowing, although we get out oars to help them along in calm weather."

"What course do you propose to take?" the merchant asked.

"When we approach the spot where she is likely to be lying, I shall order the captains of the other two ships to lie off the coast, a couple of miles distant and as far from each other, so that they can cut her off as she makes out to sea. We will follow the coast line, keeping in as close as the water will permit, and in this way we shall most likely come upon her. If we should miss her, I shall at the first dawn of morning join the others in the offing, and keep watch till she appears from under the shadow of the land."

It was now three o'clock in the morning, and an hour later the three vessels parted company, and the galley with the governor and commander of the squadron rowed for the shore. When they came close to the land, the captain ordered the oars to be laid in.

"The breeze is very light," he said; "but it is favourable, and will enable us to creep along the shore. If we continue rowing, those in charge of the ship may hear us coming, and may cut their cables, get up sail, and make out from the land without our seeing them. On a still night, like this, the sound of the sweeps can be heard a very long distance."

Quietly the vessel made her way along the shore. Over the land, the sky was red with the reflection of numerous fires, but this only made the darkness more intense under its shadow, and the lead was kept going in order to prevent them from sailing into shallow water. By the captain's orders strict silence was observed on board the ship, and every eye was strained ahead on the lookout for the pirate vessel.

Presently, all became aware of a confused noise, apparently coming from the land, but at some distance ahead. As they got further on, distant shouts and cries were heard.

"I fancy," the governor said to the captain, "the band from the town have met the pirates, and the latter are retreating to their ship."

"Then the ship can't be far off," the captain said. "Daylight is beginning to break in the east, and we shall soon be able to make her out against the sky—that is, if she is still lying at anchor."

On getting round the next point, the vessel was distinctly visible. The shouting on the shore was now plainly heard, and there could be no doubt that a desperate fight was going on there. It seemed to be close to the water's edge.

"There is a boat rowing off to the ship," one of the sailors said.

"Then get out your oars again. She is not more than half a mile away, and she can hardly get under way before we reach her. Besides, judging from the sound of the fight, the pirates must have lost a good many men, and will not be able to man all the oars even if they gain their ship."

The men sat down to their oars with alacrity. Every sailor on board felt it almost as a personal insult, that pirates should dare to enter the Venetian waters and carry on their depredations there. The glare of the burning houses, too, had fired their indignation to the utmost, and all were eager for the fight.

Three boats were now seen rowing towards the ship.

"Stretch to your oars, men," the captain said. "We must be alongside them, if we can, before they can take to their sweeps."

The pirates had now seen them; and Francis, standing at the bow eagerly watching the vessel, could hear orders shouted to the boats. These pulled rapidly alongside, and he could see the men clambering up in the greatest haste. There was a din of voices. Some men tried to get up the sails, others got out oars, and the utmost confusion evidently prevailed. In obedience to the shouts of the officers, the sails were lowered again, and all betook themselves to the oars; but scarce a stroke had been pulled before the Venetian galley ran up alongside. Grapnels were thrown, and the crew, seizing their weapons, sprang on to the deck of the pirate.

The crew of the latter knew that they had no mercy to expect, and although weakened by the loss of nearly a third of their number in the fighting on shore, sprang from their benches, and rushed to oppose their assailants, with the desperation of despair. They were led by Ruggiero Mocenigo, who, furious at the failure of his schemes, and preferring death to the shame of being carried to Venice as a pirate and a traitor, rushed upon the Venetians with a fury which, at first, carried all before it. Supported by his Moors and renegades he drove back the boarders, and almost succeeded in clearing the deck of his vessel.

He himself engaged hand-to-hand with the commander of the Venetian galley, and at the third thrust ran him through the throat;

but the Venetians, although they had yielded to the first onslaught, again poured over the bulwarks of the galley. Polani, burning to punish the man who had so repeatedly tried to injure him, accompanied them, Francis keeping close beside him.

"Ruggiero Mocenigo, traitor and villain, your time has come!"

Ruggiero started at hearing his name thus proclaimed, for on board his own ship he was simply known as the captain; but in the dim light he recognized Polani, and at once crossed swords with him.

"Be not so sure, Polani. Perhaps it is your time that has come."

The two engaged with fury. Polani was still strong and vigorous. His opponent had the advantage of youth and activity. But Polani's weight and strength told, and he was forcing his opponent back, when his foot slipped on the bloodstained deck. He fell forward; and in another moment Ruggiero would have run him through the body; had not the weapon been knocked up by Francis, who, watching every movement of the fight, sprang forward when he saw the merchant slip.

"This time, Ruggiero, my hands are free. How about your vengeance now?"

Ruggiero gave a cry of astonishment, at seeing the lad whom he believed to be lying in chains, five hundred miles away, facing him. For a moment he recoiled, and then with the cry, "I will take it now," sprang forward. But this time he had met an opponent as active and as capable as himself.

For a minute or two they fought on even terms, and then Ruggiero fell suddenly backwards, a crossbow bolt, from one of the Venetians on the poop of the vessel, having struck him full in the forehead.

Without their leader, the spirit of the pirates had fled. They still fought, steadily and desperately, but it was only to sell their lives as dearly as possible; and in five minutes after the fall of Ruggiero the last man was cut down, for no quarter was given to pirates.

Just as the combat concluded, the sound of oars was heard, and the other two galleys came up to the assistance of their consort. They arrived too late to take part in the conflict, but cheered lustily when they heard that the pirate captain, and all his crew, had been killed. Upon learning that the commander of the galley was killed, the captain next in seniority assumed the command.

In a few minutes, the bodies of the pirates were thrown overboard, the wounded were carried below to have their wounds attended to, while the bodies of those who had fallen—thirteen in number—were laid together on the deck, for burial on shore.

"Thanks to you, Francisco, that I am not lying there beside them," the merchant said. "I did not know that you were so close at hand, and as I slipped I felt that my end had come."

"You were getting the better of him up to that point," Francis said. "I was close at hand, in readiness to strike in should I see that my aid was wanted, but up to the moment you slipped, I believed that you would have avenged your wrongs yourself."

"It is well that he fell as he did. It would have been dreadful, indeed, had he been carried to Venice, to bring shame and disgrace upon a noble family. Thank God, his power for mischief is at an end! I have had no peace of mind since the day when you first thwarted his attempt to carry off the girls; nor should I have ever had, until I obtained sure tidings that he was dead. The perseverance with which he has followed his resolve, to make my daughter his wife, is almost beyond belief. Had his mind been turned to other matters, he was capable of attaining greatness, for no obstacle would have barred his way.

"It almost seems as if it were a duel between him and you to the death—his aim to injure me, and yours to defend us. And now it has ended. Maria will breathe more freely when she hears the news, for, gay and light hearted as she is, the dread of that man has weighed heavily upon her."

The governor, who from the poop of the vessel had watched the conflict, now came up, and warmly congratulated Francis upon his bravery.

"I saw you rush forward, just as my friend Polani fell, and engage his assailant. At first I thought you lost, for the villain was counted one of the best swordsmen in Venice, and you are still but a lad; but I saw you did not give way an inch, but held your own against him; and I believe you would have slain him unaided, for you were fighting with greater coolness than he was. Still, I was relieved when I saw him fall, for even then the combat was doubtful, and his men, to do them justice, fought like demons. How comes it that one so young as you should be so skilled with your weapon?"

"This is not the first time that my young friend has done good service to the state," Polani said; "for it was he who led a crew of one of my ships to the aid of Pisani, when his galley was boarded by the Genoese, at the battle of Antium."

"Is this he?" the governor said, in surprise. "I heard, of course, by the account of those who came from Venice a month since, how Pisani was aided, when hard pressed, by the crew of one of your ships, headed by a young Englishman, upon whom the state had conferred the rights of citizenship as a recognition of his services; but I did not dream that the Englishman was but a lad.

"What is your age, young sir?"

"I am just eighteen," Francis replied. "Our people are all fond of strong exercise, and thus it was that I became more skilled, perhaps, than many of my age, in the use of arms."

At nine o'clock the squadron arrived in the port, bringing with them the captured galley. As soon as they were seen approaching, the church bells rang, flags were hung out from the houses, and the whole population assembled at the quay to welcome the victors and to hear the news.

"Do you go on at once, directly we land, Francisco, and set the girls' minds at ease. I must come on with the governor, and he is sure to be detained, and will have much to say before he can make his way through the crowd."

Francis was, on his arrival at the governor's, recognized by the domestics, and at once shown into the room where the girls were awaiting him. The fact that the pirate galley had been captured was already known to them, the news having been brought some hours before, by a horseman, from the other side of the island.

"Where is our father?" Maria exclaimed, as Francis entered alone.

"He is well, and sent me on to relieve your minds."

"Saint Mark be praised!" Maria said. "We have been sorely anxious about you both. A messenger, who brought the news, said that it could be seen from the shore that there was a desperate fight on board the pirate ship, which was attacked by one galley only. We felt sure that it would be the ship that the governor was in, and we knew you were with him; and our father was so enraged at what had happened, that we felt sure he would take part in the fight."

"He did so," Francis said, "and himself engaged hand-to-hand with Mocenigo, and would probably have killed him, had not his foot slipped on the deck. I was, of course, by his side, and occupied the villain until a cross bolt pierced his brain. So there is an end to all your trouble with him."

"Is he really dead?" Maria said. "Oh, Francisco, how thankful I am! He seemed so determined, that I began to think he was sure some day to succeed in carrying me off. Not that I would ever have become his wife, for I had vowed to kill myself before that came about. I should have thought he might have known that he could never have forced me to be his wife."

"I told him the same thing," Francis said, "and he replied that he was not afraid of that, for that he should have your sister in his power also, and that he should warn you that, if you laid hands on yourself, he should make her his wife instead of you."

The girls both gave an exclamation of horror.

"I never thought of that," Maria said; "but he would indeed have disarmed me with such a threat. It would have been horrible for me to have been the wife of such a man; but I think I could have borne it rather than have consigned Giulia to such a fate.

"Oh, here is father!"

"I have got away sooner than I expected," Polani said as he entered. "The governor was good enough to beg me to come on at once to you. You have heard all the news, I suppose, and know that our enemy will persecute you no more."

"We have heard, papa, and also that you yourself fought with him, which was very wrong and very rash of you."

"And did he tell you that had it not been for him I should not be here alive now, girls?"

"No, father. He said that when you slipped he occupied Ruggiero's attention until the cross bolt struck him."

"That is what he did, my dear; but had he not occupied his attention I should have been a dead man. The thrust was aimed at me as I fell, and would have pierced me had he not sprung forward and turned it aside, and then engaged in single combat with Mocenigo, who, with all his faults, was brave and a skillful swordsman; and yet, as the governor himself said, probably Francisco would have slain him, even had not the combat ended as it did.

"And now we must have his story in full. I have not heard much about it yet, and you have heard nothing; and I want to know how he managed to get out of the hands of that man, when he had once fallen into them."

"That is what we want to know, too, father. We know what a sharp watch was kept upon us, and I am sure they must have been much more severe with him."

"They were certainly more severe," Francis said smiling, "for my right hand was chained to my left ankle, and the left hand to to my right ankle—not tightly, you know, but the chain was so short that I could not stand upright. But, on the other hand, I do not think my guards were as vigilant as yours. However, I will tell you the whole story."

The girls listened with rapt attention to the story of the capture, the escape, and of his hiding in the hold of the pirate in order to be able to give them a warning in time.

"Your escape was fortunate, indeed," the merchant said when he had finished. "Fortunate both for you and for us, for I have no doubt that Mocenigo had intended to put you to a lingering death, on his return. As for the girls, nothing could have saved them from the fate he designed for them, save the method which you took of arriving here before him."

"What are we to do for him, father?" Maria exclaimed. "We are not tired of thanking him, but he hates being thanked. If he would only get into some terrible scrape, Giulia and I would set out to rescue him at once; but you see he gets out of his scrapes before we hear of them. It is quite disheartening not to be able to do anything."

Francis laughed merrily.

"It is terrible, is it not, signora? But if I manage to get into any scrape, and have time to summon you to my assistance, be sure I will do so. But, you see, one cannot get into a scrape when one chooses, and I must be content, while I am away, in knowing that I have the good wishes of you and your sister."

"Do not trouble yourself, Maria," her father said. "Some day an opportunity may come for our paying our debts, and in the meantime Francis is content that we should be his debtors."

"And now, what are you going to do, papa?"

"I shall sail with you for Venice tomorrow. The governor will be sending one of the galleys with the news of the capture of the pirate, and doubtless he will give us all a passage in her. I shall order steps to be taken at once for rebuilding the villa, and will get it completed by the spring, before which time you will be off my hands, young lady; and I shall not be altogether sorry, for you have been a very troublesome child lately."

"It has not been my fault," Maria pouted.

"Not at all, my dear. It has been your misfortune, and I am not blaming you at all."

"But the trouble is now over, father!"

"So much the better for Rufino," the merchant said. "It will be good news to him that you are freed from the persecution of Ruggiero. And now, I must leave you, for I have arranged to ride over with the governor to the other side of the island. He has to investigate the damage which took place last evening. I hear that upwards of a score of villas were sacked and destroyed, and that many persons were killed; and while he is doing that I shall see what has to be done at our place. I don't know whether the walls are standing, or whether it will have to be entirely rebuilt, and I must arrange with some builder to to go over from here with me, and take my instructions as to what must be done."

On the following day the party set sail for Venice, where they arrived without adventure. Preparations were at once begun for the marriage of Maria with Rufino Giustiniani, and six weeks later the wedding ceremony took place. Francis did not go to sea until this was over, for when he spoke of a fresh voyage, a short time after their return, Maria declared that she would not be married unless he remained to be present.

"You have got me out of all my scrapes hitherto, Francisco, and you must see me safely through this."

As Signor Polani also declared that it was not to be thought of, that Francis should leave until after the marriage, he was obliged to remain for it. He was glad, however, when it was over, for he found the time on shore more tedious than usual. The girls were taken up with the preparations for the ceremony, and visitors were constantly coming and going, and the house was not like itself.

But even when the marriage was over, he was forced to remain some time longer in Venice. The Genoese fleets were keeping the sea, and Pisani had not, since the battle of Antium, succeeded in coming up with them. The consequence was that commerce was at a standstill, for the risk of capture was so great that the merchants ceased to send their ships to sea.

"The profit would not repay us for the risk, Francisco," the merchant said one day when they were talking over it. "If only one cargo in ten fell into their hands the profit off the other nine would be swept away; but as I see that you are longing to be afloat again, you can, if you like, join one of the state galleys which start next week to reinforce Pisani's fleet.

"The last time Pisani wrote to me he said how glad he should be to have you with him; and after your service at Antium, I have no doubt whatever that I could procure for you a post as second in command in one of the ships. What do you say?"

"I should certainly like it, signor, greatly; but, as you said before, it would be a mere waste of time for me to take service with the state, when I am determined upon the vocation of a merchant."

"I did say that, Francis, and meant it at the time; but at present trade is, as you see, at a standstill, so you would not be losing time, and, in the next place, it is always an advantage, even to a trader, to stand well with the state. Here in Venice all the great merchants are of noble family, and trade is no bar to occupying the highest offices of the state. Many of our doges have been merchants; while merchants are often soldiers, diplomatists, or governors, as the state requires their services.

"You have already, you see, obtained considerable benefit by the action at Antium. I do not say that you would derive any direct benefit, even were you to distinguish yourself again as highly as on that occasion. Still, it is always well to gain the consideration of your fellows, and to be popular with the people. Therefore, if you would like to take service with the state until this affair is decided with Genoa, and the seas are again open to our ships, I think it will be advantageous to you rather than not."

"Then, with your permission I will certainly do so, signor," Francis said. "Of course I should prefer to go as an officer on board one of the ships; but if not, I will go as a volunteer."

"You need not fear about that, Francis. With my influence, and that of the Giustiniani, and the repute you have gained for yourself, you may be sure of an appointment. Rufino would have commanded one of the ships had it not been for his marriage."

Rufino Giustiniani had indeed been most warm in his expressions of gratitude to Francis, to whom the whole family had shown the greatest attention, giving him many presents as a proof of their goodwill and gratitude.

"I am quite jealous of your English friend," Rufino had said one day to Maria. "I do believe, Maria, that you care for him more than you do for me. It is lucky for me that he is not two or three years older."

Maria laughed.

"I do care for him dearly; and if he had been, as you say, older and had fallen in love with me, I can't say how it would have been. You must acknowledge, it would be very hard to say no to a man who keeps on saving you from frightful peril; but then, you see, a girl can't fall in love with a man who does not fall in love with her.

"Francisco is so different from us Venetians. He always says just what he thinks, and never pays anyone even the least bit of a compliment. How can you fall in love with a man like that? Of course you can love him like a brother—and I do love Francisco as if he were my brother—but I don't think we should have got further than that, if he had been ever so old."

"And does Francis never pay you compliments, Giulia?"

"Never!" Giulia said decidedly. "It would be hateful of him if he did."

"But Maria doesn't object to compliments, Giulia. She looks for them as if they were her daily bread—

"Don't you, Maria—

"You will have to learn to put up with them soon, Giulia, for you will be out in society now, and the young men will crowd round your chair, just as they have done round that of this little flirt, your sister."

"I shall have to put up with it, I suppose," Giulia said quietly, "just as one puts up with other annoyances. But I should certainly never get to care for anyone who thinks so little of me, as to believe that I could be pleased by being addressed in such terms."

"From which I gather," Giustiniani said, smiling, "that this English lad's bluntness of speech pleases you more than it does Maria?"

"It pleases Maria, too," Giulia said, "though she may choose to say that it doesn't. And I don't think it quite right to discuss him at all, when we all owe him as much as we do."

Giustiniani glanced at Maria and gave a little significant nod.

"I do not think Giulia regards Francisco in quite the brotherly way that you do, Maria," he whispered presently to her.

"Perhaps not," Maria answered. "You see, she had not fallen in love with you before she met him. But I do not know. Giulia seldom speaks of him when we are alone, and if she did, you don't suppose I should tell you my sister's secrets, sir?"

The day after his conversation with Francis, Polani handed him his nomination as second in command of the Pluto, which he had obtained that morning from the seignory.

"You will be glad to hear that it is in this ship that Matteo also sails," for Matteo had come home for his brother's wedding.

"I am very glad of that," Francis said. "I wish that poor Giuseppi was also here to go with me. I shall miss him terribly. He was a most faithful and devoted follower."

"I have already sent orders, to my agent in Tunis, to spare no pains in discovering to whom the crew of the Naxos were sold. It is unfortunate that so many other captives were sold at the same time, as it will make it so much more difficult to trace our men. Those purchasing are not likely to know more than their first names, and may not even take the trouble to find out those, but may give them the first appellation that comes to hand. Therefore he has to find out who are now the masters of the whole of the captives sold at the same time, and then to pursue his investigations until he discovers the identity of the men he is looking for. Once he has found this, I will promise you there will be no delay. I have ordered him to make the best bargain in each case he can, but that at any rate he is to buy every one of them, whatever it may cost.

"I have sent him the personal descriptions of each man of the boat's crew, as given to me by their friends and relatives here, as this will be an assistance in his search. If, for instance, he hears of a Christian slave named Giuseppi living with a master some hundreds of miles in the interior, the fact that this man is middle aged will show at once that he was not the Giuseppi, age 20, of whom he is in search. I have particularly impressed upon him, in my letter, that we were especially anxious for the rescue of the captain, and the young man Giuseppi, so I hope that by the time you return from the voyage, I may have received some news of them."

Matteo was greatly pleased when he heard that he was going to sail under Francis.

"I would rather that we had both been volunteers," Francis said. "It seems absurd my being appointed second officer, while you as yet have no official position."

"I am not in the least bit in the world jealous, Francisco. With the exception of taking part in the fight at Antium, I have had no experience whatever, while you have been going through all sorts of adventures for the last two years, and always have come out of them marvellously well."

An hour after Matteo left him, a retainer of the family brought Francis a letter from Signor Giustiniani, inviting him to come to his house that evening, as many of Matteo's comrades on board the Pluto would be present. On Francis going to the palace he found assembled, not only the young men who would be Matteo's comrades as volunteers, but also the captain and other officers of the ship; and to them Signor Giustiniani personally presented Francis, while Rufino and Matteo did all they could to ensure the heartiest welcome for him, by telling everyone how greatly they were indebted to him, and how gallantly he had behaved on several occasions.

Many of the young men he already knew as Matteo's friends, and by them he was received with the greatest cordiality; but his reception by the captain, and one or two of the other officers, was much more cool. The captain, whose name was Carlo Bottini, was a distant connection of the Mocenigo family, and was therefore already prejudiced against Francis. The coolness of the other officers was due to the fact that Francis, a foreigner and several years junior to themselves, had been placed in command over their heads.

CHAPTER 15

THE BATTLE OF POLA

The squadron, consisting of four galleys, sailed for Cyprus; where Pisani had just endeavoured, without success, to expel the Genoese from Famagosta. It was towards the end of August that they effected a junction with his fleet. Pisani received Francis with great warmth, and, in the presence of many officers, remarked that he was glad to see that the republic was, at last, appointing men for their merits, and not, as heretofore, allowing family connection and influence to be the chief passport to their favour.

For two months the fleet sailed among the islands of the Levant, and along the shores of Greece, Istria, and Dalmatia; hoping to find the Genoese fleet, but altogether without success. In November, when they were on the coast of Istria, winter set in with extraordinary severity, and the frost was intense. Pisani wrote to his government asking permission to bring the fleet into Venice until the spring. The seignory, however, refused his request, for they feared that, were it known that their fleet had come into port for the winter, the Genoese would take advantage of its absence to seize upon some of the islands belonging to Venice, and to induce the inhabitants of the cities of Istria and Dalmatia, always ready for revolt, to declare against her.

The first indications of the winter were more than verified. The cold was altogether extraordinary; and out of the nineteen galleys of Pisani, only six were fit to take the sea, with their full complement of men, when the spring of 1379 began. Many of the vessels had been disabled by storms. Numbers of the men had died, more had been sent home invalided, and it was only by transferring the men from the other vessels to the six in the best condition, that the crews of the latter were made up to their full strength.

As soon as the terrible frost broke, Pisani received a reinforcement of twelve ships from Venice, these being, for the most part, built and equipped at the cost of his personal friends, Polani having contributed two of the number. With the eighteen sail, Pisani put to sea to prosecute a fresh search for the Genoese admiral, Doria, and his fleet.

The Pluto was one of the six vessels which remained in good condition at the end of the winter, thanks, in no small degree, to the energy and care which Francis had bestowed in looking after the welfare of the crew. In the most bitter weather, he had himself landed with the boats, to see that firewood was cut and brought off in abundance, not only for the officers' cabins, but to warm that portion of the ship inhabited by the men. Knowing that Polani would not grudge any sum which might be required, he obtained from his agents ample supplies of warm clothing and bedding for the men, occupying himself incessantly for their welfare, while the captain and other officers passed their time in their warm and comfortable cabins. Francis induced Matteo, and several of his comrades, to brave the weather as he did, and to exert themselves for the benefit of the men; and the consequence was, that while but few of the other ships retained enough men to raise their sails in case of emergency, the strength of the crew of the Pluto was scarcely impaired at the termination of the winter.

The admiral, on paying a visit of inspection to the ship, was greatly struck with the contrast which the appearance of the crew afforded to that of the other galleys, and warmly complimented the commander on the condition of his men. The captain received the praise as if it was entirely due to himself, and said not a single word of the share which Francis had had in bringing it about. Matteo was most indignant at this injustice towards his friend, and managed that, through a relative serving in the admiral's own ship, a true report of the case should come to Pisani's ears.

Francis was in no way troubled at the captain's appropriation of the praise due to himself. There had not, from the time he sailed, been any cordiality between Francis and the other officers. These had been selected for the position solely from family influence, and none of them were acquainted with the working of a ship.

In those days, not only in Venice but in other countries, naval battles were fought by soldiers rather than sailors. Nobles and knights, with their retainers, embarked on board a ship for the purpose of fighting, and of fighting only, the management of the vessel being carried on entirely by sailors under their own officers. Thus, neither the commander of the force on board the galley, nor any of his officers, with the exception of Francis, knew anything whatever about the management of the ship, nor were capable of giving orders to the crew. Among the latter were some who had sailed with Francis in his first two voyages, and these gave so excellent a report of him to the rest, that they were from the first ready to obey his orders as promptly as those of their own sub-officer.

Francis concerned himself but little with the ill will that was shown him by the officers. He knew that it arose from jealousy, not

189

only of the promotion he, a foreigner and a junior in years, had received over them, but of the fact that he had already received the thanks of the republic for the services he had rendered, and stood high in the favour of the admiral, who never lost an opportunity of showing the interest he had in him. Had the hostility shown itself in any offensive degree Francis would at once have resented it; but Matteo, and some of those on board, who had been his comrades in the fencing rooms, had given such reports of his powers with his weapons, that even those most opposed to him thought it prudent to observe a demeanour of outward politeness towards him.

For three months the search for the Genoese fleet was ineffectual. A trip had been made along the coast of Apulia, and the fleet had returned to Pola with a large convoy of merchant ships loaded with grain, when on the 7th of May Doria appeared off the port, with twenty-five sail.

But Pisani was now by no means anxious to fight. Zeno was away with a portion of the fleet, and although he had received reinforcements, he numbered but twenty-one vessels, and a number of his men were laid up with sickness. The admiral, however, was not free to follow out the dictates of his own opinions. The Venetians had a mischievous habit, which was afterwards adopted by the French republic, of fettering their commanders by sea and land by appointing civilian commissioners, or, as they were termed in Venice, proveditors, who had power to overrule the nominal commander. When, therefore, Pisani assembled a council of war, and informed them of his reasons for wishing to remain on the defensive until the return of Zeno, he was overruled by the proveditors, who not only announced themselves unanimously in favour of battle, but sneered at Pisani's prudence as being the result of cowardice. Pisani in his indignation drew his sword, and would have attacked the proveditors on the spot, had he not been restrained by his captains.

However, the council decided upon instant battle, and Pisani was forced, by the rules of the service, at once to carry their decision into effect. Ascending the poop of his galley, he addressed in a loud voice the crews of the ships gathered around him.

"Remember, my brethren, that those who will now face you, are the same whom you vanquished with so much glory on the Roman shore. Do not let the name of Luciano Doria terrify you. It is not the names of commanders that will decide the conflict, but Venetian hearts and Venetian hands. Let him that loves Saint Mark follow me."

The men received the address with a shout, and as soon as the commanders had regained their galleys, the fleet moved out to attack the enemy. The fight was a furious one, each vessel singling out an opponent and engaging her hand to hand.

Carlo Bottini was killed early in the fight, and Francis succeeded to the command. His galley had grappled with one of the largest of the Genoese vessels, and a desperate conflict went on. Sometimes the Venetians gained a footing on the deck of the Genoese, sometimes they were driven back, and the Genoese in turn poured on board, but no decisive advantage was gained on either side after an hour's fighting. The Genoese crew was numerically much stronger than that of the Pluto, and although Francis, with Matteo and his comrades, headed their men and cheered them on, they could make no impression on the ranks of the enemy.

Suddenly, the Genoese threw off the grapnels that attached the two ships, and hoisting their sails, sheered off. Francis looked round to see the cause of this sudden manoeuvre, and perceived for the first time that the Genoese vessels were all in flight, with the Venetians pressing closely upon them. Sails were at once hoisted, and the Pluto joined in the chase.

But the flight was a feigned one, and it was only designed to throw the Venetian rank into confusion. After sailing for two miles, the Genoese suddenly turned, and fell upon their pursuers as they came up in straggling order.

The result was decisive. Many of the Venetian ships were captured before the rest came up to take part in the battle. Others were hemmed in by numerous foes. Pisani, after fighting until he saw that all was lost, made the signal for the ships to withdraw from the conflict, and he himself, with six galleys, succeeded in fighting his way through the enemy's fleet, and gained a refuge in the port of Parenzo.

All the rest were taken. From seven to eight hundred Venetians perished in the fight, two thousand four hundred were taken prisoners, twelve commanders were killed, and five captured. The Genoese losses were also severe, and Doria himself was among the slain, having been killed by a spear thrust by Donato Zeno, commander of one of the galleys, almost at the moment of victory.

The Pluto had defended herself, for a long time, against the attacks of three of the Genoese galleys, and had repeatedly endeavoured to force her way out of the throng, but the Genoese held her fast with their grapnels, and at last the greater part of her crew were driven down below, and Francis, seeing the uselessness of further resistance, ordered the little group, who were now completely pent in by the Genoese, to lower their weapons. All were more or less severely wounded, and were bleeding from sword cuts and thrusts.

"This is an evil day for Venice," Matteo said, as, having been deprived of their weapons, the prisoners were thrust below. "I heard the Genoese say that only six of our galleys have escaped, all the rest have been taken. We were the last ship to surrender, that's a comfort anyhow."

"Now, Matteo, before you do anything else, let me bind up your wounds. You are bleeding in two or three places."

"And you are bleeding from something like a dozen, Francisco, so you had better let me play the doctor first."

"The captain is always served last, so do as you are told, and strip off your doublet.

"Now, gentlemen," he said, turning to the other officers, "let each of us do what we can to dress the wounds of others. We can expect no care from the Genoese leeches, who will have their hands full, for a long time to come, with their own men. There are some among us who will soon bleed to death, unless their wounds are staunched. Let us, therefore, take the most serious cases first, and so on in rotation until all have been attended to."

It was fortunate for them that in the hold, in which they were confined, there were some casks of water; for, for hours the Genoese paid no attention whatever to their prisoners, and the wounded were beginning to suffer agonies of thirst, when the barrels were fortunately discovered. The head of one was knocked in, and some shallow tubs, used for serving the water to the crew, filled, and the men knelt down and drank by turns from these. Many were too enfeebled by their wounds to rise, and their thirst was assuaged by dipping articles of clothing into the water, and letting the fluid from these run into their mouths.

It was not until next morning that the prisoners were ordered to come on deck. Many had died during the night. Others were too weak to obey the summons. The names of the rest were taken, and not a little surprise was expressed, by the Genoese officers, at the extreme youth of the officer in command of the Pluto.

"I was only the second in command," Francis said in answer to their questions. "Carlo Bottini was in command of the ship, but he was killed at the commencement of the fight."

"But how is it that one so young came to be second? You must belong to some great family to have been thus pushed forward above men so much your senior.

"It was a wise choice nevertheless," the commander of one of the galleys which had been engaged with the Pluto said, "for it is but justice to own that no ship was better handled, or fought, in the Venetian fleet. They were engaged with us first, and for over an hour they fought us on fair terms, yielding no foot of ground, although we had far more men than they carried. I noticed this youth fighting always in the front line with the Venetians, and marvelled at the strength and dexterity with which he used his weapons, and afterwards, when there were three of us around him, he fought like a boar surrounded by hounds. I am sure he is a brave youth, and well worthy the position he held, to whatsoever he owed it."

"I belong to no noble family of Venice," Francis said. "My name is Francis Hammond, and my parents are English."

"You are not a mercenary, I trust?" the Genoese captain asked earnestly.

"I am not," Francis replied. "I am a citizen of Venice, and my name is inscribed in her books, as my comrades will vouch."

"Right glad am I that it is so," the Genoese said, "for Pietro Doria, who is now, by the death of his brother, in chief command, has ordered that every mercenary found among the prisoners shall today be slain."

"It is a brutal order," Francis said fearlessly, "whosoever may have given it! A mercenary taken in fair fight has as much right to be held for ransom or fair exchange as any other prisoner; and if your admiral thus breaks the laws of war, there is not a free lance, from one end of Italy to the other, but will take it up as a personal quarrel."

The Genoese frowned at the boldness with which Francis spoke, but at heart agreed in the sentiments he expressed; for among the Genoese officers, generally, there was a feeling that this brutal execution in cold blood was an impolitic, as well as a disgraceful deed.

The officers were now placed in the fore hold of the ship, the crew being confined in the after hold. Soon afterwards, they knew by the motion of the vessel that sail had been put on her.

"So we are on our way to a Genoese prison, Francisco," Matteo said. "We had a narrow escape of it before, but this time I suppose it is our fate."

"There is certainly no hope of rescue, Matteo. It is too early, as yet, to say whether there is any hope of escape. The prospect looked darker when I was in the hands of Ruggiero, but I managed to get away. Then I was alone and closely guarded, now we have in the ship well nigh two hundred friends; prisoners like ourselves, it is true, but still to be counted on. Then, too, the Genoese are no doubt so elated with their triumph, that they are hardly likely to keep a very vigilant guard over us. Altogether, I should say that the chances are in our favour. Were I sure that the Pluto is sailing alone, I should be very confident that we might retake her, but probably the fifteen captured ships are sailing in company, and would at once come to the aid of their comrades here, directly they saw any signs of a conflict going on, and we could hardly hope to recapture the ship without making some noise over it."

"I should think not," Matteo agreed.

"Then again, Matteo, even if we find it impossible to get at the crew, and with them to recapture the ship, some chance may occur by which you and I may manage to make our escape."

"If you say so, Francisco, I at once believe it. You got us all out of the scrape down at Girgenti. You got Polani's daughters out of a worse scrape when they were captives on San Nicolo; and got yourself out of the worst scrape of all when you escaped from the grip of Ruggiero Mocenigo. Therefore, when you say that there is a fair chance of escape out of this business, I look upon it as almost as good as done."

"It is a long way from that, Matteo," Francis laughed. "Still, I hope we may manage it somehow. I have the greatest horror of a Genoese prison, for it is notorious that they treat their prisoners of war shamefully, and I certainly do not mean to enter one, if there is the slightest chance of avoiding it. But for today, Matteo, I shall not even begin to think about it. In the first place, my head aches with the various thumps it has had; in the second, I feel weak from loss of blood; and in the third, my wounds smart most amazingly."

"So do mine," Matteo agreed. "In addition, I am hungry, for the bread they gave us this morning was not fit for dogs, although I had to eat it, as it was that or nothing."

"And now, Matteo, I shall try to get a few hours' sleep. I did not close my eyes last night, from the pain of my wounds, but I think I might manage to drop off now."

The motion of the vessel aided the effect of the bodily weakness that Francis was feeling, and in spite of the pain of his wounds he soon went off into a sound sleep. Once or twice he woke, but hearing no voices or movement, he supposed his companions were all asleep, and again went off, until a stream of light coming in from the opening of the hatchway thoroughly roused him. Matteo, who was lying by his side, also woke and stretched himself, and there was a general movement among the ten young men who were their comrades in misfortune.

"Here is your breakfast," a voice from above the hatchway said, and a basket containing bread and a bucket of water was lowered by ropes.

"Breakfast!" Matteo said. "Why, it is not two hours since we breakfasted last."

"I suspect it is twenty-two, Matteo. We have had a very long sleep, and I feel all the better of it. Now, let us divide the liberal breakfast our captors have given us; fortunately there is just enough light coming down from those scuttles to enable us to do so fairly."

There was a general laugh, from his comrades, at the cheerful way in which Francis spoke. Only one of them had been an officer on the Pluto. The rest were, like Matteo, volunteers of good families. There was a good deal of light-hearted jesting over their meal. When it was over, Francis said:

"Now let us hold a council of war."

"You are better off than Pisani was, anyhow," one of the young men said, "for you are not hampered with proveditors, and anything that your captaincy may suggest will, you may be sure, receive our assent."

"I am your captain no longer," Francis replied. "We are all prisoners now, and equal, and each one has a free voice and a free vote."

"Then I give my voice and vote at once, Francisco," Matteo said, "to the proposal that you remain our captain, and that we obey you, as cheerfully and willingly as we should if you were on the poop of the Pluto, instead of being in the hold. In the first place, at Carlo's death you became our captain by right, so long as we remain together; and in the second place you have more experience than all of us put together, and a very much better head than most of us, myself included.

"Therefore, comrades, I vote that Messer Francisco Hammond be still regarded as our captain, and obeyed as such."

There was a general chorus of assent, for the energy which Francis had displayed throughout the trying winter, and the manner in which he had led the crew during the desperate fighting, had won for him the regard and the respect of them all.

"Very well, then," Francis said. "If you wish it so I will remain your leader, but we will nevertheless hold our council of war. The question which I shall first present to your consideration is, which is the best way to set about retaking the Pluto?"

There was a burst of laughter among the young men. The matter of fact way in which Francis proposed, what seemed to them an impossibility, amused them immensely.

195

"I am quite in earnest," Francis went on, when the laughter had subsided. "If it is possibly to be done, I mean to retake the Pluto, and I have very little doubt that it is possible, if we set about it in the right way. In the first place, we may take it as absolutely certain that we very considerably outnumber the Genoese on board. They must have suffered in the battle almost as much as we did, and have had nearly as many killed and wounded. In the second place, if Doria intends to profit by his victory, he must have retained a fair amount of fighting men on board each of his galleys, and, weakened as his force was by the losses of the action, he can spare but a comparatively small force on board each of the fifteen captured galleys. I should think it probable that there are not more than fifty men in charge of the Pluto, and we number fully three times that force. The mere fact that they let down our food to us by ropes, instead of bringing it down, showed a consciousness of weakness."

"What you say is quite true," Paolo Parucchi, the other officer of the Pluto, said; "but they are fifty well-armed men, and we are a hundred and fifty without arms, and shut down in the hold, to which must be added the fact that we are cut off from our men, and our men from us. They are, as it were, without a head to plan, while we are without arms to strike."

A murmur of approval was heard among some of the young men.

"I do not suppose that there are no difficulties in our way," Francis said quietly; "or that we have only, next time the hatch is opened, to say to those above, 'Gentlemen of Genoa, we are more numerous than you are, and we therefore request you to change places with us immediately.' All I have asserted, so far, is that we are sufficiently strong to retake the ship, if we get the opportunity. What we have now to settle, is how that opportunity is to come about.

"To begin with, has anyone a dagger or knife which has escaped the eye of our searchers?"

No one replied.

"I was afraid that nothing had escaped the vigilance of those who appropriated our belongings. As, however, we have no weapons or tools, the next thing is to see what there is, in the hold, which can be turned to account. It is fortunate we are on board the Pluto, instead of being transferred to another ship, as we already know all about her. There are some iron bolts driven in along a beam at the farther end. They have been used, I suppose, at some time or other for hanging the carcasses of animals from. Let us see whether there is any chance of getting some of them out."

The iron pegs, however, were so firmly driven into the beam, that all their efforts failed to move them in the slightest.

"We will give that up for the present," Francis said, "and look round for something more available."

But with the exception of the water casks, the closest search failed to find anything in the hold.

"I do not know whether the iron hoops of a cask would be of any use," Matteo said.

"Certainly they would be of use, if we get them off, Matteo."

"There is no difficulty about that," one of the others said, examining the casks closely. "This is an empty one, and the hoops seem quite loose."

In a few minutes, four iron hoops were taken off the cask.

"After all," Matteo said, "they cannot be of much use. The iron is rust eaten, and they would break in our hands before going into any one."

"They would certainly be useless as daggers, Matteo, but I think that with care they will act as saws. Break off a length of about a foot.

"Now straighten it, and tear a piece off your doublet and wrap it round and round one end, so that you can hold it. Now just try it on the edge of a beam."

"It certainly cuts," Matteo announced after a trial, "but not very fast."

"So that it cuts at all, we may be very well content," Francis said cheerfully. "We have got a week, at least, to work in; and if the wind is not favourable, we may have a month. Let us therefore break the hoops up into pieces of the right length. We must use them carefully, for we may expect to have many breakages."

"What next, captain?"

"Our object will, of course, be to cut through into the main hold, which separates us from the crew. There we shall probably find plenty of weapons. But to use our saws, we must first find a hole in the bulkhead. First of all, then, let there be a strict search made for a knothole, or any other hole through the bulkhead."

It was too dark for eyes to be of much use, but hands were run all over the bulkhead. But no hole, however small, was discovered.

"It is clear, then," Francis said, "that the first thing to do is to cut out some of those iron bolts. Pick out those that are nearest to the lower side of the beam, say three of them. There are twelve of us. That will give four to each bolt, and we can relieve each other every few minutes. Remember, it is patience that is required, and not strength."

The work was at once begun. The young men had, by this time, fully entered into the spirit of the attempt. The quiet and businesslike way, in which their leader set about it, convinced them that he at least had a firm belief that the work was possible; and there was a hope, even if but a remote one, of avoiding the dreaded dungeons of Genoa.

The work was slow, and two or three of the strips of iron were at first broken, by the too great eagerness of their holders; but when it was found that, by using them lightly, the edges gradually cut their way into the wood, the work went on regularly. The Pluto had been hurriedly constructed, and any timbers that were available in the emergency were utilized. Consequently much soft wood, that at other times would never have been found in the state dockyards, was put into her. The beam at which they were working was of soft timber, and a fine dust fell steadily, as the rough iron was sawed backward and forward upon it.

Two cuts were made under each bolt, wide at the base and converging towards it. The saws were kept going the whole day, and although the progress was slow, it was fast enough to encourage them; and just as the light, that came through the scuttle, faded away; three of the young men hung their weight upon one of the bolts, and the wood beneath it, already almost severed, gave; and a suppressed cry of satisfaction announced that one bolt was free.

The pieces of iron were two feet long, and were intended for some other purpose, but had been driven in when, on loading the ship, some strong pegs on which to hang carcasses were required. They were driven about three inches into the beam, and could have been cut out with an ordinary saw in two or three minutes.

"Try the others," Francis said. "As many of you get hold of them as can put your hands on."

The effort was made, and the other two bolts were got out. They had been roughly sharpened at the end, and were fully an inch across.

"They do not make bad weapons," Matteo said.

"It is not as weapons that we want them, Matteo. They will be more useful to us than any weapons, except, indeed, a good axe. We shall want at least three more. Therefore, I propose that we continue our work at once. We will divide into watches now. It will be twelve hours before we get our allowance of bread again, therefore that will give three hours' work, and nine hours' sleep to each. They will be just setting the first watch on deck, and, as we shall hear them changed, it will give us a good idea how the time is passing."

"I am ready to work all night, myself," Matteo said. "At first I had not much faith in what we were doing; but now that we have got three of these irons out, I am ready to go on working until I drop."

"You will find, Matteo, that your arms will ache, so that you cannot hold them up, before the end of the three hours. Sawing like that, with your arms above your head, is most fatiguing; and even the short spells of work we have been having made my arms ache. However, each must do as much as he can in his three hours; and as we are working in the dark, we must work slowly and carefully, or we shall break our tools."

"Fortunately, we can get more hoops off now if we want them," Matteo said. "With these irons we can wrench them off the sound casks, if necessary."

"Yes; I did not think of that, Matteo. You see we are already getting a stock of tools. Another thing is, with the point of the irons we have got off, we can wrench the wood out as fast as we saw it, and the saws will not work so stiffly as they did before. But we must not do that till the morning, for any sound like the breaking of wood might be heard by the watch, when everything is quiet."

Although all worked their best, they made but slight progress in the dark, and each worker was forced to take frequent rests, for the fatigue of working with their arms above their heads was excessive. As soon, however, as the light began to steal down, and the movement above head told them that the crew were at work washing the decks, the points of the irons were used to wrench away the wood between the saw cuts; and the work then proceeded briskly, as they relieved each other every few minutes.

At last, to their intense satisfaction, three more irons were got out.

"If anyone had told me," one of the party said, "that a man's arms could hurt as much as mine do, from working a few hours, I should have disbelieved him."

There was a chorus of assent, for none were accustomed to hard manual labour, and the pain in their arms was excessive.

"Let us have half an hour's rest, Francis, before you issue your next orders. I shall want that, at least, before I feel that I have any power in my arms at all."

"We will have an hour's rest, Matteo, if you like. Before that time they will be sending us down our food, and after we have breakfasted we can set to work again."

"Breakfast!" one of the young men groaned. "I cannot call that black bread and water breakfast. When I think of the breakfasts I have eaten, when I think of the dishes I have refused to eat, because they were not cooked to perfection, I groan over my folly in those days, and my enormous stupidity in ever volunteering to come to sea."

"I should recommend you all," Francis said, "to spend the next hour in rubbing and squeezing the muscles of your neighbours' arms and shoulders. It is the best way for taking out stiffness, and Giuseppi used to give me relief that way, when I was stiff with fencing."

The idea was adopted; and while the rest were at work in the manner he suggested, Francis, taking one of the irons, went to the bulkhead. One by one he tried the planks, from the floor boards to the beams above.

"Well, captain, what is your report?" Matteo asked as he joined the rest.

"My report is a most favourable one," Francis said. "By great good luck, the planks are nailed from the other side against the beams both above and below."

"What difference does that make, Francisco?"

"All the difference in the world. Had they been nailed on this side, there would have been nothing for it but to carry out our original plan—that is, to make holes through the planks with these irons, large enough for the saws to go through, and then to saw the wood out from hole to hole. As it is, I believe that with five minutes' work we could wrench a plank away. We have only to push the points of the irons up, between the beams and the planks, and use them as levers. The nails will be strong, indeed, if those irons, with two of us at each, would not wrench them out."

The young men all leapt to their feet, pains and aches quite forgotten in the excitement of this unexpected news, and six of them seized hold of the irons.

"Gently!" Francis said. "You must remember, there may be people going down there at present, getting up stores. Before we venture to disturb a plank, we must make the hole sufficiently large for us to spy through. This will be a very easy affair, in comparison with making a hole large enough for a saw to go through. Still, you will find it will take some time. However, we had better wait, as we agreed, till we have had our food."

CHAPTER 16

THE RECAPTURE OF THE PLUTO

As soon as the hatch had been removed, and the bread and water lowered down, and they heard heavy weights again laid on the hatch, two of the party took one of the irons and began to bore a hole, while the others proceeded to eat their food. Several times, the workers had to be relieved. The iron penetrated comparatively easily for a short distance, but beyond that the difficulty greatly increased; and it was fully four hours before one of the workers, applying his eye to the hole, said that he could see a gleam of light through.

In another quarter of an hour, the orifice was sufficiently enlarged to enable a view to be obtained of the central hold. It was comparatively light there, for the hatch was off, and they could see two men at work, opening a cask for some stores that were required.

"We must wait till it gets dark now," Francis said. "I do not think that we shall make much noise, for the nails will be likely to draw quietly; but we had better choose the time between nightfall and the hour for the crew to turn in, as there will be a trampling of feet on deck, and talking and singing, which would prevent any slight noise we might make, being heard."

"The difficulty will be to force the ends of the iron down, between the beams and the planks, so as to give us a purchase," Matteo said.

"I think we shall be able to manage that," Francis replied. "The beams are put in in the rough, and if we hunt carefully, I think we shall find a plank where we can get the irons in far enough, between it and the beam, to give us a hold."

After a careful examination, they fixed upon a plank to operate upon, and, leaving one of the irons there, so that they could find it in the dark, they lay down to sleep, or sat talking until it was dark. Before this, a glance, through the peephole, showed them that the hatch had been placed over the hatchway of the next hold, so that there was little fear of anyone coming down, unless something special was required.

"Now I think we can begin," Francis said, at last. "Do you, Paolo Parucchi, take one of the irons, I will take another, Matteo a third. We cannot possibly work more than three at the foot of a plank, though perhaps, when we have fixed them and put on the strain, two or three more hands may get at the irons; but first we will try with three, and, unless the nails have got a wonderfully firm hold, we shall certainly be able to draw them."

It took some time to fix the irons, to the best advantage, between the planks and the beam.

"Are you both ready?" Francis asked at last. "Then pull."

As Francis had anticipated, the levers did their work, and the nails yielded a little.

"It has sprung half an inch," Francis said, feeling. "Now you keep your irons as they are, while I thrust mine down farther. I have got a fresh hold. Do you shift yours."

Again the effort was made, and this time the nails drew fully two inches. Another effort, and the plank was completely free at the lower end.

"Now do you push against it as hard as you can," Francis said, "while I get my iron in between it and the beam above."

The upper nails yielded even more easily than those below.

"No farther," Francis said, when they had fairly started them, "or the plank will be falling with a crash. We must push from the bottom now, until it gives sufficiently far for you to get an iron down each side, to prevent its closing again."

"Now," he said, "push the irons higher up. That is right. Now I will loosen a bit farther at the top, and then you will be able to get your hands in at the bottom to steady it, and prevent its falling when the nails are quite drawn."

Another effort, and the plank was free, and, being drawn in, was laid down. The delight of those who were standing in the dark, and could only judge how matters were going on from Francis's low spoken orders, was extreme.

"Can we get through?"

"No," Francis replied. "It will be necessary to remove another plank first, but perhaps one of the slighter among you might manage to squeeze through, and hold the plank at the back. We shall be able to work with more freedom, if we know that there is no danger of its falling."

In a few minutes, the second plank was laid beside the first.

"What is to be done next?" Matteo asked.

"We must establish a communication with the sailors. I will take a working party of four. Paolo Parucchi, with four others, will relieve me. You, Matteo, will with the rest take the last spell. When we have entered the next compartment, we will put up the planks again, and press the nails in tightly enough to prevent their falling. Should, by some chance, anyone descend into the hold while we are working, we shall be hidden from their view. At the other end there are a number of sacks piled up, and we shall be working behind them."

Francis, and the men he had chosen, made their way to the pile of arms they had observed through their peephole, moving with great precaution, so as to avoid falling over anything. Here, with some trouble, they succeeded in finding a dagger among the heap, and they then felt their way on, until they reached the pile of sacks. These were packed to within a foot of the deck beams, and there was but just room for them to crawl in at the top.

"Whatever you do, do not bump against the beams," Francis said. "Any noise of that sort, from below, would at once excite attention. Now do you be quiet, while I find a spot to begin upon."

Commencing at a junction of two planks, Francis began, with the dagger, to cut a hole of some three or four inches across, but tapering rapidly as it went in. After waiting for some ten minutes, he touched the man lying next to him, placed his hand on the hole he had begun, and then moved aside to allow him to continue the work.

In an hour a hole was made in a two inch plank, and this was soon enlarged until it was an inch in diameter. Lying along the side of the bulkhead, so as to get his ear to the hole, Francis listened, but could hear no sound within. Then he put his mouth to the orifice and asked:

"Are you all asleep there?"

Then he listened again. Some of the men were speaking, and asking each other who it was that had suddenly spoken. No one replied; and some of them gave vent to angry threats, against whoever it might be who had just disturbed them from going off to sleep.

Directly the voices ceased again, Francis said:

"Let us have silence in there. Where is Rinaldo, the boatswain?"

"I am here," a voice replied; "but who is speaking? It sounds like the voice of Messer Hammond."

"It is my voice, Rinaldo. We have worked through from the hold at the other end of the ship, having removed some of the planks of the bulkhead. Now it is for you to do the same. We will pass you some daggers through, when we have made this hole a bit larger. You must choose one of the planks in the corner, as this will be less likely to be observed."

"They will not observe us, Messer Hammond. They never come down here at all, but pass our food down in buckets."

"Nevertheless, begin at the plank next to the side," Francis said. "Possibly someone may come down before you have finished.

You will have to remove two planks to get through. I will pass a javelin through. You can set to work with it, and bore holes through the plank close to the floor; and then, with the dagger, cut away the wood between them. When you have done them, set to at the top, close to the beams, and cut the two planks through there. There are sacks of grain piled up against them on this side, so that there is no fear of your being observed from here. The work must be carried on perfectly noiselessly, the men relieving each other every few minutes.

"When the planks are cut through, replace them in their former positions, and wedge some small pieces of wood in, so that there shall be no chance of their falling. You ought to finish the work by tomorrow. When you have done it, take no farther step until you get orders from me. It would not do to rise now, for we may be surrounded by other ships, and if we overpowered the crew, we should at once be attacked and recaptured by them. You will, therefore, remain quiet until you have orders, whether it be one day or ten. All the arms they have taken from us are lying piled here, and when the time comes, we shall have no difficulty in overpowering the Genoese, and shall, I hope, bring the Pluto safely to anchor in the port of Venice before long."

There was a murmur of delight among the sailors, pent up in their close quarters. Francis listened a moment, and heard one of the men say:

"What did I tell you? Didn't I tell you that Messer Hammond got us all out of a scrape before, when our ship was captured by the Genoese, and that I would be bound he would do the same again, if he had but the shadow of a chance."

"You did, Pietro, and you have turned out right. That is the sort of fellow to have for a captain. He is not like one of those dainty young nobles, who don't know one rope's end from another, and who turn up their noses at the thought of dirtying their hands. See how he looked after us through the winter. I wish we could give a cheer for him, but that would never do. But when we are out of this, I will give him the loudest shout I ever gave yet.

"Now then, Rinaldo, let us set to work without a moment's delay. There's a chance we aren't going to rot in the dungeons of Genoa, after all."

Convinced that the work would be carried on in accordance with his orders, Francis withdrew his ear from the hole, and, crawling over the sacks again, made his way to the pile of arms, felt about until he found two javelins, and taking these back, passed them one after the other through the hole.

"We have done our share now," he said to his comrades.

"Paolo and his party will find it a comparatively easy task to enlarge the hole sufficiently to pass the daggers through."

The party returned to the other end of the hold, removed the planks, and joined their friends. The next watch had arranged to lie down close to the planks, so that they could be aroused without waking the others.

They were soon on their feet. Francis explained to Parucchi the progress they had made, and the orders that had been given to the sailors as to what they were to do.

"When the hole is large enough, pass these five daggers in to the crew, and then come back again. I will guide you to the spot, and on my return will pick out half a dozen more daggers, in case we want them for further work."

When daylight made its way into the hold, Matteo and his watch woke, and were astonished to find that all their comrades were quietly asleep, and that they had not been awakened. Matteo could not restrain his curiosity, but woke Francis:

"Has anything gone wrong, Francis? It is daylight, and Parucchi's party, as well as yours, are all asleep, while we have not been roused!"

"Everything is going on well, Matteo, and we did not wake you, because there was nothing for you to do. We have already passed in knives and javelins to the sailors, and they are at work cutting through two planks in their bulkhead; after which we shall be able to meet in the next hold, arm ourselves, and fall upon the Genoese when the opportunity offers."

"That is excellent indeed, Francis; but I wish you had let us do our share of the work."

"It did not take us more than two hours, Matteo, to make a hole big enough to pass the javelins through, and I should say Parucchi's party enlarged it sufficiently to hand in the daggers in another hour; so you see, it would have been useless to have aroused you, and the less movement we make after they get quiet at night, the better."

"And how long will the sailors be cutting it through, do you think?"

"I should say they would be ready by this time, Matteo, but certainly they will be finished some time today."

"Then we shall soon be free!" Matteo exclaimed joyfully.

"That will depend, Matteo. We must wait till there is a good opportunity, so that we can recapture the ship without an alarm being given to the other vessels, which are no doubt sailing in company with us. And now, if you have nothing to say, I will go off to sleep again, for there is time for another hour or two. I feel as if I had not quite finished my night's rest, and the days pass so slowly here that it is as well for us to sleep when we feel the least inclination.

"By the way, Matteo, put something into that peephole we made. It is possible that they might see the light through it, and come to examine what it is. It is better to run no risk."

That day the captives were far more restless than they had been since they were taken prisoners. At first there had been a feeling of depression, too great to admit even of conversation with each other. The defeat of their fleet, the danger that threatened Venice, and the prospect of imprisonment in the gloomy dungeons of Genoa, combined to depress them on the first day of their imprisonment. On the second, their success in getting out the bolts had cheered them, and they had something to look forward to and talk about; but still, few of them thought that there was any real prospect of their obtaining their freedom. Now, however, that success seemed to lie ready to hand; now that they could, that very evening, remove the sacks, effect a junction with their crew, arm themselves with the weapons lying in sight, and rush up and overpower the Genoese; it seemed hard to remain longer in confinement. Several of them urged Francis to make the attempt that night, but he refused.

"You reckon only on the foe you see," he said. "The danger lies not from them, but from the foes we cannot see. We must wait for an opportunity."

"But no opportunity may occur," one of them urged.

"That is quite possible," Francis agreed; "but should no special opportunity occur, we shall be none the worse for having waited, for it will always be as open to us to make the attempt as it is tonight. It might succeed—possibly we could overpower the guard on deck before they could give the alarm—but the risk is too great to be run, until we are certain that no other way is open to us. In the daylight the hatch is open; but even could we free our comrades, and unite for a rush, unobserved—which we could hardly hope to do—we should find the whole of the Genoese on deck, and could not possibly overpower them before they had time to give the alarm to other vessels. At night, when we can unite, we cannot gain the deck, for the hatch is not only closed, but would almost certainly be fastened, so that men should not get down to pilfer among the stores."

"But if we cannot attack in the daytime, Messer Hammond, without giving the alarm; and cannot attack at all at night, what are we to do?"

"That is the next point to be seen to," Francis replied. "We must cut, either from this hold or from the other, a way up to the deck above. It may take us some days to do this, but that matters little. We have plenty of time for the work before reaching Genoa. The difficulty is not in the work itself, but in doing it unobserved."

"That is difficult, indeed," Matteo said, "seeing that the Genoese sailors are quartered in the forecastle above the forehold, while the officers will be in the cabins in the poop over us."

"That is so, Matteo, and for that reason, it is clear that it is we, not the sailors, who must cut through the planks above. There are no divisions in the forecastle, and it will be, therefore, absolutely impossible to cut through into it, without being perceived long before a hole is made of a sufficient size to enable us to get out. Here we may succeed better, for fortunately we know the exact plan of the cabins above us, and can choose a spot where we should not be likely to be noticed."

"That is so," Matteo agreed, "and as they will not have as many officers as we had—that is, including the volunteers—some of the cabins will not be occupied. Perhaps, by listening to the footsteps above, we might find out which are vacant."

"I thought of that, Matteo, but I doubt whether it would be well to rely upon that. Many on board ship wear soft shoes, which make but little noise, and it would be fatal to us were we to make a mistake. After thinking it over, I have decided that we had best try to cut a way up into the captain's cabin."

"But that is sure to be occupied, Messer Hammond," Parucchi said.

"Yes, it will be certainly be occupied; but it affords a good opportunity of success. As you know, Parucchi, Carlo Bottini had been a long time at Constantinople and the Eastern ports, and had a somewhat luxurious taste. Do you not remember that, against the stern windows, he had caused to be erected a low wide seat running across the cabin? This he called a divan, and spent no small proportion of his time lolling upon it. If I am right, its height was from ten inches to a foot above the deck, and it was fully four feet wide. It would therefore be quite possible to cut through the two planks at the back, without its being observed by anyone in the cabin."

There was a chorus of assent.

"Of course we must work most cautiously," Francis went on. "The wood must be cut out with clean cuts with the daggers. There must be no sawing or scraping. The beams are two feet apart, and we must cut through two planks close to them. In that way there will be no nails to remove. Of course, we shall not cut quite through until the time arrives for us to make the attempt, but just leave enough to hold the planks together. Half an hour's work will get through that, for if we were to cut through it at once, not only would there be risk of the hole being discovered by anyone sweeping the cabin, but we should be obliged to remain absolutely silent, or we should be heard immediately."

"We can begin at once, can we not?" Matteo asked. "Anything is better than sitting quietly here."

"Certainly, Matteo, if you wish. Two can work at once, one on each line. Choose the two sharpest edged of the daggers, and be sure to cut clean, and not to make a scraping noise or to try to break out pieces of wood. The work must be done in absolute quiet. Indeed, however careful you are, it is possible that some slight sound may be heard above, but, if noticed, it will probably be taken for the rats."

Matteo and another of the young men at once fell to work; but it was not until the evening of the following day that cuts were made as deep as was considered prudent. The depth of wood remaining was tested by thrusting the point of a dagger through, and it was decided that little more than a quarter of an inch remained.

Upon the following day the ship anchored, and remained for two days in some port. Provisions were brought on board and carried down into the hold, and the prisoners had no doubt that they were in harbour on the coast of either Sicily, or the south of Italy. They had not set sail many hours, when the motion of the ship told them that the wind was getting up, and by night the vessel was rolling heavily, the noise made by the dashing of the water against her planks being so great, that those below could scarcely hear each other speak. Their spirits had risen with the increase of the motion, for the opportunity for which they had been waiting was now at hand. In a gale the vessels would keep well apart from each other, to prevent the danger of a collision, and any outcry would be drowned by the noise of the wind and water.

Each night Francis had paid a visit to the sailors forward, to enjoin patience until he should give them the order for making the attempt. They had long since cut through the planks, which were only retained in their place by the pressure of the sacks behind them. He had bade them be in readiness on the first occasion on which rough weather might set in, and knew that they would now be expecting the signal.

As soon, then, as it became dark, and the hatch over the middle hold was closed; the planks were removed, and Francis and his party set to work shifting the sacks, in the corner where the sailors had cut the planks. Each sack was taken up, and placed against the pile further on, without the slightest noise, until at last

208

all were removed that stood in the way of the planks being taken down. These were carried out into the hold.

Francis entered the gap. The sailors had already been informed that the occasion had come, and that they were to remain perfectly quiet until bidden to move.

"All is prepared," he said as he entered. "Rinaldo, do you see that the men come out one by one. As each comes out a weapon will be placed in his hands, and he will be then led to the starboard side of the hold, which is free from encumbrance, and will there stand until he receives orders to move further. Remember that not the slightest noise must be made, for if any stumbled and fell, and the noise were heard above, it might be thought that some of the stores had shifted from their places, and men would be sent below to secure them. The alarm would be given, and a light or other signal shown the other ships, before we could overpower all resistance. After the men are all ranged up as I have directed, they will have to remain there for some little time, while we complete our arrangements."

As soon as the sailors were all armed, and ready for action, Francis entered the after hold, where Matteo and another had been engaged in cutting the planks quite through. They had just completed the task when he reached them, and had quietly removed the two pieces of plank. Francis had already given his orders to his companions, and each knew the order in which they were to ascend.

A dim light streamed down from the hole. Two of his comrades lifted Francis so that his head was above the level of the hole, and he was enabled to see into the cabin. So far as he could tell, it was untenanted, but it was possible that the commander might be on the divan above him. This was not, however, likely, as in the gale that was now blowing he would probably be on deck, directing the working of the ship.

Francis now gave the signal, and the others raised him still further, until he was able to get his weight upon the deck above, and he then crawled along underneath the divan, and lay there quiet until Parucchi and Matteo had both reached the deck. Then he gave the word, and all three rolled out and leaped to their feet, with their daggers in their hands, in readiness to fall upon the captain should he be on the divan.

As they had hoped and expected, the cabin was untenanted. The other volunteers now joined them, the last giving the word to Rinaldo, who soon passed up, followed by the crew, until the cabin was as full as it could contain. There were now assembled some fifty men, closely packed together.

"That is ample," Francis said, "as they will be unarmed and

unprepared. We can issue out singly until the alarm is given, and then those that remain must rush out in a body. Simply knock them down with the hilts of your swords. There is no occasion to shed blood, unless in the case of armed resistance; but remember they will have their knives in their girdles, and do not let anyone take you by surprise."

Opening the door, Francis walked along a passage, and then through an outer door into the waist of the ship. The wind was blowing fiercely, but the gale was not so violent as it had appeared to them when confined below. The night was dark, but after a week's confinement below, his eyes were able easily to make out almost every object on deck. There were but few sailors in the waist. The officers would be on the poop, and such of the crew as were not required on duty in the forecastle. Man after man joined him, until some thirty were gathered near the bulwarks. An officer on the poop caught sight of them by the light of the lantern, which was suspended there as a signal to the other vessels.

"What are all you men doing down there?" he challenged. "There is no occasion for you to keep on deck until you are summoned."

"Do you move forward with the men here, Parucchi. Knock down the fellows on deck, and rush into the forecastle and overpower them there, before they can get up their arms. I will summon the rest in a body, and we will overpower the officers."

He ran back to the cabin door, and bade the men follow him. As they poured out there was a scuffle on the deck forward, and the officer shouted out again:

"What is going on there? What does all this mean?"

Francis sprang up the ladder to the poop, followed by his men, and before the officer standing there understood the meaning of this sudden rush of men, or had time to draw his sword, he was knocked down. The captain and three other officers, who were standing by the helm, drew their swords and rushed forward, thinking there was a mutiny among their crew; but Francis shouted out:

"Throw down your weapons, all of you. We have retaken the ship, and resistance is useless, and will only cost you your lives."

The officers stood stupefied with astonishment; and then, seeing that fully twenty armed men were opposed to them, they threw down their swords. Francis ordered four of the sailors to conduct them to the captain's cabin, and remain in guard over them; then with the rest he hurried forward to assist Parucchi's party.

But the work was already done. The Genoese, taken completely by surprise, had at once surrendered, as the armed party

210

rushed in the forecastle, and the ship was already theirs. As soon as the prisoners were secured, the after hatch was thrown off, and those whose turn to crawl up through the hole had not yet arrived came up on deck.

"Rinaldo," Francis said, as soon as the crew had fallen into their places, "send a man aloft, and let him suddenly knock out the light in the lantern."

"But we can lower it down, captain, from the deck."

"Of course we can, Rinaldo, but I don't want it lowered down, I want it put suddenly out."

Rinaldo at once sent a man up, and a minute later the light suddenly disappeared.

"If we were seen to lower it down," Francis said to Matteo, "the suspicions of those who noticed it would be at once aroused, for the only motive for doing so would be concealment; whereas now, if it is missed, it will be supposed that the wind has blown it out. Now we have only to lower our sails, and we can drop unobserved out of the fleet."

"There are sixteen lights, I have just been counting them," Matteo said.

"These are probably the fourteen galleys captured with us, and two galleys as guards, in case, on their way, they should fall in with any of our ships.

"Parucchi, will you at once muster the men, and see that all are armed and in readiness for fighting?

"Matteo, do you and some of your friends assist the lieutenant."

In a few minutes, Parucchi reported that the men were all ready for action.

"Rinaldo, brail up the sails, so that we may drop into the rear of the squadron. Watch the lights of the vessels behind, and steer so that they shall pass us as widely as possible."

This was the order the men were expecting to receive, but they were surprised when, just as the last light was abreast of them, Francis gave the order for the brails to be loosed again.

"Signor Parucchi, do you tell off fifty men. I am going to lay the ship alongside that vessel, and recapture her. They will not see us until we are close on board, and will suppose it is an accident when we run alongside. No doubt they, like the Pluto, have only a complement of fifty men, and we shall overpower them before they are prepared to offer any resistance.

"No doubt they have prisoners below. Immediately we have recaptured her, I shall return on board with the rest, leaving you with your fifty men in charge of her. As soon as you have secured the Genoese, free any prisoners there may be in the hold. I shall keep close to you, and you can hear me, and tell me how many there are."

The Pluto was now edged away, till she was close to the other ship. The crew, exulting in having turned the tables on the Genoese, and at the prospect of recovering another of the lost galleys, clustered in the waist, grasping their arms. The ship was not perceived until she was within her own length of the other. Then there was a sudden hail:

"Where are you coming to? Keep away, or you will be into us. Why don't you show your light?"

Francis shouted back some indistinct answer. Rinaldo pushed down the helm, and a minute later the Pluto ran alongside the other vessel. Half a dozen hands, told off for the work, sprang into her rigging, and lashed the vessels together; while Francis, followed by the crew, climbed the bulwarks and sprang on to the deck of the enemy.

Scarce a blow was struck. The Genoese, astonished at this sudden apparition of armed men on their deck, and being entirely unarmed and unprepared, either ran down below or shouted they surrendered, and in two minutes the Venetians were masters of the vessel.

"Back to the Pluto," Francis shouted. "The vessels will tear their sides out!"

Almost as suddenly as they had invaded the decks of the galley, the Venetians regained their own vessel, leaving the lieutenant with his fifty men on board the prize. The lashings were cut, the Pluto's helm put up, and she sheered away from her prize. Her bulwarks were broken and splintered where she had ground against the other vessel in the sea, and Rinaldo soon reported that some of the seams had opened, and the water was coming in.

"Set the carpenter and some of the hands to work, to caulk the seams as well as they can from the inside, and set a gang to work at the pumps at once. It is unfortunate that it is blowing so hard. If the wind had gone down instead of rising, we would have recaptured the whole fleet, one by one."

The Pluto was kept within a short distance of the captured vessel, and Parucchi presently shouted out that he had freed two hundred prisoners.

"Arm them at once!" Francis shouted back. "Extinguish your light, and board the vessel whose light you see on your starboard bow. I will take the one to port. When you have captured her, lower the sails of both vessels. I will do the same. You will keep a little head sail set, so as to keep them before the wind; but do not show more than you can help. I wish the rest of the fleet to outrun us, as soon as possible."

The Pluto sheered off from the prize, and directed her course towards the vessel nearest to her, which she captured as easily as she had done the preceding. But this time, not only were her bulwarks stove in, but the chain plates were carried away; and the mainmast, no longer supported by its shrouds, fell over the side with a crash.

This vessel had but a hundred prisoners on board. They were wild with astonishment and delight, when they found that their vessel had been recaptured. Francis told them to keep by him through the night, as possibly he might need their assistance.

For some hours the gale increased. The Pluto lay head to it, her mast serving as a floating anchor. As soon as the lights of the Genoese squadron disappeared in the distance, Francis hoisted a lantern on his mainmast, as a signal to the other vessels to keep near him.

As soon as day broke, the galley they had last recaptured was seen, half a mile away, while the two others could be made out some six miles to leeward. The gale died out soon after daybreak, and Francis at once set his crew to work to get the mast on board, and to ship it by its stump.

It was a difficult undertaking, for the vessel was rolling heavily. It was first got alongside, two ropes were passed over it, and it was parbuckled on board. Shears were made of two spars, and the end was placed against the stump, which projected six feet above the deck. By the aid of the shears, it was hoisted erect and lashed to the stump, wedges were driven in to tighten the lashings, and it was then firmly stayed; and by the afternoon it was in readiness for sail to be hoisted again.

By this time Parucchi, with the vessel he had captured, was alongside. The Lion of Saint Mark was hoisted to the mainmast of the Pluto, and three similar banners were run up by the other vessels, the crews shouting and cheering with wild enthusiasm.

CHAPTER 17

AN UNGRATEFUL REPUBLIC

"It is glorious, Francis," Matteo said, "to think that we should have recaptured four of our ships!"

"It is very good, as far as it goes," Francis replied, "but it might have been a great deal better. If it hadn't been for the storm, we might have picked them all up one by one. Each vessel we took, the stronger we became, and I had calculated upon our capturing the greater number. But in such a sea, I don't think we could possibly capture more than we did."

"I should think not," Matteo said. "I had never dreamt of doing more than recovering the Pluto, and when you first talked about that, it seemed almost like madness. I don't think one of us had the slightest belief in the possibility of the thing, when you first proposed it."

"I thought it was to be managed somehow," Francis said. "It would have been a shame, indeed, if a hundred and fifty men were to be kept prisoners for a fortnight, or three weeks, by a third of their number."

"Well, certainly no one would have thought of making the attempt, if you had not proposed it, Francis. I believe, even if you were to propose our sailing north, and capturing Genoa, there is not a man on board but would follow you willingly, with the firm conviction that you would succeed."

"In that case, Matteo," Francis said, laughing, "it is very lucky for you that I am not at all out of my mind. Signal now to Parucchi to lower his boats, and come on board with our men. We may fall in yet with another Genoese squadron, and may as well have our full complement on board, especially as Parucchi has found two hundred men already on board the vessel we captured."

Parucchi and his men soon transferred themselves to the Pluto, and the four vessels hoisted their sails, and made for the south. They had learned, from their captives, that the squadron had already passed through the Straits of Messina, and that it was at Messina they had stopped and taken in provision two days before. Indeed, when, late in the afternoon, the sky cleared and the sun shone out, they saw the mountains of Calabria on their left.

Learning, from the captives, that no Genoese vessels had been seen in the straits as they passed through, Francis did not hesitate to order the course to be shaped for the straits, instead of sailing round Sicily, as he would have done had there been any chance of falling in with a hostile squadron, in passing between the islands and the mainland.

"I should like to have seen the face of the commander of the Genoese squadron this morning," Matteo said, "when he discovered that four of his vessels were missing. He can hardly have supposed that they were lost, for although the wind was strong, it blew nearly dead aft, and there was nothing of a gale to endanger well-handled ships. I almost wonder that he did not send back the two fully manned galleys he had with him, to search for us."

"Perhaps he did," Francis said; "but he would have been a hundred miles further north by daybreak, and it would have taken him a couple of days to get back to where we were lying."

No hostile sail was seen during the voyage back to Venice. Francis remained in command of the little squadron, for the captains, and many of the superior officers, had been transferred to the galley of the officer in command of the squadron, and Francis happened to be the only second officer on board any of the four ships.

Great care was observed when they approached Venice, as, for aught they knew, Doria's squadron might be blockading the port. The Genoese fleet, however, was still cruising on the coast of Dalmatia, capturing port after port of the Venetian possessions there.

The four vessels passed through the channel of the Lido with their colours flying. When first observed from the watchtower of Venice, they were supposed to form part of the squadron of Zeno, but as soon as they cast anchor, and the news spread that they were four of Pisani's galleys, which had been recaptured from the Genoese, the delight of the population was immense.

The ships were speedily surrounded by a fleet of boats, containing relatives and friends of those taken prisoners at the battle of Polo, and the decks were crowded with persons inquiring after their friends, or embracing with delight those whom they had, an hour before, believed to be either dead or immured in the dungeons of Genoa.

One of the first to appear was Polani, who had early received the news by a swift boat from one of his ships in the port, that the Pluto was one of the vessels entering the harbour.

"What miracle is this, Francis?" he asked, as he warmly embraced his young friend.

"Not a miracle at all, Messer Polani. The Genoese fancied that a guard of fifty men was amply sufficient to keep a hundred and fifty Venetians captives, and we taught them their mistake."

"It wasn't we," Matteo put in, as he shook hands with his kinsman. "We had no more idea of escaping than we had of flying. The whole thing was entirely the work of Francisco here."

"I might have been sure the Genoese would not keep you long, Francisco," Polani said; "and the girls and I might have spared ourselves the pain of fretting for you. But how did it all come about?"

"If you will take me to the Piazza in your gondola, I will tell you all about on the way," Francis replied. "For, absurd as it seems, I am the senior officer of the squadron, and must, I suppose, report to the council what has happened."

"Take me, too, kinsman," Matteo said. "I know Francisco so well that I am quite sure that, of himself, he will never tell the facts of this affair, and will simply say that we broke out, avoiding all mention of his share in it, and how it was that under his orders we recaptured the other ships."

"I think that a very good plan, Matteo; so do you come with us, and you shall tell me all about it, instead of my hearing it from Francis, and I will take care the council know the truth of the matter."

"The admiral got safely back, I hope?" Francis asked. "We saw that his galley, with five others, broke through the Genoese fleet and got safely away, but of course, we knew not whether the brave admiral was himself hurt."

"He arrived here safely," Polani replied; "but knowing the Venetians as you do, you will be scarcely surprised to hear that he has been sentenced to six months' imprisonment, for losing the battle."

"But that is shameful," Francis exclaimed indignantly. "I heard from our captain, who was present at the council, that Pisani was opposed to fighting, and that he was only overruled by the proveditors. It is shameful. I will go on shore and make my report, and then I will come back to you, for I swear that not another blow will I strike on behalf of the republic, as long as Pisani is in prison."

"It is a bad business, my lad," Polani said; "but you know that Pisani, popular as he is with the people, has few friends among the nobles. They are jealous of his fame and popularity, and, to say the truth, he has often irritated them, by his bluntness and his disregard for their opinion and rank. Consequently, they seized upon his defeat as an occasion for accusing him, and it was even a question in the council of taking his life, and he may be considered fortunate in getting off with the sentence of six months' imprisonment.

"I do not think he will have to remain very long in confinement. We may expect the Genoese fleet here in a few days, for the Paduan army is already moving, as we heard last night. No doubt it is going to cooperate with the fleet. Once the danger presses, the populace will demand Pisani's release. There have already been demonstrations, and shouts of 'Viva Pisani!' have been raised in the Piazza.

"At any rate, Francis, let me advise you, most strongly, not to suffer any expression of your feelings concerning him to escape you before the council. I need scarcely say it would do no good to the admiral, and would set the whole of his enemies against you. It is no affair of yours, if the governors of Venice behave ungratefully to one who deserves well at their hands, and you have made more than enough enemies by mingling in my affairs, without drawing upon yourself more foes, by your championship of Pisani."

"I will, of course, follow your counsel," Francis said; "but I will certainly serve the state no more, until Pisani is freed."

Several of the councillors were already assembled, on hearing the strange news that four of the ships, which had been captured by the Genoese, had entered port. Francis, on announcing his errand, was at once shown in to them. Polani accompanied him, explaining his presence to the council by saying:

"I have ventured, signors, to accompany my young friend here, in order that I may give you a much further detail of the affair in which he has been engaged, than you are likely to hear from his own lips. I have just come on shore from his ship, the Pluto, and have heard the story from my kinsman, Matteo Giustiniani."

"We have surely seen this young gentleman before, Messer Polani," one of the council said.

"You have, signor," Polani replied. "You may remember that he greatly distinguished himself at the fight of Antium, was sent home by the admiral with his despatches, and had the honour of receiving, from you, the thanks of the republic and the gift of citizenship."

"I remember now," the councillor said; and a murmur of assent from the others showed that they also recalled the circumstance. "Is he again the bearer of despatches, from the officer in command of the little squadron which, as it seems, has just, by some miracle, entered the port? And how is it that the officer did not present himself in person before us?"

217

"The officer has presented himself," Polani said. "Messer Hammond is in command of the four ships which have just arrived. Not only is he in command by virtue of senior rank, but it is to him that their recapture from the Genoese is entirely due."

There was a murmur of incredulity from the circle of councillors, but Polani went on quietly.

"It may seem well nigh impossible to you, signors, but what I say is strictly true. If Messer Hammond will first relate to you the broad facts of the recapture of the ships, I will furnish you with such details as he may omit."

Francis then briefly related the events which had led to the capture of the four galleys. He explained that by the death of the captain he, as second officer, succeeded to the command of the Pluto, and that afterwards being captured by the Genoese, Signor Parucchi, the sole other surviving officer, and ten gentlemen belonging to noble families and serving as volunteers on board the Pluto, were confined in one hold of that ship on her voyage as a prize to Genoa, the crew being shut up in the other; that by working at night they had effected a junction with the crew, and choosing a stormy night, when any noise that might be made would not be heard on board the ship, they made their way up to the deck above, through a hole they had cut in the planks, and overpowered the Genoese almost without resistance; that they had then, in the darkness, ran alongside another of the ships and captured her with equal ease; and Parucchi, with a portion of the crew of the Pluto, and the Venetian prisoners on board that ship, had retaken a third; while the Pluto had captured a fourth.

"It may seem to you, signors," Francis concluded, "that we might, in the same way, have recaptured the rest of our ships, and it was a bitter disappointment to me that we failed to do so; but the storm was so high, and the sea so rough, that it was only with the greatest danger and difficulty that ships could lie alongside each other. The bulwarks of all four vessels were greatly damaged, and the Pluto lost her foremast while alongside the last ship we captured, and as the storm was increasing, rather than abating, we were, to our great chagrin, obliged to let the rest escape, since in striving for more we might have lost, not only our lives, but the vessels we had taken."

"This is indeed a most notable achievement, Messer Hammond, and the restoration of four ships and their crews, at the present moment, is of great importance to the republic, threatened as she is with invasion by land and sea.

"Now, Messer Polani, if you will give us the full details of which you spoke, we shall be glad."

Polani then related to the council the full story of the means by which the crew of the Pluto had gained their liberty, showing how the recapture was entirely due to the initiative of Francis, and to the ingenuity with which he overcame all difficulties. He ended by saying:

"My kinsman, Matteo, said that should you doubt whether this account is not tinged by his friendship and partiality for Messer Hammond, Signor Parucchi, and all the gentlemen who were confined with them in the hold, can substantiate the account that he has given. He said that Parucchi's evidence would be all the more valuable, since he and the other officers were in the first place much prejudiced against Messer Hammond, deeming it an indignity that one so young, and a foreigner by birth, should be appointed to the command over the heads of others, Venetian born, of good family, and his seniors in age. The circumstances which I have related to you have, however, completely altered his opinion, and he is as enthusiastic, with respect to Messer Hammond's conduct, as are my kinsman and all on board the ship."

"I remember now," one of the council said, "that we had a letter from the admiral in the spring, and that, when describing how terribly the crews had been diminished and weakened by the severity of the winter, he said that the sole exception was the Pluto, whose crew was kept up to their full strength, and in excellent health, owing entirely to the care and attention that Messer Hammond, the officer second in command, had bestowed upon them."

"Thanks, Messer Polani," the president of the council said, "for the light you have thrown on this matter.

"Messer Hammond, it is difficult to overestimate the services that you have rendered to the state. We shall, at an early day, decide in what manner most fitly to reward them, and in the meantime you will remain in command of the squadron you have brought in."

Francis returned thanks for the promise of the president, but expressed his desire to resign the command of the squadron at once.

"I am in business," he said, "with Messer Polani, and although, for a short time, I abandoned commerce in order to sail under Admiral Pisani, I now, from various reasons, desire, as soon as my successor is appointed, to return to my work with Signor Polani.

"I desire to recommend warmly to your excellencies Signor Parucchi, who is, except myself, the sole remaining officer of the

Pluto. He seconded me most admirably in our enterprise, and himself commanded at the recapture of one of the ships. The gentlemen volunteers also worked with the greatest energy and spirit. Matteo Giustiniani has been acting as third officer, and to him also the thanks of the republic are due."

On leaving the ship, Messer Polani had despatched a boat, to carry to his house the news that Francis had returned; and when they came back from the palace they found Giulia anxiously expecting them, and a few minutes later Matteo arrived with his brother Rufino, and Maria. The latter was far more effusive in her greeting of Francis than Giulia had been.

"Matteo has been telling us all about it, Francis, and that he, and everyone else, owed their escape from the dungeons of Genoa entirely to your cleverness."

"Not so much to his cleverness, Maria," Matteo corrected, "although he is wonderful in inventing things, but to his energy, determination, and steadfastness. There was not one of us but regarded a visit to the dungeons of Genoa as a foregone conclusion, and when Francis spoke of our recapturing the Pluto, as if it were the easiest and most natural thing in the world, it was as much as we could do not to laugh in his face. However, he set about it as quietly and calmly as if he were carrying on the regular work of a ship. We gradually caught some of his spirit, and when we began to see that there was a method in his madness, did our best to carry out his orders."

"It is wonderful," Maria said; "and do you know, Francisco, that when we first knew you, after you had rescued us from the attack on the canal, I absolutely thought that, though you were brave and straightforward and honourable, yet that by the side of our own people of your age, you were rather stupid, and ever since then I have been learning how mistaken I was."

Francis laughed.

"I think your estimate of me was correct enough," he said. "You see people are often stupid one way, and sharp another. Matteo will tell you I was far behind most of those in the seminary in learning lessons, and certainly when it came to talking, and bandying jokes, I had no chance at all. I suppose that every lady I have ever spoken to, when I have been with you at entertainments, has thought me exceptionally stupid; and I am sure I am, in most things, only I suppose I have got a fair share of common sense, and a habit of thinking for myself. There was no cleverness at all in anything that Matteo is telling you of.

"It was just the same here as it was when I was in that cell near Tunis. I wanted to get out. I supposed there must be some way out, if I could but discover it, and so I sat down to think how it was to be done; and of course, after trying in my mind every possible scheme, I hit upon the right one. There certainly was nothing clever in that."

"But I have heard nothing about it yet," Giulia said; "and everyone else seems to know how it was done."

"Matteo, do you tell Giulia," Maria ordered. "I have lots of questions to ask Francis."

"By the way, Francis," Messer Polani said, "you will be glad to hear that I have succeeded in getting home your man Giuseppi. He returned two days ago, and I have no doubt is somewhere below waiting to see you."

"I will go and see him at once," Francis said, hurrying away. "I am indeed glad to know that you have rescued him."

Maria laughed, as the door closed behind Francis.

"There, Rufino," she said, turning to him, "you pretend sometimes to be jealous of Francisco Hammond; and there, you see, just when I have said I have lots of questions to ask him, and five minutes after my arrival here to greet him, he races away without a word, directly he hears that his man Giuseppi has returned."

"And he is quite right, Maria," Matteo said indignantly. "Giuseppi would give his life for Francisco, and the two have been together every day for the last six or seven years. I don't doubt the faithful fellow is crying with joy now. Francisco is quite right, not to keep him waiting for a minute."

"Perhaps I cried for joy, too, Master Matteo," Maria said.

"I believe I did see tears in your eyes, Maria; but I put them down to my own account. You would naturally be delighted to know that your brother-in-law was safe and sound, to say nothing of the fact that the family would be spared the expense of sending a thousand ducats or so to ransom him."

"A thousand ducats, Matteo! A thousand soldi would more nearly represent your value, if the Genoese did but know it. But why don't you tell Giulia your adventures, as I ordered you?"

"Because Giulia would very much rather hear them from Francisco's lips, and I have no doubt he will be equally glad to tell her himself, though certainly he is a bad hand at recounting his own doings. However, he shall have the pleasure of telling her of it, and I can fill up the details for her, afterwards."

Two days later, a decree was published by the council stating that, in consideration of the very great service rendered to the state by Francisco Hammond, a citizen of Venice, in recapturing four galleys from the Genoese, the council decreed the settlement upon him, for life, of a pension of three hundred ducats a year.

"You will not want it, Francisco," Messer Polani said, as he brought in the news, "for I intend, at the end of these troubles, to take you as a partner in my business. I told your father that I should do so; and you have not only proved yourself earnest in business, quick at learning, and full of resources, but you have vastly added to the debt of gratitude which first caused me to make the proposition, by again saving my daughters from falling into the hands of their enemy. I told your father that I should regard you in the light of a son, and I do so regard you, and as a son of whom I have every reason to be proud.

"I need no thanks, my lad. I am still, and shall always remain, your debtor. You have very much more than fulfilled my expectations, and I shall be glad to place some of the burden of my business upon your shoulders.

"There is another matter, which I have long had in my mind, but of which I will not speak just at present.

"Thus, then, the three hundred ducats, which you will receive each year from the state, may not be needed by you. Still, you are to be congratulated upon the grant, because being the recipient of a pension, for distinguished services, will add to your weight and influence in the city. And so long as you do not need it—and no man can say what may occur, in the course of years, to hinder the trade of Venice—you can bestow the sum annually upon the poor of the city, and thus increase your popularity."

"I shall be happy to do that, signor," Francis said, "although it seems to me that popularity is of little value in Venice. It has not saved the man whom, a short time since, the people hailed as their father, from unmerited disgrace and imprisonment."

"It has not, Francisco, but it has saved his life. You may take my word for it, that the proposal, absolutely made in the council, for the execution of Pisani, would have been voted had it not been for fear of the people; and it may be that you will yet see, that the voice of the people will bring Pisani from his prison, long before the expiration of his term of imprisonment. Popularity is not to be despised, for it is a great power. That power may be abused, as when one, having gained the ear of the people, leads them astray for his own base ends, and uses the popularity he has gained to attack, and hurl from power, men less eloquent and less gifted in the arts of cajoling the people, but more worthy than himself. But, used rightly, the power of swaying and influencing the people is a great one, and especially valuable in a city like Venice, where private enmities and private feuds are carried to so great an extent. Already your name is in every mouth. Your rescue of Pisani, when sorely beset by the enemy, has been the theme of talk in every house; and this feat, which retrieves, to some extent, the misfortune of Pola, will make your name a household word in Venice."

Immediately after the battle of Pola, the Venetians had entered into negotiations with Hungary, to endeavour to detach that power from the league against them. But the demands of King Louis were too extravagant to be accepted. He demanded the cession of Trieste, the recognition of the suzerainty of his crown on the part of the present doge, and all his successors, an annual tribute of one hundred thousand ducats, and half a million of ready money. This demand was so excessive that, even in their distress, the Venetians refused to accept it, and hastened on their preparations for a struggle for life or death.

Fortunately, the Genoese continued for three months, after their success at Pola, to capture the outlying possessions of Venice, instead of striking at the capital. Towards the end of July, seventeen Genoese vessels appeared off Pelestrina, burned a merchant ship lying there, and spent the day in reconnoitring positions, and in taking soundings of the shallows and canals off Brondolo. They then sailed away for Dalmatia. In less than a week six galleys again hove in sight; and Admiral Giustiniani, who was in supreme command of the forces, issued out from the Lido, with an equal number of ships, to give them battle.

On his way, however, a black object was seen in the water. As they neared it, this was seen to be the head of a swimmer. He was soon picked up, and was found to be a Venetian citizen, named Savadia, who had been captured by the enemy, but had managed to escape, and was swimming towards land to warn his countrymen that the whole Genoese fleet, of forty-seven sail, under Pietro Doria, was close at hand; and that the six ships in the offing were simply a decoy, to tempt the Venetians to come out and give battle.

Giustiniani at once returned to port, and scarcely had he done so, than the whole Genoese fleet made its appearance. They approached the passage of the Lido; but the respite that had been afforded them had enabled the Venetians to make their preparations, and the Genoese found, to their disappointment, that the channels of the Lido and Malamocco were completely closed up with sunken vessels, palisades, and chains; and they sailed away to seek another entry through which they could strike at Venice.

Had the same precautions, that had proved so effective at the Lido and Malamocco passages, been taken at all the other channels; Venice could have defied all the efforts of Doria's fleet.

The city is situated on a group of small islands, rising in the midst of a shallow basin twenty-five miles long and five wide, and separated from the sea by a long sandbank, formed by the sediment brought down by the rivers Piave and Adige. Through this sandbank the sea had pierced several channels. Treporti, the northern of these channels, contained water only for the smallest craft. The next opening was known as the port of Lido, and separated the island of San Nicolo from Malamocco. Five miles farther on is the passage of Malamocco, between that island and Pelestrina. Southwest of Pelestrina lay Brondolo, behind which stood Chioggia, twenty miles distant from Venice. The southern point of Brondolo was only separated by a small channel—called the Canal of Lombardy—from the mainland.

Unfortunately, at Brondolo the channel had not been closed. All preparations had been made for doing so, but the work had been postponed until the last moment, in order that trading vessels might enter and leave the harbour, the Chioggians believing that there was sure to be sufficient warning, of the approach of an enemy, to enable them to close the entrance in time. The sudden appearance of Doria's fleet before Brondolo upset all these calculations, and the Genoese easily carried the position. Little Chioggia, the portion of the town separated from the rest by the Canal of Santa Caterina, was captured without difficulty; but the bridge across the canal was strongly defended by bastions and redoubts, and here Pietro Emo made a brave stand, with his garrison of three thousand five hundred men.

The enemy at once erected his batteries, and, on the 12th of August, the Genoese opened fire. The Venetians replied stoutly, and for three days a heavy cannonade was kept up on both sides. Reinforcements had reached the garrison from Venice, and, hour by hour, swift boats brought the news to the city of the progress of the fight.

So far, all seemed going on well. The Genoese had suffered heavily, and made no impression upon the batteries at the head of the bridge. The days passed in Venice in a state of restless disquietude. It was hoped and believed that Chioggia could successfully defend itself; but if it fell, the consequence would be terrible.

Already the Hungarians had overrun the Venetian possessions

on the mainland, the Lord of Padua was in the field with his army, and communication was cut with Ferrara, their sole ally. Should Chioggia fall, the Genoese fleet would enter the lagoons, and would sail, by the great channel through the flats, from Chioggia to Venice; and their light galleys could overrun the whole of the lagoons, and cut off all communication with the mainland, and starvation would rapidly stare the city in the face.

Polani made all preparations for the worst. Many of his valuables were hidden away, in recesses beneath the floors. Others were taken on board one of his ships in the port, and this was held in readiness to convey Giulia and Maria, whose husband had willingly accepted Polani's offer, to endeavour to carry her off by sea with Giulia, in case the Genoese should enter the city.

The merchant made an excursion to Chioggia, with Francis, to see for himself how things were going, and returned somewhat reassured. Francis spent much of his time at the port visiting Polani's ships, talking to the sailors, and expressing to them his opinion, that the Genoese and Paduans would never have dared to lay siege to Chioggia, had they not known that Pisani was no longer in command of the Venetian forces.

"I regard the present state of affairs," he said, over and over again, "as a judgment upon the city, for its base ingratitude to the brave admiral, and I am convinced that things will never come right, until we have him again in command of our fleet.

"Giustiniani is no doubt an able man; but what has he ever done in comparison to what Pisani has accomplished? Why should we place our only hope of safety in the hands of an untried man? I warrant, if Pisani was out and about, you would see Venice as active as a swarm of bees, pouring out against our aggressors. What is being done now? Preparations are being made; but of what kind? Ships are sunk in the channel; but what will be the use of this if Chioggia falls? The canals to that place will be blocked, but that will not prevent the Genoese from passing, in their light boats, from island to island, until they enter Venice itself.

"Do you think all these ships would be lying idly here, if Pisani were in command? Talk to your comrades, talk to the sailors in the port, talk to those on shore when you land, and urge, everywhere, that the cry should be raised for Pisani's release, and restoration to command."

CHAPTER 18

THE RELEASE OF PISANI

On the morning of the 17th, the party were sitting at breakfast, when Giulia suddenly sprang to her feet.

"Listen!" she exclaimed.

Her father and Francis looked at her in surprise, but instinctively listened for whatever sound she could have heard. Then a deep, solemn sound boomed through the air.

"It is the bell of the Campanile tolling," the merchant exclaimed. "It is the signal for all citizens to take up arms. Some terrible news has arrived."

Hastily putting on his armour, the merchant started to Saint Mark's, accompanied by Francis, who put on a steel cap, which he preferred to the heavy helmet, and a breastplate. A crowd of citizens were pursuing the same direction. The numbers thickened as they approached the Piazza, which they found on their arrival to be already thronged with people, who were densely packed in front of the palace, awaiting an explanation of the summons.

There was a look of deep anxiety on every face, for all felt that the news must be bad, indeed, which could have necessitated such a call. Presently the doge, accompanied by the council, appeared in the balcony. A complete silence fell upon the multitude, the bell ceased tolling, and not the slightest sound disturbed the stillness. One of the councillors stepped to the front, for the doge, Contarini, was now seventy-two years old, and his voice could hardly have been heard over so wide an area.

"Citizens of the republic, gather, I pray you, all your fortitude and constancy, to hear the news which I have to tell. It is bad news; but there is no reason for repining, still less for despair. If Venice has but confidence in herself, such as she has throughout her history shown, when danger seemed imminent, be assured that we shall weather this storm, as we have done all that have preceded it. Chioggia has fallen!"

An exclamation of pain and grief went up from the crowd. The speaker held up his hand for silence.

"Chioggia, contrary to our hopes and expectations, has fallen; but we are proud to say, it has fallen from no lack of bravery on the part of its defenders. As you know, for six days the brave podesta,

Emo, and his troops have repulsed every attack; but yesterday an unforeseen accident occurred. While our soldiers were holding their own, as usual, a Genoese fire ship exploded in the canal behind them. The idea, unfortunately, seized the troops that the bridge was on fire. The Genoese shouted 'The bridge is in flames!' and pressed onward, and our soldiers fell back, in some confusion, towards the bridge. Here Emo, with four brave companions, made a noble stand, and for a time checked the advance of the foe; but he was driven back. There was no time to destroy the communication behind him. The enemy pressed on, and, mingled with our retreating soldiers, entered the town. And so Chioggia was taken. Our loss in killed is said to be eight hundred and sixty men; while the rest of the garrison—four thousand in number—were taken prisoners."

A loud cry of anguish burst from the crowd. Numbers of those present had relatives and friends among the garrison of Chioggia; and to all, the news of this terrible disaster was a profound blow. Venice was open now to invasion. In a few hours, the enemy might appear in her canals.

The council and the nobles endeavoured to dispel the feeling of despair. While some harangued the people from the balconies, others went down and mingled with the crowd, assuring them that all was not yet lost, that already messengers had been despatched to Doria, and the Lord of Padua, asking for terms of peace; and even should these be refused, Venice might yet defend herself until Zeno arrived, with his fleet, to their rescue. The doge himself received deputations of the citizens, and, by his calmness and serenity, did much to allay the first feeling of terror and dismay; and in a few hours the city recovered its wonted aspect of tranquillity.

The next morning the answer to the overtures was received. The Lord of Padua, who was doubtless beginning to feel some misgiving as to the final issue of the struggle, declared that he himself was not unwilling to treat upon certain terms, but that the decision must rest in the hands of his colleague. Doria, believing that Venice was now in his grasp, rejected the idea of terms with scorn.

"By God's faith, my lords of Venice," he cried, "ye shall have no peace from the Lord of Padua, nor from our commune of Genoa, until I have put a bit in the mouths of the horses of your evangelist of Saint Mark. When they have been bridled you shall then, in sooth, have a good peace; and this is our purpose and that of our commune!

"As for these captives, my brethren," he said, pointing to some

227

Genoese prisoners of rank, whom the Venetians had sent with their embassy, in hopes of conciliating the Genoese, "take them back. I want them not; for in a few days I am coming to release, from your prisons, them and the rest."

As soon as the message was received, the bell summoned the popular assembly together, and, in the name of the doge, Pietro Mocenigo described to them the terrible nature of the peril that threatened them, told them that, after the insolent reply of Doria, there was now no hope save in their own exertions, and invited all to rally round the national standard, for the protection of their hearths and homes. The reply of the assembly was unanimous; and shouts were raised:

"Let us arm ourselves! Let us equip and man what galleys are in the arsenal! Let us sally out to the combat! It is better to die in the defence of our country, than to perish here from want."

A universal conscription was at once ordered, new taxes were imposed, and the salaries of the magistrates and civil functionaries suspended. All business came to a standstill, and property fell to a fourth of its former value. The imposts were not found adequate to produce the sums required, and a new loan, at five per cent, was decreed. All subscribed to the utmost of their ability, raising the enormous sum of 6,294,040 lire. A new captain general was elected, and the government nominated Taddeo Giustiniani to the post.

The fortification of the city, with earthworks, was commenced. Lines of defence were drawn from Lido to San Spirito, and two wooden towers constructed at the former point, to guard the pass of San Nicolo. Events succeeded each other with the greatest rapidity, and all these matters were settled within thirty-six hours of the fall of Chioggia. In all respects the people, at first, yielded implicit obedience to the order of the council. They enrolled themselves for service. They subscribed to the loan. They laboured at the outworks. But from the moment the appointment of Taddeo Giustiniani was announced, they grew sullen. It was not that they objected to the new captain general, who was a popular nobleman, but every man felt that something more than this was required, in such an emergency, and that the best man that Venice could produce should be at the helm.

The sailors of the port were the first to move in the matter, and shouts for Vettore Pisani were heard in the streets. Others took up the cry, and soon a large multitude assembled in the Piazza, and with menacing shouts, demanded that Pisani should be freed and appointed. So serious did the tumult become, that the council were summoned in haste. Pisani—so popular with the lower class that they called him their father—was viewed with corresponding dislike and distrust by the nobles, who were at once jealous of his fame and superiority, and were alarmed at a popularity which could have made him, had he chosen it, the master of the state.

It was not, therefore, until after some hours of stormy debate, that they decided to give in to the wishes of the crowd, which was continually growing larger and more threatening; and it was late in the evening before the senators deputed by the council, followed by the exulting populace, hurried to the prison to apprise Pisani that he was free, and that the doge and senate were expecting him. Pisani heard the message without emotion, and placidly replied that he should prefer to pass the night where he was in reflection, and would wait on the seignory in the morning.

At daybreak on Friday, the 19th of August, the senatorial delegates and the people, accompanied by the other officers who had been involved in the disgrace of Pisani, and who had now been freed, reappeared at the gates of the prison. These were immediately opened, and Pisani appeared, with his usual expression of cheerfulness and good humour on his face. He was at once lifted on to the shoulders of some sailors, and borne in triumph to the palace, amid the deafening cheers of the populace. On the staircase he was met by the doge and senators, who saluted him cordially. Mass was heard in the chapel, and Pisani and the council then set to business, and were for some time closeted together.

The crowd waited outside the building, continuing to shout, and when Pisani issued out from the palace, he was seized and carried in triumph to his house in San Fantino. As he was passing the Campanile of Saint Mark, his old pilot, Marino Corbaro, a remarkably able seaman, but a perpetual grumbler against those in authority, met him, and elbowing his way through the crowd, drew close to him, loudly shouting at the same time:

"Now is the time, admiral, for revenging yourself, by seizing the dictatorship of this city. Behold, all are at your service. All are willing, at this very instant, to proclaim you prince, if you choose."

The loyalty of Pisani's nature was so affronted by this offer, that, in a fury of rage, he leaned forward and struck Corbaro a heavy blow with his fist, and then raising his voice shouted to those about him:

"Let none who wish me well say, 'Viva Pisani!' but, 'Viva San Marco!'"

And the populace then shouted, "Viva San Marco and our Father Pisani!"

No sooner had Pisani reached his house than the news was bruited about, that the admiral had been merely appointed governor of Lido, and that Giustiniani remained in command of the navy. The people were furious; and a deputation of 600 waited upon Pisani and said:

"We are yours. Command us as you will."

Pisani told them that it was for the republic, and not for him, to command their services. The deputation then went to the council, and declared, in the name of fifty thousand Venetians, that not a man would embark on the galleys until Pisani received his command, as captain general of all the forces of the republic, by land and sea. The Council of Ten, finding it impossible to resist the popular demand, and terrified at the idea of the tumult that a refusal would arouse, at last agreed to their request.

Fortunately for the republic, the four days which elapsed between the fall of Chioggia, and the appointment of Pisani to the supreme command, had not been utilized by the enemy. Carrara and Doria had always been at variance as to their plans of operations, and, as usual, they differed now. The Lord of Padua urged the necessity for following up their success by an instant attack upon Venice, while Doria insisted upon carrying out his original plan, and trusting as much to starvation as to military operations. He, however, gradually pushed forward two outposts, at Poreja and Malamocco, and on the latter island, at a distance of three miles from Venice, he erected a battery, many of whose shot fell at San Spirito.

Francis had borne his share in the events which had led to the installation of Pisani in the supreme command. He had at first instigated the sailors of Polani to raise a cry in the streets for the restoration of the admiral, and had gone about with two or three of his friends, mingling with knots of persons, and urging that the only hope of the republic lay in the energy and talent of Pisani. Even Matteo had joined him, although Taddeo Giustiniani was his own uncle. But, as the lad said, "what matters it about relationship now? What will become of relationship, if the Genoese and Paduans land here, raze the city to the ground, and scatter us over the face of the earth? No. When it comes to a question of ordinary command, of course I should go with my family; but when Venice is in danger, and only one man can save her, I should vote for him, whoever the other may be."

Polani had also exerted the great influence he possessed among the commercial classes, and had aided the efforts of Francis, by giving leave to the sailors of all his ships in port to go on shore. A few hours after Pisani's release the merchant, accompanied by Francis, called upon him.

"Welcome, my friends," he said heartily.

"Well, you see, Messer Hammond, that I was a true prophet, and that I have had my share of the dungeon. However, we need not talk of that now. I am up to my eyes in business."

"I have no doubt of that, admiral," Polani said. "I have called to offer every ship I have in the harbour, for the defence of the city. I myself will continue to pay their crews, as at present. Use the vessels as you like. Make fire ships of them if you will. I can afford the loss."

"Thanks, my friend," the admiral said. "We shall find a use for them, never fear.

"As for you, Messer Hammond, even in my prison I heard of your gallant feat, in recapturing the Pluto and three other ships from the Genoese, and thus retrieving, to some extent, the losses of Pola. I hope to wipe off the rest of the score before long. I shall find a command for you, in a day or two. Age and rank go for nothing now. I am going to put the best men in the best position.

"I have just appointed that old rascal, Corbaro, vice admiral of the Lido. He is a grumbling old scoundrel, and would have had me get up a revolution today, for which I had to knock him down; but he is one of the best sailors Venice ever turned out, and just the man for the place."

"I would rather act as a general aide-de-camp to you, admiral, than have a separate command, if you will allow me," Francis said. "I am still too young to command, and should be thwarted by rivalry and jealousies. I would, therefore, far rather act under your immediate orders, if you will allow me."

"So be it, then, lad. Come to me tomorrow, and I have no doubt I shall have plenty for you to do. At present, I cannot say what course I may adopt, for in truth, I don't know what position I shall hold. The people do not seem content with my having only the government of Lido; but for myself, I care nothing whether I hold that command, or that of captain general. It is all one to me, so that I can serve the republic. And Giustiniani is an able man, and will no doubt do his business well.

"You do not think so, young man?" he broke off, when Francis shook his head.

"I do not, indeed, sir. He has erected two wooden towers at the mouth of the Lido, which the first stone from a Genoese ballista would knock to splinters; and has put up a fence to San Spirito, which a Genoese soldier in full armour could jump over."

"Well, we shall see, Messer Hammond," the admiral said, smiling. "I fear you have one bad quality among your many good ones, and that is that you are a partisan. But go along now. I have no more time to spare to you."

No sooner had Pisani obtained the supreme command, than he set to work in earnest to provide for the safety of the city, the reorganization of the navy, and the conversion of the new levies into soldiers and sailors. The hulls of forty galleys, which were lying in the arsenals, were taken in hand, and two-thirds of them were equipped and ready for sea in three days.

The population was full of ardour and enthusiasm, and crowded to the offices to register their names for service. The women brought their jewels, to be melted down into money; and all vied with each other in zeal.

Pisani's first task, after seeing the galleys put in hand, was to examine the defences Giustiniani had erected. He at once pronounced the two wooden towers—of which Francis had spoken so disrespectfully—to be utterly useless, and ordered two tall towers, of solid masonry, to be erected in their stead.

Giustiniani was indignant at this condemnation of his work; and he and his friends so worked upon the minds of those who were to carry out the work, that they laid down their tools, and refused to embark upon such useless operations. The news was brought to Pisani by one of his friends, and, starting in his gondola, he was soon upon the spot.

He wasted no time in remonstrating with the workmen on their conduct, but, seizing a trowel, lifted a heavy stone into its place, shouting:

"Let him who loves Saint Mark follow my example!"

The success of the appeal was instantaneous. The workmen grasped their tools. A host of volunteers seized the stones and carried them to their places. When they were exhausted, fresh workmen took their places, and in the incredibly short time of four days, the two castles were finished.

The workmen were next set to level the paling and earthwork, from Lido to San Spirito, and in the course of a fortnight the lofty and massive stone walls were erected. By this time, something like a fleet was at Pisani's disposal. In spite of the conduct of Taddeo Giustiniani, Pisani, with his usual magnanimity, gave him the command of three large ships, mounting the heaviest guns in the arsenal. The light boats were under the command of Giovanni

Barberigo. Federigo Cornaro was stationed with a force of galleys at San Spirito. Nicholo Gallieano was charged with the defence of the Lazaretto, San Clemente, Santa Elena, and the neighbourhood; while on the strand between Lido and Malamocco, behind the main wall, were the mercenaries, eight thousand strong, under Jacopo Cavalli. Heavy booms were placed across all the canals by which it was likely that the enemy's fleet might advance.

Francis found his office, under the energetic admiral, no sinecure. He was kept constantly moving from one point to the other, to see that all was going on well, and to report the progress made. The work never ceased, night or day, and for the first week neither Francis, nor his commander, ever went to bed, contenting themselves with such chance sleep as they could snatch.

Having wasted eight precious days, the enemy, on the 24th of August, advanced to the attack. A Genoese force, under Doria's brother, landed upon San Nicolo; while the Paduans attacked San Spirito and Santa Marta. They found the besieged in readiness. Directly the alarm was given, the Venetians flocked to the threatened points, and repulsed the enemy with slaughter.

The latter then attempted to make a junction of their forces, but Cornaro with his galleys occupied the canal, drove back the boats in which they intended to cross, and defeated the attempt. Doria had felt certain that the movement, which was attempted under cover of night, would succeed, and his disappointment was extreme.

The Lord of Padua was so disgusted that he withdrew his troops to the mainland. Doria remained before Venice until the early part of October, but without making another attack. Indeed, the defences had long before become so formidable, that attack was well-nigh hopeless. At the end of that time he destroyed all his works and fell back upon Chioggia, and determined to wait there until Venice was starved into surrender.

The suffering in the city was intense. It was cut off from all access to the mainland behind, but occasionally a ship, laden with provisions from Egypt or Syria, managed to evade the Genoese galleys. These precarious supplies, however, availed but little for the wants of the starving city, eked out though they were by the exertions of the sailors, who occasionally sailed across the lagoon, landed on the mainland, and cut off the supplies sent from Padua and elsewhere to the Genoese camp.

The price of provisions was so enormous, that the bulk of the people were famishing, and even in the houses of the wealthy the pressure was great. The nobility, however, did their utmost for their starving countrymen, and the words of Pietro Mocenigo, speaking in the name of the doge to the popular assembly, were literally carried into effect.

"Let all," he said, "who are pressed by hunger, go to the dwellings of the patricians. There you will find friends and brothers, who will divide with you their last crust."

So desperate, indeed, did the position become, that a motion was made by some members of the council for emigrating from the lagoons, and founding a new home in Candia or Negropont; but this proposal was at once negatived, and the Venetians declared that, sooner than abandon their city, they would bury themselves under her ruins.

So October and November passed. Carlo Zeno had not yet arrived, but by some letters which had been captured with a convoy of provisions, it was learned that he had been achieving the most triumphant success, had swept the seas from Genoa to Constantinople, had captured a Genoese galleon valued at three hundred thousand ducats, and was at Candia.

This intelligence revived the hopes of Venice, and on the 16th of November Luigi Moroceni was despatched to order him, in the name of the government, peremptorily to hasten to the rescue of Venice. Almost at the same time, Giovanni Barberigo, with his light craft, surprised and captured three of the enemy's vessels, killing many of the sailors, and taking a hundred and fifty prisoners. The success was not in itself important, but it raised the hopes of the Venetians, as being the first time they had taken the offensive. Pisani himself had endeavoured to reconnoitre the position of the enemy, but had each time been sharply repulsed, losing ten boats and thirty men upon one occasion, when the doge's nephew, Antonio Gradenigo, was also killed by the enemy; but in spite of this, he advised government to make a great effort to recover Chioggia.

He admitted that the chances of failure were great. Still, he maintained that success was possible, and it was better that the Venetians should die fighting than by hunger.

As the result of his expeditions, he had found that Doria had at least thirty thousand men, fifty great ships, and from seven to eight hundred light craft. Moreover his troops were in high spirits, well fed, and well cared for, and should therefore be, man to man, more than a match for the starving soldiers of Venice. Nevertheless, there was a possibility of success, as Zeno would doubtless arrive by the time the siege had fairly commenced.

After much debate, the council determined that the

undertaking should be attempted. To stir the people to the utmost exertion, the senate, on the 1st of December, published a decree that the thirty plebeians, who should most liberally meet the urgent necessities of the state by the proffer of their persons or estates, should, after peace was made, be raised to the rank of nobility, and summoned to the great council; that thirty-five thousand ducats of gold should be distributed annually among those who were not elected, and their heirs, forever; that any foreign merchant, who should display peculiar zeal for the cause of the republic, should be admitted to the full privileges of citizenship; and that, on the other hand, such Venetians as might endeavour to elude a participation in the common burdens, and hardships, should be held by so doing to have forfeited all their civil rights.

Seventy-five candidates came forward. Some offered money, some personal service or the service of their sons and relatives; some presented galleys and offered to pay their crews. Immense efforts were made, and by the 21st of December sixty ships, four hundred boats of all sizes, and thirty-four war galleys were equipped. The doge, although just seventy-three years old, signified his wish to assume the supreme command of the expedition, Pisani acting as his lieutenant and admiral.

During the long weeks the siege continued, Francis saw little of the Polanis, his duties keeping him constantly near Pisani, with whom he took such meals as the time would afford, sleeping in his house, in readiness for instant service. Maria had returned to her father's house, for her husband was in command of the outpost nearest to the enemy, and was therefore constantly away from home. Maria's spirits were higher than ever. She made light of the hardships in the way of food, bantered Francis when he came on his business engagements, and affected to treat him with extreme respect, as the trusted lieutenant of Pisani. Giulia, too, kept up her spirits, and no one would have thought, listening to the lively talk of the two girls with their father and Francis, that Venice was besieged by an overwhelming force, and reduced to the direst straits by hunger.

The greater part of Polani's ships were now in the service of the state. Those which remained, were constantly engaged in running across to the Dalmatian coast, and bringing in cargoes of provisions through the cordon of the Genoese galleys.

The light gondola which, after being repaired, had been lying for two years under cover in Messer Polani's yard, had again been made useful. Giuseppi had returned to his old work, and he and another powerful oarsman made the light boat fly through the water, as Francis carried the orders of the admiral to the various posts. He had also been in it upon several of the reconnoitring expeditions, in the canals leading to Chioggia, and although hotly chased he had, on each occasion, left his pursuers behind. The evening before the expedition was to start Pisani said to him:

"I think you have brought me more news, with that fast little craft of yours, than I have been able to obtain even at the cost of some hard fighting, and a good many lives. I wish that you would make an excursion for me tonight, and find out, if you can, whether the enemy have moved their position since the last time I reconnoitred them. I particularly wish to learn if they have strong forces near the outlets of the channels of Chioggia, and Brondolo, and the Canal of Lombardy. You know my plans, and with such a host of recruits as I shall have with me, it is all important that there should be no failure at first. Veterans can stand defeat, but a reverse is fatal to young troops. Heaven knows, they will have enough to bear, with wet, cold, exposure, and hunger, and success will be necessary to keep up their spirits. Do not push your adventure too far. Run no risk if you can help it. I would not, for much, that harm befell you."

Francis at once accepted the commission, and left the admiral in order to make his preparations.

"Giuseppi," he said, as he took his place in the boat, "I want you to find for me, for service tonight, a gondolier who is a native of Chioggia, and who knows every foot of the country round, and every winding of the canals. He must be intelligent and brave, for the risk will be no slight one."

"I think I know such a man, Messer Francisco; but if he happens to be away, there will be no difficulty in finding another, for there are many fishermen here who escaped before the Genoese captured Chioggia."

"When will you see him?"

"As soon as you have landed me at Messer Polani's."

"Go and fetch him, Giuseppi; and if you can find one or two old fishermen of Chioggia, bring them also with you. I want to gain as much information as possible regarding the country."

"Is it true that the fleet starts tomorrow, Francisco?" Maria asked as he entered. "Everyone says so."

"It is quite true. There will be no further change. The orders have been all issued, and you may rely upon it that we are going to sea."

"And when will you return?"

"That's another matter altogether," Francis laughed. "It may be a week, it may be three months."

"But I thought we were going to fight the Genoese galleys. It does not seem to me that a week is wanted to do that. A day to go to Chioggia, a day to fight, and a day to return. What can you want more than that for?"

"I do not think that we are going to fight the Genoese galleys," Francis answered. "Certainly we shall not do so if we can help it. They are vastly stronger than we are; but I do not know that we need fear them for all that."

"What do you mean, Francisco? You do not mean to fight—they are vastly stronger than you are—and yet you do not fear them. You are not given to speak in riddles; but you have puzzled me this time."

"Well, I will explain myself a little," Francis said; "but you must remember that it is a secret, and not to be whispered to anyone."

"That is right," Maria said. "I love a secret, especially a state secret.

"Giulia, come and sit quite close, so that he can whisper it into our ears, and even the walls shall not hear it.

"Now, sir, explain yourself!"

"I will explain it without telling you," Francis said. "Have you not gone to see African lions, who were very much stronger and fiercer than yourself, and yet you did not fear them?"

"Because they have been in cages," Maria said. "But what has that to do with it?"

"It explains the whole matter," Francis said. "We do not mean to fight the Genoese fleet, if we can help it; but we are going to try to put them in a cage, and then we shall not be afraid of them."

"Do not trifle with us, sir," Maria said sternly. "How can you put Genoese galleys in a cage?"

"We cannot put them in a cage, but we can cage them up," Francis said. "Pisani's intention is, if possible, to close all the entrances to the canals round Chioggia. Thus, not only will the Genoese galleys be unable to sally out to attack us, but the whole of the Genoese army will be cooped up, and we shall then do to them what they have been doing to us, namely, starve them out!"

"Capital, capital!" Maria said, clapping her hands. "Your Pisani is a grand man, Francisco. And if he can do this for us, there is nothing which we would not do to show our gratitude. But you won't find it easy; besides, in the game of starving out, are we likely to win? The contest will not be even, for they start on it full men and strong, while our people are half starved already."

"I do not regard success as certain," Francis replied; "and Pisani himself acknowledges the chances are very great against us. Still, it is possible; and as nothing else seems possible, we are going to attempt it."

Polani looked grave, when he heard of the mission which Francis was going to undertake. Giulia's bright colour fled at once, and Maria said angrily:

"You have no right to be always running into danger, Francisco. You are not a Venetian, and there is no reason why you should be always running risks greater than those which most Venetians are likely to encounter. You ought to think of us who care for you, if you don't choose to think of yourself."

"I did not volunteer for the service," Francis said. "I was asked by the admiral to undertake it, and even had I wished it, I could hardly have refused. The admiral selected me, not from any merit on my part, but because he knows that my boat is one of the fastest on the lagoons, and that I can easily run away from any of the Genoese rowboats. He particularly ordered me to run no unnecessary risks."

"That is all very well," Maria said; "but you know very well that you will run risks, and put yourself in the way of danger, if there is a chance of doing so.

"You should tell him not to go, father!"

"I cannot do that, Maria; for the service he has undertaken is a very important one to Venice. Everything depends upon the success of Pisani's attempt, and undertaken, as it is, against great odds, it is of the utmost importance that there should be no mistake as to the position of the enemy. Whether Francis was wise or not, in accepting Pisani's offer that he should act as his aide-de-camp, may be doubted; but now that he has undertaken it, he must carry out his orders, especially as it is now too late to make other arrangements, did he draw back.

"If you will come into my room, Francisco, I will give you a chart of the passages around Chioggia. You can study that, and you will then the better understand the information you may receive, from the men you are expecting."

Half an hour later Giuseppi arrived with the gondolier he had spoken of, and two old fishermen, and from their explanations, and a study of the map, Francis gained an exact idea of the localities. From his previous expeditions he had learned where the Genoese were generally posted, and something of the strength of the forces at the various points.

In truth, they kept but a careless watch. Feeling convinced that the Venetians possessed no forces capable of attacking him, and that their surrender must now be a matter of a few days only, Doria took no precautions. His troops were all quartered in the houses of Chioggia, his galleys moored alongside its quays, and the utmost he did was to post small bodies of men, with rowboats, at the entrances to the passages from the sea, and up the lagoons, to give warning of any sudden attempt on the part of Barberigo, with his light flotilla, to make a dash at the galleys, and endeavour to burn them.

Having obtained all the information he could from the old fishermen, Francis dismissed them.

"It is evident," he said to Giuseppi, "that we can hardly hope to succeed in passing the boats at the entrance to the canal seaward, or by going up the lagoon. The only plan that I can see is for us to land on the island of Pelestrina, which is held by us, to carry the boat across it, and to embark in the Malamocco channel. In this way, we should be within their cordon of boats, and can row fearlessly either out to the entrances, or to Chioggia itself. We are not likely to be detected, and if we are, we must make a race of it to Pelestrina."

The gondolier agreed that the scheme was practicable, and Francis ordered Giuseppi and him to remove the burdens, and every bit of wood that could be dispensed with from the gondola, so as to facilitate its transport.

CHAPTER 19

THE SIEGE OF CHIOGGIA

Late in the afternoon, Francis embarked in his gondola, and in an hour and a half landed at Pelestrina. He was well known, to those posted there, as the bearer of Pisani's orders, and as soon as it became dark, Rufino Giustiniani, who was in command, ordered a dozen men to carry the light gondola across the island to the Malamocco channel. While this was being done, Francis went to Rufino's tent, and informed him of what was going on in Venice, and that the whole fleet would set sail on the morrow.

"We heard rumours, from the men who brought our rations, that it was to be so," Rufino said; "but we have heard the same story a dozen times. So, now, it is really true! But what can the admiral be thinking of! Sure he can't intend to attack Doria with this newly-manned fleet and rabble army. He could not hope for victory against such odds!"

"The admiral's intentions are kept a profound secret," Francis said, "and are only known to the doge and the Council of Ten."

"And to yourself," Rufino said laughing.

"The admiral is good enough to honour me with his fullest confidence," Francis said; "and in this matter, it is so important that the nature of the design should be kept wholly secret, that I cannot tell it even to you!"

"You are quite right, Francisco; nor do I wish to know it, though I would wager that Maria, and her pretty sister, have some inkling of what is going on."

Francis laughed.

"The signoras are good enough to treat me as a brother," he said, "and I will not affirm that they have not obtained some slight information."

"I will warrant they have!" Rufino said. "When my wife has made up her mind to get to the bottom of a matter, she will tease and coax till she succeeds.

"Ah, here is Matteo! he has been out posting the sentries for the night."

The two friends had not indulged in a talk for some weeks, though they had occasionally met when Francis paid one of his flying visits to the island.

"I have just seen your boat being carried along," Matteo said, as he entered the tent. "I could not think what it was till I got close; but of course, when I saw Giuseppi, I knew all about it. What are you going to do—scout among the Genoese?"

"I am going to find out as much as I can," Francis said.

"It's a capital idea your bringing the boat across the island," Matteo said. "You are always full of good ideas, Francis. I can't make it out. They never seem to occur to me, and at the present time, especially, the only ideas that come into my mind are as to the comfortable meals I will eat, when this business is over. I never thought I cared much for eating before, but since I have had nothing but bread—and not enough of that—and an occasional fish, I have discovered that I am really fond of good living. My bones ache perpetually with lying on the bare ground, and if I escape from this, without being a cripple for life from rheumatism, I shall consider myself lucky, indeed. You are a fortunate fellow, Francisco; spending your time in the admiral's comfortable palace, or flying about in a smooth-rowing gondola!"

"That is one side of the question certainly," Francis said, laughing; "but there is a good deal of hard work, too, in the way of writing."

"I should not like that," Matteo said. "Still, I think you have the best of it. If the Genoese would come sometimes, and try and drive us off the island, there would be some excitement. But, except when the admiral wishes a reconnaissance, or Barberigo's galleys come down and stir them up, there is really nothing doing here."

"That ought to suit you exactly, Matteo, for never but once did I hear you say you wanted to do anything."

"When was that?" Rufino asked, laughing.

"Matteo conceived a violent desire to climb Mount Etna," Francis said, "and it needed all my arguments to prevent his leaving the ship at Girgenti, while she was loading, and starting to make the ascent."

"He would have repented before he had gone a quarter of the way up," Rufino said.

"I might have repented," Matteo replied stoutly, "but I would have done it, if I had begun. You don't know me yet, Rufino. I have a large store of energy, only at present I have had no opportunity of showing what I am made of.

"And now, how do you intend to proceed, Francisco? Have you any plan?"

"None at all," Francis replied. "I simply want to assure myself that the galleys are all in their usual places, and that the Genoese are making no special preparations against our coming."

"I have seen no unusual stir," Rufino said. "Their ships, as far as one can see their masts, seem all in their usual position. I fancy that, since Barberigo carried off two of them, they have put booms across the channels to prevent sudden attacks. I saw a lot of rowboats busy about something, but I could not make out exactly what they were doing; but still, I fancy they were constructing a boom. Their galleys keep a sharp lookout at night, and you certainly would not have succeeded in passing them, had you not hit upon this plan of carrying your boat over.

"Your greatest danger will be at first. When once you have fairly entered the inner canals, you are not likely to be suspected of being an enemy. They will take you for Chioggian fishermen late. We often make out their returning boats near the town. No doubt Doria is fond of fresh fish. Otherwise you would be detected, for the Genoese boats are, of course, quite different to ours, and even in the dark they would make out that you belonged to the lagoons.

"Ah, here is supper! It is not often that I should have anything to offer you, but one of my men managed to catch three or four fish today, and sold them to me at about their weight in silver. However, I have some good wine from my own cellars, and a man who has good wine, fish, and bread can do royally, whatever this grumbling brother of mine may say."

Half an hour later, a soldier brought the news that the gondola was in the water, and Francis bade adieu to his friends, and started at once.

"Row slowly and quietly," he said, as he took his seat. "Do not let your oars make the slightest splash in the water, until we are well across to the opposite shore. They may have a guard boat lying in the channel."

The light craft made her way noiselessly across the water. Once or twice they heard the sound of oars, as some Genoese galley passed up or down, but none came near enough to perceive them, and they crossed the main channel, and entered one of the numerous passages practicable only for boats of very light draught, without being once hailed. A broad shallow tract of water was now crossed, passable only by craft drawing but a few inches of water; then again they were in a deeper channel, and the lights of Chioggia rose but a short distance ahead.

They paused and listened, now, for they were nearing the ship channel, and here the enemy would, if anywhere, be on the alert. Coming across the water they could hear the sound of voices, and the dull noise made by the movement of men in a boat.

"Those are the galleys watching the boom, I expect," Francis said.

"Now, Philippo, we can move on. I suppose there is plenty of water, across the flats, for us to get into the channel without going near the boom."

"Plenty for us, signor; but if the boom goes right across the channel, heavy rowboats would not be able to pass. There are few shallower places in the lagoons than just about here. It may be that in one or two places even we might touch, but if we do, the bottom is firm enough for us to get out and float the boat over."

But they did not touch any shoal sufficiently shallow to necessitate this. Several times Francis could feel, by the dragging pace, that she was touching the oozy bottom; but each time she passed over without coming to a standstill. At last Philippo said:

"We are in the deep channel now, signor. The boom is right astern of us. The town is only a few hundred yards ahead."

"Then we shall be passing the Genoese galleys, directly," Francis said. "Row slowly as we go, and splash sometimes with the oars. If we go quickly and noiselessly past, they might possibly suspect something, but if we row without an attempt at concealment, they will take us for a fisherman's boat."

Soon the dark mass of Genoese ships, with their forests of masts, rose before them. There were lights in the cabins, and a buzz of talking, laughing, and singing among the crews on board.

"What luck today?" a sailor asked them as they rowed past, twenty or thirty yards from the side of one of the ships.

"Very poor," Giuseppi replied. "I think your ships, and the boats lying about, and the firing, have frightened the fish away from this end of the lagoons."

It was half a mile before they passed the last of the crowd of vessels.

"Would you like me to land here, signor?" Philippo said. "There would be no danger in my doing so. I can make my way, through the streets, to the house of some of my relatives, and find out from them whether there are any fresh movements among the Genoese. I will not enter any house; for aught I know there are soldiers quartered everywhere; but I am sure not to go many yards before I run against someone I know."

"I think it will be a very good plan, Philippo. We will lie under the bank here, and wait your return."

It was not more than twenty minutes before the gondolier was back.

"I have spoken to three men I know, signor. They are agreed that there are no movements among the enemy, and no one seems to have an idea that the Venetians are about to put to sea. Of course, I was cautious not to let drop a word on the subject, and only said we had managed to get through the enemy's cordon to learn the latest news, and I expected to earn a ducat or two by my night's work."

"That is excellent," Francis said. "Now, we will row out to the sea mouths of the channels, to assure ourselves that no ships are lying on guard there, for some are going in or out every day to cruise along the coast. A few may have taken up their station there, without attracting notice among the townspeople."

The opening of the passage known as the Canal of Lombardy was first visited. To gain this, they had to retrace their steps for some distance, and to row through the town of Chioggia, passing several boats and galleys, but without attracting notice. They found the mouth of the canal entirely unguarded, and then returned and rowed out to the mouth of the Brondolo passage. Some blazing fires on the shore showed that there were parties of soldiers here, but no ships were lying anywhere in the channel.

After some consultation they determined that, as no watch seemed to be kept, it would be shorter to row on outside the islands, and to enter by the third passage to be examined, that between Pelestrina and Brondolo. Here, however, the Genoese were more on the alert, as the Pelestrina shore was held by the Venetians. Scarcely had they entered the channel, when a large rowboat shot out from the shadow of the shore and hailed them.

"Stop rowing in that boat! Who are you that are entering so late?"

"Fishermen," Philippo shouted back, but without stopping rowing.

"Stop!" shouted the officer, "till we examine you! It is forbidden to enter the channel after dark."

But the gondoliers rowed steadily on, until ahead of the boat coming out. This fell into their wake, and its angry officer shouted threats against the fugitives, and exhorted his men to row their hardest.

"There are two more boats ahead, signor. They are lying on their oars to cut us off. One is a good deal further out than the other, and I don't think we shall gain Pelestrina."

"Then make for the Brondolo shore till we have passed them," Francis said.

The boat whirled off her course, and made towards the shore.

The Genoese galleys ahead at once made towards them; but in spite of the numerous oars they pulled, the craft could not keep up with the racing gondola, and it crossed ahead of them. In another five minutes' rowing, the three galleys were well astern, and the gondola again made out from the shore, her head pointing obliquely towards Pelestrina. The galleys were now fifty yards behind, and although their crews rowed their hardest, the gondola gradually gained upon them, and crossing their bows made over towards Pelestrina.

"We are out of the channel now," Philippo said, "and there will not be water enough for them to follow us much further."

A minute or two later a sudden shout proclaimed that the nearest of their pursuers had touched the ground.

"We can take it easy now," Giuseppi said, "and I am not sorry, for we could not have rowed harder if we had been racing."

A few minutes later, the light craft touched the mud a few yards distant from the shore.

"Is that you, Francisco?" a voice, which Francis recognized as Matteo's, asked.

"All right, Matteo!" he replied. "No one hurt this time."

"I have been on the lookout for you the last hour. I have got a body of my men here, in case you were chased. We heard the shouting and guessed it was you."

"If you have got some men there, Matteo, there is a chance for you to take a prize. A galley rowing twelve or fourteen oars is in the mud, a few hundred yards out. She was chasing us, and ran aground when at full speed, and I imagine they will have some trouble in getting her off. I suppose she draws a couple of feet of water. There! Don't you hear the hubbub they are making?"

"I hear them," Matteo said.

"Come along, lads. The night is cold, and I don't suppose the water is any warmer, but a skirmish will heat our blood."

Matteo, followed by a company of some forty men, at once entered the water, and made in the direction of the sounds. Five minutes later, Francis heard shouts and a clashing of weapons suddenly break out. It lasted but a short time. Matteo and his band soon returned with the prisoners.

"What! Have you waited, Francisco? I thought you would be on the other side of the island by this time."

"I was in no particular hurry, Matteo; and besides, I want my boat; and although two men can lift her easily enough, she would be a heavy weight to carry so far."

"You shall have a dozen, Francisco. It is owing to you we have taken these prisoners, and that I have had my first bit of excitement since I came out here.

"Sergeant, here are a couple of ducats. When you have given the prisoners into safe custody, spend the money in wine for the company.

"The water is bitterly cold, I can tell you, Francisco; but otherwise I am warm enough, for one's feet stick to the mud, and it seems, each step, as if one had fifty pounds of lead on one's shoes. But come along to my brother's tent at once. Your feet must be cold, too, though the water was only a few inches deep where you got out of your boat. A glass of hot wine will do us both good; and it will be an hour before your boat is in the water again. Indeed, I don't see the use of your starting before daybreak."

"Nor do I, Matteo; but I must go, nevertheless. Pisani knows how long it will take me to get to Chioggia and return. He will allow an hour or two for me to reconnoitre, and will then be expecting me back. As it is, I shall be two hours after the time when he will be expecting me, for he knows nothing about the boat being carried across this island, and will make no allowance for that. Moreover, Polani and his daughters will be anxious about me."

"Oh, you flatter yourself they will be lying awake for you," Matteo said, laughing. "Thinking over your dangers! Well, there's nothing like having a good idea of one's self."

Francis joined in the laugh.

"It does sound rather conceited, Matteo; but I know they will be anxious. They took up the idea it was a dangerous service I was going on, and I have no doubt they fidgeted over it. Women are always fancying things, you know."

"I don't know anyone who fidgets about me," Matteo said; "but then, you see, I am not a rescuer of damsels in distress, nor have I received the thanks of the republic for gallant actions."

"Well, you ought to have done," Francis replied. "You had just as much to do with that fight on board Pisani's galley as I had, only it happened I was in command.

"Oh, there is your brother's tent! I see there is a light burning, so I suppose he has not gone to bed yet."

"All the better," Matteo said. "We shall get our hot wine all the quicker. My teeth are chattering so, I hardly dare speak for fear of biting my tongue."

Francis was warmly welcomed by Rufino Giustiniani.

"I need hardly ask you if you have succeeded in reconnoitring their positions, for I know you would not come back before morning had you not carried out your orders.

"Why, Matteo, what have you been doing—wading in the mud, apparently? Why, you are wet up to the waist."

"We have captured an officer, and fourteen men, Rufino. They will be here in a few minutes. Their boat got stuck fast while it was chasing Francisco; so we waded out and took them. They made some resistance, but beyond a few slashes, and two or three thumps from their oars, no harm was done."

"That is right, Matteo. I am glad you have had a skirmish with them at last. Now go in and change your things. I shall have you on my hands with rheumatism."

"I will do that at once, and I hope you will have some hot spiced wine ready, by the time I have changed, for I am nearly frozen."

The embers of a fire, outside the tent, were soon stirred together, and in a few minutes the wine was prepared. In the meantime, Francis had been telling Rufino the incidents of his trip. In half an hour, the message came that the gondola was again in the water, and Francis was soon on his way back to the city.

"I was beginning to be anxious about you," was Pisani's greeting, as, upon being informed of his return, he sprang from the couch, on which he had thrown himself for an hour's sleep, and hurried downstairs. "I reckoned that you might have been back an hour before this, and began to think that you must have got into some scrape. Well, what have you discovered?"

"The Genoese have no idea that you are going to put to sea. Their ships and galleys are, as usual, moored off the quays of Chioggia. The entrance to the Canal of Lombardy, and the Brondolo passage, are both quite open, and there appear to be no troops anywhere near; but between Pelestrina and Brondolo they have rowboats watching the entrance, but no craft of any size. There are a few troops there, but, so far as I could judge by the number of fires, not more than two hundred men or so."

"Your news is excellent, Francisco. I will not ask you more, now. It is three o'clock already, and at five I must be up and doing; so get off to bed as soon as you can. You can give me the details in the morning."

The gondola was still waiting at the steps, and in a few minutes Francis arrived at the Palazzo Polani. A servant was sleeping on a bench in the hall. He started up as Francis entered.

"I have orders to let my master know, as soon as you return, signor."

"You can tell him, at the same time, that I have returned without hurt, and pray him not to disturb himself, as I can tell him what has taken place in the morning."

Polani, however, at once came to Francis' room.

"Thank Heaven you have returned safe to us, my boy!" he said. "I have just knocked at the girls' doors, to tell them of your return, and, by the quickness with which they answered, I am sure that they, like myself, have had no sleep. Have you succeeded in your mission?"

"Perfectly, signor. I have been to Chioggia itself, and to the entrances of the three passages, and have discovered that none of them are guarded by any force that could resist us."

"But how did you manage to pass through their galleys?"

"I landed on this side of Pelestrina, and had the gondola carried across, and launched in the channel inside their cordon; and it was not until we entered the last passage—that by Brondolo—that we were noticed. Then there was a sharp chase for a bit, but we outstripped them, and got safely across to Pelestrina. One of the galleys, in the excitement of the chase, ran fast into the mud; and Matteo, with some of his men, waded out and captured the officer and crew. So there is every prospect of our succeeding tomorrow."

"All that is good," Polani said; "but to me, just at present, I own that the principal thing is that you have got safely back. Now I will not keep you from your bed, for I suppose that you will not be able to lie late in the morning."

Francis certainly did not intend to do so, but the sun was high before he woke. He hurriedly dressed, and went downstairs.

"I have seen the admiral," Polani said as he entered, "and told him that you were sound asleep, and I did not intend to wake you, for that you were looking worn and knocked up. He said: 'Quite right! The lad is so willing and active, that I forget sometimes that he is not an old sea dog like myself, accustomed to sleep with one eye open, and to go without sleep altogether for days if necessary.' So you need not hurry over your breakfast. The girls are dying to hear your adventures."

As he took his breakfast, Francis gave the girls an account of his expedition.

"And so, you saw Rufino!" Maria said. "Did he inquire after me? You told him, I hope, that I was fading away rapidly from grief at his absence."

"I did not venture upon so flagrant an untruth as that," Francis replied.

"Is he very uncomfortable?"

"Not very, signora. He has a good tent, some excellent wine, an allowance of bread, which might be larger, and occasionally fish.

As he has also the gift of excellent spirits, I do not think he is greatly to be pitied—except, of course, for his absence from you."

"That, of course," Maria said. "When he does come here, he always tells me a moving tale of his privations, in hopes of exciting pity; but, unfortunately, I cannot help laughing at his tales of hardship. But we were really anxious about you last night, Francisco, and very thankful when we heard you had returned.

"Weren't we, Giulia?"

Giulia nodded.

"Giulia hasn't much to say when you are here, Francisco, but she can chatter about you fast enough when we are alone."

"How can you say so, Maria?" Giulia said reproachfully.

"Well, my dear, there is no harm in that. For aught he knows, you may be saying the most unkind things about him, all the time."

"I am sure he knows that I should not do that," Giulia said indignantly.

"By the way, do you know, Francisco, that all Venice is in a state of excitement! A proclamation has been issued by the doge, this morning, that all should be in their galleys and at their posts at noon, under pain of death. So everyone knows that something is about to be done, at last."

"Then it is time for me to be off," Francis said, rising hastily, "for it is ten o'clock already."

"Take your time, my lad," the merchant said. "There is no hurry, for Pisani told me, privately, that they should not sail until after dark."

It was not, indeed, until nearly eight o'clock in the evening, that the expedition started. At the hour of vespers, the doge, Pisani, and the other leaders of the expedition, attended mass in the church of Saint Mark, and then proceeded to their galleys, where all was now in readiness.

Pisani led the first division, which consisted of fourteen galleys. The doge, assisted by Cavalli, commanded in the centre; and Corbaro brought up the rear, with ten large ships. The night was beautifully bright and calm, a light and favourable breeze was blowing, and all Venice assembled to see the departure of the fleet.

Just after it passed through the passage of the Lido, a thick mist came on. Pisani stamped up and down the deck impatiently.

"If this goes on, it will ruin us," he said. "Instead of arriving in proper order at the mouth of the passages, and occupying them before the Genoese wake up to a sense of their danger, we shall get there one by one, they will take the alarm, and we shall have their whole fleet to deal with. It will be simply ruin to our scheme."

Fortunately, however, the fog speedily lifted. The vessels closed up together, and, in two hours after starting, arrived off the entrances to the channels. Pisani anchored until daylight appeared, and nearly five thousand men were then landed on the Brondolo's shore, easily driving back the small detachment placed there. But the alarm was soon given, and the Genoese poured out in such overwhelming force that the Venetians were driven in disorder to their boats, leaving behind them six hundred killed, drowned, or prisoners.

But Pisani had not supposed that he would be able to hold his position in front of the whole Genoese force, and he had succeeded in his main object. While the fighting had been going on on shore, a party of sailors had managed to moor a great ship, laden with stones, across the channel. As soon as the Genoese had driven the Venetians to their boats, they took possession of this vessel, and, finding that she was aground, they set her on fire, thus unconsciously aiding Pisani's object, for when she had burned to the water's edge she sank.

Barberigo, with his light galleys, now arrived upon the spot, and emptied their loads of stone into the passage around the wreck. The Genoese kept up a heavy fire with their artillery, many of the galleys were sunk, and numbers of the Venetians drowned, or killed by the shot.

Nevertheless, they worked on unflinchingly. As soon as the pile of stones had risen sufficiently for the men to stand upon them, waist deep, they took their places upon it, and packed in order the stones that their comrades handed them, and fixed heavy chains binding the whole together.

The work was terribly severe. The cold was bitter. The men were badly fed, and most of them altogether unaccustomed to hardships. In addition to the fire from the enemy's guns, they were exposed to a rain of arrows, and at the end of two days and nights they were utterly worn out and exhausted, and protested that they could do no more. Pisani, who had himself laboured among them in the thickest of the danger, strove to keep up their spirits by pointing out the importance of their work, and requested the doge to swear on his sword that, old as he was, he would never return to Venice unless Chioggia was conquered.

The doge took the oath, and for the moment the murmuring ceased; and, on the night of the 24th, the channel of Chioggia was entirely choked from shore to shore. On that day, Corbaro succeeded in sinking two hulks in the passage of Brondolo. Doria, who had hitherto believed that the Venetians would attempt nothing serious, now perceived for the first time the object of Pisani, and despatched fourteen great galleys to crush Corbaro, who had with him but four vessels. Pisani at once sailed to his assistance, with ten more ships, and the passage was now so narrow that the Genoese did not venture to attack, and Corbaro completed the operation of blocking up the Brondolo passage. The next day the Canal of Lombardy was similarly blocked; and thus, on the fourth day after leaving Venice, Pisani had accomplished his object, and had shut out the Genoese galleys from the sea.

But the work had been terrible, and the losses great. The soldiers were on half rations. The cold was piercing. They were engaged night and day with the enemy, and were continually wet through, and the labour was tremendous.

A fort had already been begun on the southern shore of the port of Brondolo, facing the convent, which Doria had transformed into a citadel. The new work was christened the Lova, and the heaviest guns in the Venetian arsenal were planted there. One of these, named the Trevisan, discharged stones of a hundred and ninety-five pounds in weight, and the Victory was little smaller. But the science of artillery was then in its youth, and these guns could only be discharged once in twenty-four hours.

But, on the 29th, the Venetians could do no more, and officers, soldiers, and sailors united in the demand that they should return to Venice. Even Pisani felt that the enterprise was beyond him, and that his men, exhausted by cold, hunger, and their incessant exertions, could no longer resist the overwhelming odds brought against him. Still, he maintained a brave front, and once again his cheery words, and unfeigned good temper, and the example set them by the aged doge, had their effect; but the soldiers required a pledge that, if Zeno should not be signalled in sight by New Year's Day, he would raise the siege. If Pisani and the doge would pledge themselves to this, the people agreed to maintain the struggle for the intervening forty-eight hours.

The pledge was given, and the fight continued. Thus, the fate of Venice hung in the balance. If Zeno arrived, not only would she be saved, but she had it in her power to inflict upon Genoa a terrible blow. Should Zeno still tarry, not only would the siege be raised, and the Genoese be at liberty to remove the dams which the Venetians had placed, at such a cost of suffering and blood; but there would be nothing left for Venice but to accept the terms, however onerous, her triumphant foes might dictate, terms which would certainly strip her of all her possessions, and probably involve even her independence.

Never, from her first foundation, had Venice been in such terrible risk. Her very existence trembled in the balance. The 30th passed as the days preceding it. There was but little fighting, for the Genoese knew how terrible were the straits to which Venice was reduced, and learned, from the prisoners they had taken, that in a few days, at the outside, the army besieging them would cease to exist.

At daybreak, on the 31st, men ascended the masts of the ships, and gazed over the sea, in hopes of making out the long-expected sails. But the sea was bare. It was terrible to see the faces of the Venetians, gaunt with famine, broken down by cold and fatigue. Even the most enduring began to despair.

Men spoke no more of Zeno. He had been away for months. Was it likely that he would come just at this moment? They talked rather of their homes. The next day they would return. If they must die, they would die with those they loved, in Venice. They should not mind that. And so the day went on, and as they lay down at night, hungry and cold, they thanked God that it was their last day. Whatever might come would be better than this.

Men were at the mastheads again, before daylight, on the 1st of January. Then, as the first streak of dawn broke, the cry went from masthead to masthead:

"There are ships out at sea!"

The cry was heard on shore. Pisani jumped into a boat with Francis, rowed out to his ship, and climbed the mast.

"Yes, there are ships!" he said. And then, after a pause: "Fifteen of them! Who are they? God grant it be Zeno!"

This was the question everyone on ship and on shore was asking himself, for it was known that the Genoese, too, were expecting reinforcements.

"The wind is scarce strong enough to move them through the water," Pisani said. "Let some light boats go off to reconnoitre. Let us know the best or the worst. If it be Zeno, Venice is saved! If it be the Genoese, I, and those who agree with me that it is better to die fighting, than to perish of hunger, will go out and attack them."

In a few minutes, several fast galleys started for the fleet, which was still so far away that the vessels could scarcely be made out, still less their rig and nationality. It would be some time before the boats would return with the news, and Pisani went ashore, and, with the doge, moved among the men, exhorting them to be steadfast, above all things not to give way to panic, should the newcomers prove to be enemies.

"If all is done in order," he said, "they cannot interfere with our retreat to Venice. They do not know how weak we are, and will not venture to attack so large a fleet. Therefore, when the signal is made that they are Genoese, we will fall back in good order to our boats, and take to our ships, and then either return to Venice, or sail out and give battle, as it may be decided."

The boats, before starting, had been told to hoist white flags should the galleys be Venetian, but to show no signal if they were Genoese. The boats were watched, from the mastheads, until they became specks in the distance. An hour afterwards, the lookout signalled to those on shore that they were returning.

"Go off again, Francisco. I must remain here to keep up the men's hearts, if the news be bad. Take your stand on the poop of my ship, and the moment the lookouts can say, with certainty, whether the boats carry a white flag or not, hoist the Lion of Saint Mark to the masthead, if it be Zeno. If not, run up a blue flag!"

CHAPTER 20

THE TRIUMPH OF VENICE

Francis rowed off to the ship, got the flags in readiness for hoisting, and stood with the lines in his hand.

"Can you make them out, yet?" he hailed the men at the mastheads.

"They are mere specks yet, signor," the man at the foremast said.

The other did not reply at once, but presently he shouted down:

"Far as they are away, signor, I am almost sure that one or two of them, at least, have something white flying."

There was a murmur of joy from the men on the deck, for Jacopo Zippo was famous for his keenness of sight.

"Silence, men!" Francis said. "Do not let a man shout, or wave his cap, till we are absolutely certain. Remember the agony with which those on shore are watching us, and the awful disappointment it would be, were their hopes raised only to be crushed, afterwards."

Another ten minutes, and Jacopo slid rapidly down by the stays, and stood on the deck with bared head.

"God be praised, signor! I have no longer a doubt. I can tell you, for certain, that white flags are flying from these boats."

"God be praised!" Francis replied.

"Now, up with the Lion!"

The flag was bent to the halyards and Francis hoisted it. As it rose above the bulwark, Pisani, who was standing on a hillock of sand, shouted out at the top of his voice:

"It is Zeno's fleet!"

A shout of joy broke from the troops. Cheer after cheer rent the air, from ship and shore, and then the wildest excitement reigned. Some fell on their knees, to thank God for the rescue thus sent when all seemed lost. Others stood with clasped hands, and streaming eyes, looking towards heaven. Some danced and shouted. Some wept with joy. Men fell on to each other's necks, and embraced. Some threw up their caps. All were wild with joy, and pent-up excitement.

Zeno, who, in ignorance of the terrible straits to which his countrymen were reduced, was making with his fleet direct to Venice, was intercepted by one of the galleys, and at once bore up for Brondolo, and presently dropped anchor near the shore. As he did so, a boat was lowered, and he rowed to the strand, where the Venetians crowded down to greet him. With difficulty, he made his way through the shouting multitude to the spot, a little distance away, where the doge was awaiting him.

Zeno was of medium height, square shouldered and broad chested. His head was manly and handsome, his nose aquiline, his eyes large, dark, and piercingly bright, and shaded by strongly-marked eyebrows. His air was grave and thoughtful, and in strong contrast to that of the merry and buoyant Pisani. His temper was more equable, but his character was as impulsive as that of the admiral. He was now forty-five years of age—ten years the junior of Pisani. Zeno was intended for the church, and was presented by the pope with the reversion of a rich prebendal stall at Patras. On his way to Padua, to complete his studies at the university, he was attacked by robbers, who left him for dead. He recovered, however, and went to Padua. He became an accomplished scholar; but was so fond of gambling that he lost every penny, and was obliged to escape from his creditors by flight. For five years he wandered over Italy, taking part in all sorts of adventures, and then suddenly returned to Venice, and was persuaded by his friends to proceed to Patras, where his stall was now vacant.

When he arrived there, he found the city besieged by the Turks. In spite of his clerical dignity, he placed himself in the front rank of its defenders, and distinguished himself by extreme bravery. He was desperately wounded, and was again believed to be dead. He was even placed in his coffin; but just as it was being nailed down, he showed signs of returning life. He did not stay long at Patras, but travelled in Germany, France, and England.

Soon after he returned to Patras he fought a duel, and thereby forfeited his stall. He now renounced the clerical profession, and married a wealthy heiress. She died shortly afterwards, and he married the daughter of the Admiral Marco Giustiniani.

He now entered upon political life, and soon showed brilliant talents. He was then appointed to the military command of the district of Treviso, which the Paduans were then invading. Here he very greatly distinguished himself, and in numberless engagements was always successful, so that he became known as Zeno the Unconquered.

When Pisani was appointed captain general, in April, 1378, he was appointed governor of Negropont, and soon afterwards received a separate naval command. He had been lost sight of for many months, prior to his appearance so opportunely before Brondolo, and he now confirmed to the doge the news that had been received shortly before. He had captured nearly seventy Genoese vessels, of various sizes, had cruised for some time in sight of Genoa, struck a heavy blow at her commerce, and prevented the despatch of the reinforcements promised to Doria. Among the vessels taken was one which was carrying three hundred thousand ducats from Genoa.

He reported himself ready with his men to take up the brunt of the siege forthwith, and selecting Brondolo as the most dangerous position, at once landed his crews. The stores on board ship were also brought ashore, and proved ample for the present necessities of the army.

In a few days, he sailed with his galleys and recaptured Loredo, driving out the Paduan garrison there. This conquest was all important to Venice, for it opened their communication with Ferrara, and vast stores of provisions were at once sent by their ally to Venice, and the pressure of starvation immediately ceased.

The siege of Brondolo was now pushed on, and on the 22nd of January the great bombard, the Victory, so battered the wall opposite to it that it fell suddenly, crushing beneath its ruins the Genoese commander, Doria.

The change which three weeks had made in the appearance of the Venetian forces was marvellous. Ample food, firing, and shelter had restored their wasted frames, and assurance of victory had taken the place of the courage of despair. A month of toil, hardship, and fighting had converted a mob of recruits into disciplined soldiers, and Zeno and Pisani seemed to have filled all with their own energy and courage. Zeno, indeed, was so rash and fearless that he had innumerable escapes from death.

One evening after dusk his own vessel, having been accidentally torn from its anchorage near the Lova Fort by the force of the wind and currents, was driven across the passage against the enemy's forts, whence showers of missiles were poured into it. One arrow pierced his throat. Dragging it out, he continued to issue his orders for getting the galley off the shore—bade a seaman swim with a line to the moorings, and angrily rebuked those who, believing destruction to be inevitable, entreated him to strike his flag. The sailor reached the moorings, and, with a line he had taken, made fast a strong rope to it, and the vessel was then hauled off into a place of safety. As Zeno hurried along the deck, superintending the operation, he tumbled down an open hatchway, and fell on his back, almost unconscious. In a few moments he would have been suffocated by the blood from the wound in his throat, but with a final effort he managed to roll over on to his face, the wound was thus permitted to bleed freely, and he soon recovered.

On the 28th of February, he was appointed general in chief of the land forces, and the next day drove the Genoese from all their positions on the islands of Brondolo and Little Chioggia, and on the following morning established his headquarters under the ramparts of Chioggia, and directed a destructive fire upon the citadel. As the Genoese fell back across the bridge over the Canal of Santa Caterina, the structure gave way under their weight, and great numbers were drowned. The retreat of the Genoese was indeed so hurried and confused, and they left behind them an immense quantity of arms, accoutrements, and war material, so much so that suits of mail were selling for a few shillings in the Venetian camp.

So completely were the Genoese disheartened, by the change in their position, that many thought that the Venetians could at once have taken Chioggia by assault; but the leaders were determined to risk no failure, and knew that the enemy must yield to hunger. They therefore contented themselves with a rigorous blockade, cutting off all the supplies which the Lord of Padua endeavoured to throw into the city. The Venetians, however, allowed the besieged to send away their women and children, who were taken to Venice and kindly treated there.

The army of Venice had now been vastly increased, by the arrival of the Star Company of Milan, and the Condottieri commanded by Sir John Hawkwood. The dikes, erected across the channels with so much labour, were removed, and the fleet took their part in the siege.

On the 14th of May there was joy in Chioggia, similar to that which the Venetians had felt at the sight of Zeno's fleet, for on that morning the squadron, which Genoa had sent to their assistance under the command of Matteo Maruffo, appeared in sight. This admiral had wasted much valuable time on the way, but had fallen in with and captured, after a most gallant resistance, five Venetian galleys under Giustiniani, who had been despatched to Apulia to fetch grain.

The Genoese fleet drew up in order of battle, and challenged Pisani to come out to engage them. But, impetuous as was the disposition of the admiral, and greatly as he longed to avenge his defeat at Pola, he refused to stir. He knew that Chioggia must, ere long, fall, and he would not risk all the advantages gained, by so many months of toil and effort, upon the hazard of a battle. Day after day Maruffo repeated his challenge, accompanied by such insolent taunts that the blood of the Venetian sailors was so stirred that Pisani could no longer restrain them. After obtaining leave from the doge to go out and give battle, he sailed into the roadstead on the 25th. The two fleets drew up in line of battle, facing each other. Just as the combat was about to commence a strange panic seized the Genoese, and, without exchanging a blow or firing a shot, they fled hastily. Pisani pursued them for some miles, and then returned to his old station.

The grief and despair of the garrison of Chioggia, at the sight of the retreat of their fleet, was in proportion to the joy with which they had hailed its approach. Their supply of fresh water was all but exhausted. Their rations had become so scanty that, from sheer weakness, they were unable, after the first week in June, to work their guns.

Genoa, in despair at the position of her troops, laboured unceasingly to relieve them. Emissaries were sent to tamper with the free companies, and succeeded so far that these would have marched away, had they not been appeased by the promise of a three days' sack of Chioggia, and a month's extra pay at the end of the war. Attempts were made to assassinate Zeno, but these also failed. The Genoese then induced the pope to intercede on their behalf; but the council remembered that when Venice was at the edge of destruction, on the 31st of December, no power had come forward to save her, and refused now to be robbed of the well-earned triumph.

On the 15th of July, Maruffo, who had received reinforcements again made his appearance; but Pisani this time refused to be tempted out. On the 21st a deputation was sent out from Chioggia to ask for terms, and though, on being told that an unconditional surrender alone would be accepted, they returned to the city, yet the following day the Genoese flag was hauled down from the battlements.

On the 24th the doge, accompanied by Pisani and Zeno, made his formal entry into Chioggia. The booty was enormous; and the companies received the promised bounty, and were allowed to pillage for three days. So large was the plunder collected, in this time, by the adventurers, that the share of one of them amounted to five hundred ducats. The republic, however, did not come off altogether without spoil—they obtained nineteen seaworthy galleys, four thousand four hundred and forty prisoners, and a vast amount of valuable stores, the salt alone being computed as worth ninety thousand crowns.

Not even when the triumphant fleet returned, after the conquest of Constantinople, was Venice so wild with delight, as when the doge, accompanied by Pisani and Zeno, entered the city in triumph after the capture of Chioggia. From the danger, more imminent than any that had threatened Venice from her first foundation, they had emerged with a success which would cripple the strength, and lower the pride of Genoa for years. Each citizen felt that he had some share in the triumph, for each had taken his share in the sufferings, the sacrifices, and the efforts of the struggle. There had been no unmanly giving way to despair, no pitiful entreaty for aid in their peril. Venice had relied upon herself, and had come out triumphant.

From every house hung flags and banners, every balcony was hung with tapestry and drapery. The Grand Canal was closely packed with gondolas, which, for once, disregarded the sumptuary law that enforced black as their only hue, and shone in a mass of colour. Gaily dressed ladies sat beneath canopies of silk and velvet; flags floated from every boat, and the rowers were dressed in the bright liveries of their employers. The church bells rang out with a deafening clang, and from roof and balcony, from wharf and river, rang out a mighty shout of welcome and triumph from the crowded mass, as the great state gondola, bearing the doge and the two commanders, made its way, slowly and with difficulty, along the centre of the canal.

Francis was on board one of the gondolas that followed in the wake of that of the doge, and as soon as the grand service in Saint Mark's was over, he slipped off and made his way back to the Palazzo Polani. The merchant and Giulia had both been present at the ceremony, and had just returned when he arrived.

"I guessed you would be off at once, Francisco, directly the ceremony was over. I own that I, myself, would have stayed for a time to see the grand doings in the Piazza, but this child would not hear of our doing so. She said it would be a shame, indeed, if you should arrive home and find no one to greet you."

"So it would have been," Giulia said. "I am sure I should not have liked, when I have been away, even on a visit of pleasure to Corfu, to return and find the house empty; and after the terrible dangers and hardships you have gone through, Francisco, it would have been unkind, indeed, had we not been here. You still look thin and worn."

"I think that is fancy on your part, Giulia. To my eyes he looks as stout as ever I saw him. But certainly he looked as lean and famished as a wolf, when I paid that visit to the camp the day before Zeno's arrival. His clothes hung loose about him, his cheeks were hollow, and his eyes sunken. He would have been a sight for men to stare at, had not every one else been in an equally bad case.

"Well, I thank God there is an end of it, now! Genoa will be glad to make peace on any terms, and the sea will once more be open to our ships. So now, Francisco, you have done with fighting, and will be able to turn your attention to the humbler occupation of a merchant."

"That will I right gladly," Francis said. "I used to think, once, I should like to be a man-at-arms; but I have seen enough of it, and hope I never will draw my sword again, unless it be in conflict with some Moorish rover. I have had many letters from my father, chiding me for mingling in frays in which I have no concern, and shall be able to gladden his heart, by writing to assure him that I have done with fighting."

"It has done you no harm, Francisco, or rather it has done you much good. It has given you the citizenship of Venice, in itself no slight advantage to you as a trader here. It has given you three hundred ducats a year, which, as a mark of honour, is not to be despised. It has won for you a name throughout the republic, and has given you a fame and popularity such as few, if any, citizens of Venice ever attained at your age. Lastly, it has made a man of you. It has given you confidence and self possession. You have acquired the habit of commanding men. You have been placed in positions which have called for the exercise of rare judgment, prudence, and courage; and you have come well through it all. It is but four years since your father left you a lad in my keeping. Now you are a man, whom the highest noble in Venice might be proud of calling his son. You have no reason to regret, therefore, that you have, for a year, taken up soldiering instead of trading, especially as our business was all stopped by the war, and you must have passed your time in inactivity."

In the evening, when the merchant and Francis were alone together, the former said:

"I told you last autumn, Francis, when I informed you that, henceforth, you would enter into my house as a partner in the business, when we again recommenced trade, that I had something else in my mind, but the time to speak of it had not then arrived. I think it has now come. Tell me, my boy, frankly, if there is anything that you would wish to ask of me."

Francis was silent for a moment; then he said:

"You have done so much, Signor Polani. You have heaped kindness upon me altogether beyond anything I could have hoped for, that, even did I wish for more, I could not ask it."

"Then there is something more you would like, Francisco. Remember that I have told you that I regard you as a son, and therefore I wish you to speak to me, as frankly as if I was really your father."

"I fear, signor, that you will think me audacious, but since you thus urge upon me to speak all that is in my mind, I cannot but tell you the truth. I love your daughter, Giulia, and have done so ever since the first day that my eyes fell on her. It has seemed to me too much, even to hope, that she can ever be mine, and I have been careful in letting no word expressive of my feelings pass my lips. It still seems, to me, beyond the bounds of possibility that I could successfully aspire to the hand of the daughter of one of the noblest families in Venice."

"I am glad you have spoken frankly, dear lad," the merchant said. "Ever since you rescued my daughters from the hands of Mocenigo, it has been on my mind that someday, perhaps, you would be my son-in-law, as well as my son by adoption. I have watched with approval that, as Giulia grew from a child into a young woman, her liking for you seemed to ripen into affection. This afternoon I have spoken to her, and she has acknowledged that she would obey my commands, to regard you as her future husband, with gladness.

"I could not, however, offer my daughter's hand to one who might reject it, or who, if he accepted it, would only do so because he considered the match to be a desirable one, from a business point of view. Now that you have told me you love her, all difficulties are at an end. I am not one of those fathers who would force a marriage upon their daughters, regardless of their feelings. I gave to Maria free choice among her various suitors, and so I would give it to Giulia. Her choice is in accordance with my own secret hopes, and I therefore, freely and gladly, bestow her upon you. You must promise only that you do not carry her away altogether to England, so long as I live. You can, if you like, pay long visits with her from time to time to your native country, but make Venice your headquarters.

"I need say nothing to you about her dowry. I intended that, as my partner, you should take a fourth share of the profits of the business; but as Giulia's husband, I shall now propose that you have a third. This will give you an income equal to that of all but the wealthiest of the nobles of Venice. At my death, my fortune will be divided between my girls."

Francis expressed, in a few words, his joy and gratitude at the merchant's offer. Giulia had inspired him, four years before, with a boyish love, and it had steadily increased until he felt that, however great his success in life as Messer Polani's partner, his happiness would be incomplete unless shared by Giulia. Polani cut short his words by saying:

"My dear boy, I am as pleased that this should be so as you are. I now feel that I have, indeed, gained a son and secured the happiness of my daughter. Go in to her now. You will find her in the embroidery room. I told her that I should speak to you this evening, and she is doubtless in a tremble as to the result, for she told me frankly that, although she loved you, she feared you only regarded her with the affection of a brother, and she implored me, above all, not to give you a hint of her feelings towards you, until I was convinced that you really loved her."

Two months later, the marriage of Francis Hammond and Giulia Polani took place. There were great festivities, and the merchant spent a considerable sum in giving a feast, on the occasion, to all the poor of Venice. Maria told Francis, in confidence, that she had always made up her mind that he would marry Giulia.

"The child was silly enough to fall in love with you from the first, Francisco, and I was sure that you, in your dull English fashion, cared for her. My father confided to me, long since, that he hoped it would come about."

Francis Hammond lived for many years with his wife in Venice, paying occasional visits to England. He was joined, soon after his marriage, by his brother, who, after serving for some years in the business, entered it as a partner, when Messer Polani's increasing years rendered it necessary for him to retire from an active participation in it.

Some months after his marriage, Francis was saddened by the death of Admiral Pisani, who never recovered from the fatigue and hardships he suffered during the siege of Chioggia. He had, with the fleet, recovered most of the places that the Genoese had captured, and after chasing a Genoese fleet to Zara, had a partial engagement with them there. In this, Corbaro, now holding the commission of admiral of the squadron, was killed, and Pisani himself wounded. He was already suffering from fever; and the loss of Corbaro, and the check that the fleet had suffered, increased his malady, and he expired three days later.

Venice made peace with Genoa, but the grudge which she bore to Padua was not wiped out until some years later, when, in 1404, that city was besieged by the Venetians, and forced by famine to surrender in the autumn of the following year; after which Zeno, having been proved to have kept up secret communications with the Lord of Padua, was deprived of his honours and sentenced to a year's imprisonment. Thus, in turn, the two great Venetian commanders suffered disgrace and imprisonment.

As she had been patient and steadfast in her time of distress, Venice was clement in her hour of triumph, and granted far more favourable terms to Padua than that city deserved.

At the death of Messer Polani, Francis returned with his wife and family to England, and established himself in London, where he at once took rank as one of the leading merchants. His fortune, however, was so large, that he had no occasion to continue in commerce, and he did so only to afford him a certain amount of occupation. His brother carried on the business in Venice, and became one of the leading citizens there, in partnership with Matteo Giustiniani. Every two or three years Francis made a voyage with his wife to Venice and spent some months there, and to the end of his life never broke off his close connection with the City of the Waters.

www.ingramcontent.com/pod-product-compliance
Lightning Source LLC
Chambersburg PA
CBHW020632260626
47157CB00008B/2711